BLOOD HOLLOW

ALSO BY WILLIAM KENT KRUEGER

The Devil's Bed
Purgatory Ridge
Boundary Waters
Iron Lake

BLOOD HOLLOW

WILLIAM KENT KRUEGER

ATRIA BOOKS
New York London Toronto Sydney

ATRIA BOOKS
1230 Avenue of the Americas
New York, NY 10020

For information address Atria Books, 1230 Avenue of the Americas, New York, NY 10020

Library of Congress Cataloging-in-Publication Data

Krueger, William Kent.
Blood hollow / William Kent Krueger—1st Atria Books hardcover ed.
p. cm.
ISBN 0-7434-4586-4—ISBN 0-7434-4587-2 (pbk.)—ISBN 0-7434-8867-9 (ebook)
1. O'Connor, Cork (Fictitious character)—Fiction. 2. Private investigators—Minnesota—Fiction. 3. Minnesota—Fiction. I. Title.

PS3561.R766B58 2004
813'.54—dc22 2003062803

First Atria Books hardcover edition February 2004

10 9 8 7 6 5 4 3 2

Manufactured in the United States of America

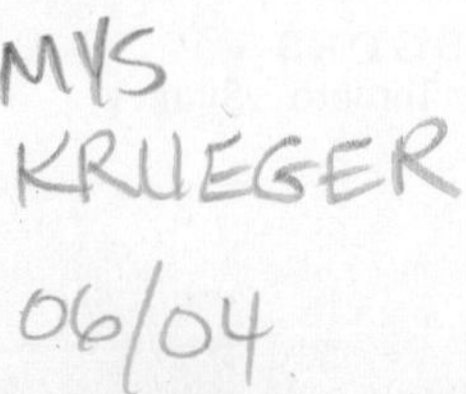

For Diane, of course;
and
for my children, Seneca and Adam,
who cracked my heart wide open and crept inside.

ACKNOWLEDGMENTS

Where the law is concerned, I plead ignorance. So I'm grateful that during the writing of this book I received help from others far more knowledgeable than I. Thanks to the Honorable Kevin Eide of Minnesota's First Judicial District Court, Assistant Ramsey County Attorney Tami McConkey, and former Pine County Sheriff Steve Haavisto for their expert advice and guidance in matters of the law and its enforcement.

In addition to my usual gang of cohorts in Crème de la Crime—Carl Brookins, Julie Fasciana, Michael Kac, Jean Miriam Paul, Charlie Rethwisch, Susan Runholt, Tim Springfield, and Anne B. Webb—I am also indebted to Joci Tilsen for her astute reader's eye and excellent suggestions.

Good editors are the angels of this art, and I have been blessed with help from two of the best: George Lucas, who saw me through the early chaos; and Emily Bestler, who helped me fill the dark holes at the end.

A special note of thanks to my late agent, Jane Jordan Browne, whose honesty, intelligence, compassion, and grit set her apart and above. God bless you, Jane.

And finally thanks to Jim and Elena Theros and the staff of the St. Clair Broiler for the coffee, the quiet, and that little corner sanctuary we all know as booth #4.

ACKNOWLEDGMENTS

JANUARY

1

JANUARY, AS USUAL, was meat locker cold, and the girl had already been missing for nearly two days. Corcoran O'Connor couldn't ignore the first circumstance. The second he tried not to think about.

He stood in snow up to his ass, more than two feet of drifted powder blinding white in the afternoon sun. He lifted his tinted goggles and glanced at the sky, a blue ceiling held up by green walls of pine. He stood on a ridge that overlooked a small oval of ice called Needle Lake, five miles from the nearest maintained road. Aside from the track his snowmobile had pressed into the powder, there was no sign of human life. A rugged vista lay before him—an uplifted ridge, a jagged shoreline, a bare granite pinnacle that jutted from the ice and gave the lake its name—but the recent snowfall had softened the look of the land. In his time, Cork had seen nearly fifty winters come and go. Sometimes the snow fell softly, sometimes it came in a rage. Always it changed the face of whatever it touched. Cork couldn't help thinking that in this respect, snow was a little like death. Except that death, when it changed a thing, changed it forever.

He took off his mittens, deerskin lined with fleece. He turned back to the Polaris snowmobile that Search and Rescue had provided for him, and he pulled a radio transmitter from the compartment behind the seat. When he spoke through the mouth hole of his ski mask, his words ghosted against the radio in a cloud of white vapor.

"Unit Three to base. Over."

"This is base. Go ahead, Cork."

"I'm at Needle Lake. No sign of her. I'm going to head up to Hat Lake. That'll finish this section."

"I copy that. Have you seen Bledsoe?"

"That's a negative."

"He completed the North Arm trail and was going to swing over to give you a hand. Also, be advised that the National Weather Service has issued a severe weather warning. A blizzard's coming our way. Sheriff's thinking of pulling everybody in."

Cork O'Connor had lived in the Northwoods of Minnesota most of his life. Although at the moment there was only a dark cloud bank building in the western sky, he knew that in no time at all the weather could turn.

"Ten-four, Patsy. I'll stay in touch. Unit Three out."

He'd been out since first light, and despite the deerskin mittens, the Sorel boots and thick socks, the quilted snowmobile suit, the down parka, and the ski mask, he was cold to the bone. He put the radio back, lifted a Thermos from the compartment under the seat of the Polaris, and poured a cup of coffee. It was only lukewarm, but it felt great going down his throat. As he sipped, he heard the sound of another machine cutting through the pines to his right. In a minute, a snowmobile broke through a gap in the trees, and shot onto the trail where Cork's own machine sat idle. Oliver Bledsoe buzzed up beside Cork and killed the engine. He dismounted and pulled off his ski mask.

"Heard you on the radio with Patsy," Bledsoe said. "Knew I'd catch you here." He cast a longing look at Cork's coffee. "Got any left?"

"Couple swallows," Cork said. He poured the last of the coffee into the cup and offered it to Bledsoe. "All yours."

"Thanks."

Bledsoe was true-blood Iron Lake Ojibwe. He was large, muscular, a hair past fifty, with a wide, honest face and warm almond eyes. Although he was now an attorney and headed the legal affairs office for the tribal council, in his early years he'd worked as a logger and he knew this area well. Cork was glad to have him there.

Bledsoe stripped off his gloves and wrapped his hands around the warm cup. He closed his eyes to savor the coffee as it coursed down his throat. "Anything?" he asked.

"Nothing," Cork said.

"Lot of ground to cover." Bledsoe handed the cup back and glanced north where the wilderness stretched all the way to Canada. "It's a shame, nice girl like her, something like this." He dug beneath his parka and brought out a pack of Chesterfields and Zippo lighter. He offered a cigarette to Cork, who declined. He lit up, took a deep breath, and exhaled a great white cloud of smoke and wet breath. He put his gloves back on and let the cigarette dangle from the corner of his mouth. Nodding toward the sky in the west, he said, "You hear what's coming in? If that girl didn't have bad luck, she'd have no luck at all."

Cork heard the squawk of his radio and picked it up.

"Base to all units. It's official. We've got us a blizzard on the doorstep. A real ass kicker, looks like. Come on in. Sheriff says he doesn't want anyone else lost out there."

Cork listened as one by one the other units acknowledged.

"Unit Three. Unit Four. Did you copy? Over."

"This is Unit Three. Bledsoe's with me. We copy, Patsy. But listen. I still haven't checked Hat Lake. I'd like to have a quick look before I head back."

"Negative, Cork. Sheriff says turn around now. He's pulling in the dogs and air search, too. Weather service says it's not a storm to mess with."

"Is Wally there?"

"He won't tell you anything different."

"Put him on."

Cork waited.

"Schanno, here. This better be good."

Cork could see him, Sheriff Wally Schanno. Grim, harried. With a missing girl, a whale of a blizzard, and a recalcitrant ex-sheriff on his hands.

"I'm just shy of Hat Lake, Wally. I'm going to check it out before I turn back."

"The hell you are. Have you taken a good look behind you?"

Glancing back to the west, toward the cloud bank that was now looming high above the tree line, Cork knew time was short.

"It would be a shame to come this far and not make it that last mile."

"Bring yourself in. That's an order."

"What are you going to do if I don't? Fire me? I'm a volunteer."

"You want to stay on Search and Rescue, you'll come back now. You read me, Unit Three?"

"Loud and clear, Sheriff."

"Good. I expect to see you shortly. Base out."

Schanno sounded weary deep down in his soul. Cork knew that the sheriff would turn away from the radio to face the family of the missing girl, having just reduced significantly the chances of finding her alive. For Cork, being out there in the cold and the snow with a blizzard at his back was infinitely preferable to what Sheriff Wally Schanno had to deal with. Once again, he was exceedingly glad that the badge he himself had once worn was now pinned to the chest of another man.

"Guess that about does it," Oliver Bledsoe said.

"I'm going to check Hat Lake."

"You heard the sheriff."

"I've got to know, Ollie."

Bledsoe nodded. "You want a hand?"

"No. You go on back. I won't be more than half an hour behind you."

"Schanno'll skin you alive."

"I'll take my chances with Wally."

Cork climbed onto the seat, kicked the engine over, and shot east in a roar of sparkling powder.

He hated snowmobiles. Hated the noise, a desecration of the silence of the deep woods that was to him a beauty so profound it felt sacred. Hated the kind of people snowmobiling brought, people who looked at the woods as they would an amusement park, just another diversion in the never-ending battle against boredom. Hated the ease with which the machines allowed access to a wilderness that could swallow the ignorant and unwary without a trace. The only value he could see in a snowmobile was that it allowed him, in a situation like this, to cover a large area quickly.

By the time he reached Hat Lake, the dark wall of cloud

behind him stretched north and south from horizon to horizon, completely blotting out the late afternoon sun. The sight gave Cork chills that had nothing to do with the temperature. He found no sign of a snowmobile on the trail that circled the lake. Exactly what he'd suspected, but he wanted to be certain. The wind rose at his back. He watched ghosts of snow swirl up and pirouette across the lake ice. Except for the dancing snow and the trees as they bent to the rising wind, nothing moved. Not one flicker of life across the whole, frigid face of that land.

2

HE DIDN'T BEAT the blizzard.

The trail climbed gradually over a ridge that roughly paralleled the Laurentian Divide, the spine of upper Minnesota, determining whether creeks and rivers ran north toward Hudson Bay or south toward the watershed of the Mississippi River. When Cork finally topped the ridge, he met the storm in a blast of wind. The machine he straddled shuddered under him like a frightened pony, and he plunged into blinding white, unable to see more than a few feet ahead.

Using the trees that lined the corridor as guides, he kept to the trail. Most of the time he rode due west, battling the wind head-on. Whenever his way turned to the north or to the south, the trees provided a little shelter and gave him some relief. Dressed for bitter cold, he could, if he had to, simply hunker down and wait out the storm. It wouldn't be pleasant, but it would be possible. He knew the area, knew that if he felt in grave danger, he could easily radio his position and a Sno-Cat would probably be dispatched. In all this, he understood he was more fortunate than the missing girl.

At last, he drew alongside a huge open area where the blowing snow was a maelstrom, a blinding swirl across the frozen expanse of Fisheye Lake. The trail circled the lake, but snowmobilers often cut a straight path across rather than follow the parabola of the shoreline. Cork knew if he did the same, he'd save himself a good twenty minutes, which at the moment seemed like a long time. He checked his compass, took a bearing, revved his snowmobile, and charged onto the ice.

On the flat, frozen lake, a bleached wall blotted out the rest of the world. There was no up or down, no left or right, no ahead or behind; there was only a hellish, acid brilliance blasting at him from every direction. He gripped the compass in his hand and kept the nose of the snowmobile lined up with the bearing point he'd chosen. In a few minutes, he would reach the far shoreline and the relative shelter of the trees.

He hadn't counted on seeing the missing girl.

He jerked the machine hard to the left. The snowmobile tipped. He let go his hold, flew off the Polaris. The ice was like concrete and sent a bone-rattling jolt down his body when he hit. He rolled several times before he came to rest on his back staring up (was it up?) into blinding white. For a moment, he lay perfectly still, putting together what his perception had taken in but his mind hadn't fully processed, then he staggered to his feet.

Had he actually seen the girl materialize in front of him? Something had been there, little more than a gray wraith barely visible behind the curtain of snow.

"Charlotte!" He shouted into a wind that ate the word. "Charlotte!"

He turned, then turned again. He moved a few steps forward. Or was he going back? The compass had flown from his hand when he spilled off the snowmobile, and he had no idea of direction.

"Charlotte Kane!" he tried again.

No matter which way he turned, the wind screamed at him. He lifted his goggles. The driving snow attacked his eyeballs, a thousand sharp needles, and bitter fingers seemed to pry at his sockets. He squeezed his eyes shut and tried again to recall exactly what he'd seen in the instant before he'd lost control.

There had been something directly ahead of him, a vague gray shape, no more. Why had he thought it was the girl? He realized that if it were Charlotte Kane, he hadn't had enough time to turn aside before he hit her, yet he'd felt no impact. Had the blizzard simply played a cruel trick on him?

He had no idea where the Polaris was, and nearly blind in the white, he began to grope around him.

This was exactly what Schanno had been afraid of, losing one of the search team. Cork, in his arrogance, believing that he might yet find the missing girl, had only made matters worse. Unless he was able to locate the snowmobile or the radio, Search and Rescue would have no idea where he was, no knowledge that he'd screwed himself, tumbled onto the ice of Fisheye Lake and got lost in a whiteout there. He was about to become another weight on the shoulders of the other searchers.

He tried not to panic, telling himself he could wait out the storm. But that was a supposition, not a known. For all he knew, the blizzard could last a week. Where would he be then?

He'd just resettled the goggles when he saw it again out of the corner of his eye, the flicker of gray behind the white.

"Charlotte!" He stumbled in that direction.

Blindly, he groped ahead a dozen steps, then another glimpse of the phantom, left this time, and he turned and hit his shinbone against the snowmobile, which was sitting upright, half-buried in a drift that was growing deeper even as Cork stood there, amazed and grateful.

The compass was hanging from the handgrip. Cork did a three-sixty, one last scan of the small circle his eyes could penetrate. He took his bearing, kicked the machine into action, and headed toward safety.

It took him another hour to reach the graded road that led him to Valhalla on Black Bear Lake.

Valhalla was the Northwoods retreat of Dr. Fletcher Kane, a widower, and his sister, Glory. The main structure was a lodge-like affair, two stories, five bedrooms, three baths, a couple of stone fireplaces, and fifty-five windows. All the numbers added up to a piece of property worth a million plus dollars situated at the end of a graded road twenty miles from Aurora, Minnesota, the nearest town, and about as far from any neighbors as a person could get in that stretch of woods. In addition to the house, a small guest lodge had been constructed a hundred yards south on the shoreline of Black Bear Lake. It was in the guesthouse that Wally Schanno had set up the base for the search and rescue operation. Since leaving that morning, Cork had been back once, near noon, to gas up and to grab a quick sandwich.

The guesthouse had been a hub of activity then. This time when he pulled up on his Polaris, the place was dead. A dozen other snowmobiles were parked among the trees. The trailers that had brought the machines stood empty and unconnected, the hitches buried in snow, the trucks and SUVs that had hauled them gone. The only vehicles remaining were Cork's old red Bronco and a Land Cruiser from the Tamarack County Sheriff's Department.

The driving snow made it difficult to see much of anything. Still, Cork could make out the big house and a tall, lone figure standing in a lighted window, staring toward the frozen lake.

A wonderful warmth hit Cork the moment he stepped into the guesthouse. He threw back the hood of his parka and pulled off his ski mask. All day he'd been cold, but not until the heat of the room hit him and made his icy skin tingle did he let himself acknowledge fully just how cold. And hungry. For along with the heat came the good smell of hot stew.

Rose McKenzie, Cork's sister-in-law, was the only other person in the room. She was a heavy, plain-looking woman, as good-hearted as anyone Cork had ever known. She'd lived with the O'Connors for more than fifteen years, had come to help raise their children, and in the process had become a beloved and integral part of their lives. When she'd learned of the search that was to be undertaken, she'd offered to do what she could to help. Because she had a reputation as a marvelous cook, it had been obvious from the start how she could best contribute.

She turned from the stove. "Thank God. I was worried. You're the last one in."

Cork hung the parka on a peg beside the door. The polished floorboards of the guesthouse were marred by dozens of wet boot prints. "The others?"

"They all left a few minutes ago, following Freddie Baker's plow. You need to leave pretty soon, too, before the road drifts over."

"Not until I've had some of that stew."

"That's why I kept it hot."

Coming in from the cold affected Cork in the usual way. He headed to the bathroom, where he stood at the toilet for a full minute relieving himself. When he came back, Rose had a filled bowl, a napkin, and a spoon on the table.

"Can I get you something to drink?"

"I'm fine with just the stew, Rose."

He leaned to his bowl. Steam, full of the smell of beef and carrots and onions and parsley and pepper, rose up against his face. Cork thought heaven couldn't smell any better.

"Where's Wally? Up at the house?" he asked.

Rose moved to the sink and began to wash the last of the dishes, except for what Cork was using. "Yes," she said.

"How are Fletcher and Glory doing?"

She turned, wiping her fleshy hands on her apron, one Cork recognized from home. She crossed to a window and looked toward the big house. "They're scared," she said.

There was a history of bad blood between Fletcher Kane and Cork. Glory was a chilly enigma that no one, not even Rose who was her friend, quite seemed to understand. Yet Cork had put aside his personal feelings because he was a parent himself, and the idea of a child, anyone's child, lost in that kind of hell left a metallic taste of fear in his own mouth that even Rose's wonderful stew couldn't wash away.

"I hated coming in," he said.

"Everybody did."

The guesthouse had a small kitchen and dining area that opened onto a larger living room with a fireplace. The living room had been set up for the search. The radio sat on a big table near a window. Beside it lay the search log and other documents, including a blown-up photograph of the missing girl, a pretty teenager with black hair and a reserved smile. A topographical map of the area had been taped to the wall. Cork could see the pins in the map, each search team denoted by a pin with a particular color. They'd covered what ground they could, but that was the problem. Charlotte Kane had vanished in the night on a snowmobile without telling anyone where she was going. She left a New Year's Eve party that she'd thrown at Valhalla without her father's consent. She was seventeen and intoxicated. Twenty-one inches of snow had fallen after her departure. Trackers—volunteers from the U.S. border patrol—had blown away the powder, what they called blue smoke, and had been able to say only that she'd headed to the graded road where she'd connected with a heavily used snowmobile trail that eventually branched in a dozen directions, and each branch in a dozen more. There was no guarantee that she'd even kept to the trails. With a full tank of gas, she could have made it halfway to North Dakota or all the way to Canada. It was an enormous area, an impossible area, to cover thoroughly.

"The air-scent dogs?" Cork asked.

Rose shook her head. "Nothing." She headed back to the sink.

"Thanks," Cork said.

"For what?"

"Coming out. Helping."

"A lot of folks have helped."

"You're still here."

"Somebody has to feed you. Jo would never forgive me if I let you starve or freeze to death." As soon as she said it, she looked sorry. She put a hand to her forehead. "That wasn't funny."

"It's okay, Rose."

The door opened and a cold wind blasted Deputy Randy Gooding into the room and a lot of snow with him. He took a moment and breathed deeply the warm air inside.

"And I thought winters in Milwaukee were tough," he finally said.

Gooding was tall and wiry, late twenties, good-looking in a square-jawed way, and possessed of a friendly disposition. Although he'd been in Aurora less than two years, he seemed to have fit nicely into the pace of life there. Like Cork, he was a man who'd fled the city for the north country, looking for a simpler way of life.

Gooding acknowledged Cork with a nod. "Sheriff wanted me to check, make sure you made it in okay."

"Is he up at the house?"

Gooding tugged off his gloves and his dark blue stocking cap. "Him and Father Mal. Dr. Kane's not happy that the plug's been pulled on the search."

Cork put his spoon down and wiped his mouth with his napkin. "If it were my daughter, I wouldn't be happy either."

"How's Glory?" Rose said.

Gooding breathed into his hands. "She's sedated herself pretty well," he said. "Blue Sapphire gin."

"It's hard to blame her," Rose said.

Gooding shook his head. "Tough on the doc, dealing with it all himself. He just stands at the window staring out as if that'll make her materialize somehow."

Rose turned to the stew pot and stirred with a wooden spoon. "I took some food up earlier. I'm not sure they ate anything. They'll be hungry eventually."

"The sheriff wants everybody ready to move," Gooding said. "He's afraid the snow's going to close in right behind Baker's plow."

Rose glanced at Cork, and he knew before she spoke what she was going to say. "Somebody should stay. Those folks should not be left alone out here."

"Father Mal's planning on staying," Gooding said.

"Father Mal can't cook. He can't even boil water right."

Cork said, "I think he figures to offer a different kind of sustenance, Rose."

She gave him a sharp look. "I understand that. But they'll all need to eat. It's hard to hold on to hope when you're hungry."

The door banged open, and once again the storm muscled its way in with the men who entered. Sheriff Wally Schanno carried on with the conversation he'd been having with Father Mal Thorne.

"With this storm blowing like it is, I can't guarantee we'll be back tomorrow."

"All the more reason I should stay," the priest said. "These people shouldn't be alone at a time like this."

Side by side, the two men were distinct contrasts. Schanno was tall and gaunt, his face gouged by worry. He was in his midsixties, but at that moment, he looked far older. Father Mal Thorne was younger by twenty years. Although he was a much smaller man, his compact body seemed to hold double its share of energy. Broad-chested and in good condition, he always reminded Cork of a tough pugilist.

Schanno noticed Cork. "Thought I told you to skip Hat Lake and come straight in."

"I made it back in one piece, Wally."

The sheriff looked too tired to argue. "See anything?"

Cork thought about the gray visage behind the snow, the sense that he'd been guided back to his snowmobile, that somehow Charlotte had tried to reach out to him.

"No," he finally said.

"Well, we're all accounted for now. Let's get this show on the road before we get stuck out here."

"I'm staying," Rose said.

Schanno began to object. "Goll darn it—"

"Thank you, Rose," Father Mal broke in. He smiled at her, and there were boyish dimples in his cheeks. "But you don't have to do that."

"They've got enough on their minds without worrying about fixing food or cleaning up. You, too. Your hands will be full, Father."

Mal Thorne considered it and decided in the blink of an eye. "All right."

Schanno opened his mouth, but the priest cut him off.

"The longer you stand here arguing, Wally, the worse that road gets."

"He's right, Sheriff," Gooding said.

Schanno gave in and nodded unhappily.

Cork stood up. He began to gather his dirty dishes to take them to the sink.

"I'll take care of those," Rose said. She hugged him. "Give my love to Jo and the kids."

"I'll do that. And I'll see you tomorrow. You, too, Mal." He put on his parka and his deerskin mittens. "I'm ready."

Schanno dug keys out of his pocket and handed them to his deputy. "You take the Land Cruiser. I'm riding with O'Connor."

Gooding shrugged. "Whatever you say." He opened the door and pushed his way into the storm.

Cork stood in the open doorway a moment, looking back at Rose and Father Mal. They were only two people, but he had a sense of something huge about them and between them, a vast reservoir of strength that neither the blizzard nor the long vigil they were about to keep could empty.

"Shut the damn door," Father Mal said.

The Bronco was buried in a drift that reached to the grill.

"You get in and get 'er started," Schanno shouted over the wind. "I'll clear the snow."

Cork grabbed the brush from beneath the front seat and tossed it to Schanno, then got in and turned the key. The starter ground sluggishly.

"Come on," Cork whispered.

The engine caught and roared to life. Cork kicked the defrost up to full blast. Schanno cleared the snow from the windows and the tailpipe and climbed into the Bronco.

"Damn," the sheriff said, hunching himself against the cold.

Cork couldn't agree more.

In a couple of minutes, Gooding eased the Land Cruiser forward, and Cork followed slowly.

Dark had come early, descending with the storm. Cork could barely see the taillights ahead of him. The glare of his own headlights splashed back off a wall of blowing snow that appeared solid as whitewashed concrete.

He knew Schanno was right to have been concerned about the road, knew that in a blizzard, snow became fluid in the way it moved. It ran like water around tree trunks, eddied against buildings, filled in depressions. It had already flowed into the trench that Freddie Baker had plowed not more than half an hour before, and as he followed in Baker's wake, Cork felt a little like Pharaoh of the Exodus with the Red Sea closing in.

"What is it, Wally?"

"What's what?"

"You rode with me, not with Gooding. I'm guessing you wanted to talk."

Schanno took his time answering. "I'm tired, Cork. Worn to the nub. I figured you'd understand, that's all." He let out a deep breath. "Hell of a way to start a year."

It was the second day of January.

The interior of the Bronco was lit from the reflection of the headlights off the snow. Schanno leaned forward, peering hard ahead. His face was gray and deeply hollowed. Skeletal.

"Hell of a way to end a career," he said.

He was talking about the fact that in a few days a man named Arne Soderberg would be sworn in as Tamarack County sheriff, assuming the responsibilities for that office for the next four years.

"You've done a good job, Wally."

"I did my share of stumbling. We both know that." Schanno pulled off his gloves and put his big hands on the dash, as if preparing himself for an impact. "Soderberg. He's no cop. Should be you taking the badge."

"I didn't want the badge," Cork reminded him. "Even if I'd run, there's no guarantee I'd have won."

"You'd have won," Schanno said. "You betcha, you'd have won."

"You're not sorry to be leaving, are you, Wally?"

"Today, not at all." Schanno took his right hand off the dash and rubbed his forehead for a moment. The winter air had dried and cracked the skin of his fingers. "I told Garritsen when he comes tomorrow he should bring along his cadaver dog."

They hit an open area, and the wind slammed against the side of the Bronco with the force of a charging moose. Cork yanked the steering wheel to keep from plowing into a snowbank.

He didn't want to talk about cadaver dogs.

"You and Arletta got plans?" he asked.

"Going to spend the rest of the winter in Bethesda, enjoying our grandkids."

"Looking forward to retirement?"

Schanno thought about it for a minute. "I'm looking forward to not being the guy who calls in the cadaver dog."

3

AFTER HE DROPPED Schanno off at the sheriff's office, Cork headed for home. The people of Aurora had seen this kind of storm many times before, seen worse. They'd sealed themselves behind heavily insulated walls and double-paned windows and settled down to wait. Cork's Bronco was the only thing that moved against the wind, and it moved slowly.

An enormous snowdrift blocked the door to Cork's garage. He left the Bronco parked in the drive and waded to the side door of the house. As he stepped into the kitchen, he could feel how knotted his whole body had become from fighting the blizzard. He breathed out deeply, trying to relax.

"Dad!"

The soft gallop of little feet across the living room floor. A moment later, his seven-year-old son burst into the kitchen. Stevie raced toward his father and threw his small arms around Cork's waist. The force of Stevie's greeting nearly knocked Cork off balance.

"You're cold," Stevie said. He smiled up at his father.

Cork laughed. "And you're not." There were crumbs at the corner of his son's mouth, and the scent of food ghosted off his breath. "You smell good enough to eat."

"Mom fixed soup and grilled cheese sandwiches."

"You mean she burned soup and cheese sandwiches," Jenny said, as she came into the kitchen. At seventeen, Cork's daughter was slender and bookish, trying fiercely to be independent.

She'd recently emerged from a Goth phase during which she'd dyed her hair the color of night and her entire wardrobe was black. She'd returned to wearing clothes with color, and her hair was very near its natural shade of blonde.

Cork's wife was right behind her. "I admit everything was a little overdone," Jo said.

"Overdone? Mom, you cremated dinner," Jenny said, but with a smile.

Cork eased from his son's grasp, hung up his parka, and laid his mittens on the counter. Then he gave Jo a long hug.

"Hungry?" she asked.

"For burned food?" He laughed softly. "That's okay. Rose fed me."

"Where is Aunt Rose?" Stevie looked with concern toward the window beyond which raged the storm. "Didn't she come home with you?"

"She stayed out at Valhalla to help Dr. Kane and his sister. Father Mal stayed, too. They're fine, Stevie."

"You didn't find Charlotte?" Jo said.

He shook his head.

"Know what we're going to do tonight?" Stevie danced with excitement. "Fix popcorn and watch *The Lion King.*" It was his favorite video.

"Sounds great, buddy."

Jo put her hand on his cold cheek. Her hair was like winter sun, a shining white-blonde. Her eyes were pale blue. When she was angry, they could become cold and hard and pierce Cork like shards of ice, but right now they were warm and liquid with concern. "Why don't you go up and take a good, hot shower?"

"Thanks. Think I will." He took one step, then stopped abruptly and asked, "Where's Annie?" For he'd suddenly noticed the absence of his middle child.

"Relax," Jo said. "She's at the Pilons. Mark and Sue insisted she stay the night with them rather than try to make it home in the storm. Go on now. That shower will do you good."

Upstairs in the bathroom, he turned on the water, then stood at the sink, looking into the mirror. As the glass steamed over, his own image was obscured, and he saw again the lone figure of Fletcher Kane at the window of the big cabin, staring at the frozen lake, with nothing to hold to but the thinnest of hopes.

"You okay in there?" Jo called from beyond the door.

Cork realized he'd been standing a long time gripping the solid porcelain of the sink. "I'll be out in a minute."

After his shower, he came downstairs to the smell of fresh popcorn and found his family already gathered in front of the television. Stevie was in his pajamas.

Cork sat on the sofa with his son snuggled against him, spilling pieces of popcorn into his lap. He paid little attention to the video. He was seeing instead the empty white trails that had been in front of him all day, and he was thinking, was there somewhere he should have looked but hadn't? He was surprised when the movie seemed to have ended so quickly.

"Time for bed," Jo said to her son.

"I'll take him up," Cork offered.

"You're sure?"

"I'm sure. Come on, buddy. How about a piggyback ride?"

Stevie wrapped his arms and his legs tightly about his father and rode Cork's back upstairs to bed. Cork tucked him in, sat down, and began to read from *The Tales of King Arthur.* Stevie lay staring up at the ceiling, his hands behind his head.

"Does it hurt to die?" he asked suddenly.

Cork lowered the book. At seven, Stevie had already withstood blows that some people lived their whole lives never having to face. Cork believed his son was strong deep down and he answered honestly.

"It does sometimes."

"Annie says it's like sleep. And then you wake up with the angels."

"It might be like that. I don't really know."

"Angels are white, like snow."

Stevie said it as if he knew it was the truth, and Cork, who knew the absolute truth of nothing, didn't argue.

He read until Stevie's eyes closed and his breathing was deep and regular, then he closed the book and listened to the wind push against the house as if seeking a way to enter. He pressed the covers tightly around his son, gave him a gentle kiss, and turned out the light.

Jo was already in bed. She had an open folder on her lap, a legal file. She wore a long, yellow sleep shirt that Jenny had given her for Christmas. Across the front in black letters was printed LAWYERS DO IT IN COURT. In Cork's eyes, she was a beautiful woman, his wife, and he looked at her with appreciation, as if he'd almost lost her but now here she was, a gift.

Jo looked up from her reading. "Is Stevie asleep?"

Cork nodded.

"Rose called. She's fine."

"At least the lines are still up," Cork said. "That's something."

"You look exhausted. Why don't you call it a night?"

"Not sure I can sleep."

"Do you want to talk?"

"I don't know what there is to say." He stood at the end of their bed. "Schanno's calling in a cadaver dog. Not that it will do any good. Way too cold. He just wants to be certain in his own mind, and the Kanes', that he's tried everything. If Charlotte Kane's out there, she'll be frozen under that snow until the spring melt." Cork hesitated, then said what was on his mind. "I wanted to ask Mal Thorne something today. I wanted to ask him why his God lets things like this happen."

"His God?"

"His idea of God. Doesn't he preach a loving God every Sunday?" Cork didn't know for sure, because church was a place where he'd refused to set foot for the last three years.

Jo gave him a look that seemed full of compassion, not censure. "Do you really want to argue theology right now?"

She was right. It wasn't God he was angry with.

"I'm going to walk a little," he said.

"I'll be here."

He headed downstairs and found Jenny standing at the living room window. He glanced where she looked and he was startled by her dark reflection in the glass. For the briefest instant, he saw again the shape of the wraith that had appeared to him on the ice of Fisheye Lake, a form that was both real and not real, that he'd sensed was Charlotte and yet was not Charlotte. Had they connected, two souls lost in a frigid hell?

" 'Rage against the dying of the light,' " Jenny said.

"What's that?"

"It's from a poem by Dylan Thomas."

Jenny was an honors English student and an avid reader. She dreamed of being a great writer someday. She had a knack for remembering passages and seemed to have an appropriate literary reference for any occasion. Cork studied her reflected face, pale and serious in the window.

"Will you find her?" she asked.

He didn't like the way she'd phrased her question, as if the responsibility for saving Charlotte Kane were his personally. He wanted to tell her that he'd done his best. That they all had. That it was no one's fault.

"I don't know," he said.

Across the street, John O'Loughlin came out of his house and trudged to where his Caravan sat buried against the curb. He cleared the door on the driver's side, stepped in, and started the engine. Then he got out and scraped his windows. Finally, he tried to ease the vehicle forward. The tires just spun. O'Loughlin got out again, pulled a shovel from the back of the van, and dug at the snow in front of the wheels. Cork couldn't imagine what would take a man out into a storm like that. He considered bundling up and going over to give a hand, but he knew that even if O'Loughlin made it out of the drift in front of his house, he'd just get stuck somewhere else. In a couple of minutes, Cork's neighbor gave up and went back inside.

"Do you know her well?" he asked.

Jenny shook her head. "I used to talk to her a little at church, but she hasn't come for a long time."

"How about school?"

"She's a senior. We hang out in different crowds. She's rich. Pretty. You know."

"She's always seemed very nice. Quiet. Smart, I hear. Very smart." Though how smart was it to ride a snowmobile alone into the wilderness in the dead of night?

"Smart, yeah, but she's been kind of out of control for a while," Jenny said. "Partying a lot, running with Solemn Winter Moon."

"Solemn," Cork said. He knew the kid well. Ojibwe, good-looking, troubled. An enticing guide for a young woman who wanted a quick walk on the wild side.

"There's something else," Jenny began, then hesitated.

"What is it?" he said.

"It's just that . . ." She bit her lip and weighed the wisdom of proceeding.

Cork waited.

"I had a class with her last term. Creative writing, one of my English electives. Mostly we wrote poetry. We read some of it aloud in class, but a lot of it we didn't. We kept these poetry journals that we only shared with the teacher and a poetry partner. Charlotte was my poetry partner. I saw what she didn't share with the class. What she read out loud was fine and all, but what she wrote in her journal was really different. Way better than anything else any of us wrote. But very dark."

"Dark how?"

"You know that artist Hieronymus Bosch?"

"The guy who paints those weird nightmare things, right?"

"Yeah. That was Charlotte's poetry. Really beautiful, you know, but scary." She looked at her father, her blue eyes troubled. "She went out in the middle of the night, right? Alone?"

"That's the way it looks."

"Dad, a lot of her poetry was about death and suicide."

"I don't think that's such an unusual fascination for a teenager, Jen."

"There was one I remember all about resurrection and death."

"She's Catholic. Death and resurrection, that's pretty much what it's all about."

"No, she looked at it the other way around. Resurrection, then death. It was this poem about Lazarus, about how Jesus, when he raised Lazarus from the dead, didn't do the guy any favors. Lazarus had gone through death once, and now he was just going to have to go through it again. In the poem, he's really pissed off. It ended something like,

> 'Death take my hand and lead me to that dark bed
> From which I neither rise,
> Nor remember,
> Nor dream,
> Nor dread.' "

The wind let loose a fist that slammed against the house, and the whole structure quivered.

"Dad, you don't think she might be, like, trying to kill herself?"

He put his arm around her. "I'd hate to think so."

They watched the storm a while together, then Jenny said, "I'm going to bed."

Cork kissed the crown of her hair. " 'Night, sweetheart."

He called John O'Loughlin to find out if there were some emergency, and if so, some way he could help. O'Loughlin said it wasn't an emergency, really. He was completely out of coffee, and the idea of facing a morning of shoveling without a cup of java was frightening. Cork said he always had a pot ready by six, and told his neighbor to come on over.

He started toward the front door to secure it for the night. But he imagined Charlotte Kane struggling to get in out of the cold only to find every door locked against her. He couldn't bring himself to throw the bolt.

Jo was waiting for him in the bedroom, her book closed on the nightstand. Cork put on his flannel pajamas and slipped under the covers beside her. She put a hand softly on his chest. "Are you all right?"

Cork stared up at the ceiling, as Stevie had done earlier. "I saw something out there today." He told her about his experience in the whiteout.

"If it was so vague, why do you think it was Charlotte?"

"Crazy, huh?"

"I didn't say that."

"I felt it was Charlotte, that's all. At the same time, it wasn't. She was different somehow."

"One of the *manidoog* taking her shape?" She was speaking of the spirits the Ojibwe, whose blood ran through Cork's veins, believed resided in the forests, and she was not speaking lightly.

"I just can't help feeling she was trying . . ." He thought about it. "It's hard to explain, but I think she reached out somehow, you know?"

"You believe she's dead?"

"Yes."

Jo studied his profile. Cork could feel her eyes on him.

"There's something else, isn't there?" she said.

"Yeah." Cork took a deep breath. "Children do stupid things, Jo. Dangerous things. Even the best of them. Sometimes I wonder if we really know our children."

"We know them, Cork."

"It could be Jenny out there. Or Annie. God knows we've had our share of close calls. I think about Fletcher and Glory, what they've got to face, and the truth is, I'm so damned relieved it's not us. Isn't that awful?"

"I'd say it's only human." She kissed his forehead lightly. "You're a good man. You've done your best. We all have. So much is out of our hands, out of anyone's hands." She reached to the lamp on the nightstand and turned out the light. Then she put her arms around her husband. "Sleep," she told him. "Just sleep now. You've earned it."

He believed he'd no more earned his sleep than Fletcher and his sister had earned their worry. But his own children were safe in bed. And his wife's warm arms cradled him. And although these were things that every day he took for granted, that night they felt like the rarest of treasures.

"Sleep," Jo whispered. "Sleep."

And Cork decided he could.

APRIL

WHEN HE WAS TWENTY-ONE YEARS OLD and wild, before he settled down to study law, Oliver Bledsoe cut off half his right foot. He did it with a McCullough chain saw. He was employed at the time on one of Hutch Gunnar's logging crews operating out of Babbitt, hired to limb and buck, which meant that he carefully walked the felled trees, trimming off their branches and cutting the trunks into sections to be hauled to the mill. In those days, he often showed up for work nursing a hangover. That morning, he showed up drunk. It was late autumn, and a light snow had fallen the night before. A hunter's snow. Bledsoe, as he mounted the first downed tree, was amazed at the dreamy beauty of the woods around him. He was amazed, too, at his own agility as he scampered down the trunk, cutting to the right and to the left, swinging his McCullough nimbly as if he were some kind of dancer in some kind of dream. So deeply enraptured was he, and numbed from the alcohol, that he didn't feel at all the cut of the chain saw as it sliced through the steel toe of his Wolverine boots. He didn't even realize he'd carved off a good chunk of his own flesh and bone until he saw his blood staining the sheet of snow on the ground below him.

The accident turned out to be a wake-up call for Bledsoe, who exchanged his chain saw for a stack of law books and became a damn fine lawyer.

Although he liked to claim he'd cut off half his foot, in truth, it was maybe a tenth—his two smallest toes and a couple of inches north of that. And while he always made it known to his opponents on the basketball court that they were playing against a cripple, he still had the best outside jump shot Cork O'Connor had ever seen.

Cork and Bledsoe sat in the men's steam room of the Aurora YMCA. Father Mal Thorne was with them, and Randy Gooding, too. They were part of the team officially known as the St. Agnes Saints, but usually they referred to themselves as the Old Martyrs, because on Saturday mornings during basketball season, week after week in the name of the church, they sacrificed themselves on the court. Although Cork's faith had lapsed, playing with the Old Martyrs was one of the few ties he maintained with St. Agnes. It was something he did for his body; his soul was not an issue. He enjoyed the company of the men, liked how the games brought them together in an easy fellowship. Afterward, the team generally gathered in the steam room to let the wet heat melt the ache out of their weary muscles.

"More steam?" Mal Thorne asked. He got up from his bench and poured a bit of cool water from a bucket over the thermal mechanism mounted on the wall.

Father Mal Thorne's nose followed a crooked line. It had been broken more times than he could remember during his Golden Gloves boxing days, and later when he was the middleweight intramural champ at Notre Dame. A thin braid of scar tissue crowned his left eyebrow, but there were also two long scars across his chest clearly unrelated to boxing. How they'd happened, no one knew. The priest refused to talk about it. As a cop, Cork had seen a lot of men in holding cells or on their way to prison with similar scars, usually the result of a knife slash. He knew that Mal had run a homeless shelter on South Michigan Avenue in Chicago, a tough territory. He'd heard rumors that the scars had been delivered by hoodlums trying to rob the shelter and that Mal had used his pugilist's skills to disabuse them of the notion. Cork had never pushed the priest for an explanation. A man's past was his own affair, and he dealt with his scars in his own way. Mal Thorne wasn't tall, but he was fast and aggressive, and a natural leader on the court, so usually he played point guard.

The wall vents began to hiss hot vapor, and Mal sat down.

"Heard you on the radio yesterday, Cork, tearing into Randy's boss," Bledsoe said.

He was talking about Sheriff Arne Soderberg who'd taken over the office from Wally Schanno in January.

"Tearing into Arne Soderberg?" Mal laughed. "I'd have loved to hear that. What did you do, Cork?"

It had been during Olaf Gregerson's weekly call-in radio program *All Around Aurora*. Sheriff Soderberg was the guest. He'd spent most of the initial interview crowing about his accomplishments in just the few weeks he'd been in office. Once the phone line opened up for calls, Cork seized the opportunity to call and point out some of the cold realities that underlay the sheriff's glowing assertions.

"I'll tell you what he did," Bledsoe said. "Old Arne claims that in the couple months he's been sheriff, crime in Tamarack County has declined thirty percent over the preceding seven-month period."

"Not true?" Mal said.

"Probably true," Cork put in. "What I pointed out was simply that every winter, after the summer tourists and the fall color gawkers have gone, crime in Tamarack County drops, and after the fishing opener in the spring and all the tourists come back, the crime rate climbs back up. Arne's taking credit for a pattern we've seen for years."

"That was only the beginning," Bledsoe said. "Cork took him to task for laying off officers and cutting programs in order to look good financially to the electorate when he runs for the state legislature, which everybody knows is his next move."

Gooding said, "He came back from the radio station ready to draw blood, and he took a bite out of anyone in the department who looked cross-eyed at him. Thanks a lot, Cork."

"Sorry."

"No, I mean it. Thanks a lot. Somebody needed to say those things."

Gooding, who sat next to Cork, stood up and began to stretch. His body was lithe and unmarred. That didn't mean he had no scars. Cork knew that the wounds people carried didn't always show on the skin. He was younger than the others, not quite thirty. Before coming to Aurora, he'd been with the FBI, assigned to the Milwaukee field office. He'd told Cork he left because the job turned out to be all paperwork, that he was a small-town boy at heart, and that he liked the idea of serving folks who would know him as a person, not just a badge. He was religious, very Catholic, a little pious maybe, but these days Cork tended to think that of almost anyone who attended church regularly. He sang in the St. Agnes choir and headed the youth program, where the kids adored him. He'd struck up a particularly good friendship with Annie, Cork's middle child, because at one time he'd been in the seminary, and Annie, for as long as anyone could remember, had dreamed of being a nun. Annie insisted that she connected with him on a spiritual level, but it probably didn't hurt that he was drop-dead gorgeous. An affable man, still a bachelor, he was considered a catch in Aurora, but so far as Cork knew he was seeing no one. He was the tallest of the Old Martyrs, and he played center.

Cork felt his own scars were insignificant, two bullet holes, an entrance wound the size of a dime on his right shoulder and a slightly larger exit wound on his back just below his right scapula. The bullet had shattered bone and loosed a flood of blood and had almost killed him, but unless someone pointed them out, he usually forgot about them.

Mal Thorne said, "You don't think much of our new sheriff, Cork?"

Sweat dripped from the end of Cork's nose. He sat naked on a towel, his back against the tiles of the steam room wall. The other men were all hazy figures through the hot fog. "For him the job's about politics, not law enforcement."

"Ever regret your decision not to run?"

"Not for a minute," Cork said.

The door of the steam room opened. Cool air sifted in.

"Gooding? Deputy Gooding? You in there?"

"Yo, Pender. What's up?" Gooding said.

"Sheriff wants you," Pender called back.

"Hey, man. It's my day off."

"He says get your ass to the office now."

"Is there overtime in it?"

"Close the damn door, Pender," Bledsoe said. "You're letting the North Pole in."

"Not until I see Deputy Gooding stepping out."

"Talk to him, Randy. It's getting cold in here. I just saw a penguin waddle by."

"I'm coming, Pender. Close the door."

Gooding stood up, and the steam swirled as he moved.

"Think I'm done, too," Cork said. He got up from the cedar bench. "Who do we play next week?"

"Team from the casino," Bledsoe said. "The Five Card Studs."

In the locker room, Randy Gooding and Deputy Duane Pender stood huddled in a corner near the showers. Gooding nodded a couple of times and finally said, "I'll be out of here in ten." Pender strode quickly out. Gooding went straight to his locker without bothering to shower.

When Soderberg became sheriff, he reorganized the department, cutting out the specialized units that Cork and Wally Schanno had created to focus on particular areas of crime prevention and investigation. That had pissed off a number of veteran officers, including Captain Ed Larson, who'd headed major crimes investigation for years and who, along with several others, had resigned. Now Gooding, because of his FBI training, generally handled the responsibility of investigating serious crimes, but he had no special rank or title and got no extra pay for it. He did it, he said, because he loved the work, something Cork understood.

"What's up, Randy?" Cork asked. "Pender looked pretty serious."

Gooding glanced around to confirm that they were alone. "Couple of hikers found a body buried in snow up on Moccasin Creek. Young. Female."

"Charlotte Kane?"

"Won't know for certain until we get there. But that's sure what I'm thinking."

"Where on Moccasin Creek?"

Gooding started to answer but caught himself. "Unh-uh. No way. I can tell what you're thinking. Cork, this kind of thing isn't your business anymore." He opened his locker and began to dress. "Don't take this wrong, but when I worked the field office in Milwaukee, we had a couple old agents who'd retired and couldn't stand it. Those guys were always dropping by the office, adding their two cents to everything. Became a real pain in the ass."

"I froze for nearly a week trying to find her."

"Sixty other people did, too. You don't see them clamoring for a glimpse of the body."

"Where on Moccasin Creek?"

"Look, you show up and the sheriff's going to know who clued you in. He'll ream me."

"I'll swear it wasn't you."

"He's not stupid."

"Jury's still out on that one. Come on, Randy. Where?"

Gooding stroked his beard, a trim strip of reddish hair that formed a triangle around his mouth. He often said that tolerance of facial hair was one of the things he liked about working on a rural police force. He shook his head and gave in. "Footbridge about a quarter mile north of the trailhead off County Five."

"I know it."

The deputy slipped a T-shirt over his head, then bent to put on his boots. When he'd tied them, he straightened and shot Cork a guilty look. "Give us a head start at least."

As Gooding exited, Mal Thorne came around the corner from the steam room, a towel wrapped around his waist. He glanced at Gooding's back, then at Cork, who was just beginning to dress. "Neither of you showering? What's so important?"

"A body's been found in the snow up on Moccasin Creek."

"Where's that?"

"Just east of Valhalla."

"A woman's body?"

"Yes."

"Charlotte Kane?"

"Can't say for sure. But I don't know of any other women who've disappeared here in the last few months."

"I'd like to go with you."

Cork didn't answer.

"You're going," the priest said. "That's why you're not showering."

"It's a closure thing for me," Cork said.

"I've got plenty of reason, too."

Cork started to object but realized Mal Thorne had given every bit as much of himself as Cork had in the bitter, cold days during the search for Charlotte Kane. He nodded toward the priest's locker.

"Better get dressed then. I'm not taking you naked."

5

"YOU'RE QUIET," Cork said after they'd ridden a long time in silence. "Sure you want to do this?"

Because he never went to church anymore, Cork didn't relate to Mal Thorne as a priest. They just played basketball together. Mal had come to Aurora a couple of years earlier to assist the aging pastor of St. Agnes. He was an energetic man, well liked, and had done an excellent job managing the parish. Whether he was capable of handling what he might see on Moccasin Creek was something Cork didn't know.

Mal said, "I've just been thinking. If it is Charlotte Kane's body out there, in a way it may be a blessing."

"How do you figure that?"

"Fletcher and Glory are desperately in need of resolution, one way or another."

"Kane's in need of resolution in a lot of ways, you ask me."

The priest studied him. "I gather from some of the things Rose has said to me that you and Fletcher aren't on the best of terms."

Cork turned onto County 5, a narrow strip of asphalt heavily potholed during the freeze and thaw at the end of winter. They were driving through the Superior National Forest, far north of Aurora. The April sun was bright and promising through the windshield of Cork's old Bronco.

"I'm pretty sure Fletcher blames my father for the death of his own father."

Surprise showed on the priest's face. "How so?"

"You know my father was sheriff here a long time ago."

"I'd heard that, yes."

"Fletcher's father was a dentist. When Fletcher and I were kids, his old man killed himself. Turned out my father was investigating a complaint of sexual assault lodged by one of Harold Kane's female patients."

"And Fletcher holds your father responsible?"

"He's never said as much, but his actions have spoken pretty eloquently."

They thundered over an old wooden bridge and Cork began to slow down, watching for the turnoff. He knew it would come up suddenly around a sharp bend.

"Rose tells me things are rough for them," Cork said.

Mal nodded. "Fletcher's totally withdrawn. And Glory loved that girl as if she were her own daughter. I think if she didn't have Rose to lean on, she'd have fallen apart completely by now."

"The death of a child." Cork shook his head. "I can't think of anything more devastating."

"They have a lot of people praying for them."

"Might as well be throwing pennies down a wishing well."

The priest gave him a long look. "Someday I'd like to know the whole story."

"What story?"

"The one that ends with you angry at God."

"And someday I'd like to know the other story," Cork said.

"Which one is that?"

"The one that ends with a guy as obviously capable as you are exiled to a small parish buried in the Northwoods. You must've really pissed off God or somebody."

"Maybe the choice was my own."

"Yeah," Cork said. "Right."

A brown road sign marked the trailhead at Moccasin Creek. Cork pulled into the graveled parking lot. Snow still lay banked along the edges in small dirty humps, the last of the great piles that had been plowed during winter and that had been melting slowly for weeks. The lot was filled with vehicles, mostly from the Tamarack County Sheriff's Department. Cy Borkmann, a heavy man and a longtime deputy, stood near his cruiser, smoking a cigarette. Not far away, another man, a stranger, sat in a red Dodge Neon. The door of the Neon stood wide open. The man sat hunched over, legs out of the car, feet on the wet gravel of the lot, staring at the ground.

Cork parked next to Borkmann's cruiser and got out. "Morning, Cy."

The deputy smiled, and his already big cheeks mounded some more. "Hey, Cork. Father Mal. What're you guys doing here?"

"We heard the news. Dropped by to see if we could help."

Borkmann's smile faded. He shook his head, and the sack of skin below his chin wobbled. "Sheriff said to keep everybody but authorized personnel out. You're not exactly authorized these days."

Borkmann had been a deputy long before Cork was sheriff. They'd always got on well. But things had changed, and Borkmann had his orders.

Cork nodded toward the man in the Neon. "Who's that?"

"Found the body."

"Looks a little shook up. Mind if I talk to him?"

Borkmann thought it over. "Sheriff didn't say anything about that. Go ahead."

Cork walked to the man, who looked up without interest. He appeared to be in his late twenties with dark, heavily oiled hair and the kind of deep tan that told Cork he was not from anywhere near Minnesota.

"Cork O'Connor." He offered the man his hand.

"Jarrod Langley."

"I understand you found the body."

"My wife did."

Cork looked around.

"She's back at the lodge," Langley said. "I left her there when I called the sheriff's office."

"You're not from around here," Cork said, noting the accent.

"Mobile," Langley said. "Alabama. On our honeymoon." He picked up a piece of gravel and tossed it a couple of times in his hand. "I wanted to go to Aruba. Suzanne wanted to go north. She never saw snow before."

They'd missed the pretty snow by a few weeks. What was left on the ground now were isolated patches littered with dead pine needles and branches and other debris shaken from the trees by the spring winds. Uneven melt left the snow pockmarked and cancerous looking. In those places where the sun shone steadily all day long, the wet earth was laid bare and the black mud looked like pools of crude oil.

"How'd you find the body?" Cork said.

"We were going for a hike. Figured if we couldn't ski or snowmobile at least we could walk. Got down there to the bridge and Suzanne saw something sticking out of the snow along the creek. She climbed down to see what it was. Hollered back up to me that she'd found a big machine. She thought it was a snowmobile. Next thing I know, she's screaming her head off." He threw the piece of gravel he'd been holding, heaved it across the lot, where it embedded itself in a gritty snowbank. "Hell of a honeymoon."

"I can imagine," Cork said.

Langley looked at him, squeezing his eyes a little against the bright sunlight. "You one of the sheriff's people?"

"Retired," Cork said. "In a manner of speaking. Mr. Langley, anybody offer you coffee?"

"No."

"Would you like some?"

"Sure."

Cork went back to where Borkmann and the priest stood together. "Cy, you used to carry a Thermos of coffee in your cruiser."

"Still do," Borkmann said.

"How about giving that man a little. Might not settle his nerves, but it can't hurt."

Borkmann looked at Jarrod Langley and nodded. "Good idea."

When the deputy headed toward the Neon with the Thermos in his hand, Cork said to Mal Thorne in a low voice, "Let's go." He started quickly for the trail along Moccasin Creek. Without a word, the priest followed.

The trail access was through a break in the pine trees that enclosed the parking lot and began with a fairly steep incline ending at the creek. Cork led the way. The ground was thawed and muddy and full of boot prints. In a few minutes, the two men reached the footbridge where melting snow and ice had turned the little stream beneath into a milky torrent.

Nine people worked the scene, nearly a third of the whole department. Deputies Jackson, Dwyer, and Minot were using a hand winch hooked to the trunk of a big red pine to pull the snowmobile out of the creek and up the bank. Deputy Marsha Dross was documenting the scene with video while Pender did the same with a still camera. Johannsen and Kirk were working with a tape measure. Randy Gooding hunkered at the water's edge, half hidden by a boulder that sat on a thick plate of melting snow. Also on that plate, jutting from behind the boulder like a couple of bread sticks, was a pair of jean-clad human legs.

Sheriff Arne Soderberg stood looking over Gooding's shoulder. Soderberg never wore a uniform. He preferred, in the normal course of his duties, to dress in trim three-piece suits, crisp white shirts, silk ties. On the street, he could easily have been mistaken for a successful banker or stockbroker from the Twin Cities. He was a few years younger than Cork, but his hair was already a magnificent silver, which he had razor cut once a week. He was a good-looking man—strong jaw, piercing blue eyes, a charming, practiced smile—and he photographed well. He had no experience with law enforcement. It was widely known that he was simply being groomed by the Independent Republicans for higher office and that the job as sheriff was an opportunity for Soderberg to prove himself as a public servant before moving on to grander things. For years, he'd been on the family payroll, a vice president in his father's company, Soderberg Transport, a huge enterprise that dominated trucking on the Iron Range and much of the rest of northern Minnesota. His enthusiasm for politics coincided with the age at which most men experienced a midlife crisis. Cork suspected public office might have been the answer for a man who could buy an expensive sports car anytime he wanted.

Cork and Mal crossed the bridge and worked their way down the creek bank toward Gooding and Soderberg. The deputies who knew Cork well gave him a nod, but no one said a word about his presence. Until Soderberg raised his head.

"O'Connor. What the hell are you doing here?"

The sheriff wore something a bit more appropriate to the work at hand than his usual three-piece suit. He sported a new Pendleton shirt and jeans that carried a sharp crease. Despite the April mud, he'd somehow managed to keep his Gore-Tex boots spotless.

Cork had been certain that after their heated exchange on Olaf Gregerson's radio program Soderberg would not be happy to see him. Anger, however, wasn't what Cork saw in that first moment his eyes locked on the sheriff. Instead there was a look of horror, the expression of someone whose senses brought to him a reality his sensibility couldn't deal with. Cork figured the dead girl must be a gruesome sight.

"I heard about Charlotte Kane," Cork said.

He'd reached the boulder and could now see what Gooding and the sheriff saw. The body lay on a bed of snow crystals like a fish in a meat market display. She was fully clothed, still wearing her down parka. The skin of her face and hands seemed well preserved, and Cork figured the body had been frozen all winter.

From Soderberg's reaction, Cork had assumed the worst, but he'd been wrong. Even in death, Charlotte Kane was lovely to look at. Her hair was long and black, sleek from the snow around her melting under the April sun. Cork remembered how, whenever she'd stopped at Sam's Place for a burger or a shake, she'd always been extremely polite. She'd been a quiet, lovely young woman. Now her face was pale, relaxed, her arms crossed over her chest, as if she were only in a long, deep sleep. Seeing her this way, Cork felt an overwhelming sadness for her and her family.

And something more, something he hadn't felt in months. The tug of a dark shape from behind a curtain of solid white, an unseen hand that reached out to him.

"Pender," Soderberg hollered. "Pender, get these men out of here."

Cork looked back at the footbridge, then at the snowmobile being hauled up the bank, and finally at the place where the body lay. "Looks like her Arctic Cat flew right off the bridge," he said. "Must've come hell-bent down that hill."

Gooding nodded. "And she couldn't negotiate the bridge. She'd been drinking, we know that."

The bridge was well marked and wide enough for an easy crossing. Cork recalled what Jenny had told him about Charlotte the night she'd disappeared, about the girl's dark poetry and fascination with suicide.

Soderberg stepped in front of Cork, eclipsing the body. "I want you out of here, O'Connor. This isn't your concern." He looked around. "Where the hell is Pender?"

"What's that?" Cork pointed toward a scrap of brightly colored paper just visible in the snow a few feet away.

"I was just going to check it." Gooding wore surgical gloves and he reached over and pulled out a red, white, and green wrapper. "Pearson's Nut Goodie," he said. He brushed away a bit of snow and brought up some torn cellophane. "Beef jerky." He widened the cleared area and uncovered the remnant of a Doritos bag, pieces of frozen orange rind, and a Corona beer bottle with a couple of inches of pale liquid still in the bottom.

Gooding looked up at Cork. "What do you make of that?"

Soderberg, who still appeared shaken, said, "Maybe she was trapped by the storm and ate to keep her strength up, hoping to get found."

Cork studied the body, its peaceful repose. There was a detail that bothered him. "Take a good look at her, Arne. Notice anything?"

Soderberg swung his attention back to Cork and to the priest, who stood observing at a slight distance. "Out of here, O'Connor. And look, Father, I'm sorry, but you need to leave, too. Pender," he cried. "Pender, where the hell are you?"

"Here, Sheriff." Duane Pender emerged from the shadow under the footbridge, zipping his fly as he came. He stepped carefully among the rocks and pockets of snow along the creek bank. "Nature called," he said with a look of chagrin.

"Escort these men back to the parking lot," Soderberg ordered. "O'Connor, I'd appreciate it if you didn't give my deputy any trouble."

Cork said, "Where are her gloves, Arne?"

"What?"

"Her gloves."

Soderberg looked down at her hands, which were white and bare.

"If she'd driven that snowmobile out here without gloves on, her hands would have been frozen long before she got to Moccasin Creek," Cork said.

Soderberg nodded to Gooding. "Check her coat."

Gooding went through the pockets of her parka and came up empty-handed. He sifted the snow around her body and shook his head.

"Why would she have the presence of mind to bring food with her but not gloves? And one more thing," Cork said. "That bottle of Corona. Hard to believe it would have survived the crash in one piece."

"But not out of the question," Soderberg countered.

"Maybe not. How'd she open it?"

"How do you usually get a beer open? You twist off the damn top."

"That's a Corona, Arne. They don't make a twist top. Unless you find an opener around here, you gotta wonder."

Soderberg said, "I thought I told you to get these men out of here, Pender."

Deputy Pender was new to the sheriff's department. He hadn't served under Cork. To him, Corcoran O'Connor was just a guy who ran a burger joint on Iron Lake. Because Pender was a Baptist, the priest had no special authority as far as he was concerned. He jerked his head in the direction of the trail up to the parking lot. "You heard the sheriff."

"Are you going to bag that stuff?" Cork asked, indicating the things Gooding had uncovered near the body.

"O'Connor." Soderberg put out a hand, as if to move Cork bodily from the scene. Cork glared at the hand, and Soderberg drew up short of actually touching him.

"I'll bag it," Gooding said.

Cork turned and started up the bank. The priest held back.

Mal Thorne asked, "Sheriff, when are you going to tell her parents?"

"I don't know yet."

"I'd like to be there when you do."

Soderberg shook his head. "I don't think—"

"Arne," Cork said, "have you ever had to tell a mother or father that their child is dead?"

In reply, the sheriff simply glared. It may have been meant to demonstrate Soderberg's perturbation, but more probably it was meant to disguise the fact that he'd never had to shoulder that particular burden.

Cork said, "When you do, I think you'll be glad to have someone like Mal there with you."

"When I want your advice, I'll ask for it." To his credit, Soderberg spoke civilly to the priest. "I'll think about it, and I'll let you know."

"I'll be at the rectory."

Soderberg turned an angry eye on Pender. "When you get to the parking lot, relieve Borkmann and send him down here. I want a word with him."

They walked up the trail, slowly because of the slippery terrain and because there was something heavy on them now. Cork thought about Soderberg, about the anguish on his face as he'd stared down at the body of Charlotte Kane. It occurred to him that the sheriff had probably never dealt with death in this way before. He wondered how Soderberg liked the responsibility of the job now.

The priest let out a deep sigh that had nothing to do with the effort of the climb. "Is Rose home?"

"I think so," Cork said. "Why?"

The priest kept his eyes on the mud. "Glory's going to need her."

6

Cork spent the afternoon working on Sam's Place, getting ready for the tourist season. Sam's Place was an old Quonset hut that had long ago been converted to a burger stand on the shore of Iron Lake, just beyond the northern limits of Aurora. Beginning in early May until late October, Cork, with the help of his daughters, catered to the hungry fishermen and tourists and locals. For an ex-lawman, it was a quiet existence, but one Cork had come to appreciate.

He was thinking about Charlotte Kane as he worked, about how peaceful she'd looked in death. He'd heard that freezing wasn't a bad way to go, that people who froze to death experienced a false warmth at the end, a final euphoria. Maybe that's how it had been for Charlotte. He hoped so. However, that didn't explain why she had no gloves with her, or who'd opened the curiously unbroken Corona bottle. Cork had considered from several angles the food wrappers found in the snow near the body. He would love to have a look at the autopsy, to know if any of that junk food was in her stomach when she died. Because more and more, the circumstances caused him to consider the possibility that she had not been alone at the end.

He'd already pulled away the plywood that had covered the serving windows all winter, and was just preparing to clean a squirrel's nest from the lakeside eave, when his cell phone chirped.

"Cork O'Connor," he answered.

There was nothing but static on the phone, which didn't surprise him at all. Technologically speaking, Aurora was at the edge of a frontier. The demand for cell phones wasn't great enough yet to warrant the building of relay towers that would easily service the area. North of Aurora, cell phones didn't work at all. In town, reception was often sketchy at best. Usually, Cork didn't even bother to carry his cell phone with him.

"Hello," he said. "You're not coming in well."

Within the scratchy static, he made out Rose's voice and two phrases. "Glory Kane . . ." and ". . . needs your help."

Glory Kane opened the door before he knocked. Cork was surprised to see that she seemed perfectly sober.

Glory was in her midthirties, a good thirteen years younger than her brother. Aside from the surname they shared, there was little about the two Kanes that was alike. Fletcher was tall, awkward looking, already gone bald. Glory was a small woman, with long black hair, and lovely features. When she did the full nine yards of makeup, she was absolutely stunning. For a while after she'd arrived in Aurora with Fletcher, she'd often taken the time to look that way. Little by little, however, she had abandoned the enormous effort it must have taken to paint over and powder smooth her pain, and now her face was different. It bore the beaten expression of a war veteran, the sometimes vacant stare of someone who'd survived a long and bitter campaign. Very often, this was simply the effect of the booze, for it was no secret that Glory Kane drank. She wasn't obnoxious in her drunkenness. Usually, she holed up in her brother's big house, and no one saw her for days. In the Kane household, she seemed to cover much the same territory that Rose did with the O'Connors, and to care about Charlotte as deeply as Rose did her own nieces and nephew. This might have been the reason she had allowed Rose closer than anyone else in Aurora. That and the fact that Rose didn't have a judgmental bone in her body.

"Thank you for coming," she said, and stood back to let him enter.

Like Cork and a lot of others who now lived in Aurora, the Kanes had returned after a long absence. Fletcher and Glory had been gone longer than most, thirty-five years. Fletcher, when he left, had been Cork's age, thirteen. Glory had been conceived, but not yet born, visible only as an obvious rounding of her mother's belly. So far as Cork knew, no one had heard a word from them after they'd gone. Any relatives they'd had in Tamarack County had died or departed long ago. They had no old friends and no apparent reason that compelled their return. The middle-aged Fletcher, now a widower, had simply showed up unannounced one day a couple of years earlier, bringing with him his daughter, his sister, and enough money to be one of the richest men on the Iron Range. He'd settled into life in Aurora without any word about what had happened to him in the nearly four decades of his absence. The facts known about him were few. He was a physician, a plastic surgeon, but he no longer practiced. He speculated in real estate and land development instead. He supported the Independent Republican party with heavy donations. And he guarded his privacy fiercely, something guaranteed to raise an eyebrow in any small town.

In addition to building Valhalla, his isolated retreat, he'd bought one of the grandest houses in Aurora, the old Parrant estate, which occupied the entire tip of the finger of land called North Point. The house was huge, gray stone, surrounded by cedars and an enormous expanse of lawn that ran down to the shore of Iron Lake. Cork knew the Parrant estate well. One snowy night a few years before, he'd been the one who found Judge Parrant in his study with most of his head blown away.

Glory led him into the living room. Rose was already seated on the couch. She made room for Cork beside her.

"You know about Charlotte," he said.

Glory nodded.

"I'm sorry," Cork said.

"Thank you." It was obvious she'd been crying, but she seemed to have composed herself. Cork figured Rose had been a big help.

Glory generally kept to herself. Except for her regular attendance at St. Anges, she was seldom seen in public. This spawned all kinds of gossip. Rose listened to none of it, and from the beginning had made an effort to befriend her. Once or twice a week, she came visiting, and the two women talked over coffee. After Charlotte disappeared, Glory stopped going to church and Rose became very nearly her only contact with the world outside the stone walls of her brother's home. Glory was an intelligent woman and talked about books, religion, politics, but not, Rose said, about her life before she came to Aurora.

"You used to be sheriff," Glory said.

"That's right."

"Rose thinks you might know something about finding people."

"I suppose I do."

"When Sheriff Soderberg told us there was going to be an autopsy on Charlotte, Fletcher was furious. He's a doctor. He knows what they do to a body during an autopsy. He argued. If Father Mal hadn't been here to intervene, I think he might have become violent. He went into his office, locked the door, stayed there until the sheriff and Father Mal had gone. He wouldn't open it when I knocked. A little while later, he stormed out of the house. I haven't heard from him since. That was several hours ago."

"You're worried about his safety?"

"In his state of mind, I'm afraid he could do something drastic."

"And you want me to find him before he does?"

"Yes."

"Why not the sheriff's people?"

"I know he wouldn't talk to them, and they might only upset him more."

In the days of Judge Parrant, the house had been a dark place, full of hunting trophies and a suffocating silence. The trophies were gone but Cork still felt the silence there, thick in all the rooms he could not see.

"He might not want me looking for him," Cork said.

"But I do."

"I mean, he might not want *me* looking for him."

Glory's hands worked over each other, as if she were washing them, desperate to be clean. "I know he doesn't like you. I don't know why, but that doesn't matter now. I just want to be certain he's okay."

Cork said, "All right."

Glory took a white Bible from the coffee table and held it in her hands. "Rose and I have been talking. There are those who believe it takes three days for the spirit to adjust to the reality of death, three days to let go completely of the body. For Charlotte, three days was a long time ago. I understand that's not Charlotte they're working on in the morgue, but Fletcher doesn't see it that way."

Cork said, "Any idea where he might have gone?"

In the face of this simple question, Glory seemed completely lost.

"We've been over that, Cork," Rose said. "Glory has no idea."

"Does he have an office somewhere?" Cork prompted.

"Only here," Glory said.

"How about a bar he likes?"

"Fletcher doesn't drink."

"Friends?"

"Fletcher has associates. He has acquaintances. But he has no friends."

"Is there someplace that's special to him? Valhalla maybe?"

"He hates Valhalla. After Charlotte disappeared, he couldn't stand going back there."

"Could he be out driving somewhere, thinking?"

"He gets car sick."

"May I use your phone?" Cork said.

"There." Glory indicated a cordless on a table near the kitchen doorway.

Cork took the phone and stepped into the kitchen where he could speak in private. On the wall next to the refrigerator hung a large frame with several photographs, each with its own opening in the matte. They were all of Kane and his daughter in a happier time, smiling. On snowmobiles, on mountain bikes, on a tennis court, on a beach, and one in formal attire beside a wall hung with red bougainvillea. They appeared to have done a lot of things together, and seemed to have genuinely enjoyed each other's company. Physically, they were an unusual pairing—Charlotte, dark-haired and lovely, with a smile that showed braces; her father bald, long-limbed, and homely. Cork thought the girl had been lucky to have inherited what must have been her mother's beauty, because her father was so extraordinarily odd-looking. The photos appeared to have been taken before the Kanes moved to Minnesota, because there were mountains behind the snowmobiles, and the beach was on the ocean. Cork wondered why he'd never seen Kane and his daughter doing things together in Aurora. Had something happened to come between them, to ruin the joy they'd shared? The death of Kane's wife, perhaps? Cork didn't know the details, but maybe it had been a particularly difficult ordeal and the memory was painful. Perhaps that was why there were no pictures of Charlotte's mother.

He dialed the sheriff's office and spoke with Deputy Marsha Dross, who was on desk duty. Fletcher Kane hadn't been there. Cork called the morgue at Aurora Community Hospital where the autopsy would be performed, but he got no answer. He called and spoke with Arne Soderberg at home, who said that since he'd left the Kanes' house several hours earlier, he hadn't seen or heard from the man. Cork went back to the living room.

"Glory, is there a working telephone at Valhalla?"

"I think so. We never had the service canceled. But you're wasting your time, Cork."

"It's one more place we can eliminate."

Glory gave him the number.

Cork let the phone ring ten times. He was just about to hang up when the receiver at the other end was lifted. No one spoke.

"Fletcher?" Cork said.

He heard only the sound of breathing, heavy but not labored.

"Fletcher, it's Cork O'Connor."

There was a long moment of silence, followed by a single word uttered like a curse.

"Butchers."

Glory didn't accompany Cork. Fletcher, she said, wouldn't listen to her. Cork suspected Fletcher wouldn't listen to him either, but he agreed to try.

He wasn't surprised that Glory didn't know the roots of her brother's enmity toward the O'Connor name. It had occurred in a time when Glory was still contentedly inside her mother's womb.

Cork remembered Harold Kane as a spidery man, long-limbed, with bulging eyes, and soft hands that smelled of antiseptic. On a Saturday morning when Cork and Fletcher were both thirteen years old, Harold Kane had locked himself in his dental office on Oak Street, sat in the chair where his patients usually reclined, and put a bullet in his head.

In a small town like Aurora, suicide was the kind of event that lingered a long time in the collective memory. When it came to light that Sheriff Liam O'Connor had been investigating Dr. Kane because one of his patients had alleged that the dentist molested her while she was anesthetized in his office, there was a good deal more to remember than the desperate act itself. Because the man died before all the evidence could be considered and formal charges brought, his guilt or innocence was never established. That didn't matter. In the mind of the town, his response was proof enough. He was, in public opinion, tried and convicted.

A few weeks later, Fletcher Kane's pregnant mother left town, taking her son away from the vicious tongues.

Cork all but forgot the Kanes, but Fletcher had not forgotten the O'Connors. An incident occurred soon after the Kanes' return that signaled to Cork the deep resentment the man must have felt all those years as a result of his father's death.

Access to Sam's Place was via a narrow, gravel road that branched off a street on the outskirts of Aurora. Before it crossed the Burlington Northern tracks, the road passed through land privately owned by Shorty Geiger. Sam Winter Moon, the old Ojibwe after whom the establishment was named, had obtained easement rights through Geiger's land and across the Burlington Northern tracks. On Sam's death, when the Quonset hut and surrounding property passed to Cork O'Connor, there was a clause that required renegotiation of the easement agreement. In Aurora, not much happened in a hurry, and no one rushed to litigation. But shortly after Fletcher Kane returned, Cork received notice that access to Sam's Place could no longer occur as it had in the past. A development company had purchased Shorty's land and intended to put a fast-food franchise there, a move that would pretty much insure the end of Sam's Place. Jo mounted a marvelous legal battle and won back the easement rights. The franchise was never built. In the litigation process, Jo discovered that the major investor in the development company was none other than Fletcher Kane.

Cork pulled into the muddy drive of Valhalla, deep in the woods north of Aurora. It was hard dark by then, and his headlights flashed on the back end of Fletcher Kane's silver Cadillac El Dorado. He parked, killed his lights, and got out.

The night was still, but the lake was thawing. Beyond the pine trees, it moaned and cracked and made Cork think of a great animal awakening.

A bright three-quarter moon lit the scene. There were no lights on in the big cabin, nor in the guesthouse. Cork took a flashlight from the glove compartment of his Bronco, but he didn't turn it on. He approached the big cabin, carefully mounting the wooden steps built into the hillside. With its grand deck that overlooked the water, the cabin seemed like a ghost ship anchored among the black trunks of the pines. He crossed the deck to the screen door and saw that the heavy inside door was open. The room beyond it was completely dark.

As he stood at the threshold, Cork became aware of a strong odor all around him that was out of place among the fresh scent of spring pines.

Kerosene.

"Fletcher," he called toward the black inside.

He heard movement, then a metallic squeak. In the dark of the room, a small circle of glowing red rotated into sight. Cork interpreted the squeak to come from the mechanism of a swivel rocker. He was pretty sure the red glow came from the end of a lit cigar.

"Fletcher?"

"What are you doing here?"

"Glory asked me to come. She's worried."

"Tell her I'm touched. Now go away."

"I'm not leaving until we talk."

"I don't want to talk to you, O'Connor."

Kane's speech was slurred, and despite what Glory said about her brother not drinking, it was clear to Cork that's exactly what Fletcher had been doing. The whole situation struck Cork as odd. Glory, who drank, was sober. Fletcher, who didn't, was drunk.

"I know how hard this must be for you, Fletcher," he said.

"You have no idea."

"I have daughters. I know it would just about kill me to lose one."

"But you haven't lost one."

"I know you loved Charlotte. And that's why I know you're going to do the right thing for her."

"The right thing?" The tip of his cigar bloomed red as he took a deep draw amid the strong odor of kerosene that was everywhere.

"Do you know why Arne requested an autopsy?"

"All I heard was that he wanted to butcher my girl."

"In situations like this, an autopsy is almost automatic."

"Situations like what?"

"A death in which drinking might have played a part. In Charlotte's case, there's probably something even more compelling."

Although he could not see Kane clearly, he could see the dark shape and how still it was.

"They found some food wrappers and a beer bottle next to Charlotte's body. An autopsy could probably tell the sheriff if it was Charlotte who did the eating and drinking."

"What do you mean *if* it was Charlotte?" He thought about it. "Somebody was with her?"

"Maybe."

"Then why didn't the son of a bitch do anything to help?"

"I suppose there are several possibilities."

A long silence, then Kane struck on the darkest of the implications. "Somebody wanted her dead?"

"That's one of the possibilities."

"Who?"

"A question the autopsy could help answer."

Cork watched the glowing ember descend, and he heard the tiny squeal of the tobacco as Fletcher Kane ground out the cigar in an ashtray. A moment later, a small lamp came on.

Kane sat in a rocker. Over the years, he'd grown to resemble his father, a man of elongated proportions and bug eyes. He put Cork in mind of a giant grasshopper.

"I want to be alone, O'Connor." When Cork didn't move, Kane said, "You can tell Glory I'm fine."

Cork walked to his Bronco, but he didn't get in. He stood watching Valhalla, worried that it might yet go up in flames. In a few minutes, however, he saw Kane at a window, a tall, bent figure, staring down at the lake. Kane's mouth moved, speaking words Cork couldn't hear. Below him, as if in reply, the lake ice moaned.

7

CORCORAN O'CONNOR was three-quarters Irish and one-quarter Ojibwe. Except for a few years in college, and as a cop in Chicago after that, he'd lived his whole life in the town of his birth. He'd been raised Catholic, baptized at St. Agnes, received his first communion and was confirmed there. He'd served as an altar boy, sung in the choir, spent his share of time in the confessional. Being Catholic had been important to him once. For several years, however, he'd refused to set foot in church, and didn't give a hoot about the commandment of keeping the Sabbath holy.

On that April Sunday afternoon, Cork stood at the frozen edge of Iron Lake with Sam's Place at his back. The sun was high, its warmth soaking into the earth, melting the ice that still held the deeper soil prisoner. The air was laced with a fragrance that augured spring. He'd come with his tools and with half a mind to work on the old Quonset hut, but he knew he wouldn't disturb the peace of that afternoon. Even though he was at odds with God, he couldn't ignore the fact that on such a day there was a sacred feeling to everything.

Part of it was the place itself, that small parcel of land Sam Winter Moon had deeded to Cork. It was bounded on the north by the Bear Paw Brewery and on the south by a copse of poplars that held the ruins of an old foundry. West lay the tracks of Burlington Northern and beyond that the streets on the outskirts of Aurora. East, below the sun and beneath a thinning layer of ice, lay the deep, clear water of Iron Lake. There may have been places more beautiful, but none in Cork's thinking that were more special. Whenever he stood on that little stretch of shoreline, he could feel Sam Winter Moon's spirit there.

Sam had been his father's good friend. When Liam O'Connor died, shot dead in the line of duty as Tamarack County sheriff, Sam Winter Moon had stepped in and guided fourteen-year-old Corcoran O'Connor into manhood. Sam had done it without fanfare, as if the fatherless were the natural concern of every man. Summers in high school, Cork had worked at Sam's Place, learning his way around the grill, the state laws governing cleanliness, the rules of simple bookkeeping. Suffusing all their time together was the spirit of Sam Winter Moon's own manhood, a quiet strength couched within a gentle humor that was decidedly Ojibwe in its sensibility. In those days, despite the death of his father, Cork still practiced his Catholicism. The murder of Sam Winter Moon, a brutal killing for which Cork blamed both himself and God, had been the first of a series of tragedies that had hardened Cork's heart against the spirit of his baptism and the church of his confirmation.

Still, on such a day as this, standing at the edge of Iron Lake with the sweet, distant breath of spring breaking over his face, Cork couldn't help but feel gratitude. He remembered the words his Grandmother Dilsey, a full-blood Ojibwe, had once taught him. *Great Spirit! We honor you this day, and we thank you for life and for all things. Mother Earth! We honor you this day, and we thank you for life and for all things. You are our mother. You feed us, you clothe us, you shelter us, and you comfort us. For this we thank you and honor you.*

It seemed to Cork to cover things as well as any prayer of thanksgiving he'd ever heard.

The sound of an approaching car brought him around. Jo's Toyota mounted the grade over the railroad tracks and pulled into the gravel parking lot. Jo wasn't alone. Dorothy Winter Moon was with her.

In appearance, Dot Winter Moon reminded Cork a good deal of her uncle Sam Winter Moon. She was tall, solid, her hair black, but with a bit of red in it that came out in the proper light, like a second personality. She wore a Grateful

Dead T-shirt with the sleeves cut away, and her arms were muscular.

When she was sixteen, Dot had left the Iron Lake Reservation and headed south to the Twin Cities. She came back four years later with a boy child, her maiden name, and no inclination to explain herself. She'd done her best raising her son, Solemn, but the early years had been tough going. She wasn't very successful at holding on to a job, mainly because she was hardheaded, not particularly customer oriented, and didn't believe in apologies. She didn't ask for them, didn't give them. She was scrupulously honest and forthright, however, and she expected the same of others. She finally found her niche working on a road crew for the county. The men on the crew gave her a hard time at first, a woman on male turf, but Dot gave as good as she got, and then some, and it wasn't long before she was one of the boys. Eventually, she ended up driving an International dump truck spring through fall with a plow on the front in winter. She wasn't a striking woman, but there were probably men who found her attractive, in a hard sort of way. She had a wide, sun-darkened face, a strong slender body, eyes that over the years had taken on a perpetual squint from working outside.

Cork put down his saw and smiled at the women. "Hey there, Dot. Been a while."

"Cork." Dot reached out and shook his hand so hard the bones grated.

"What's up?"

"Cops been at my place," Dot answered. "Looking for Solemn. Sons of bitches wouldn't say why."

"Was Solemn there?"

"Haven't seen him for a couple of days. I told them that."

"Has he been in any trouble lately?"

"Not that I know of."

"They have a warrant?"

"No."

"How many of them?"

"Three."

Jo said, "My first thought was that since they've found Charlotte's body, they're just interviewing everyone who was at the party the night she disappeared."

"Maybe," Cork said. But he thought, *not three of them.*

"It would be good to know for sure," Jo said.

"Did you call Arne?"

She nodded. "I tried. He wasn't available. No one at the Department was able to offer me an explanation."

"You're sure you don't have any idea what this might be about, Dot?"

For all her strength, Dorothy Winter Moon looked suddenly vulnerable.

If it hadn't been for Sam Winter Moon, young Solemn would often have been left to fend for himself while his mother worked to make a living. Summers, Solemn hung out at Sam's Place helping with the things that were within a small boy's capability. He cleaned the grounds, swept the Quonset hut, Windexed the windows. When he wasn't helping, he was fishing from the dock on Sam's property or swimming in the lake. Whenever Cork stopped by to pass the time with his old friend Sam, Solemn was there, a thin boy, good-looking, who didn't smile much but who loved to tell knock-knock jokes that Sam never failed to appreciate.

Still, there was a dark side to Solemn, even then. Sam knew it. There was something that came into the boy and filled him with anger, a hot, bubbling churn that put fire in his eyes and gave his movements a fast, jerky quality like bursts of flame. Eventually, Sam could tell when his great-nephew was ready to erupt. On those days, he sent young Solemn onto the lake in a rowboat to fish alone, and told him not to come back until he had a full stringer of sunnies. The solitude, the warm sun, maybe just the passage of time itself usually opened young Solemn up and let loose whatever it was that had entered him. By the time he came back and tied up at the dock, the dark look was gone, and the boy who loved Sam and loved knock-knock jokes was fully returned.

Unfortunately, Sam wasn't always around when Solemn went into one of his moods, and his great-nephew often got into trouble. Fights, mostly. Public disturbances. Cork, who was sheriff then, often had young Solemn in his office awaiting the arrival of Dot or Sam. In those days, the transgressions were usually minor. Solemn wasn't a liar; he never denied his guilt. He wasn't a thief; he never stole anything. He was, in his dark moments, simply ruled by an impulse to strike out, and when the moment had passed, he was full of contrition. Generally, an apology would do the trick, or sometimes if property had been involved, a bit of time and labor served in repairing the damage. Solemn never tried to duck his sentence.

The spring Solemn turned sixteen, Sam Winter Moon died, died in Cork's arms with his chest opened up from a shotgun blast. It happened at a place called Burke's Landing during a tense conflict between whites and Anishinaabeg over fishing rights on Iron Lake. Without Sam's firm, loving hand to hold him in place, Solemn spun off into space. The trouble he got into became more serious. He became a kid with an unhealthy reputation.

Cork knew the boy needed help. He remembered only too well how Sam Winter Moon had come into his own life after his father died and had guided him through the long journey of his grief. Solemn needed someone to step forward in the same way. That someone should have been Cork. But Sam's death had nearly destroyed Corcoran O'Connor. Both the whites and the Anishinaabeg blamed him for the bloodshed at Burke's Landing. Cork blamed himself, too, so it was pretty much unanimous. After that, for a while, his life fell apart. He lost his job as sheriff and his self-respect. He nearly lost his wife and family as well. He viewed Solemn's plight from the distance of his own isolation and suffering. Although he knew he should help, he'd been unable to scrape himself off the bottom of his own dark hole, and Solemn was left to find his way alone.

Cork studied Dorothy Winter Moon, and she flinched under his stare.

"Why do they want to talk to Solemn, Dot?"

"Used to be I'd know. Used to be he'd tell me when shit was going to hit the fan. Not anymore. He's been gone for the last two days, vanished, then the sheriff's people show. I thought it might be serious this time, so I took the day off and looked for him. Then I went to Jo."

Dot had often turned to Jo when Solemn's impulses put him on the wrong side of the sheriff's people. For many years, Jo had represented both the Iron Lake Reservation and the Ojibwe people in court actions. This hadn't endeared her to the citizens of Aurora, but the Ojibwe trusted her as they would one of their own. So far, Jo had always been able to negotiate Solemn's freedom in court.

Jo said, "I was hoping you might use your influence to get a few answers, Cork."

"My influence is limited these days."

"Would you see what you can do?"

"Sure." As Cork gathered his tools, he said, "I've got to warn you, Dot, this may be all about Charlotte Kane, and it could be serious. Wasn't Solemn her boyfriend for a while last fall?"

"They broke up."

"And then she disappeared. And her body was found a few days ago, and now Solemn's taken off. The police may see a connection."

"But it was a snowmobile accident. Everybody says."

"He's just thinking like a cop, Dot," Jo said. "Look, I'll drop you back at your car, then why don't you go on home. When I hear from Cork, I'll give you a call. If Solemn shows up in the meantime, or if he contacts you, let me know."

Dot nodded. It was obvious that the possibility Cork raised had shaken her. She walked toward Jo's Toyota with her head down, staring at the gravel under her feet.

Jo asked Cork quietly, "Do you really think that might be it?"

He shrugged. "Like you said, just trying to think like a cop."

When Charlotte Kane moved to Aurora with her father, everyone remarked on her beauty, which she must have inherited from her mother. They remarked on her manners, her reserve (very Kane-like), her intelligence. And when, in her senior year of high school, she began to run with Solemn Winter Moon, they remarked on her disastrous choice in a young man.

For several weeks, beginning with the homecoming dance in early November when they were first seen together as a couple, until around Christmas, when word filtered through town that it was all over, they were a hot gossip item. She, the shy beauty; he, the bad boy off the rez. She, the kindling; he, the fire. At nineteen, Solemn had a reputation not just for his impulsive behavior but also for his conquests. His hair was panther black, and he wore it long, so that it hung down his back like a moonlit river. He was lean, good-looking, with a brooding Brandoesque quality to his face. As far as Cork knew, Dot had never said a word about Solemn's father, but it was clear that something more than Indian blood ran through his veins. Solemn used all of this, the good looks, the mystery, the lure of being part of a culture that to whites was mythic and forbidden, to hook and reel in the attractive bored tourist women deserted by their husbands who spent whole days away fishing Iron Lake. No complaints had ever been lodged against Solemn, but the town knew him as a kind of Ojibwe Romeo, and a lot of folks were disappointed when a girl as polite and sensible as Charlotte fell for the Indian's line. If there were any evidence concerning her death that pointed at Solemn Winter Moon, Cork feared many in the town would render a verdict of guilty long before a trial ever took place.

When he arrived at the sheriff's department, he found Deputy Duane Pender on desk duty. Pender told him that Arne Soderberg had been in earlier but wasn't anymore. That was all Pender would tell him.

"Do you expect him back?"

"Can't tell you that."

"You don't know?"

Pender didn't reply, just gazed at Cork with a face stolid as a guard at Buckingham Palace.

"All right. Then how about telling me why Arne had people out at Dorothy Winter Moon's place at sunup looking for Solemn."

"You'd have to talk to the sheriff about that."

"And he's not in."

"Now you're getting the picture."

Behind Pender, Randy Gooding came into view. He was carrying a stack of papers, and when he saw Cork he stopped and listened to the exchange. Cork figured it probably wouldn't have made a big difference if Gooding had been on duty at the desk. Probably, they were all under instructions to keep quiet. The difference would have been that Gooding wouldn't have played it like a game.

"Any way I might be able to get word to the sheriff that I'd like to talk to him?"

"Can't think of one."

Cork glanced at his watch. "Any possibility he'd be at home?"

"I can't help you there."

Cork saw Randy Gooding offer the ghost of a nod.

"Thanks, Duane," Cork said. "You've been more of a help than you know."

Pender's face took on a slightly troubled look as he considered how this could possibly be.

The Soderbergs lived behind a red brick wall. The wall stood only waist high, but it made a statement. Every year, once the earth warmed enough to welcome new roots, the yard behind the wall became a showcase of annuals that were ordered by Arne's wife, Lyla, and delivered by the truckload. Lyla always did something different—new flowers, new arrangements, complex and beautiful patterns. The grounds around the Soderbergs' big, brick Tudor were so perfect by summer that even the birds knew better than to crap on Lyla's lawn.

Cork paused at the iron gate and looked toward the end of North Point Road where Fletcher Kane's house was barely visible behind the cedars of the old estate. He hadn't seen Kane since they'd spoken at Valhalla, and he wondered how the man was holding up.

As he walked the flagstone path to the front door, Cork heard voices raised inside the house. It was a warm April afternoon, a few windows were open, and the harsh tones of the exchange carried easily out to the yard. The words weren't clear, but the two sides involved in the argument were. Arne and Lyla. Everyone in town knew that the Soderbergs' marriage was hanging by a thread, held together for the sake of Arne's political ambitions and Lyla's concern over what people would think.

Cork stepped onto the porch. As he reached toward the doorbell, the front door whipped open, and Tiffany Soderberg flew outside. She ran headlong into Cork, who stood with his arm outstretched. She uttered a little cry of surprise and stumbled back a step.

He barely knew Tiffany, although he'd often seen her around

Aurora over the years. She was Jenny's age, but Jenny seldom mentioned her. She was a honey-haired young woman, pretty. She dressed well, dressed like money, as did her mother. When she got over looking startled, she looked irritated.

"Yes?"

"Sorry, Tiffany. Didn't mean to scare you. I came to talk to your father."

She glanced back into the house. "He's . . . um . . . busy."

"This won't take long."

"Who is it?" Lyla spoke from somewhere near the front door but out of sight.

Tiffany rolled her eyes. "Mr. O'Connor. He wants to talk to Dad."

The door opened wider, and Lyla loomed behind her daughter.

Lyla had once represented Minnesota in the Miss America pageant. She had long, blonde hair, long legs that were tanned even in winter, and long, beautifully manicured nails. She had a notoriously short temper, however. She was wearing a sunflower yellow sweater and Guess jeans, both of which hugged nicely the body that had been a substantial part of her ticket to Atlantic City.

"What can I do for you?" she asked. It was clear that what she really wanted to do for Cork was shove him back out the front gate.

"I'd just like a few minutes of Arne's time."

"Friendly or official?"

"I'd say it leans more toward official."

"My husband's done for the day."

Cork wanted to advise her that for the sheriff there was never an end to a day.

Arne stepped into view behind Lyla. "I'm here."

Soderberg wore khaki slacks and a dark blue polo shirt. He was dressed for relaxing, although his face looked as if he'd been doing anything but.

"I'm gone," Tiffany said. She slipped past Cork and hurried to the driveway where Lyla's custom gold PT Cruiser was parked. The vehicle was a beauty, the only one like it in the county, and Lyla drove it everywhere.

"Dinner at six-thirty," Lyla called. "And don't you dare put a ding in my car, young lady."

"Whatever," Tiffany said with a flutter of her hand. She started the Cruiser, backed onto the street, and was gone.

Lyla gave Cork a cold look. Before it melted, she saved a little of the chill for her husband. Then she vanished back inside the house.

Arne came onto the porch and closed the door. "What is it, O'Connor?"

"I talked with Dorothy Winter Moon a little while ago. She said your people showed up at her place first thing this morning looking for Solemn. I'm wondering what you want him for."

"We'd like to talk with him, that's all."

"What about?"

"I'd rather not say."

"I was just down at your office. Lid's tight on everything there. Feels like something big. I'm wondering if you've got evidence you believe ties Solemn to Charlotte Kane's death. Something from the autopsy?"

Soderberg crossed his arms and leaned back against his door. He looked like he'd just dropped a million dollars into the bank. "You'll find out when everyone else does. You have no special status here, O'Connor."

"It was just a friendly inquiry, Arne."

Soderberg straightened and reached for the door. "I've got a lot to do. I've given you all the time I'm going to."

"Do you think it was murder, Arne? And do you think it was Solemn Winter Moon?"

Soderberg let go of the knob and swung back toward Cork. "I'll tell you what I think. I think I'm going to be able to close the book on Charlotte Kane's death very soon. And I don't need your help, and I don't want your interference."

8

Dot and Solemn Winter Moon lived on the Iron Lake Reservation, on a newly paved road a few miles south and east of the little town of Alouette. For years, she and Solemn had lived in an old but well-maintained trailer with a ceramic deer poised on the narrow apron of lawn in front. The stiff, painted deer always baffled Cork, because Dot Winter Moon didn't seem like a ceramic deer kind of woman. After the profits from the Chippewa Grand Casino began to be distributed among the Iron Lake Band of Ojibwe, Dot replaced the trailer with a nice, two-bedroom rambler with cedar siding. She kept the deer.

No one answered Cork's knock. The bright blue Blazer that Dorothy Winter Moon drove was parked next to the house. Cork knocked again, harder, then he circled to the backyard, where a trail ran through a narrow stand of red pines toward the glimmer of a little lake that was called, by mapmakers dry of inspiration, Lake 27. From somewhere in that direction came the bark of a dog. Cork headed down the trail.

He was upwind of the lake, and upwind also of Dot's big dog Custer. Custer was a golden retriever, as dumb a mutt as Cork had ever seen. And far too friendly to be of any use to Dot for protection. The dog came bounding up the trail from the lake and pranced around Cork playfully with his tongue hanging out of his mouth like a pink salmon fillet.

"Hey there, Custer." Cork put out a hand and roughed the dog's long fur. "Where's Dot?"

"Down here," he heard her call from beyond the end of the trees.

He found her on a flat gray rock at the water's edge. She sat cross-legged, smoking a cigarette and sipping a can of Molson. It was nearing evening. The day had cooled and she wore a jean jacket with DOT in letters made of brass studs across the back. Her side of the lake lay in shadow. Sunlight carved an arc across the water midway out, and everything beyond that was gold.

"Come 'ere, Custer," she called. "Come to mama."

The dog responded, bounded onto the rock, and lay down at her side.

"Jo tried calling," Cork explained. "Didn't get an answer."

"Sorry." Dot tapped her ash into a small tin can on the rock next to her. It didn't have a label, but it looked to Cork to be an empty tuna can. It was full of butts. "Came out here to think." She puffed out smoke through a little part in her lips. "I've sure made a mess of things."

"You think so?" Cork said.

She was looking across the lake where the gold and the shadow met. "Always wanting to do things my way. The hell with everybody else. Folks told me a long time ago Solemn needed professional help. I don't know, maybe he could have used a father at least, but I didn't want to bring in some shiftless son of a bitch just to play ball with him, you know?"

"He had the next best thing to a father. He had Sam."

"He sure could've used Sam these last few years. Me, too." She snuffed out her cigarette on the rock and added the butt to the others in the can. "You find out anything?"

"I'm pretty sure they want to talk to him about Charlotte. I'd guess there's enough evidence to suggest her death wasn't an accident."

She finished her beer with a long swallow, set the can upright carefully on the rock, balled her hand into a fist, and crushed the can with a single blow.

"I don't exactly know what they have," Cork went on, "but they're interested in Solemn. It doesn't look good that he's disappeared."

Dot picked up a pack of Salem Lights that lay beside her on the rock. She pulled one out and lit it with a green, disposable

Bic. She shook her head, scattering the smoke. "That's not unusual for him. He gets into one of his moods, he leaves for a while. He comes back when he's ready."

"Any idea where he goes?"

She shrugged. "His business. I've never pushed him on it."

"Arne Soderberg's smug, so whatever it is they have, it must be pretty solid."

She was quiet. At first, Cork thought she was looking at the lake again, but then he saw that her eyes were closed. Custer resettled himself, laid his head on his paws, and blinked at Cork.

"I've always been afraid that someday whatever it is that gets into him would get him into serious trouble. But this." She hugged her legs, laid her forehead against them. "Christ."

"If you hear from him, try to make him understand that it's important to come in and talk to the sheriff. Jo will be happy to go with him."

Dot lifted her head, nodded. "Thanks."

He got up, and Custer jumped to his feet.

"No, you stay here," Dot said to the dog. She put her arm around his neck and pulled him next to her.

Cork left her beside the lake, left her staring out at the water. As he walked away, he couldn't help thinking of Fletcher Kane who, when Cork last left him, had been staring across his own lake of sorrow.

Cork headed through Alouette, along back roads, until he was well into the woods that edged the north boundary of the reservation. He slowed down and finally saw what he was looking for, a cut through the trees on the left side of the road, an old access. He pulled in and made his way carefully between the trunks of pines so close to the edge of the track that they threatened to scrape the paint off his Bronco. It was a quarter mile to the cabin.

Summers, Sam Winter Moon had lived in the back of the Quonset hut on Iron Lake so that he could run his burger stand. But early fall through late spring, he lived in his old cabin near the headwaters of Widow's Creek. It was a small, rustic affair, a single room heated by an old, potbellied stove, no electricity or running water, and an outhouse. In the years after his father died, Cork had spent a lot of time there with Sam, learning much about himself from a man who was a patient teacher.

As Cork drew near, he saw a black Ford Ranger parked in front of the cabin.

Sunlight, low in the sky, broke through the pine trees and hit the cabin in bright splashes. Except for the incessant cawing of a crow somewhere in the high branches of the trees, and the gurgle from Widow's Creek a dozen yards north, the woods were quiet. No one answered his knock, and Cork opened the door. He'd been inside only once since Sam died, and that was to retrieve an important item that Sam had bequeathed to him. A bear skin. Entering now, smelling the place—the old logs and the sooted stove, leather bindings and wool blankets—Cork traveled back instantly across more than three decades to his adolescence. He felt a great happiness inside him, thinking about Sam. The room was neatly kept, and Cork had a pretty good idea of why.

He stepped outside and found himself staring into the black maw of a shotgun barrel.

"What are you doing here?" Solemn Winter Moon said.

He was a little taller than Cork, wore jeans, a flannel shirt with the sleeves rolled back, a green down vest. His long, black hair was pulled into a ponytail. Cork couldn't help seeing behind his dark good looks and his distrusting eyes the face of the boy who'd fished for sunnies from the dock at Sam's Place.

"Looking for you," Cork said.

Solemn lowered the barrel of the shotgun. A grouse lay in the dirt at his feet, the feathers messed and bloodied by buckshot.

"Yeah? Why?"

"I was hoping to get to you before the police did." Cork waited. "You don't seem surprised, Solemn."

"What do they want?" His question seemed more an afterthought.

"To talk about Charlotte Kane, I'd guess."

"Ancient history."

"It's a current affair now. I think the sheriff believes someone killed her, and you may be the number one suspect on his list. Look, I'm here to help, not to take you in."

Cork watched his eyes, looking for a sign of the fire that might signal some impulsive action. The kid seemed pissed, but not out of control.

"Why'd you take off?" Cork asked.

"It's what I do sometimes."

"Bad timing. Looks pretty suspicious." The crow stopped cawing. The still of the evening wrapped around them, and Cork felt the goodness of the place. "Come here to think?"

Solemn didn't answer.

"You can feel him out here, can't you? I sure can."

Cork looked for a crack in the front the kid put up, but Solemn remained hard.

"He saved my life once. Did you know that?"

No sign whether Solemn knew or not, whether he even cared.

"It was in the fall, a year after my father died. Sam asked me to help him build a bear trap, something he'd never tried before. We set it a mile or so down Widow's Creek, near that meadow full of blueberries. You know the one?" Solemn gave no reply, but his face altered a bit, a splinter of acknowledgment. "The bear sprung the trap, but it was such a goddamned huge animal it got away. Sam went after it and took me with him. I'd never hunted a bear before. We tracked it for a day and a half. Finally we got into a rocky area where even Sam couldn't track and we turned back. I remember that Sam was happy he wasn't going to have to kill a creature as magnificent as we knew that bear was.

"Toward evening, coming back, we hit a thick patch of sumac, bloodred stuff. We'd passed it earlier. This time Sam sensed something. He told me to wait, and he headed into the sumac. I waited, like he said. Then I heard a rustling in all those red leaves. I thought Sam was coming back. But it wasn't him. The biggest black bear I've ever seen charged out, coming right at me. It had circled. Bears sometimes do that. I was paralyzed. Couldn't move. That huge bear reared up on its hind legs, claws longer than my fingers. I was sure it was going to rip me apart.

"Then Sam shot it. At first, nothing happened. Finally the bear wavered, stumbled back, fell. It tried to get up, defend itself, but it couldn't. Sam came out of the sumac, spoke to the bear, something in Ojibwe I didn't understand. And he finished the kill. I could tell it made him sad to do it."

Solemn cradled the shotgun in a hunter's safe stance, barrel toward the earth. He looked at the place where the barrel pointed.

"I loved him, too, Solemn. Almost like he was my father. And he'd tell you what I'm telling you. Talk to the sheriff. Jo says she'll go with you if you'd like. The choice is yours."

Cork turned and started away.

"You going to tell anyone?" Solemn called after him.

"No."

"Not even my mother?"

"Not if you don't want me to. Okay if I tell her you're fine?"

Solemn thought about it. "Yeah."

Cork paused before he got into his Bronco. "In everything we remember, Sam's still alive. In every decision we make, he's still with us. But you know that. It's why you come here."

The light was fading as Cork pulled away. Solemn was still standing in front of the cabin, his figure darkening along with the day, his shotgun pointed at nothing. The truth was Cork hated leaving him alone that way. But there was nothing more he could do. Solemn Winter Moon was no longer a boy.

9

CORK CAME HOME TO DISASTER. Rose was leaving. She had a suitcase packed and sitting beside the front door. The children were gathered around her, looking at her with sad eyes.

"You're going somewhere?" Cork said.

Rose opened her purse to double-check the contents. "Ellie Gruber called. Her sister broke a hip. Ellie's going to stay with her for a while to help out. She asked me if I'd be willing to take care of things at the rectory until she's back."

"A broken hip," Cork said. "That could be quite a while."

"It could be."

Rose didn't seem concerned, but to Cork—and to the children, judging by their faces—it felt as if the O'Connors were being orphaned.

"Where's Jo?"

Rose snapped her purse shut. "Working late. Don't worry. Meat loaf and potatoes are in the oven. Green beans are on the stove. A list of meals for the week is posted on the fridge. You girls know your way around the kitchen, and I expect you to help take care of things while I'm gone. And, Stephen, there's plenty you can do, too."

Rose wore a green print dress, a plain thing that gave little definition to her plump body. Her dust-colored hair was brushed but, as always, still looking a little ruffled. She wore no makeup. She wasn't a woman particularly beautiful to the eye, but to anyone who knew her, her beauty was obvious in many ways.

She looked at the children, at the funereal expressions they wore, and she laughed. "For goodness' sake, I'm not dead. I'm just going over to the rectory at St. Agnes. You'll do fine."

In the gloom of the gathering dark outside, Father Mal Thorne pulled up to the curb in his yellow Nova, parked, and walked to the house. Rose opened the door to him.

"Evening, Cork. Kids," Mal said. "Thanks for doing this, Rose."

"No problem, Father."

"Honestly, I don't think it's necessary, but Mrs. Gruber, you know how she is."

"Ellie's absolutely right. You can't take care of everything, especially with Father Kelsey to consider."

Mal was only one of the priests who lived at the rectory. Father Kelsey was the other, a man long past the age when he should have retired. In serving the parish in Aurora and the mission on the Iron Lake Reservation, most responsibilities fell to Mal.

"I appreciate this." He glanced at the faces of the children. "And I appreciate what you're all giving up, too."

Jo's Toyota swung into the driveway and stopped quickly. Jo got out and hurried to the house.

"Oh, good. I didn't miss you." She hugged her sister. "You take good care of the Fathers."

"And you take care of things here."

"We'll be fine," Jo said.

Rose hugged and kissed each of the children and Cork, then said to the priest, "We'd best be off. Have you eaten?"

He picked up her suitcase. "I figured we could scrounge something from the refrigerator."

"Nonsense. I'm sure Ellie has the shelves well stocked. I'll put together a decent meal." She turned back at the opened door. "Bye, dears."

The children lifted limp hands in farewell.

Jo closed the door and laughed when she saw the look on their faces. "My God, you'd think she was going to the other side of the world. Come on, let's get dinner on the table."

As the children headed toward the kitchen, Jo turned to Cork. "Did you talk with Dot?"

"Yes. And Solemn."

"Solemn? You found him? Where?"

"He asked me not to say and I gave my word."

"Is he willing to talk to the sheriff?"

"I don't know. I told him I thought it was the best thing, but Solemn makes up his own mind. I also told him you'd go with him if he decides to see Soderberg."

"Good. What about Dot?"

"I called from Alouette, told her Solemn was fine."

"Thanks." She put a hand on his cheek. "You're terrific, you know that?"

"Never hurts to hear."

When the table was set, they gathered and said grace. It was quiet during the meal.

"How was school?" Jo asked of everyone in general.

Jenny shrugged.

Annie said, "Okay."

Stevie moved his meat loaf around with his fork. "I miss Aunt Rose."

"It will only be for a little while," Cork said. "She's only a few blocks away. She'll come to see us, and you can visit her at the rectory anytime you want."

There was a knock at the side door. Cork got up to answer it. In the kitchen, he flipped the switch to the light outside and opened the door. Solemn stood there blinking, darkness hard against his back.

Solemn looked at Cork, then past him. "Is Mrs. O'Connor here? I'm ready to talk to the sheriff."

Jo practiced law out of an office in the Aurora Professional Building, but she also maintained an office in her home, on the first floor of the O'Connor house. She led the way, and Solemn followed. Cork brought up the rear. When they were all inside, he closed the door behind them.

"Have a seat, Solemn," Jo said. She switched her desk lamp on, pulled a legal pad and a pencil from her desk drawer, and sat down. "Does your mother know you're here?"

"No. I don't want her to know. This doesn't involve her."

"She has a different view. But we'll worry about that later. What we need to try to figure out now is why the sheriff wants to see you. Any idea?"

"He does." Solemn poked a finger at Cork, who stood near the bookshelves.

"I know what Cork thinks, but I also want to cover any other possibilities. Is there anything that, as your legal counsel, I should know?"

"Nothing."

"You're sure?"

"I told you. Nothing."

"All right. Then let's think about you and Charlotte Kane. Cork believes the sheriff has come up with something that connects you in some way with Charlotte's death. Any idea what that might be?"

"No."

Jo glanced at Cork.

Cork spoke to Solemn. "If Arne's thinking clearly, he knows there are three essentials in making a case. Motive, opportunity, and a physical connection with the crime."

Jo said, "Let's begin with motive. It's no secret, Solemn, that you and Charlotte were seeing each other for a while last fall."

"We broke up."

"When?"

"Couple of weeks before Christmas."

"Why?"

"You know." He shrugged.

"I don't know. Tell me about it."

"We just broke up, that's all."

"Was it a mutual decision?"

"It was Charlotte's idea."

"Was she seeing somebody else?"

Solemn shot a dark look at her but said nothing.

"Who was she seeing?"

It was a few moments before he answered.

"I don't know. Some married guy, I think."

Jo and Cork exchanged a glance.

"Why do you think he was married?" Jo asked.

"She wouldn't talk about him. Acted like it was some big secret thing nobody could know about. Married, I figured."

"Okay. How did you feel about it when she broke up with you?"

"What's that got to do with anything?"

"Motive, Solemn," Cork said. "Jo's trying to think like the sheriff so she can stay ahead of him. If he's pegged you for Charlotte's death, he has to have a motive. Scorned love is pretty classic."

"I got over her. Long time ago."

"Back then though," Jo said. "How was it?"

"Hard. Okay? It was hard."

"You loved her?" Jo asked.

"I was into her pretty heavy."

"Charlotte's death occurred following a New Year's Eve party at Valhalla. Were you there?"

"Yeah."

"Invited?"

"No. I heard about it. I showed up, had a few beers."

"Did you see Charlotte?"

"Sure."

"Did you talk to her?"

"Yeah."

"About what?"

"This. That. You know."

"About the breakup?"

"Yeah. A little."

"Was it a civil conversation?"

"What's civil?"

"Like we're having right now."

"She didn't ask me so many questions."

"Did you raise your voice?"

"It was a loud party."

"Did you threaten her?"

"I might have called her a bitch. Something like that."

"Did you touch her?"

"I may have bumped into her. It was crowded."

"You didn't touch her in any other way?"

"I took hold of her arm. She pulled away. But that was it, swear to God. Why are you asking all this?"

"When Charlotte disappeared, did the sheriff's people talk to you?"

"Yeah. They talked to everyone who was at the party."

"Did you tell them what you told me?"

"Maybe I didn't say anything about touching her."

"My guess is that they're talking with everyone again, this time a little more thoroughly, and I'll bet if they didn't know before about your interaction with Charlotte, they know now. I'm just making sure I know what they know. What happened after you argued?"

"I left."

"What time was that?"

"Around eleven."

"Where'd you go?"

"Benoit's Bar. I had a couple more beers there, then took off."

"They served you?" Cork said. "You're underage."

"Like they care."

"Did anybody see you at the bar?" Jo said.

"Yeah, I could rustle up a few."

"What time did you leave Benoit's?"

"Few minutes before midnight. That stupid ball in Times Square hadn't dropped yet."

"Where'd you go?"

"Home."

"Straight home?"

"Straight home."

"You got there what time?"

"Twelve-fifteen maybe."

"And then what?"

"Nothing. I crashed. Woke up around noon the next day."

"Was Dot home with you?"

"No. It was New Year's Eve. She was out partying with some guys on her crew. Then it snowed and she had a plow to drive. She poked her head in my room when she got home. Six, maybe seven A.M."

Jo glanced at Cork.

"What?" Solemn asked.

"Six hours when you were alone," Cork said. "And nobody to vouch for your actions during that time."

Solemn took a moment to put it together, then said, "Oh, shit."

"Motive and opportunity," Cork said. "But Arne's got to have something more, something that connects you directly with Charlotte's death."

Jo said, "Let's go find out what."

10

RANDY GOODING was working late. He seated Jo, Cork, and Solemn at one of the desks in the common area that the deputies used for interviews and for doing paperwork, then asked them to wait while he called the sheriff.

It was going on nine o'clock, and there wasn't much action in the department. Marsha Dross was on the front desk. She'd smiled cordially and said hello, but she studiously avoided looking at them after that. Pender came in from patrol, saw them, smiled in a knowing way and whispered something to Gooding. Gooding scowled in return. Pender sauntered on by, whistling off-key, and headed toward the locker room.

Despite what Lyla Soderberg had said about her husband being done for the day, Arne showed up fifteen minutes later dressed in a charcoal three-piece, looking like a real estate broker prepared to close a million-dollar deal.

"Let's do this in my office," he said. Then to Gooding, "Go get the stuff."

Gooding left and walked toward the back of the department, toward what Cork knew was the evidence room.

Cork got up and started into the sheriff's office with Jo and Solemn. Soderberg put a hand on his chest and stopped him. "Not you. The kid's got counsel. You have no business in there. You wait out here."

Jo nodded to Cork, and gave him a *don't start anything* look. She went into Soderberg's office with Solemn, and the sheriff followed. Cork watched the door close. He caught Marsha Dross eyeing him. She turned quickly away.

"What's up, Marsha?" He'd hired the deputy, the first woman to work as a law officer in Tamarack County. He crossed the room and stood near her.

"Not much, Cork. Quiet night, all things considered." She tapped the front of a manila folder with the sharp tip of her pencil, making a constellation of dots.

"I mean in there." He nodded toward the sheriff's closed door.

"That's department business, Cork. You know I can't talk about it. Why don't you get yourself a cup of coffee and relax."

Cork wandered to the coffeemaker, a big Hamilton Beach. There was barely a cup left in the pot. He poured himself the last of it, strong-smelling stuff that had probably been on the burner for hours. Because he knew where all the supplies were, he set about making a fresh pot.

He was spooning Folgers into the filter when Randy Gooding returned carrying a brown cardboard box marked CHARLOTTE KANE #2731. Gooding glanced his way, then went into Soderberg's office and closed the door behind him. Cork turned on the coffeemaker, picked up his disposable cup, and sipped from the bitter swill he'd poured earlier.

A few minutes later, a loud thump came from the wall of the sheriff's office, knocking a framed photograph of Iron Lake off the wall. When the frame hit, glass shattered across the floor. The door to Soderberg's office flew open, and Solemn burst out, his eyes gone wild. He slammed into the side of the nearest desk and sent papers flying. He turned in a frantic circle, looking like a scared young buffalo surrounded by hunters. Then he shot toward the security door.

"Stop him," Soderberg shouted.

By then it was too late. Solemn was already beyond the waiting room and headed toward the sanctuary of the night outside.

Marsha Dross gave pursuit immediately. Randy Gooding stumbled out of Soderberg's office, a trickle of blood running from the corner of his mouth. He followed Dross. Duane Pender rushed from the rear of the department, clearing his weapon from its holster as he ran.

Jo was out now, too, and when she saw the gun in Pender's hand, she yelled, "Jesus, don't shoot him."

It was impossible to tell if Pender heard. He was out the door and hot on Winter Moon's trail.

Cork doubted they would catch him. Solemn had a decent head start and was in good shape. He was also a man who knew the dark, and Cork counted on the dark to welcome him and keep him safe.

The office was suddenly very quiet. Cork walked to Jo, who stood looking a little dazed.

"So," he said. "How'd it go?"

They sat together in Soderberg's office, waiting to see if the sheriff's people would be able to take Solemn into custody immediately. Arne Soderberg was hovering over Dispatch, personally coordinating the movements of his deputies as they searched. Cork and Jo had the office to themselves.

On the wall behind the sheriff's desk hung an enlarged, framed photograph of Arne Soderberg with his father, Big Mike. As his moniker implied, the elder Soderberg was a continent of muscle and bone with a huge, self-satisfied smile. Big Mike was a legend on the Iron Range, having taken over his own father's small trucking operation and turned it into the biggest transport company north of the Twin Cities. Big Mike wanted a son who would storm the north country in the way he had, but his wife delivered to him a boy who, everyone agreed, never quite made the grade. Although Arne talked like a winner, his performance never equaled his promise. He had played second string quarterback for Hibbing High School, graduated in the middle of his class from Concordia College in Moorhead, dropped out of the MBA program at St. Thomas University in St. Paul, and had gone instead to a second-rate law school. It had taken him three attempts to pass the bar. Big Mike's connections got him a job with a prestigious Twin Cities law firm, but Arne was never partner material. After five unremarkable years, he left the firm and returned to Tamarack County to work in his father's company.

There was one small family photo on his desk, a posed thing with a background that suggested spring. Arne with a grin like he had a couple of fishhooks stretching the corners of his lips, Lyla looking ingenue perfect, and Tiffany vaguely bored.

Cork sat in a chair positioned where he could look out the window at the bell tower of Zion Lutheran a block away. During his own tenure as sheriff, he'd often sat that way, staring out the window as he wrestled with a problem. The view was one thing that never changed, and it made him feel comfortable. The tower was a spectral presence against the empty night.

"It was my fault," Jo said. "Arne was waiting to ambush Solemn and I walked the kid right into it."

"What's Arne got?"

"First of all, the autopsy. X rays showed an elongated skull fracture, more consistent with a blow from something like a club or a bar than from hitting her head on a rock in the accident. Also, there were signs of sexual activity, from the bruises it looks like some pretty rough play, so rape isn't out of the question. After that, Randy Gooding began taking a good look at the evidence he gathered at Widow's Creek. Some food wrappers—"

"Junk food. And the autopsy showed that none of it was in her stomach, right?"

"That's right. There was a beer bottle, too."

"A Corona."

"I don't know. But Solemn's fingerprints were all over it."

"Damn."

"Once they had that, they went out to Valhalla and did a thorough search. In the wood box of the guesthouse, they found a big, open-end wrench with dried blood on it. *S.W.M.* was etched on the shaft. Guess whose fingerprints were all over that."

"And the blood was Charlotte's?"

"Bingo. So they already had motive and a physical connection. All they needed to establish was opportunity. After we'd given them that in spades, they brought out the evidence box and sprung the trap."

"A lot of drama, but what the hell was Arne thinking?" Cork said. "He gave you information he should never have let you have at this point."

Jo shook her head. "I think he really believed he could get a spontaneous confession out of Solemn, à la Perry Mason."

"No wonder Solemn took off." Cork stood up and walked to the window. There was a playground in the park between the sheriff's department and the Lutheran church. A wind had risen, and in the light from streetlamps, Cork could just make out the swings moving slowly back and forth, as if the ghosts of children were at play. "How did Solemn react?"

"You saw for yourself."

"I mean before he split."

Jo thought a moment. "Surprised."

"Surprised by the evidence or surprised that they had it?"

"I wish I could say."

Soderberg came in, looking grim and determined. "We just impounded his truck from in front of your place. Wherever he's going, he's going on foot."

"You need us for anything, Sheriff?"

"Go on home." He turned and left.

Jo got up from her chair. "I guess it's time I called Dot."

They didn't say much as they drove home. It was late, and many of the houses on the streets were already dark. Aurora was usually a quiet place, something Cork valued, and at night especially, the silence could be deep as death itself. Jo stared out her window. As they passed under streetlights, her white-blonde hair flashed with a startling, neon brilliance. Her face, in profile, appeared troubled. Finally she said, "Pretty damning."

"Also pretty convenient," Cork said. "Everything laid out for Arne. *A-B-C*."

"How many times have you told me that people who commit crimes, especially crimes of passion, don't think very clearly. It's entirely possible that Solemn left all that evidence behind."

"You sound like the prosecutor. You think he did it?"

"He ran."

"He's scared."

"He has reason to be. They've already got a lot against him." She repositioned herself so that she faced Cork more directly. She put a hand lightly on his leg. "I know that Solemn is important to you because of Sam Winter Moon. But we both know he's impulsive, sometimes violently so."

"He's been in his share of fights, but he's never come close to killing anyone."

"Cork, he never told us he didn't kill her."

"We never asked." Cork laid his hand over hers. "Will you defend him?"

She laughed with surprise and drew away. "You've got to be kidding. This is going to be a murder charge. I've never defended someone accused of murder."

Cork slowed a moment and looked steadily at her. Even in the dark, he could see how ice blue her eyes were, and how intense. "He trusts you."

"There's a lot more to winning in a courtroom than trust." She looked away. "The best person in Tamarack County for something like this is Oliver Bledsoe."

They turned onto Gooseberry Lane and Cork saw immediately that Solemn's truck was gone. When they got inside the house, Jenny and Annie both greeted them with anxious faces.

Before either of his daughters could say a word, Cork asked, "Stevie?"

"We put him to bed hours ago," Annie said. "He's sound asleep. Randy Gooding was here. He was looking for Solemn Winter Moon. He said there's a warrant for his arrest."

"Because they think he killed Charlotte Kane," Jenny jumped in.

"And then a tow truck came and took his truck away," Annie added, a bit breathlessly.

"Did he kill Charlotte?" Jenny asked. There was disbelief, and maybe a little fear, in her voice.

Jo took off her jacket, opened the entryway closet, and reached for a hanger. "The sheriff has evidence that points in that direction."

Jenny leaned back against the wall and stared down at the rug. "When they first started going out, it seemed like it was Solemn just playing her. By the end, I remember wondering who was playing who." She shook her head. "But, Jesus, killing her?"

"He's innocent until proven guilty, Jen," Cork said.

She looked at him with those crystal blue eyes that were her mother's. "Not Solemn Winter Moon, Dad. Not in this town."

11

SAM WINTER MOON used to say white people were just like puppies. If one peed on a tree, all the others had to pee on it, too. The morning after Solemn vanished into the night, Cork found out just how true Sam's words were.

Jo had a court case first thing, and she left in the gray light before sunrise to prepare. Cork made sure the kids got up, had breakfast, and were off to school on time. They drank Minute Maid orange juice, ate Cocoa Puffs and Kix, and complained because Rose always had a hot breakfast for them. When they were finally out the door and on their way, Cork thought a hot breakfast did sound like a good idea, and he hopped in his Bronco and headed for the Broiler.

Johnny Papp's Pinewood Broiler was an institution in Aurora, a gathering place for locals as far back as Cork could remember. His father, during his tenure as sheriff, often started his day there, rubbing elbows with the loggers and construction crews and merchants and resort owners of Tamarack County. Most of them were descended from the early Voyageurs and the immigrants—Finns, Germans, Slavs, Irish, and a dozen other nationalities who'd come in the old days, lured by the promise of a good life built on the wealth of the great white pines and the rich iron ore deposits of the Mesabi and Vermilion Ranges. Only a very few ended up rich, but most immigrants were able to build good lives, create homes, and establish history. The problem was that as they moved in, they shoved aside an entire group of people who had occupied that land for generations. The white men called them the Chippewa, which was a bastardization of one of the names by which they were known, Ojibwe. They were part of the Anishinaabe Nation whose territory, by the time the white settlers arrived, stretched from the eastern shores of the Great Lakes to the middle of the Great Plains. The Anishinaabeg saw themselves as stewards of the land with no more right or need to possess the earth than the hawks did the air currents that held them aloft. Land ownership was a white man's concept, and it was accomplished through a series of treaties and underhanded business dealings that robbed the Anishinaabeg blind.

But all this was a long time ago, long before the Broiler regulars were born, and to them it was ancient history and of no relevance to their lives. Unless the uppity members of one of the tribal bands decided to push the issue. Which happened on occasion. Usually with an outcome that pleased no one.

When Cork stepped into the Broiler that morning, the talk was of Solemn Winter Moon. Everyone seemed to know about the accusations and about Solemn's flight. Cork bellied up to the counter, called to Sara, a young waitress with tanning-booth brown skin and dyed blonde hair, for a cup of coffee and a stack of buckwheat cakes, then he turned to listen to what was being said at the nearest table.

Jeeter Hayes was holding forth. Jeeter was head of a crew that did tree work for the Tamarack County Department of Parks and Recreation. He was a big man with an enormous number of tattoos that made his arms look, from a distance, like the green hide of an alligator. He had a small head for such a large frame, and Cork had always suspected that the size was an indication of how little that skull had to hold. Everyone at Jeeter's table seemed to have a story of a social or criminal trespass by Solemn, and every story seemed to be worse than the last.

Jeeter finally looked in Cork's direction. "I heard he did things to her before he killed her. That true, Cork?"

"You want details, ask Arne Soderberg." Cork sipped his coffee and wondered where the hell his pancakes were.

"I heard your wife's defending him."

"You want to know, ask her."

"I always kind of liked Jo," Jeeter said. The way he said it made it sound vaguely dirty. "We all do, don't we, boys?" He nodded, but the other men only looked at him, as if wondering where this was going. "We don't like it when she pushes something for them out there on the rez, but she's almost one of us by now, you know?" Jeeter stood up, walked to the counter, and sat on the stool next to Cork. "Defending a guy like Winter Moon, after what he did to Charlotte Kane, that'll set a mean hook in a lot of folks' thinking. Am I right?"

Cork said, "The kid hasn't been formally charged yet, and you've already got him convicted and hung, Jeeter."

Jeeter narrowed his eyes on Cork. "A man who'd piss on a cross, hell, I imagine nothing's beyond him."

Solemn had never pissed on a cross. He had, however, admitted to vandalizing St. Agnes Church, which included urinating in the baptismal font and spray-painting graffiti across one of the church walls. He'd written *Mendax*. The vandalism had taken place late at night, a few weeks before Christmas. In a door-to-door canvass of the neighborhood following the incident, the sheriff's deputies found someone who'd seen Solemn's truck parked on the street in front of the church. When they went out to Dot's place to talk to Solemn, the deputies found a can of black spray paint in his truck. Solemn didn't even try to deny his guilt.

Jo had defended him. Solemn claimed to have been drunk and to have acted alone, but Jo had a question for him he couldn't answer and it made her believe he was not telling the whole truth. She asked him what *Mendax* meant. He told her he didn't know. "Liar," she said. He swore he was telling the truth. "No," Jo told him. "Loosely translated, the word means liar." When she asked him why he'd put that particular word on the wall of St. Agnes, he refused to reply. It was Jo's belief that Solemn hadn't done the deed on his own. She thought he'd been talked into it and was covering for his accomplice. She believed the most likely candidate was his girlfriend Charlotte Kane, who was bright, Catholic, and at that time, displaying a wildness that surprised everyone. Solemn insisted on taking the fall alone. He apologized in person and in writing, and he spent a day taking the spray paint off the wall. He also agreed to shovel the walks of St. Agnes free of charge during the rest of the winter.

At the counter of the Broiler, seated next to Cork, Jeeter opened his hands and said with great innocence, "I'm just going on history here, O'Connor. Just looking at the road that kid's already traveled and torn up behind him."

Cork said, "I took you in a few times for drunk and disorderly back when I wore a badge, Jeeter. Does that mean you're ripe for killing somebody?"

Jeeter leaned close. Cork could smell the char of crisp bacon on his breath. "You want to know the truth, I don't have to wait until a jury says he's guilty. I know it already. Indian bucks, see, they love the idea of doing a white woman. Get 'em drunk and, hell, anything's game." His words were not spoken loud, but they were spoken into a hush that had settled over the Broiler.

Cork looked across the room at the faces of people he knew, but who sometimes seemed like strangers. No one contradicted Jeeter Hayes.

"This conversation's over, Jeeter," Cork said.

Jeeter sat up. "And if I keep talking, what? You'll arrest me? You know, I'm thinking it's a hell of a good thing you're not sheriff around here anymore. What with you being a half-breed. You know what else? Those times you hauled me in, if it hadn't been for your badge, you and me, we might've gone a few rounds. I would've liked that."

Johnny Papp intervened at that moment, dropping a plate of steaming cakes on the counter between the two men. "Go on back to your table, Jeeter," Papp said. "Let the man eat in peace."

"Sure," Jeeter said after a long moment. "I got work to do anyway." He stood up and headed toward the register. "Come on, boys. We got a lot of rotten trees to take care of and time's a wastin'."

After they'd gone, Johnny Papp said, "Sorry, Cork."

"Not your fault, Johnny." He slid off the stool and picked up his check.

"What about your cakes?"

"I'm not hungry anymore."

Papp reached across the counter and took the check from Cork's hand. "Then don't worry about paying."

"I drank your coffee."

"It's on me." Papp crumbled the check. "And for the record, Jeeter Hayes is a jackass, and everybody knows it."

The day was overcast. A chill wind came out of the northwest, straight out of Canada. Now and then, a wet snowflake splattered against the windshield of Cork's Bronco, probably just the lingering echo of winter, but in that far north country, you never knew for sure. He was on his way to Sam's Place, to work on getting things ready for the May opening. The grayness wedged its way into his mood, and by the time he arrived, he was feeling pretty lousy.

Long ago, after he bought the Quonset hut for a song from the Army National Guard, Sam Winter Moon had divided the building into two sections. In the front, he'd installed a gas grill, a freezer, a sink, storage shelves, and a food prep area. He cut out two serving windows in the south wall, and between them he hung a wood-burned and hand-painted sign that read SAM'S PLACE. During tourist season, the rear of the Quonset hut was his home. It consisted of a kitchen, a bathroom, a living area with an eating table and chairs that Sam had made from birch, a desk for doing business, and a bunk. There were bookshelves, too, for Sam loved to read.

Cork opened the door and stepped inside. The curtains were drawn over the windows, and the room was dark. Cork lifted his hand toward the light switch, but stopped when a voice said, "Don't."

"Solemn?" Cork let his hand fall, the switch untouched. It wasn't so much that he'd recognized the voice immediately as he understood the rightness of the situation, that Solemn should seek shelter in yet another place where Sam Winter Moon had dwelt.

"Close the door."

Cork did. His eyes were adjusting, and he could make out Solemn lurking in the entryway to the bathroom. He had something in his hand that Cork assumed must be a firearm.

"You can put the gun down."

"Gun?" Solemn laughed quietly. He came forward into what little light filtered through the curtains, and Cork saw that what he held was a hammer. Solemn aimed the handle at him. "Bang."

"Been here all night?"

"Most of it."

"Hungry?"

Solemn seemed surprised by the question.

"I haven't eaten yet," Cork said. "I was thinking of fixing some eggs. You want, I'll fix enough for both of us."

Solemn looked at him, making some kind of assessment. "I could eat," he said.

Cork drew open the curtains over the sink to let in some light. He opened the refrigerator, where he kept a small supply of food—eggs, milk, butter, cheese, fruit, bread—in case he got hungry while he was readying the place for the tourist season. During the time when Cork's life fell apart and he and Jo were separated, he'd lived in Sam's Place. The pans and utensils he'd used then were still in the drawers and on the shelves. Many of them were left from the time when Sam had lived there.

"You haven't changed things much," Solemn said.

Cork lit a burner on the stove and put a frying pan over it. He dropped in a pat of butter, then broke six eggs into a bowl, added a little milk, salt and pepper, and began to beat the mixture with a fork.

"Never saw much that needed changing," he said over his shoulder. "Sam put things together pretty well."

"Even smells the same," Solemn said. "Fry oil."

Cork poured the beaten eggs into the hot pan. He took a grater from a drawer and began to grate cheese onto a cutting board.

"Coffee?" he said.

"Sure."

"In the cupboard, in a jar." He nodded to his right. "Don't have a drip coffeemaker. You'll have to let it perk on the stove."

Solemn took the old aluminum pot from the back burner and set about making the coffee.

"When's the last time you were here?" Cork asked. With a spatula, he rolled the eggs carefully in the pan, cooking them gradually to keep them from becoming stiff and dry.

"Three years ago. Before Sam died."

"You've never come by since I took over the place."

"Figured it wouldn't be the same."

"Almost nothing ever is."

Solemn looked around. "You've done a good job of keeping it up."

"I spend a lot of time out here, even in winter. I use it as a getaway."

"From what?"

"Bills. Phone calls. Life."

Solemn lit a burner and put the coffeepot on the stove. "There's a good spot for ice fishing about a hundred yards out."

"I know," Cork said.

Solemn walked to the table and sat down. Cork scraped the grated cheese off the cutting board into the eggs and stirred to melt it.

"I watch sometimes," Solemn said.

"Watch what?"

"You. Here. With your kids. I stand out there in the trees." He waved toward the copse of poplars to the south.

"What are you looking for?"

Solemn shrugged.

"What you had here once with Sam maybe?"

Solemn didn't answer.

Cork turned the flame down low and put a lid over the frying pan. "When the coffee's ready, we'll eat." He took a chair and sat near Solemn. "Why'd you run last night?"

"Because they think I killed Charlotte and because that asshole looked at me and grinned like I was some kind of rat he had in a cage."

"The sheriff?"

"Yeah."

"It was Gooding you slugged."

"Was it? I don't remember much. I just knew I had to get out of there."

"How do you feel about it, knowing that Charlotte was murdered?"

Despite his moments of fire, Solemn, like many Ojibwe, could wipe all emotion from his face in an instant, become absolutely unreadable, and that moment he did. But that in itself was a sign. He had something to hide. Was it guilt? Or had he genuinely cared about Charlotte and didn't want Cork or anyone else to know?

The coffee began to perk. Cork went to the cupboard and pulled down a couple of plates and cups. He took flatware from the drawer and put the things on the table. He let the coffee perk until the color was deep brown.

"Why don't you pour us some," he said to Solemn, "and I'll get the eggs."

At first they ate in silence. Solemn's predicament didn't affect his appetite. He stuffed the food into his mouth in huge forkfuls, and he followed each bite with a deep gulp of coffee. It was the way a hungry teenager ate, as if every meal were the last. Cork, as he watched Solemn, saw so much about the young man that was still not formed, but forming.

"What are you going to do now?" Cork finally asked.

"I don't know. Talking to the sheriff sure didn't do me any good."

"At least you know where you stand."

"Yeah. In deep shit." He spoke around a mouthful of eggs. "I'm thinking of going to Canada."

"Your truck's been impounded."

"Hell, I could walk from here."

"Then what?"

"I don't know. I'll figure something."

"Not much of a plan."

Solemn stopped eating and for a moment poked idly at his food. "What do you think I should do?"

Cork looked at him, looked deeply into the eyes that were not quite Indian or quite white, into the face that was not quite that of a grown man. And he asked the question no one had bothered to ask yet. "Did you kill her?"

Solemn put his fork down. "No."

"Then my advice is to turn yourself in."

"Are you kidding?" Solemn's look began to turn dark. "They've got enough right now to put me behind bars forever."

"You run, it seems to me you'll be putting yourself in a different kind of cage, one that's not any better."

"No way." Solemn scooted his chair back and jumped up. He began to pace the room. "I need money."

"If that's what you came to me hoping for, you've made a mistake."

"I wasn't asking. But I'm in this mess because I listened to you."

"You were already in this mess. Now, if you want my help, I'll give it. That means going at this thing head-on, not running away."

Solemn had a frightened look in his eyes, as if he were watching the door to freedom close on him. "It's all lies. I didn't do anything."

"Then somebody's gone to a lot of trouble to make it look like you did. I'll do my best to find out who."

"Your best?" His voice was tight, climbing in pitch.

"That's all I can offer. But I'll make you a promise. I'll stay with you the whole way. You won't go through this alone."

Solemn looked as if he couldn't decide between laughing or crying. "Is that supposed to mean something? Who the hell do you think you are? You make hamburgers, for Christ sake."

Cork waited a moment, then said calmly, "So did Sam."

Solemn spun angrily away.

"Do you see anyone else stepping forward, Solemn? I'm willing to help, but the choice is yours. This is what I'm going to do. I'm going to leave here and go get Jo. We'll come back. If you're still here, we'll all head to the sheriff's office together. If you're not . . . well, Solemn, I guess you're on your own."

Cork got up from the table and headed to the door. He turned back with his hand on the knob. Solemn was watching him now.

"While I'm gone," Cork said, "how about you do up those dishes."

12

CORK PARKED IN FRONT of Pflugelmann's Rexall Drugstore across from the county courthouse. He found Jo in the courtroom of Judge Daniel Hickey. She sat at the plaintiff's table, jotting notes while Ed Mendez, the defendant's attorney, argued something about "interpretation of the trust language." Hickey looked bored. The clients weren't present, and the courtroom was mostly deserted. Cork sat behind Jo, on a bench in back of the railing that blocked off the spectator area. He waited a few minutes for an opportunity to make his presence known to Jo. It came when the judge asked to have a look at a document Mendez held. As defense counsel approached the bench, Cork leaned across the railing and handed Jo a scrap of paper on which he'd scribbled a note. She read it and nodded.

When Mendez started away from the bench, Jo stood. "Your Honor, I apologize, but I'd like to request a ten-minute recess. A rather pressing personal matter."

Hickey, a little man with a white billy goat beard, shook back the sleeve of his robe and glanced at his watch. "Any objection, Ed?"

Mendez thought a moment. "No, that's fine."

"All right. Ten minutes I think we can handle, Jo. Court is in recess until nine-forty." He sealed his pronouncement with a tap of his gavel, and he yawned as he left the bench.

Jo turned to Cork.

"Not here." He motioned her to an empty corner of the courtroom.

"Where is he?" Jo asked.

"At Sam's Place," he whispered. "He spent the night there. He's ready to turn himself in."

Jo shook her head. "I told you. I can't represent him."

"No, you said you won't. That's different. He needs our help."

"I can't just leave here. I'm in the middle of a hearing." She waved toward the judge's bench.

"Solemn's just a kid, Jo, and he's scared. He could bolt at any moment. Couldn't you ask Hickey for a continuance or something?"

Jo pressed the tips of her fingers to her forehead and closed her eyes a moment. "Look, talk to Oliver Bledsoe. He really is Solemn's best hope. He's here today. Courtroom B. Cork, I'm sorry, but I can't help Solemn, not in the situation he's in right now."

"Will you at least go with me to talk to Ollie?"

Jo looked at her watch. "If he's free."

They were in luck. Bledsoe was standing in the hallway outside Courtroom B, consulting his Palm Pilot.

Cutting off a part of his foot had turned out to be a blessing for Oliver Bledsoe. He'd been a young man without much direction beyond earning a good paycheck and spending it having a good time. While recovering from the logging accident, he'd decided to make some significant changes in his life. The first thing he did was to enroll in college. He completed his B.A. at the University of Minnesota at Duluth in three years and applied immediately to law school. He graduated from William Mitchell School of Law in St. Paul, second in his class. He could have had his choice of law firms. Instead, he opened a storefront legal office on East Franklin Avenue in the Phillips neighborhood of Minneapolis, an area that at the time contained the largest population of urban Indians in the United States. He represented people who often had little hope and even less money. His practice ranged from simple wills to defending clients accused of murder. Eventually, he made a name for himself. His one-person law office grew over time to include half a dozen lawyers, some of whom had left lucrative positions to work in what they considered the front lines of American justice. After twenty years, Oliver Bledsoe had been persuaded to return home to head up the new legal affairs office for the Iron Lake Band of Ojibwe. Because of the casino profits, he was better paid now, but his clients and their problems were little changed.

Bledsoe glanced up when Cork and Jo approached, and he smiled.

"Got a minute?" Cork said.

"Just."

"You heard about Solemn Winter Moon?"

"You'd have to be deaf not to."

"He wants to turn himself in. He'll need representation."

Bledsoe's eyes shifted toward Jo.

She held up her hands in objection. "I can't. I've never handled a criminal charge that serious."

Bledsoe shook his head. "I'm afraid I can't help him either."

"You've got the experience," Cork said.

"But I'm not in a position to help. Cork, I represent the Iron Lake Band of Ojibwe. I officially represent them. You know better than anyone how tenuous the relationship is between the rez and the rest of Tamarack County. Solemn's antics feed into some of the worst stereotypes white people have about Indians. I can't risk the possibility that people will associate him as an individual and the mess he's got himself into with my official representation of the reservation. If Solemn's civil rights were being violated, or, shoot, if I really believed he was being wrongly accused—"

"You don't?" Cork said.

"It's my understanding there's plenty of evidence against him."

"He's still entitled to the best representation possible."

"Look, why don't you try Bob Carruthers? He's a good, experienced criminal attorney."

"Experienced," Jo said. "Good would be a stretch."

Bledsoe looked at his watch. Cork was becoming irritated that in this house of the law, time seemed more important to everyone than justice. But he kept his mouth shut.

"I'm sorry," Bledsoe said. "I'm due in court. Good luck." He headed away.

Cork swung his gaze to Jo. He could see her tense a moment, then give a little sigh. "All right," she said. "I'll go with Solemn while he turns himself in so that he's got someone to advocate for him, but I'm not agreeing to take his case. I'll help just until we can get a lawyer capable of doing a good job of representing him in this thing."

"Thanks."

"Yeah," Jo said without enthusiasm. "I don't know what the hell I'm going to tell Judge Hickey."

The occasional snowflake had turned to a dismal drizzle of cold rain by the time Cork and Jo pulled up to Sam's Place. Iron Lake had disappeared behind a gloom of mist. As they walked across the lot, they felt the wet gravel like slush under their feet. Cork pushed open the door of the Quonset hut and called, "Solemn?"

There was no answer.

He looked in the front where the rain dripped down the glass of the serving windows, but Solemn was not hiding there. He turned back to Jo.

"You told me he didn't exactly promise he'd stay," Jo said. "You tried to help. What more could anyone ask?"

Cork stood in the room where he thought he'd made a connection with Solemn. He felt that he'd somehow failed the young man, although he couldn't have said exactly how. He glanced at the kitchen sink and saw that it was empty. Before he'd vanished, Solemn had done the last thing Cork had asked of him. He'd washed the dishes.

MAY

13

ON A SUNNY SPRING MORNING a few days after the autopsy, on a hillside in Lakeview Cemetery, Charlotte Kane was buried. If she'd still had sight, her eyes would have beheld a wonderful view from the few feet of earth that were to be hers forever. Spread out below her was Iron Lake. In winter, it would be hard and white as a beaver's tooth, and in summer so blue it would seem like a fallen piece of the sky. If she'd still had her senses, she'd have felt the touch of the wind off that lake and smelled the cool, deep scent that was the breath of a million pines. Cork had always believed that if you were going to be stuck somewhere forever, that hillside was a pretty good place. Not many people were asked to attend the simple graveside ceremony. Rose and the Soderbergs were among them. Rose had spoken with Glory about a visitation, some way for the folks of Aurora—or of St. Agnes, at least—to pay their respects, but Glory wanted nothing of the kind. Apparently, what Glory wanted most was to be gone, because the morning after the funeral, she left town. Without a word to anyone. Not that there were many who would have cared. Rose told Cork that when she stopped by the old Parrant place to call on Glory, Fletcher had given her the news. "Gone," was all he would say. And no idea where. Cork could see that Rose was puzzled by her friend's abrupt departure, and perhaps a little hurt that Glory hadn't said good-bye.

* * *

April warmed gradually into May. The ice on Iron Lake retreated and then was gone. The aspens and poplars budded, and above them geese wedged their way home to the Boundary Waters and to the lakes of Canada beyond.

The Anishinaabeg called May *wabigwunigizis,* which means month of flowers. It was the season in which Grandmother Earth awakened and the storytellers fell silent, waiting to speak the sacred histories until after the wild rice had been harvested and the snow had returned and Grandmother Earth slept again.

It was tick season. The news was full of reports and warnings of Lyme disease, and doctors' offices were crowded with patients concerned about every little rash.

It was softball season, and Cork's favorite team, the Aurora High Voyageurs, for which his daughter Annie pitched, were predicted to take the conference title.

It was the opening of fishing season, the beginning of months when tourists flocked to Aurora lured by walleye and the beauty of the great Northwoods naked of snow.

And it was, as always, the season of love.

"Dad?" Annie said.

"Yeah?"

"What do guys want?"

It was Saturday afternoon. Cork was standing on a stool in Sam's Place, checking the consistency of the mixture for the shake machine. Business had been slow that day, which was good because Annie had seemed preoccupied.

"Big question," Cork replied. "With lots of answers, depending."

"I mean, what do guys look for in a girl?"

She was Cork's middle child, fifteen years old, and had developed a bit later than her friends the slopes and curves that might catch a young man's eye. She had never dated, channeling all her energy into sports, especially softball. She was a decent student, although academics were far less important to her than they were to her sister, Jenny. Lately, however, her grades had been slipping and Cork wondered if the current conversation might be a clue as to the reason. It was an unusual topic to be discussing with Annie. Usually they talked sports. But Cork gave it his best shot.

"I can't speak for all guys. I fell in love with your mother because she was strong, independent, smart. I liked that. She laughed at my jokes, too."

Annie leaned on the counter of her serving window. She wore jeans and a dark blue sweatshirt with VOYAGEURS printed across the front. She'd begun to let her reddish hair grow out, and it was at an unruly, in-between stage that made it look like licks of flame were bursting out all over her head.

"She was pretty, though. Right?" Annie asked.

Cork put the lid back on the shake maker and climbed down from the stool. "I thought so. But, you know, love has a way of making people beautiful. To each other anyway." He put the stool in the corner next to a stack of cartons that held potato chips.

Annie was quiet a moment. "Do you think I'm pretty?"

He looked at her. Sunlight cleaved her face, and the freckles of her left cheek were like a field of russet flowers. "Gorgeous," he said.

"Seriously?"

"Seriously. Gorgeous."

"Oh, Dad."

He could see that she was pleased. She went back to looking out the window, at the lake that was a huge, sparkling sapphire.

"We were talking about sex at youth group the other night. Like, not officially or anything," she added, catching the look on her father's face. "A few of us after. We asked Randy about it, you know, to put him on the spot, see if we could embarrass him."

She was speaking of Gooding, who headed the youth program at St. Agnes.

"Did it work?"

"Oh yeah. He got all red in the face. It was sweet." She used *sweet* the way kids did when they meant devilishly enjoyable.

"What did he say?"

She scraped a finger idly along the window glass. "That men mostly want a woman they can respect and who'll respect them back. Respect is important, huh?"

"I'd say so."

She looked at him coyly. "When you told me why you fell in

love with Mom, respect wasn't one of the things you mentioned."

"Respect preceded the love," he said, thinking quickly.

Annie laid her head on her arms like a tired dog and thought awhile. "Gwen Burdick got her navel pierced and she wears these short tops so you can see her belly button ring. Guys seem to like that, but it seems to me that's got nothing to do with respect."

Cork almost said that there were a lot of things guys liked that had little to do with respect, but he didn't want to open a door to a subject he wasn't comfortable pursuing.

"I'm thinking of getting my ears pierced."

"Have you talked to Mom?" Cork opened a carton of chips and took out a half dozen small bags. He began to clip them on the display near the other serving window.

"Yeah, she says ears are okay but it stops there."

Thank God for Jo, Cork thought.

Two days later, Annie showed up for work an hour late wearing dark lipstick that made her look like a vampire who'd just feasted, and sporting dark eye shadow that made her lids appear to be bruised. Gold studs twinkled from her earlobes. She wore a tight red top and jeans that hugged her butt. She went about her business as if nothing were unusual. About her makeup and clothing, Cork judiciously held his tongue, thinking that he'd talk things over with Jo first. About the pierced ears, he said, "Looks good, kiddo."

Jenny, who was also working, was blunter. "You look like a KISS groupie. Why don't you let me help you with your makeup?"

"Who died and made you fashion queen?"

"Fine. You want to date zombies, you've got the right look. You decide you want to date guys, let me know and I'll give you the benefit of my excellent taste."

In the evening, a little before seven, Annie took a break and stepped outside. Cork watched her walk down to the dock, bend, and study her reflection in the water of Iron Lake. He hoped that she saw deeper than that awful layer of makeup, saw what he saw, her unbridled laughter, her grace when she moved on the ball field, her shining spirituality. It was what he hoped some young man would see someday, but Annie was probably right. Boys were more apt to be impressed by exposed midriffs and pierced navels.

Randy Gooding drove up in his Tracker, parked, and came to the serving window. "Hey, Cork, Annie around?"

"Taking a break down by the lake. What's up?"

"I need to talk to her about the youth group car wash next weekend. She's in charge, she tell you?"

"I think so."

"All right if I go on down?"

Cork thought of warning him about Annie's new look but decided against it. "Go ahead."

After Gooding left, Jenny said, "I'd buy a ticket to see the look on his face."

They watched Gooding saunter down to the dock. Annie was so engrossed studying her reflection that she didn't hear him coming. Gooding called to her as he neared. She straightened up and turned to him, an expectant smile on her face. Gooding stopped dead in his tracks. For a moment, he just stared. His back was to the Quonset hut and neither Cork nor Jenny could see his face, but it must have been something awful because Annie's response was a look of horror. Gooding finally spoke, and Annie took off, running in the direction of Aurora and home.

Cork rushed from Sam's Place and hurried to the dock. "What happened?"

Gooding stared fiercely in the direction Annie had fled. "My God, Cork, didn't you see her?"

"Yeah, I saw her."

"And you didn't say anything?"

"Like what?"

"Like she's just asking for trouble."

Cork knew a lot of men thought that way, a lot of cops, but it surprised him coming from Gooding. And because it was Annie, it pissed him off, too.

"It's a look, Randy. Christ, just a look. She's not asking for anything."

"Maybe not, but that kind of look can get a girl hurt, even a good kid like Annie."

"Did you tell her?"

"You bet I did."

"What the hell were you thinking?" Cork stepped back and let the boil of his own blood cool. "This doesn't sound like you, Randy. That was Annie you sent off in tears. She thinks the world of you."

Gooding watched Cork's daughter as she grew smaller with every stride that carried her away, and slowly his face changed.

"What's going on, Randy?"

Gooding kept his eyes on Annie until she merged with all that was indistinct in the distance.

"Randy?"

"You're right. I shouldn't have spoken to her that way. It's just . . ."

"Just what?"

"Look, it wasn't Annie I was seeing. It was Nina." He rubbed his temple with his fingertips and seemed genuinely pained. "You got a minute?"

"I've got all the time it takes for a good explanation."

It was dusk and everything was bathed in hues of faded blue. Gooding shifted his feet, and the old boards of the dock squeaked under his weight. He pulled on the short red hairs of his beard and stared east where the evening star was already visible.

"I don't know if I ever told you this, but I grew up in a children's home," he said. "Most of us there were orphans."

"I didn't know." Cork's anger softened and he said, "Must've been tough."

"It was okay, really. We felt like family, a lot of us. There was one girl in particular who was the nearest thing to a sister I ever had. Nina. Nina van Zoot. From Holland, Michigan. After we left, Nina and I kept in touch. She went to Chicago. I went briefly into the seminary, then finished school in Ann Arbor and decided to join the Bureau. I requested assignment to the field office in Chicago, mostly because Nina was there. They didn't have an opening, so I ended up at the Milwaukee field office. That was fine. Couple of hours from Nina, I figured.

"In her letters, she'd told me she was working for the church, but when I visited her, I found out that was a lie. She'd been telling me what I wanted to hear. The truth was that she was in the life. A prostitute. Broke my heart, Cork. I tried to help. Nina's smart. She could have done anything she set her mind to. But she wanted none of it. Had herself a world-class pimp. Guy who told her she was gold, and she fell for it. My god, what a fall."

He paused a moment, looked down at the dock, shook his head.

"When I saw Annie, all made up like that, for a moment all I saw was Nina."

"I guess I can understand."

Gooding's face was soft blue, troubled in the evening light. "I left the seminary, stopped preparing for the priesthood because I didn't have it in me to forgive. I still haven't forgiven Nina. And that pimp of hers, I hope he rots in hell."

Cork waited a moment, then said, "I think you're right. You probably would have made a terrible priest. But you're a pretty good cop."

Gooding opened his hands. "What do I say to Annie now?"

"Why don't you let us do a little damage control first?"

Gooding nodded, still looking bereaved. "God, I feel horrible."

"She's young. She'll recover."

Gooding took a step as if to walk away, but paused and, his voiced weighted heavily, said, "I wasn't completely off base, Cork. You know it as well as I do. Even a good kid like Annie, looking like that, she'll give men the wrong idea."

"We'll talk to her, Randy."

"All right." He walked slowly back to his Tracker.

Cork closed down Sam's Place immediately, and he and Jenny headed home. Jo met them at the door.

"Annie here?" Cork asked.

"She came in a few minutes ago, crying, ran upstairs. She's locked herself in her bedroom. What happened?"

"Randy Gooding said something."

"Randy? What could he possibly have said?"

"She got her ears pierced today."

"I knew she was planning on it."

Jenny said, "Did you get a good look at her face, Mom?"

"No. Why?"

"She tried makeup. She looks like an extra from *Night of the Living Dead*. And she was dressed straight out of Slutsville."

"Randy took it on himself to tell her she was asking for trouble," Cork said. "He wasn't very diplomatic about it. Did you try to talk to her?"

"I knocked. She told me to go away."

"What if I tried?" Cork said.

"Give her a little time to herself."

There was a knock. Cork turned, saw Gooding on the front porch beyond the screen door, and he stepped outside. Randy stood there looking like a big, awkward kid.

"Cork, I was wondering if you'd give something to Annie for me."

Randy handed him a large sheet torn from a sketch pad. In addition to the standard training offered all recruits, the FBI had tapped a special talent in Gooding and trained him as a sketch artist. These days he drew for his own pleasure. Although he called himself a hack, he was quite good and was sometimes convinced to give his drawings as gifts. What he handed Cork was a lovely charcoal sketch of Annie, sans makeup and earrings.

"It's a kind of apology," he explained.

"Is this recent?"

"A while ago. I've done sketches of most of the kids in the youth group, just for my own enjoyment, but I've never given any of them away. I screwed up big time, and I wanted to do something special for Annie."

"I'll see that she gets it."

"How's she doing?"

"I'm guessing her mascara's run all the way down to her chin."

"Man, I'm so sorry. But look, there's something that might help cheer her up. I have it on good authority that Damon Fielding has been trying to work up the nerve to ask her out."

"Damon Fielding?"

"Brad and Cindy Fielding's son."

"I know who he is. Set a conference record for stolen bases last year. Fast kid. How do you know he's interested in Annie?"

"He's treasurer of the youth group, and he's horrible at keeping secrets."

"Nice kid," Cork said.

"They don't make 'em any nicer."

"I'll let her know. But you still owe her a personal apology."

"She'll have it."

Gooding walked down the steps into the deepening gloom as night overtook Aurora.

Cork went back to the living room, where Jo and Jenny were waiting. "I'm going up to talk to Annie. Okay?"

"I think it would be all right now," Jo said.

Upstairs, he tapped at her door. At first there was no answer. Then Annie called out in a small voice, "Yes?"

"It's Dad. May I come in?"

"Just a minute."

He waited. In her room, there was a tiny click and a little welcome mat of light slipped under her door. A moment later, she opened up.

He hadn't exaggerated to Gooding. Black mascara ran down each of Annie's cheek in a wide, crooked line. The whites of her beautiful brown eyes were red from crying. Her hair was a mess. She left the doorway, went to her bed, and sat down, all slumped over. Cork sat beside her and put Gooding's sketch facedown on the floor.

"I just talked with Randy Gooding."

"Here?" She seemed alarmed.

"He came by to apologize."

She covered her face with her hands. "I don't want him to see me like this."

Cork put his arm around her. "He won't."

"Oh, Daddy." She fell against him and buried her face in his chest. "I messed up."

"No, you didn't."

She pulled away and reached toward her ears. "I'm going to take these awful things out. I'm never going to wear them again."

"Now wait a minute." Cork gently gripped her wrists, restraining her. "Your mother has pierced ears. Do you think that's so awful?"

"No." She lowered her hands and Cork let go.

"Before you ran into Randy, were you happy with what you'd done?"

"Yes."

"Then stick with it."

Annie thought it over. "You think I should?"

"Absolutely." He reached out and blurred one of the black mascara lines with his finger. "You might want to talk to Jenny. Get some pointers on makeup."

She shook her head adamantly. "I'm not wearing makeup anymore."

"Not a bad choice," Cork said. "You're beautiful without it."

"Really?"

"Cross my heart."

Annie kissed him on the cheek. "Thanks."

"Randy left this for you."

He gave her the drawing, and her face broke into a wonderful smile.

"One more thing," Cork said. "I have it on good authority that Damon Fielding wants to ask you out."

"Damon?"

"That's what I hear."

Her eyes danced. "Radical."

Cork left her sitting on her bed, with Gooding's offering in her hands and the prospect of Damon Fielding in her thinking.

After Gooding's reaction to Annie, Cork thought a lot about Charlotte Kane, considered if maybe something had gone terribly wrong with a quiet young woman's attempt to be desirable, and, as Gooding had feared, she'd become involved in something way over her head and dangerous, perhaps with the married man Solemn believed she was seeing. He wanted to talk more with Solemn about that possibility, but the young man had vanished completely. From discussions with Dorothy Winter Moon, Cork knew that she'd given her son nothing. She claimed not to have seen Solemn at all since his disappearance. If she was telling the truth, Solemn was flat broke. His truck was still in the impound lot, so he had no transportation. He had no clothes but those he'd been wearing when Cork had last seen him. So what had become of Solemn Winter Moon?

Periodically, Cork visited the old cabin on Widow's Creek, looking for an indication that Solemn might have returned to the place where he'd spent good times with Sam. Early one sunny Sunday morning in the middle of May, he drove to the rez, through Alouette, and up north toward Widow's Creek. The wild grass was high on the narrow track that led between the pines to Sam's old cabin. Cork parked and went inside. The place smelled musty and abandoned. He saw that a spider had spun a web in one of the kerosene lanterns and had already trapped and bound in silk a bounty of tiny prey. As he stood in the middle of the empty cabin, he heard a scurrying under the bunk. He understood. The cabin was gradually being taken over. In the end, the woods would reclaim the land and the materials Sam had borrowed to build his little home.

He walked to the creek. The snowmelt was over, and the water was clear now, fed by a spring that bubbled from a rocky hillside about a mile northeast. Sam had erected his cabin beside a little waterfall below which the creek widened into a pool a dozen feet across. The water Sam drew from the pool he used for everything—drinking, cooking, bathing. All winter long, even when the deep cold put a hard shell of ice over the creek, Sam kept a hole cleared in the pool. The bucket with which he carried water was still there, sitting upright on a flat rock on the bank. Cork glanced inside. A black snake lay coiled at the bottom. It lifted its head toward Cork. The fork of its tongue tasted the air. It was a harmless racer, not dangerous at all. Still, its presence in the bucket startled Cork and left him feeling uneasy.

He looked around once more and was about to return to his Bronco when something caught his eye and his ear. A couple of hundred yards south along the creek, a dozen crows circled, dropped, and rose. They cawed furiously in the way of those scavengers when they were squabbling over carrion. Their cries grated against the stillness of the woods and added to Cork's sense of disquiet. He began to make his way through the bog myrtle that grew thick along the banks of Widow's Creek. It didn't take him long to realize he was following a faint trail that had recently been broken through the thorny shrub growth.

Everything about the scene felt a degree off, as if the whole compass of that place had been shifted. His uneasiness deepened into a true sense of menace, and he found himself wishing he'd brought his rifle.

The crackle of the brush as he pushed through alerted the crows. At his approach, they scattered. They'd been feeding on something at the center of a patch of ostrich ferns grown a yard high. Cork could see an outline of crushed greenery, but the growth was too thick and too high for him to be able to make out immediately what was there. The size, however, was about right for a human body. He caught a glimpse of soft tan like a leather coat, and almost immediately was assaulted by the smell of rotting flesh. He steeled himself and went forward.

It was death, all right, but not exactly as he'd anticipated. The carcass of a yearling whitetail lay on a bed of bloodied ferns. Its throat had been shredded, its stomach cavity ripped open, emptied. Cork suspected it had been brought down by wolves who'd feasted and left the rest for scavengers. He stood awhile looking down at the raw flesh that was so thick with flies it appeared to be covered by rippling black skin. What was it he'd expected? What was it he'd feared? That it would be Solemn he'd find there? And why was that? Because death would have explained easily how Solemn had been able to drop so completely off the face of the earth. And because a shadow had come over all of Cork's thinking now, a darkness that shaded all his expectations with foreboding.

The crows cried at him bitterly from the branches in the pines where they'd fled. Cork left the place and walked back to his Bronco, unable to shake the sense that in these woods there was a great deal that wasn't right.

14

CORK'S SENSE OF UNEASINESS PERSISTED. Because it had arisen in the woods, and because it seemed to be something that came out of a place in his own sensibility that defied logic, he finally decided to seek counsel with a man who understood such things.

Henry Meloux was one of the Midewiwin, a Mide, a member of the Grand Medicine Society. He was an old man, very old, who lived alone in a cabin on a section of the rez far north on Iron Lake. Late one sunny afternoon when he'd enlisted the help of both Annie and Jenny to run Sam's Place, Cork drove north out of Aurora, along back highways, until he reached a place at the edge of a graveled county road where a double-trunk birch marked the entrance to a footpath through the pines. Cork parked his Bronco, got out, and began to walk the trail. After a while, he knew he'd passed from land under control of the U.S. Forest Service onto that which belonged to the Iron Lake Ojibwe. Three-quarters of a mile in, he danced across a string of rocks that spanned a stream called Wine Creek. The name came from the color of the water, a reddish hue due to the iron-rich area through which it flowed and the seepage from bogs along its banks. A few minutes later, he broke from the trees into a clearing that extended all the way to a narrow peninsula called Crow Point that jutted into Iron Lake. Cork could see Meloux's cabin on the point. The structure was as old as Meloux and just as sturdy. It was built of cedar logs, with a board roof covered with birch bark. The bark worked as well as shakes or shingles and was easier to replace. Smoke came from a stovepipe that thrust up from the roof, and even at a distance, Cork could smell the spices of a stew.

The cabin door stood wide open.

"Henry?"

He received no answer and he stepped inside. Meloux's cabin was a reflection of time itself. The walls were adorned with many items that harkened to an earlier day. A bow strung with the sinew of a snapping turtle, a deer-prong pipe, a small toboggan. There was also a cheesecake calendar, circa 1948, from a Skelly gas station. Nailed to a post near the potbellied stove was a color Polaroid of Henry Meloux standing with the activist Winona LaDuk. And lying on Meloux's bunk was the most recent Lands' End catalogue

The stew simmered in a cast-iron pot on the stove. Fish, wild rice, onions, and mushrooms, spiced with sage and pepper. The table was set with two bowls and two spoons. Cork wasn't surprised that Meloux had set a place for him. The old man had an uncanny knack for knowing when he was going to receive a visitor.

The barking of a dog came from somewhere near the end of the point. Walleye, Henry Meloux's old yellow hound. The barking became louder, and Cork figured Meloux was on his way up from the lake. He stepped outside. The low afternoon sun shone directly in his eyes, and for a moment, he was blinded. He put up his hand to block the light, and he saw two silhouetted figures walking together with the dog trotting alongside them. Meloux was obvious, small and just a little stooped, but the other wasn't clear to Cork. As they came nearer, Cork saw exactly who it was that accompanied the old man, and he let his surprise show.

Solemn Winter Moon smiled when he saw Cork in the doorway. He nodded and said, "It must be time."

Meloux put another bowl and spoon on the table and dished up stew. The men ate without speaking, Meloux filling the quiet of the one room with the sound of his slurping as he sucked from his spoon. He'd tossed Walleye a big ham bone, and the dog gnawed contentedly in the corner. When they'd eaten, Cork took a pack of Lucky Strikes he'd bought at the Food 'N Fuel on his way out of Aurora and held the cigarettes out to Meloux. The old Mide accepted the offering. Without a word, he stood up, and Cork and Solemn followed. Meloux walked outside, led them down a path toward the lake, between two rock outcroppings to a place where sooted stones ringed a circle of ash. The lake spread before them, water the color of apricots, reflecting a sky full of the afterglow of sunset. Meloux sat on a maple stump, the other two on the ground. Walleye, who'd trotted along, circled tightly a couple of times and, with a tired groan, eased himself onto the dirt near his master. From the pack Cork had given him, Meloux took one cigarette. Carefully, he tore open the paper and let the tobacco fall loose into his palm. He pinched the tobacco and sprinkled a bit to the west, to the north, to the east, and to the south. He took another pinch and offered it to the sky, and then a final sprinkling offered to the earth. When this was done, he took another cigarette for himself, then passed the pack to the others. Meloux wedged a wrinkled hand into the pocket of his bib overalls and drew out a small box of wooden matches. One after another, the men lit up and smoked for a while, letting the silence that had begun with the meal linger. In the apricot light, Cork studied Solemn's face.

There was something very different about the young man. Since Sam's passing, the muscles around Solemn's eyes were always tense, wary, waiting, expecting the approach of something bad. That tension was gone now. Cork had the feeling he was finally seeing Solemn's eyes clearly. And they were beautiful eyes, dark brown and sparkling.

Meloux sat with the lake at his back. He blew smoke into evening air that smelled of pines and also, in that particular place, of the char and ash of many fires.

Without looking directly at Solemn, Meloux said, "I think you are right. I think it is time."

Solemn seemed to divine Cork's confusion. "We're talking about what I ran from," he said. "It's time to go back and face it."

"I was beginning to think you were dead," Cork said.

Solemn laughed. "In a way, I was. After you left me alone at Sam's Place that day, I got to thinking about my chances with the law. I knew what people thought of me. I didn't see any way I was going to get a break. Man, I could feel those iron bars closing in. I got scared and ran. I followed the lake north, thinking I'd make it to Canada, figure what to do from there. But I didn't get to Canada. I ran into Henry instead."

The old Mide shook his head. "You ran into Walleye."

Solemn pointed toward the trees northwest along the lake. "Out there in the woods beside Half Mile Spring. Walleye wouldn't let me pass. A few minutes later, Henry showed up."

Meloux said, "I thought Walleye must have scared up a rabbit. Turned out to be a scared rabbit in a young man's skin."

He grinned, and Solemn laughed.

"I gave him shelter," Meloux said. "And food. I heard his story. I let him stay, and I burned cedar, and considered what should be done. The nephew of Sam Winter Moon, that is something to think about. If he were a man truly, I would have told him to turn and face his problems. But I could see he wasn't. And then I understood." The old man took a draw on his cigarette, and let the smoke out slowly. *"Giigwishimowin."*

Cork knew the word, knew of the rite. In the days before white people disrupted the Anishinaabe way, *giigwishimowin* was the experience that marked a male's passage into manhood. When the time was right, usually sometime in his teens, a young man was sent out into the forest alone to fast and to seek a vision that would guide him for the rest of his life. Not until Kitchimanidoo, the Great Spirit, had granted him that vision showing him the path he was to follow and that would lead him in harmony with creation, did he return to his village. He left as a boy and came back as a man, in his own eyes and in the eyes of his people.

"I explained it to him, because it was a thing he had never heard of," Meloux said.

"A modern Shinnob." Solemn smiled at his ignorance. "Mumbo jumbo, I thought. But I figured whatever it took to keep my ass out of jail. Henry led me into the woods. We walked for a couple of hours. I didn't have a clue where we were going, where we were. Finally Henry stopped and said, 'Here.' That's all. A man of few words."

"You don't have to speak much if you speak well," Meloux replied.

"We were in this big hollow with a stream running through," Solemn went on. "I asked Henry what I was supposed to eat. He said, 'Nothing.' I asked him what exactly I was supposed to do. He said 'Nothing.' I asked him when he would come back. He said, 'When it's time.' And then he left.

"At first, I was just bored, you know. Time dragged by. Night came. I went to sleep. Maybe I dreamed, I don't remember. The next day I got hungry. I thought about looking around for something to eat, but Henry told me to eat nothing, so that's what I did. When I got thirsty, I drank from the stream. I sat, thought, slept, thought some more. Day after day. Man, my stomach growled like a bear. The nights got pretty cold. The only visitors I had were blackflies and wood ticks. A lot of times, I was close to just packing it in. But what then? There wasn't anyplace for me to go. I lost track of the days. My thinking began to get confused. Henry tells me I was out there for sixteen days when it finally happened, when I finally had my vision.

"I was sitting up against a big rock beside the stream when He walked out of the forest. He came to where I was and smiled. He sat down and we talked."

Solemn's eyes were alive with the color of the sky and the lake, the color of a fire that burned beyond the horizon but still lit everything.

"Who was it?" Cork finally asked.

"You're going to love this," Solemn said. "It was Jesus."

Cork looked at Meloux, who seemed unperturbed at this startling declaration.

"Jesus?" Cork said.

"The Son of God," Solemn said.

"He appeared to you?"

"We had a good, long talk."

Cork peered hard at Solemn's face. He saw no indication that it was a joke, a hoax, a diversion. In fact, what he saw in those dark eyes was utter calm.

Cork said, "What was he wearing?"

"Jeans. An old flannel shirt. Minnetonka moccasins, I think."

"He was dressed like a Minnesota tourist?"

"Maybe in Mexico He wears a sombrero," Solemn said.

Cork felt fire on his fingers, and he realized he'd forgotten about his cigarette. The ember had burned all the way down to the point where it was singeing his skin. He dropped the cigarette and jerked his hand to his mouth to suck away the pain.

"Did he give you a message to deliver?"

"We just talked."

Cork blew on his fingers. "About what?"

"He told me He understood what it was like to be accused of a crime you didn't commit. He told me it was okay to be afraid, but that all things occurred for a purpose, and to believe that all of this was happening for a reason."

"Did he tell you the reason?"

"Just to believe."

"What happened then?"

"He told me he knew I was tired and that I should lie down and sleep. So I did. When I woke up, he was gone."

"When you woke up," Cork said.

"You think it was just a dream," Solemn said.

Cork looked toward Henry Meloux. "What do you think?"

Meloux finished his own cigarette, ground the ember against the side of the maple stump, and threw the butt into the ashes inside the stone ring.

"The concern on a vision quest is this: Has the vision guided the life? Solemn Winter Moon went into those woods lost. When he came out, he had found himself. Look at him, Corcoran. You can see the change for yourself."

"Henry, do you really think Jesus visited Solemn?"

The old Mide gave it some consideration. "In a thing like this," he finally said, "what one man thinks, or even what many men think, isn't important. A life has been changed. A good man walks with us today. This is always a reason to be glad."

Cork looked back at Solemn. "Just like that, it happened?"

"Just like that," Solemn replied. He licked his fingers, pinched the ember of his cigarette to extinguish the glow, and tossed the butt into the ashes with Meloux's. "I figure your coming here is a sign that it's time to go back."

Solemn stood up, then Henry and Cork. Walleye, when he saw the others rise, yawned and stretched, and slowly got to his feet.

"Migwech," Solemn said to Henry. *Thank you.*

Henry, a man of few words, closed his eyes, and nodded once.

15

Cork and Solemn walked back toward the Bronco as night swept the light from the sky. Cork was careful because the way was growing dark. They came to Wine Creek. As they prepared to cross, Solemn spoke at his back.

"You don't believe me."

"I believe you believe what you saw," Cork said.

"But it wasn't real, right? Just a dream. Or maybe a hallucination brought on by the fast."

Cork turned back. "What did he look like? What was the color of his hair?"

"Black."

"Long or short?"

"Long."

"Eyes?"

"Dark brown, kind of like walnuts, but so soft you could lie down in them."

"You've just described a Shinnob. Isn't it possible that you did hallucinate? Or you know the Shinnob sense of humor. Maybe somebody played a joke on you that, in your weakened condition, you bought hook, line, and sinker."

"What I saw was real. It's important that you believe it."

"What's important is what the sheriff's people are going to believe. Put yourself in their place. A guy with your background bolts in the middle of a murder investigation, and next thing they know, you claim to have talked with Jesus Christ.

They're going to think one of two things. Either you're trying something you hope will give you a shot at an insanity plea. Or you really are crazy."

"Because people don't talk to Jesus?" Solemn said.

"Because Jesus doesn't just step out of the woods wearing Minnetonka moccasins."

"I'm here to tell you that sometimes He does."

Solemn leaned very close to Cork so that his face was less than a foot away. For an uncomfortably long time, he looked into Cork's face, something the Ojibwe did not normally do. To look into the eyes of another was a piercing of sorts. And Cork felt pierced.

"What did *you* see," Solemn finally said.

"I don't know what you're talking about."

"It's in your eyes. You saw something, too, but don't understand it. What?"

Was Solemn referring to the gray visage that had guided Cork to safety during the whiteout on Fisheye Lake? How could he know?

"You're wrong." Cork turned away, studied the creek in the dark, looking for the stones over the water.

"You told me before that if I turned myself in, you'd stand by me," Solemn said. "Will you?"

"Yes."

"Even though you don't believe me."

"I believe you didn't kill Charlotte."

"I appreciate that." Then Solemn said something strange. "What's ahead won't be easy."

"That's exactly what I've been trying to tell you," Cork said. "You're in deep shit."

"I mean for you. I've talked with Jesus. I have that to give me strength and comfort. But I know that you doubt God."

"For me, God doesn't matter. What matters is that I gave you my word."

His foot found the first stone, and he crossed Wine Creek.

From the pay phone in the waiting area of the sheriff's department, Cork called Jo at home. He called Dot Winter Moon but got her answering machine and left her a message. Finally, he called Sam's Place to apologize to his daughters for having deserted. When they heard his reason, they didn't give him a hard time, and they agreed to close.

Randy Gooding came out of the secured area and seated himself on the hard plastic bench where Cork sat waiting for Jo.

"Winter Moon's taking all this pretty calmly."

"He's had time to think things over."

Gooding scratched the back of his head. "How'd you find him?"

"Doesn't matter."

"You convince him to come in?"

"That was his idea."

Gooding nodded. "Sheriff's on his way. We had some trouble tracking him down. He was at a swank dinner thing out at the Four Seasons. He'll probably show up in a tux."

"Nobody in Aurora wears a tux except to their wedding."

Gooding smiled slightly. "Having Winter Moon in custody is such an occasion for Arne, I wouldn't be surprised if he took the time to stop by home and put one on. He's been taking a lot of grief for letting Winter Moon get away. But if he closes this case, he's got his future wrapped up like a big, fat cigar."

Cork leaned forward and clasped his hands. "Solemn didn't do it."

"Sure a lot of evidence that says otherwise."

The front door opened and Jo walked in. She'd come in a hurry. She had on jeans and a gray sweatshirt. Her reading glasses were still propped on top of her head. She held Stevie by the hand. In the years when he'd have been old enough to remember, Stevie had never been in the sheriff's office. His eyes were like two big, shiny chunks of coal as he took the place in.

"I didn't have anybody to leave him with," Jo said in response to Cork's look of surprise. "The girls are at Sam's Place, and Rose is at the rectory."

"No problem," Cork said. "Come on over and sit with me, Stevie."

The moment Jo appeared, Randy Gooding had politely stood up. Stevie settled himself in the spot vacated by Gooding.

"Where's Solemn?" Jo asked.

Gooding said, "We've got him in a holding cell at the moment. The sheriff hasn't arrived yet."

"Did anybody talk to him?"

"I read him his Miranda rights, but he'd already been strongly cautioned against making any statements without an attorney present." Gooding cast a glance at Cork. "He was pleasant but he didn't say anything."

"I'd like to see him."

"I'd rather you waited until the sheriff—"

Arne Soderberg swept through the front door. It wasn't a tux he was wearing, but it was a dark blue suit that probably cost enough money for Cork to have damn near retired on it. The sheriff's eyes quickly took in everyone in the waiting area, but he spoke only to Gooding.

"He's in lockup?"

"Yes."

"Question him yet?"

"He asked to have an attorney present."

Soderberg looked at Jo. "Lost cause, counselor. County attorney says we've already got enough to nail him."

"That's what county attorneys are supposed to say," Jo replied.

Soderberg finally deigned to speak to Cork. "You bring him in?"

"Solemn came in on his own. I just provided the transportation."

"Fine." Soderberg smiled and clapped Gooding on the shoulder. "Great day, Randy. Great day. Shall we go have a talk with Winter Moon?"

Soderberg and Gooding started toward the security door. Jo looked at Cork.

"I'll stay here and keep Stevie company," he told her. "You see to Solemn."

Jo spoke quietly, but with great firmness. "I'm not taking his case, Cork. I'll just see him through things until he can secure representation, that's all."

"He wants you to represent him."

"That's tough. He's getting somebody else."

"Try telling him that."

Jo gave him a cold eye, but he knew it wasn't even half the chilly look Solemn would get when he made his request.

"Where do they keep the bad guys?" Stevie asked once everyone had gone.

"Just because someone's under arrest that doesn't make him a bad guy. The police sometimes make mistakes, too."

It was nearing his bedtime, and Stevie settled against his father and yawned. "Can I see the jail?"

"Not tonight."

"Were you ever in jail?"

"Lots of times. But fortunately, I always had the key." He tickled his son's cheek.

Stevie laughed and pushed at his father's hand. "Will Mom be long?"

"I don't know. Maybe."

Stevie slid down, laid his body out along the bench and put his head on his father's lap. Cork stroked his son's hair. It was oily, in need of a shampoo. By the time they all got home that night, it would be too late for washing. Tomorrow would have to do.

"Solemn is a funny name," Stevie said. He stared at the bright light in the ceiling, his dark eyes reflecting the glare. He seemed mesmerized. Or more likely, just tired.

"I suppose," Cork said.

Stevie's eyes continued to glaze over. In a few minutes, his eyelids began to droop under the weight of his weariness. He finally let them close.

It was almost an hour before Jo came out again. She walked slowly toward the bench where Cork sat cradling Stevie's head in his lap. Her normally sharp blue eyes seemed dulled, a little bewildered.

"Are you okay?" Cork asked.

"I'm not sure," she said.

"What happened?"

She spoke as if she couldn't quite believe what she was saying. "I agreed to take his case."

A wind came up and blew all night long. Jo lay in bed next to Cork, listening to the trees groan and shiver, to the wind as it rushed through the leaves with a sound like floodwaters. The curtains did a frantic dance. Finally she got up and closed the bedroom windows. When she came back to bed, she said, "By morning all the lilac blossoms will be gone."

Cork took her hand as she slid back under the covers. "How're you doing?"

"Worried. I don't think I'm the right person to help Solemn. I don't know if there's anything I can do."

"You haven't had time to think about it much. I'm sure when you do, you'll know the way."

"The evidence is pretty damning."

"Then why'd you take his case?"

Jo sucked in a long breath and shook her head. "I looked into those eyes and I couldn't say no."

"Something's happened to him, there's no doubt about it."

Jo rolled to her side and studied Cork's face. "Do you believe his story?"

"He believes his story. What I believe is that he didn't kill Charlotte Kane, no matter what the evidence looks like. What about you?"

"I wish I knew what to think. About his story, his innocence."

"You looked into his eyes, and you couldn't say no. What does that tell you?"

"That I'm getting soft in my old age." She laid her arm across his chest. "Oh, Cork, I don't know how I can do this by myself. With the work I'm doing for my other clients, I already feel overwhelmed."

"What do you need?"

She thought a moment. "Well, I suppose an investigator would help. Someone who can do interviews, and track down leads, and help me think about evidence and all the things I don't know about a homicide case. I need you, Cork."

"I'll find a way to swing it." Cork lifted her hand to his lips and softly kissed her palm. "You've got yourself a gumshoe, ma'am."

In the relative quiet that had come with the closing of the windows, Cork heard a slight sniffle at the bedroom door. He rose up on his elbows and saw the small, dark shape of Stevie in the doorway.

"What is it, buddy?"

"I keep hearing things."

Stevie heard things even when there was nothing to hear. Cork and Jo never chided him for the fears caused by night noises, real or imagined. They'd decided the best way to help their son was to let him know he was never alone.

"I'll go," Jo said. "I can't sleep anyway."

She went to the door, put her arm around her son, and the two of them walked back down the hallway.

The wind pushed through the trees outside like something huge and panicked. Alone, Cork lay staring at the ceiling, thinking about Solemn Winter Moon, about the evidence, about what Jo would be up against. He finally sat up and turned on the light on the nightstand. He pulled a pencil and a notepad from the drawer and set about making a list of all the factors stacked against Solemn.

1. Breakup with Charlotte Kane.
2. Seen arguing with Charlotte at the New Year's Eve party.
3. No alibi.
4. Murder weapon is his; his prints all over it.
5. Fingerprints on a beer bottle at the scene of Charlotte's death.

He looked at his list and knew that in Aurora these were not the only things that could influence the thinking of a jury. He added two more notations.

6. Troubled past.
7. Solemn is an Indian.

He drew a line under these items to separate the page and began to list the factors that might help Solemn's case.

1. No confession. Denies guilt.

This was important, because despite what movies and television said about the value of forensic evidence in securing a conviction, the truth was that in the vast majority of homicide cases the killer's confession was the most damning exhibit the prosecution could present in a murder trial.

2. No eyewitnesses.

At the moment, there was no one who could actually place Solemn at the scene when the crime occurred. That meant that all the evidence against him so far was circumstantial, and a good defense attorney could mount an effective attack on that basis alone. Still, with circumstantial evidence, what a jury would finally decide was anyone's guess.

Cork tried to think if there was anything else working in Solemn's favor. Only one possibility occurred to him, and he wrote it down.

3. Talked with Jesus.

Cork looked at that one a long time, weighing the effect it might have on anyone's thinking about the case. Solemn seemed to believe truly in what he'd experienced, and that belief had changed him dramatically. But it might be that not everyone would see that change, or believe it to be sincere. Maybe Cork's own thinking was influenced by his love of Sam Winter Moon and by what he thought he owed Sam's great-nephew. In a town like Aurora, once the opinion about a thing was set, changing that opinion was like trying to reverse the rotation of the earth. Solemn was a wild kid, a troublemaker, a hoodlum. It wouldn't be a hard stretch at all to believe he'd killed Charlotte Kane. He was also the desecrator of St. Agnes, and the fact that he claimed to speak to Jesus might well be the final blasphemy.

Cork drew a line through his third notation under the list of things helpful to Solemn's case, and assigned it number eight under the things against. Then he looked at what he'd put together. Jo was right to be concerned. On paper, Solemn was already a goner.

16

THE NEXT MORNING, as soon as he'd seen the children off to school, Cork went to St. Agnes to talk to Mal Thorne. He tried the rectory first. When he knocked, Rose opened the door.

She'd been absent from the O'Connor house for over a month, and Cork had seen her only two or three times in that period, not very recently. The children and Jo stopped by the rectory regularly, and they saw her every Sunday morning, but a stop at St. Agnes was never on Cork's agenda. Now he stood at the doorway to the priests' residence and looked at Rose as if he were seeing a stranger. For a moment, he simply stared at her, speechless.

She smiled. "Hello, Cork."

"Rose?"

She laughed, reached out, and hugged him.

"You've lost weight," he said.

"A few pounds."

"New dress?"

"Yes. My old clothes tend to hang on me these days."

"Your hair's different."

"I've decided to let it grow a bit."

That wasn't all that was different. There was a light in her eyes, a rosy aura about her, even a subtle, enticing fragrance that was the faintest hint of perfume, something that, to Cork's knowledge, Rose never wore.

"Come in, won't you?" she said.

From inside the rectory came the blare of the television. *The Price Is Right*. Father Kelsey, Cork figured, because the old priest was nearly deaf and Rose never watched television during the day. Cork held back. "I'm looking for Mal. Is he in?"

"He's working in his office in the church this morning."

"Think he'd mind if I dropped by?"

"You? In St. Agnes? He'd welcome that like a miracle."

"I'll just go on over then." Cork took one last look at his sister-in-law. "You know, you look wonderful, Rose."

"Why, thank you, Cork."

Walking to the church, Cork mulled over the change in Rose. He considered that maybe just getting out of the O'Connor house had made the difference, but that was unconvincing. There was something else going on.

Mal Thorne was at his desk, shoving around the mouse for his computer. Cork knocked at the door, and the priest looked up. The pleasant surprise of seeing Corcoran O'Connor at his door carved a wide smile on his face.

"Well, come on in." He stood up and bounded toward Cork, his hand already out in greeting.

"I stopped by the rectory first. Rose said I'd find you here."

"Just finished brewing up a pot of coffee. Join me?"

"Thanks."

Mal went to a small table pushed against the wall where a framed charcoal drawing of St. Agnes hung.

"Nice picture," Cork said. "Where'd you get it?"

"Randy Gooding. A Christmas present. Remarkable, isn't it?" Mal lifted the pot from the coffeemaker and poured some into a disposable cup. "All I've got is this powdered creamer crap."

"Black'll do." Cork took his coffee. "Rose seems to be doing fine covering for Ellie Gruber."

"Are you kidding? Rose is a saint." The priest tipped the jar of creamer and tapped some into his own coffee. "I've never seen anybody handle Father Kelsey with such a firm, loving hand. Don't get me wrong. Mrs. Gruber is fine. It's just that there's something special about Rose. But I'm sure you know that."

Cork sipped from his cup. The coffee was hot and strong, just as he liked it. "Whatever it is she does here, it agrees with her. She looks terrific."

"She's absolutely lovely." He became intent on stirring his coffee with a white plastic spoon, as if he'd said too much. He indicated a chair to Cork, and he sat back down in the swivel chair he'd been using at the computer. "What's up?"

Cork sat down. "Solemn Winter Moon turned himself in last night."

The priest was about to take a sip, but he paused. "Does Fletcher Kane know?"

"I'm sure he does by now. Mal, there's a strange twist to all this."

"How so?"

"Solemn claims he's had a vision. He claims he talked with Jesus."

"A prayer talk?"

"No, like we're having right now."

"Jesus in the flesh?"

"That's what he says."

"When?"

"While he was out in the woods."

Cork told him about Henry Meloux, *giigwishimowin,* and Solemn's visitation in the clearing.

When Cork finished, Mal swirled his coffee for a moment, then said, "Minnetonka moccasins?"

"That's what he claims."

"Why did you come to me with this?"

"I was hoping you might talk to Solemn."

"The man who urinated in the baptismal font."

"Please. Just talk to him."

"To what end?"

"I'd like your reaction to what he says and to the change in him."

"Change?"

"Talk to him. You'll see what I mean."

"How do I get in?"

"I'll have Jo arrange it. She's agreed to represent him. He's scheduled to be arraigned later this morning. Maybe this afternoon you could see him."

"I suppose it couldn't hurt."

"Thanks." Cork gulped down the last of his coffee.

Mal Thorne stood up with him as he prepared to go. "Do you believe it's possible he talked with Jesus?"

Cork said, "What I believe doesn't matter."

"I think it does," the priest said. He placed his thick hand gently on Cork's shoulder. "I think it does more than you realize."

17

AT 11:00 A.M., SOLEMN WINTER MOON was arraigned in the Tamarack County courthouse on a single charge of assaulting an officer. Dressed in the blue uniform and wearing the plastic slippers of a county jail inmate, handsome with his long black hair down his back, Solemn stood before Judge Norbert Olmstead and entered a plea of not guilty.

Nestor Cole, the county attorney, had a narrow face and eyes that lay alongside his thin nose like two stewed oysters. He wore black-rimmed glasses that made him look more like a science teacher than a lawyer. Everyone knew he had a good shot at a judgeship when the next vacancy arose, provided he kept a reasonable profile and didn't blow anything too important. He vehemently maintained that Solemn was a flight risk. Near the end of his argument, he slapped his hand down on the table, but his timing was a hair off and the gesture seemed overly theatrical.

Jo argued that Solemn's first absence wasn't flight; he often sought solitude at Sam Winter Moon's old cabin. She contended that the second instance was panic, understandable in light of the questionable tactics the sheriff had used in questioning her client. Both times, she pointed out, Solemn returned of his own accord.

Cork knew that public sentiment ran against Solemn, that he would probably be charged eventually with Charlotte's death, and that it would be smart to hold on to him until a formal murder charge could be made. Judge Olmstead, a hunched man with a twitching right eye that made him look like a nervous pickpocket, set bail at $250,000.

Jo was on her feet instantly. "For assaulting an officer?"

"Counselor," the judge broke in. "I was thinking half a million. You persuaded me to be lenient." He banged his gavel to seal his decision and told both attorneys that he wanted to see them in chambers to discuss a date for the scheduling conference.

Fletcher Kane had come to the arraignment. He sat alone at the back of the courtroom. Although he didn't say a word, the force of his presence was clear in the way Judge Olmstead kept glancing in his direction. Once that impossible bail had been set, Kane unfolded his hands and rose from the bench on which he sat. No emotion showed in his face as he ambled out of the courtroom.

Dorothy Winter Moon had taken the morning off from her county job. She'd done herself up carefully and come to court looking as if she handled realty papers all day long instead of wrestling the wheel of a dump truck that could haul ten tons. When bail was set, she said under her breath (but loud enough for Judge Olmstead to hear if he'd cared to take note), "You lousy son of a bitch Republican bastard." Jo explained to Dot and to Solemn that the only alternative to coming up with $250,000 in cash would be to have a bondsman post bail. In order to arrange that, someone would have to be willing to fork over to the bondsman a nonrefundable twenty-five grand.

Dot clearly looked distressed. "I'll come up with it somehow," she said.

"Keep your money, Ma," Solemn said. "I'm not afraid." He kissed her just before the deputies led him away.

After Solemn was gone, Dot turned to Jo. She wiped at her eyes with a rough knuckle. "He's Indian. And he never goes to church. Why would Jesus talk to him?"

Cork didn't arrive at Sam's Place until almost noon. As he pulled up, a boat with a couple of fishermen aboard putted toward the dock and tied up there. Cork hurried inside and began to ready things for customers.

Shortly before three o'clock, Mal Thorne parked in the graveled lot and walked to the serving window. Jenny wasn't due for another half an hour, and Cork was still handling things alone. Mal waited until Cork finished with his only customers at the moment, a man and woman who'd ordered chocolate sundaes, then he stepped up and leaned in the window.

"I just came from talking with Solemn Winter Moon," he said.

"Well?"

"You know, Cork, when I was running the mission in Chicago, I had a regular there, an old man who called himself Jericho. I don't have the slightest idea if that was his real name or simply what he went by. He had no family so far as I ever knew, no home. He was a harmless old guy. Always wore a tam, like he was Scottish or something. Anyway, despite his life on the streets, Jericho was basically a happy man. Why? He said he had a talk with God every day and that set the tone. Not prayer talk, mind you."

"Like Solemn claims to have had with Jesus?"

"Exactly. I often asked him what God said to him, but he wouldn't tell me. Well, one day I get a call from Cook County General. Jericho's been admitted, hit by a flower delivery truck. He's in pretty bad shape, and they don't think he's going to make it. He's asking for me. So I go to his bedside, give him Last Rites. When I'm done, he crooks his finger, signals me down close, and he whispers in my ear, 'You always wanted to know what God said to me. Well, Father, I'll tell you. I never understood a word because He always talked in Hebrew.'

"The point is this," the priest went on. "Did it matter whether his talks with God were delusional? They made him happy."

"You think Solemn is delusional?"

"I think whatever he's experienced, it's changed him for the better, and to me that's all that matters."

"But you don't really believe he talked with Jesus."

"God makes His presence known in many ways. In acts of love, in selfless acts of courage, in everyday human compassion. There's no reason not to believe that God's hand was at work in whatever changed young Winter Moon. But I have to say this. I've prayed desperately, devoutly, passionately for much of my life and I've never had the kind of vision Solemn claims to have had. As a priest, I've got to accept the possibility, but as a man, I'm full of doubt." He saw the concern in Cork's face. "What did you expect? That I'd somehow give my blessing?"

"I just figured you'd be a better judge than me, that's all."

"By the way, he asked me to bring him a Bible. I said I would."

A van swung into the parking lot, scraping gravel as it slid to a stop. Half a dozen teenagers piled out.

"Looks like you've got your hands full," Mal said. "I'm outta here."

"Thanks."

The priest held up a moment more. "It would be easy if we all had visions, or if we all believed in those who did. My own feeling is that faith was never meant to be easy."

A few minutes before five, Cork spotted Jo's Toyota bumping over the Burlington Northern tracks. There was a lull at the moment, so he stepped outside to greet her. When she got out of her car, Cork could see from the taut look on her face that she was concerned about something.

"I just came from the reservation," she told him. "I talked to George LeDuc and Ollie Bledsoe about the possibility of bail for Solemn coming out of some of the casino funds."

"No go, huh?"

She shook her head. "I thought it was worth a try. But I also picked Ollie's brain while I was at it. I couldn't figure out why Nestor Cole didn't charge Solemn with murder. He's had plenty of time to prepare, and he's got everything to make a good case for second-degree homicide, intentional or unintentional. He could put Solemn away for at least a dozen years. More if he argued particular cruelty, which would be a good argument, since it appears that whoever killed Charlotte had themselves a little feast while they watched her freeze to death."

"What did Bledsoe say?"

"He thinks Nestor Cole is probably preparing to take everything before a grand jury to see if a charge of murder in the first will fly. If the jury declines to indict, he's out nothing. If they do hand down an indictment but he doesn't convict, he can still shrug his shoulders and say it was the grand jury's decision to go for the whole ball of wax, not his. That way he doesn't risk losing his shot at a judgeship." She looked angry. "Solemn may be looking at spending his life in prison, and the jackasses in charge of justice around here can only think of politics."

"You look tired."

"There's a lot I'm trying to get a handle on. I won't know everything that the prosecution has until Cole finally decides to charge Solemn with homicide, but I'd like to have some idea of what we'll be up against. I thought I'd head over to the jail and talk to Solemn again. I was hoping you might be able to spring yourself free and come with me."

Cork glanced back at the serving window. There was a lanky kid leaning on the counter talking with Jenny, but he didn't seem to be in a hurry to order.

"Jenny," Cork called. "Can you handle things alone for a while?"

"Sure, Dad." She smiled and waved to her mother.

Duane Pender escorted Solemn to the interview room where Cork and Jo were waiting. Before he closed the door, Pender said, "The prisoners get fed in half an hour. Winter Moon's still talking to you then, he goes hungry."

"You like being a hardass, don't you, Duane?" Cork said.

Pender shrugged. "I didn't send him an invitation to stay here. And I don't make the rules." He closed and locked the door.

Solemn looked calm and rested. He folded his hands on the table.

"How are you doing?" Jo asked.

"Good. Father Mal stopped by to see me this afternoon. We had a long talk. He said you asked him to come, Cork. Thanks."

Jo offered Cork a *what in the hell* kind of look, and he realized he hadn't said a word to her about consulting the priest.

"Solemn, I want you to know how a few things stand," Jo said. "I'm almost certain you'll be charged in Charlotte Kane's death. I think that won't occur until after a grand jury hearing."

"But you'll defend me."

"Not before the grand jury. Only the prosecution has an opportunity to appear there. The question they'll consider is whether there's enough evidence to charge you with first-degree murder. If they hand down an indictment, that's when you'll go to trial and I'll defend you. Now if the county attorney doesn't get an indictment, he'll probably charge you with second-degree murder. If that happens, we may have some leeway."

"What kind of leeway?"

"A plea bargain is one possibility."

"I would have to admit to something."

"Yes."

"Then there won't be a bargain. I didn't have anything to do with Charlotte's death."

"Let's talk about Charlotte." Jo brought out a small notepad and a silver Cross ballpoint pen. "You told us before that you thought Charlotte was seeing someone else while you were dating. That's why she broke up with you. You said you thought it might have been a married man. Why did you think that?"

Solemn sat for quite a while, thinking. He was composed and didn't seem in any hurry to reply. The room had no windows. The air was warm and stuffy. Cork felt a trickle of sweat crawl down from his armpit. Jo watched Solemn, the point of her pen resting against the notepad.

"I know a lot of Shinnobs who have next to nothing, but they're still happy," Solemn finally said. "Charlotte had everything, but she was one of the saddest people I ever knew. You wouldn't have guessed it, looking at her. I mean, she seemed to have the perfect life, but the truth was she didn't like herself at all. Sometimes she seemed desperate to be loved."

"Did you love her?" Jo said.

"In the beginning, what I felt came mostly from below the waist." He said it with regret. "But in the end, yeah, my heart got caught up in it."

"Did she love you?"

Solemn thought it over. "At first, I figured I was just her walk on the wild side. A good, quiet Catholic girl, straight-A student, finally looking for a thrill. But from the things she said, I finally decided she was seeing me for the shock value. Using me to get at someone. Probably the guy she was really interested in."

"And you still felt strongly about her?"

"The head and the heart, you know, they don't always see eye to eye."

"Did she give you any indication who the guy was?"

"No."

"But you think he was married."

"From the way she acted, all secretive, I figured married was the reason."

"Think back. Did she ever say anything that might have been a clue to his identity?"

Solemn closed his eyes for a while. "No."

"Okay. Tell me about Charlotte."

"Tell you what?"

"Anything that you might think is relevant."

Solemn thought a moment. "She was beautiful, but didn't see herself that way. She always needed compliments. She was depressed a lot. Took some kind of medication for it. She had this fixation with death. She told me she tried suicide once. She believed she would die young." Solemn looked down. "She was sure right about that."

"How about drugs?"

"Yeah. And booze. But she worked hard not to let it show."

Jo wrote in her notebook, then looked up.

"Let's talk about your wrench," she said. "The one that was used to kill Charlotte. Did you know it was missing?"

"Yes."

"When?"

"A couple of days after Charlotte disappeared. My fan belt was squealing. I thought the alternator was a little loose. I've got a tool chest built into the bed of my pickup, and I went there to get a pry bar. The hasp on the chest was broken. I went through everything. Only thing missing was the wrench. I went to Hardware Hank's and bought a new one. New hasp, too."

"Before that, when was the last time you checked your tool chest?"

Again he closed his eyes and spent time being sure. "I don't remember."

"Do you have a receipt for the hasp and wrench?"

"I probably threw it away."

Cork said, "Remember who waited on you?"

"Sure. It was old man Springer."

Cork glanced at Jo. "I'll talk to him, see if he remembers."

Jo nodded. "Okay. How about the bottle found at the scene? The night Charlotte disappeared, did you have a Corona?"

He smiled at her. "Corona's my favorite beer. Everyone knows that. I drink it all the time."

"Were you drinking it at Valhalla?"

"Yeah."

"What did you do with your empty bottles?"

Solemn scratched his cheek while he puzzled that one. "I don't remember."

"Okay."

"Wait. When I was leaving, I took a beer with me out to the truck. I had to pee, and I set the bottle down in the snow while I took care of business. I don't remember picking it up."

"Good." Jo looked seriously at Solemn. "Did you have sex with Charlotte Kane?"

"Yes. And right from the beginning. She knew what she was doing. That surprised me. She didn't seem the type."

"I mean that night. Did you have sex with her on New Year's Eve, before she disappeared?"

"No, we were history by then."

Jo said, "Tell me about the break-in at St. Agnes. It wasn't you alone, was it? I'm betting Charlotte was with you that night."

"Yeah, but it was my truck that got reported, and when they grabbed me I didn't see any reason to bring her into it."

"The break-in, your idea or Charlotte's?"

"Hers. But I did the damage."

"Why *Mendax?* Why 'liar'?"

"I don't know. She was pissed."

"At the church?"

"I got the feeling it was the priest."

"Father Mal? Why?"

He shrugged. "A lot of the time, she was hard to figure."

"Did she talk about him?"

"No."

"What did she talk about?"

"Reincarnation. She was real big on that. Always talking about her other lives, things that had happened in them."

"Like what?"

"Awful things, mostly. She claimed that in her first life, she was raped as a child. In her second, she was a prostitute."

"She believed this?"

"Oh, yeah."

"And in her next life, she was murdered," Cork said. "What kind of karma is that?" He remembered the poem Jenny had told him about, the one Charlotte had written. Lazarus, angry at being raised from the dead. Given what he knew now, he thought he had a better sense of the girl's perspective.

"It's almost dinnertime," Solemn said. "And I am hungry. Mind if we call it?"

"One more question. In your statement, you admitted arguing with Charlotte at her home shortly before Christmas. Her father overheard. He claims you threatened her. Is that true?"

"No. What I said was that someday somebody was going to tear her heart out like she'd torn mine."

"That was it? No threat?"

"Just something to hurt her. Like she needed more of that."

"I think we're through for now. If there's anything you need, just let me know." Jo lifted the wall phone and called Pender.

The deputy opened up and stepped in. "Come on, Winter Moon. Got a dinner reservation for you." He held a small, black Bible in his hand. "Oh, and the priest stopped by, brought this for you. Sheriff asked me to check it out before I gave it to you." With a snort, he handed the Bible to Solemn. "Believe me, there's nothing in here that'll do the likes of you any good."

"You're quiet," Cork said as they drove home.

"Just thinking about Charlotte. She wasn't exactly the young woman we all thought she was." Jo looked out the window. "I feel sorry for her, Cork. And a little guilty that none of us saw how troubled she was."

"We have our own children to worry about."

"And who worries about the Charlotte Kanes?"

After a little while, Cork said, "I'd love to know exactly what Nestor Cole has, what he intends to base his case on."

"From the documents I've been able to look at so far," Jo said, "it goes something like this. At the party, just before midnight, Charlotte made it clear that she was going to the guesthouse to grab her snowmobile for a ride, some kind of crazy way to see the New Year in. But according to the statements of some of the kids at the party, the snowmobile didn't actually leave until around one A.M. In the meantime, Charlotte had sex with someone. Probably she was assaulted with Solemn's wrench after leaving the guesthouse, since there was no blood found inside. If she bled outside, the snowfall covered it. She was carried to the snowmobile, driven to Moccasin Creek where the 'accident' was staged. After that, someone calmly feasted on junk food and watched while the girl froze to death. Then her assailant either walked back to Valhalla, only a mile or so away, or went to a vehicle parked in the lot at the trailhead.

"So, Nestor has the bottle found at the scene with Solemn's prints all over it, and the murder weapon with his prints on that as well. There's the argument at the party, and the fact that Solemn has no alibi. It's still circumstantial. I keep thinking there's something else, something we don't know about, and probably won't until Solemn's charged."

Cork paused for the traffic light at the intersection of Oak and Fox.

"I keep asking myself if Solemn didn't kill Charlotte, who did?" he said.

"And why."

"Let's start with why. Maybe that will lead us to who."

Jo said, "In making the case against Solemn, I'm sure the prosecution's going to say it was scorned love. Maybe what's a good motive for Solemn would be good for someone else. Maybe the man she was having the affair with?"

"That would make sense. When I saw her at the creek, she looked peaceful, her arms across her chest. She seemed composed, almost tenderly so, as if whoever killed her had put her gently to rest. If that's true, it might point to someone with very mixed emotions about her, someone who loved her, and maybe killed her in a moment of jealous rage. That would fit with some of the other things we know. He killed her with an object at hand, Solemn's wrench. And the beer bottle that points to Solemn's guilt, I don't see how that could have been planned. Just Solemn's bad luck that he left it in the snow. All of which would point toward not a lot of forethought in the killing. It could be that he arrived at the party, saw Solemn's truck, assumed that Solemn and Charlotte were an item again, and went ballistic."

"On the other hand," Jo said, "maybe he'd wanted to kill her. Maybe she wasn't satisfied with an illicit affair and wanted more. She threatened to go public if he—what?—didn't leave his wife and marry her? At the party, he finally saw his chance and killed her."

A car honked behind them and Cork realized the light had changed to green.

Jo leaned back against the headrest and stared out her window at the familiar houses of Aurora. She could probably give the names of the families who lived in them. When she spoke again, she sounded weary and sad. "This seems unreal, somehow. Do you realize we're talking about Aurora, Cork, about someone we may see every day on the street? It feels dirty, speculating this way. Is this how the police always look at people in an investigation?"

"The good cops," Cork said. "The ones who realize anybody can be driven to kill under the right circumstances. It's not a cop's job to pass judgment. Once you put judgment aside, uncomfortable speculations become bearable. So," he said. "Who?"

"I don't know."

"Think about the adults she normally comes into contact with. Who would they be?"

Jo thought. "Teachers."

Cork nodded. "A good possibility. Affairs like that happen all the time. Who else?"

"Employer."

"Maybe. But with Kane's money, I doubt if Charlotte ever had a job."

"A family friend."

"Worth checking out."

Jo fell silent. Cork could feel her shutting down, turning away from the speculation.

"I don't like this thinking," she said.

"Nobody does. But it's what you do if the truth is what you're after." Cork hesitated a moment, then asked, "What do you think her anger at Mal was all about?"

"Don't even go there, Cork." Jo shoved at the empty air in front of her, pushing away the thought. "This makes me sick. I can't do it."

"That's why you asked me to help," Cork said. "Because I can."

Jo was silent for a long time. As Cork turned onto Gooseberry Lane, she reached out and laid her hand on his arm. "I'm concerned about pursuing this line of investigation right now. I'm afraid all it will do is stir people up. Until we see what Nestor Cole's plan is, especially if he's thinking grand jury, I'd like you to hold off asking questions, especially any that might probe an affair. I don't want to prejudice the whole county against us even before we start."

"The question will still be hanging out there unanswered, Jo. Who killed Charlotte?"

"My job is to keep Solemn out of jail."

"A few minutes ago you asked me who watched out for the Charlotte Kanes."

"She's dead, Cork. I can't help her now."

In his mind's eye, he saw a dark figure beckoning to him from a lonely place.

"The dead can't speak for themselves," he said. "They've got no way to ask for justice. What's left behind in the details of their deaths is the only hope they have for pointing the way toward the truth, and someone ought to pay attention." He slowed down and looked at Jo. "It's called due diligence, Jo. It's what a good cop does. He considers all the possibilities, turns over all the stones, and he tries to do it without prejudice. Arne won't do that. He's not a cop. Like everybody else, he thinks Solemn is guilty and that's all there is to it. The truth will have to be found by someone else. And, sweetheart, at the moment, it looks like there's just you and me."

"I understand what you're saying. I do. And it's one of the things I love about you. But I'm still going to ask that you wait a little while before you stir things up. Just a while. Okay?"

Cork didn't reply.

"Okay?"

He pulled into the driveway and shut off the engine. In the pale evening light that filtered through the trees and fell across the car, he looked at Jo. She was beautiful to him in so many ways. He loved her so much that sometimes it made him ache. Often when he was alone at Sam's Place, out of the blue he would think of her, and it always felt as if his heart had suddenly ballooned and filled his whole chest. But looking at her now, he understood they were two very different people, and there were some things deep in the heart of each of them that the other could never touch, would never understand. It made him sad, but he didn't say so. Instead he said, "I'll do my best to behave myself."

18

THE NEXT MORNING, Cork paid a visit to Aurora High. He stopped at the office first, spoke with Jake Giles, the assistant principal, and was given both a schedule of the classes Charlotte Kane had taken while attending the high school and a list of her extracurricular activities. Then Cork went to see Juanita Sherburne.

Sherburne was the school psychologist. Her office was on the second floor of the new consolidated high school that had been built three years earlier just west of town, near the gravel pit. An athletic woman, Sherburne could often be seen jogging along Lakeshore Drive with her husband and their two Afghan hounds. The Sherburnes were avid canoeists and regularly led groups of students into the Boundary Waters Canoe Area Wilderness, north of Aurora. She was fortyish, had short black hair, and despite her vaguely Hispanic features, spoke with a flat, nasal accent that pinned her upbringing to somewhere in the heart of the Wisconsin dairy land. In addition to her duties as the school psychologist, she coached the girls' softball team.

"Cork." She stood up from her desk and reached out to shake his hand.

"I probably should have made an appointment, Juanita. I'm wondering if I could talk to you for a few minutes."

"About Annie, I assume."

"Annie?"

"Those slipping grades. Isn't that why you're here?"

"Should I be concerned?" Cork said.

The office was spare, neat. Tan filing cabinets lined the walls, and above them hung photographs of the teams she'd coached over the last five years. Behind her, the window opened toward the west where, visible beyond a line of white birch, stood the tall conveyor of North Star Aggregate's gravel pit.

Cork waited until the woman took her seat, then he sat down, too.

"I don't think it's anything to worry about, Cork. She's a little distracted these days. I see it on the ball field, too. I've just chalked it up to normal teenage stuff. You know, boys, social status, boys. Does she have a boyfriend?"

"She just started dating Damon Fielding."

"Damon? Very nice. Well, there you go. I wouldn't worry unless her grades don't rebound, but I believe they will. Annie's not a frivolous young woman. She's serious in the things she cares about."

"Used to be just sports and religion," Cork said.

"If you'd like, I'll talk to her about it, see if I can get her to focus a little more on her studies. And her pitching."

"I'd appreciate it."

"I have a selfish motive. She's a big part of a winning season for the Voyageurs. Is that all?"

"There's something else," Cork said.

The bell rang and the hallway outside her office became a crazy river of bodies with currents running every which way.

"Just a moment." She got up and closed the door.

"I'm very concerned about another young woman I know. She's only seventeen, and I believe she may be having an affair with a married man."

"What's your interest?"

"I'm concerned is all. Wouldn't you be?"

She returned to her desk and sat down. "What can you tell me about her?"

"Poor self-esteem. Depressed. She tried suicide once. Fixation with death."

"Compulsive sexual behavior?"

"Possibly."

"Drugs? Self-injury? Eating disorder?"

"Drugs, yes. I don't know about the others. Why?"

"These are all signs that might be indicative of sexual abuse. Generally speaking, the more severe the symptoms, the more long-term the abuse."

This made Cork sit back.

"I'm not saying they are," she hastened to add. "Many teenagers exhibit some of these symptoms. It's a question of number and degree. I'd have to do a complete assessment."

"If you saw these things in one of your students, you'd be required to report it, wouldn't you?"

"If I saw it. The thing is, adolescents who've been sexually abused can be very good at hiding the symptoms from general view."

"If it was sexual abuse, who might be the perpetrator?"

"Well, statistically speaking, it's most likely a family member." The chaos in the hall died away, and the psychologist's office dropped into a well of silence. She gave him a long look. "Annie wasn't the reason you came."

"No."

"Can you tell me who?"

"I'd rather not, unless I'm sure."

"I understand, Cork. But a young woman in this situation desperately needs help and usually doesn't know how to ask for it."

"It's a bit more complicated than you realize."

"This kind of thing is always complicated."

"I'm wondering if a teacher might be involved."

"A teacher here?"

"If it's a teacher, it would be here."

She gave her head a faint shake. "The symptoms you've described are more consistent with long-term abuse, something that began before this girl ever entered high school."

"A girl like this, though, would she be more vulnerable to a sexual relationship with an adult?"

"Possibly."

"So she could be involved with a teacher, someone who had nothing to do with her earlier abuse?"

"I suppose so, yes. Cork, I wish you'd tell me who this is so I can help."

"She's beyond help, Juanita."

The woman puzzled for a moment, then a light came into her eyes. "Jo's defending Solemn Winter Moon. You're wondering about Charlotte Kane."

"I don't think Solemn had anything to do with the girl's death."

"He's a troubled kid."

"I still don't think he did it. Solemn believes that before her death, Charlotte was seeing someone, maybe a married man."

"A teacher, you think? Someone here? I hope that's not what you've come to me for. I won't even begin to speculate on something like that, Cork."

"I understand. But, Juanita, if Solemn is innocent, there's a murderer still out there somewhere. Maybe even walking the halls of Aurora High. You've already said that a student-teacher liaison isn't an impossibility."

"One that ends in murder is."

"I'm not asking you to accuse anyone, just help my thinking. It may save an innocent young man. Could it have been a teacher?"

"I'm sure that kind of thing goes on in schools somewhere, but not here. I'm not going to continue this conversation."

"Just hear me out."

"We're done."

Cork started to argue but saw how tense she'd become. "All right. I didn't mean to put you in a professionally awkward position. I'm just trying to save a boy I believe is innocent."

"I understand."

Cork stood up and offered his hand. Her face slowly relaxed.

"I heard Solemn claims he talked with Jesus," she said. "Is it true?"

"Where'd you hear that?"

"Around. I also heard that Jesus was wearing Minnetonka mocassins."

"That's what Solemn says."

She allowed herself a brief smile. "That's funny. I always figured Him for a Birkenstock kind of guy."

That night after Cork got home from Sam's Place, Jo cornered him in the kitchen.

"Annie said she saw you lurking in the halls at school today."

"I didn't see her," Cork said. "How come she didn't say hello?"

"Are you kidding? Acknowledging the existence of one of your parents at school? What planet are you from?" Jo was about to make a pot of decaf French roast coffee. As she lifted the bag to pour the beans into the grinder, she asked, "So, what were you doing there?"

"I had a talk with Juanita Sherburne about Charlotte Kane."

"Cork, you didn't." She dumped beans all over the counter. "After you promised."

"I said I would behave myself. And I did. I was very polite."

"You're splitting hairs. And you're splitting them because you know you're wrong. Oh, Cork." Angrily, she began to gather the spilled beans. "If we have to go to trial, and even before we've selected a jury you've turned this whole town against us—"

"Charlotte may have been sexually abused."

That made her pause.

"Why do you say that?"

"Some of the things Juanita told me. I think Charlotte exhibited a number of telling symptoms."

Jo looked thoughtful and troubled. "Did you talk about who it might have been?"

"Not specifically. But according to Juanita, usually it happens among family members."

"Family, as in . . . ?"

"The only family we know about is Fletcher and Glory, so maybe we start there."

She shook her head. "I think we should leave it alone, Cork."

"Fletcher's a widower. No lady friends. He's certainly an odd duck. And remember what Solemn said about Charlotte being so secretive. Maybe it's the reason she hid so much, and why the one person who should have known she was troubled did nothing. Jo, I'm not accusing him. I'm just saying we should check it out."

"Due diligence?" She gave the words a sarcastic sting. "It's a dangerous speculation, Cork."

"Look, this girl had problems. Someone somewhere along the line messed her up. Maybe that same someone killed her. Or maybe someone else preyed on her and then killed her. The more we know about Charlotte, the better we'll be able to understand what happened."

"How did Juanita react to your questions?"

Cork paused a moment. "When she understood I was asking about Charlotte, she clammed up."

"She didn't want to go there with you, right? And she's a professional. Imagine what the average citizen of Aurora will think. Solemn already has a lot of black marks against him in Tamarack County. If jurors know that we're casting aspersions on their friends, their neighbors, God knows who all, even before Solemn's been charged, they're going to be sworn onto that grand jury already prejudiced against him. And us. They may not admit it to themselves, but the prejudice will be there. The fact is that the character of their town is being called into question, and they'll be looking for the easiest way back to normalcy. In their minds, I guarantee you, that way will be to indict and then convict Solemn."

"That's a lot of speculation, Jo."

"I know how juries think. That's part of what I do. It may be that the questions you ask lead nowhere. Suppose Charlotte was sexually abused. Does that mean it necessarily had anything to do with her death?"

"Jo, they're going to charge Solemn with murder eventually. First-degree, second-degree, whatever. I promised him I would help. This is how I do that."

"I understand that, Cork. And I hope you understand that I'm trying to handle a very delicate situation here, a balance between my client's needs at this point, the prejudice of this community, the long-term effect of every move we make, and the fact that you can't even sneeze in this town without everyone knowing it.

"Charlotte's been dead for several months. Will another week or two change anything? Once Solemn's been officially charged you can ask your questions. People will expect it then. They may not like it any better, but they'll understand."

"You ask for my help and then you ask me to sit on my hands."

"I know."

Cork stooped and picked up a bean that had fallen to the floor. He looked at it, hard and black in the palm of his hand. That was him inside.

"All right," he said. He threw the bean onto the counter and turned toward the side door.

"Where are you going?" Jo asked.

"I need to be by myself for a while."

He opened the kitchen door.

"Cork," Jo said to his back. "It's good information. I'm sure it will be a big help if we have to go to the mat for Solemn. Thank you."

"Yeah."

He stepped out under the early night sky and walked away into the gathering dark.

19

THE FIRST MIRACLE occurred a few days later, on Memorial Day.

Every year on that holiday, weather permitting, the O'Connors had a backyard barbeque. They invited friends and neighbors, and over the coals of a couple of grills, they cooked up hamburgers and hot dogs that they served with Rose's famous potato salad. Everyone who came brought a dish to share. Cork nestled beer and pop in a half-barrel full of ice, and the kids made lemonade from real lemons. The pièce de résistance was a tub of vanilla ice cream handmade in an oak bucket filled with ice and rock salt, and everyone had to take a turn at the crank.

Memorial Day weekend was a big one for tourists. Cork could have made a tidy profit keeping Sam's Place open, but for him family came first. If he was going to flip burgers, he'd just as soon do it in the company of people he loved for people he cared about.

Rose was late. She had planned to come early with Father Mal so that she could help the rest of the O'Connor clan get everything ready. When she hadn't arrived by one, Jo called the rectory. The phone rang half a dozen times before Father Kelsey picked up. He'd been invited, as always, but Father Kelsey seldom left the rectory anymore. He preferred the comfort of his easy chair in front of the television.

The priest said that Rose and Father Mal had left some time ago after Mal got a phone call. Something odd at the cemetery.

Father Kelsey didn't know what kind of oddness, or why anyone would call out the priest, or what made Rose feel she needed to accompany him.

Cork was about to start the coals when Jo reported all this to him and asked if he'd mind popping over to the cemetery to check things out. As Cork headed toward his Bronco, Stevie ran to him begging to go along.

Lakeview Cemetery occupied the crown of a big hill at the southern end of town. The site was surrounded by a black wrought iron fence, built tall so that deer couldn't jump it to feed on the flowers inside. Because this was Memorial Day, Cork expected to see a number of people there, paying their respects to loved ones who existed now only in memory, but he was surprised to find the cemetery looking nearly deserted.

Gus Finlayson, the cemetery groundskeeper, stood smoking a pipe under a burr oak tree just inside the gate. Cork stopped. "Where is everybody?"

"Way to the other side," Gus said. "You ain't heard?"

"What?"

"Best go on and see for yourself."

Cork drove ahead, threading his way down the narrow lanes between the rows of gravestones. He soon saw the place, dozens of cars parked on a hillside at the distant end of the cemetery. As Cork approached, Stevie stuck his head out the window.

"It smells pretty," he said.

And it did. The air was redolent with the scent of roses.

Cork parked behind Mal Thorne's Nova. Just ahead of that was a sheriff's department Crown Victoria. Randy Gooding stood next to the cruiser, his arms crossed. Mal and Rose were with him.

"What's up?" Cork said.

Gooding nodded down the hillside where a crowd had gathered. "Check it out."

Cork glanced at Mal, who looked a little mystified. Rose glowed and seemed about to speak, but she held herself back.

Cork descended the hill with Stevie at his side. A quiet murmur came from the gathering. In the gaps between people, Cork glimpsed deep red, like a pool of blood, at the center of things. He found an open space and moved in. It was not blood but rose petals, thousands of them, a foot deep over the grave and covering the grass around it in a circle several yards wide.

Then he looked at the gravestone.

Fletcher Kane had paid a pretty penny for the stone that marked his daughter's grave, bought her a white marble obelisk six feet tall. Carved in relief above Charlotte's name was a beautiful angel with eyes cast toward heaven.

"Look, Dad," Stevie said. "The angel is bleeding."

Not exactly bleeding, Cork thought. Weeping. Tears of blood, it seemed, dark red trickles that ran glistening from the angel's eyes all the way down the white face of the stone into the petals that lay deep around the base.

A few of the crowd were on their knees, praying. Most of the others simply stared at the weeping angel with a quiet reverence. Cork turned away and walked back up the hill.

"Where did the petals come from?" he asked.

Gooding shrugged. "The question of the day."

"It's like they fell from the sky." Rose lifted her hands, as if to catch any petals that might yet flutter down. "And the angel, Cork. Did you see the tears?"

"I'd take a sample of those tears, if I were you," Cork said to Gooding.

"I already have. Over great objection from the true believers down there."

The priest gave Cork a dazzling smile. "Don't you feel it? Something absolutely amazing has happened here."

"Amazing all right," Cork said. "Someone's gone to a lot of trouble. Did Gus Finlayson see anything?"

Gooding shook his head. "It was like this when he opened the gate this morning. Says there was nothing last night when he locked up."

"Does Arne know?"

Gooding said, "Sheriff's over in Hibbing, spending the day with Big Mike and the rest of his family. I didn't see any reason to haul him back here for this. No harm done, so far as I can see. I'm guessing at some point somebody will come forward and we'll find out it was just some kind of extravagant gesture."

"No one will," Rose said. There was a look in her eyes that was a little like madness. Cork wasn't sure he'd ever seen her so happy.

Stevie climbed back up the hill, cradling something in the palm of his hand. "They look like red teardrops," he said of the three delicate petals he held. "Can I keep them?"

"I think it would be all right," Cork said. "Let's get on home, buddy. Your mom will be wondering." He turned to Rose and Mal. "You guys coming?"

"We'll be along," Rose said in a dreamy voice.

The girls, when they heard, had to see for themselves. They came back with Rose and Mal Thorne, excited and mystified. Then Jo had to go, too.

In a day that was normally filled with talk about baseball and fishing and gardens and remembrances of the past, most conversations centered on what had quickly been dubbed "the angel of the roses."

It was dusk before the gathering in the O'Connors' backyard broke up and people drifted home. Rose and Mal Thorne lingered, sitting across from each other at the picnic table, talking in quiet tones. Mal sipped from a can of Leinenkugel, Rose from a coffee mug. Jenny and Stevie were finishing a game of croquet. Annie was devouring the last hot dog. Cork stood just inside the sliding back door, watching the scene in his yard. Jo came from the kitchen, put her arm around him.

"Annie's still eating?" she said.

"She's a growing girl, an athlete. And she does like to eat. She told me she wants to be a professional sin eater when she grows up."

"A what?"

"A sin eater. It's something Mal told her about. Back in the Middle Ages, rich people hired poor folk to feast over the bodies of their dead loved ones. Basically a ritual eating of sins so the rich would go to heaven."

"And the poor people?"

"Fat and damned, I guess." He saw Jo's look of concern. "Relax. She was only joking."

"A grotesque joke. Why would Father Mal tell her such a bizarre story?"

"Why don't you ask him?"

With a small frown, Jo regarded her sister and the priest.

"What is it?" Cork asked.

Mal leaned across the picnic table and said something. Rose laughed and lightly touched his hand.

"She's in love with him."

"Rose? With Mal?"

Jo nodded.

"She told you?"

"She didn't have to."

Cork could see it now. A comfortable intimacy between the two of them. Almost like a married couple. In truth, the revelation didn't surprise him much. He thought back and realized that he'd noted the signs but simply hadn't put them all together. Jo, of course, had been way ahead of him on that.

"Do you think Mal knows?"

"I don't know. Men can be so blind. Maybe a priest even more so."

"What are you going to do?"

"It's her life."

"You're not going to talk to her?"

"If she wants to talk to me, she will."

"Nothing we can do?"

"Be there for her when she needs us."

"I'm sorry, Jo." He put his arms around her. "You okay?"

"Yes."

"Mind if I slip out for a while?"

"Where?"

"I want another look at the angel of the roses."

Gus Finlayson was preparing to lock the gate when Cork arrived at the cemetery.

"Hold on dere, Cork," the old Finn shouted, waving the Bronco down.

"Five minutes, Gus, that's all I need."

Gus leaned in the window and shook his head. "Been a hell of a long day, that's for sure, and it ain't gonna get any longer if I got anything to say about it."

"Everybody cleared out?"

" 'Cept the sheriff. He's still out dere."

"At Charlotte's grave?"

"Yah."

"If you lock the gate, how's he going to get out?"

"He's got a key. The department copy."

Cork had forgotten. Not surprising. He couldn't remember ever having cause to use it himself when he'd been sheriff.

The cemetery was going dark at Finlayson's back. The rows of stone markers, rigid and charcoal colored, reminded Cork of a military brigade standing watch over the dead.

"How about letting me in and I'll come out with him?"

Finlayson puffed out his cheeks but gave in easily. "I'd argue, but I'm too pooped. Pull on in. Sheriff's somewhere over to the other side of the cemetery."

"Thanks, Gus."

As he approached Charlotte's grave the smell of the rose petals was astonishing, the fragrance both pleasing and overpowering. Mal Thorne had asked him earlier, didn't he feel it? Didn't he feel that something remarkable had occurred? He wasn't entirely sure what he felt, but what he thought was that the hands that had created this event were made of flesh and blood, and sooner or later the mind behind it, and the motive, would reveal itself.

Soderberg's BMW sat under a linden tree. The sheriff was nowhere in sight. Cork parked in the middle of the lane, blocking traffic if there'd been any. He got out and stood awhile, taking in the hillside and Iron Lake in the distance. The sky was the color of an old nickel, and everything under it lay in a dim light that was not day nor yet night. Everything around Cork was absolutely still. He had the feeling he was looking at an underexposed black-and-white photograph, one that didn't give away what the photographer had intended to capture.

Then he saw the flare of a match reflected off the shiny marble pillar thirty yards down the hill.

Soderberg drew meditatively on his cigarette and didn't turn at Cork's approach. When Cork spoke his name, the sheriff jumped, a cloud of smoke shot from his mouth, and he dropped his cigarette. The ember exploded in a small burst of sparks in the grass at his feet.

"Jesus Christ, O'Connor."

"Sorry, Arne."

"What the hell are you doing here?"

"Same as you, I imagine. Trying to understand the angel of the roses. Thought you were in Hibbing."

"I was until I heard about this." Soderberg picked up his cigarette. There was still enough glow to the ember to salvage a smoke if he'd wanted. Apparently he didn't. He just held the cigarette in his fingers. "It doesn't take a genius to figure it out," he said.

"You have a theory?"

Soderberg looked the graves over and nodded to himself. "The Ojibwe."

Cork almost laughed. "What are you talking about?"

"Winter Moon claims he talked with Jesus. He gets his Indian friends to do this. Big miracle." Soderberg waved his hands in a gesture of magic. "Poof, everyone believes he's pure and blessed and how could they ever convict him of murder? You realize what all the roses for these petals must have cost? The casino brings in that kind of money. Hell, it's pocket change to those people."

"Show me the receipt, Arne," Cork said. Although he had to admit it might be a plausible theory, if you thought the Iron Lake Ojibwe gave a hoot and a holler about Solemn Winter Moon.

Soderberg lifted his foot and snuffed out the cigarette against his sole. Rather than toss the butt out among the petals, he put it in his pocket and turned uphill toward his car.

"I need to follow you out, Arne."

"Hurry up then." Soderberg started walking.

Cork took a last look at the scene around him. The light was almost gone, but there was enough left so that he could clearly see the eyes of the angel. For a moment, he could have sworn that the angel looked right back at him.

20

A STRONG NORTH WIND came up in the night, bending the trees and causing the houses of Aurora to creak. Near dawn, a brief summer rain fell. The wind had died, and the sky was clear the next morning when a news van from KBJR in Duluth parked outside Lakeview Cemetery waiting for Gus Finlayson to open the gate. Behind it, a line of cars backed up along the road, mostly the curious from outside town who hadn't heard of the angel of the roses in time to make the trip on Memorial Day. Gus was late, and the news van began honking its horn. It wasn't long before all the horns were honking. The caretaker finally pulled up in his old Volvo and got out looking groggy, stuffing his shirttail into his pants. He fumbled with the lock and swung the gate wide.

Cork was in line with the others, but he knew long before he reached Charlotte's grave that something wasn't right. The incredible fragrance, beautiful and overpowering the day before, was missing.

What greeted the visitors that morning disappointed everyone. The powerful night wind had swept the cemetery clean of rose petals, and the rain had washed the tears from the angel's eyes.

From the cemetery, Cork headed to the Pinewood Broiler to get himself some breakfast. When he stepped inside that morning, he found the talk to be all about the roses. He shot the bull a few minutes with a table full of retired iron miners, then he noticed Randy Gooding sitting at the counter by himself.

Gooding lived alone in the upper of a duplex on Ironwood Street, a block from St. Agnes. Cork often encountered him having breakfast at the Broiler, which was also near the church.

"How's it hanging, Randy?"

Gooding looked up from his plate that held the last of a Denver omelet, and he smiled. "Morning, Cork."

Without waiting for an invitation, Cork took the stool next to the deputy. "Eggs over easy, Sara," he said to the waitress. "Hash browns, toast—"

"Burned, right?" Sara said.

"Charred. And coffee. Oh, and his breakfast's on me." He jabbed a thumb toward Gooding.

"Trying to bribe an officer of the law?" Gooding said.

Gooding wasn't wearing his uniform. He was dressed in a dark blue polo shirt and white Dockers. Next to his plate was a small notepad with a pen lying beside it. From the furious scribble across the pad, Cork guessed that Gooding had been hard at work on something. The occasional doodles were roses, lovely roses.

"You on duty?"

"Day off." Gooding finished the last bite of his omelet and carefully wiped his mouth with his paper napkin.

Cork tapped the notepad. "Working on the angel of the roses?"

"Yeah. Nothing criminal about what's happened, and the sheriff made it clear that he doesn't want any official time put in on it. But it's got me intrigued."

"Have you been up there this morning?"

Gooding nodded. "I used the department's key and let myself in at first light. Gone, blown away in the night, all the petals, that wonderful fragrance. And the tears gone, too." He shook his head sadly.

Sara set a cup in front of Cork and poured his coffee.

"Thanks," he said. Then to Gooding, "What do you make of it?"

"Let me show you something." Gooding shoved his plate, coffee cup, and notebook to the side. He reached down to a small, white paper bag on the floor by his stool and took out a single long-stemmed red rose. "I just came from talking with Ray Lyons."

Lyons owned North Star Nursery and supplied a good deal of the stock that went into the gardens of Tamarack County.

Gooding broke the rose and scattered the petals over the counter. "There are enough here to cover a couple of square inches one layer deep."

"Okay."

"You saw the grave yesterday, how deep all the petals lay. I did a rough calculation this morning. It would take a couple of thousand roses to supply enough petals to do the trick."

Cork let out a low whistle.

Gooding nodded. "I lost a lot of sleep last night considering how that many roses would get here. UPS? FedEx? What?"

"Did you run that question by Lyons?" Cork noticed his coffee cup still had the ghost of a lipstick print along the lip. He wiped it clean with his napkin, then took a sip.

"Yeah. He says they could have come from a wholesaler almost anywhere. Up from the Twin Cities, Duluth, over from Fargo. Could even have come directly from one of the big suppliers down in Miami. Good time of year to order a lot of roses. Big South American crops coming in, but no big holiday to generate demand. You'd get a good price."

"How would they get to Aurora?"

"They come in bunches of twenty-five, in containers they call Florida boxes, usually shipped by the gross. Generally they're kept fresh with cold packs, so they don't need special refrigeration or anything. Lyons said usually there's nothing on the packaging that would make them stand out from other freight, so they wouldn't necessarily be noticed."

"Anybody with a sizeable truck could have picked them up at an airport or a freight depot?"

"Exactly." He reached into the white sack again and pulled out a plastic bag full of wilted petals. "I left a bunch of these with Lyons. He's going to see if he can identify the variety, give me some idea of where they might have come from."

"So you're among those who think there's a logical explanation for the roses?" Cork said.

Gooding put back everything he'd taken from the white sack. "You know anything about the miracle of Our Lady of Fatima?"

"Not much."

"At one point during the visitations, a shower of rose petals fell from the sky. Same thing happened in the fifties when a Filipino nun went on a fast for world peace. Documented." He reached for his coffee cup and signaled Sara for a refill. "In eighteen fifty-one, blood and pieces of meat rained down out of a cloudless sky on an army post near San Francisco. In Memphis, Tennesee, in eighteen seventy-seven, live snakes fell by the thousands. Stones showered down on Chico, California, for a full month in nineteen twenty-one. There are hundreds of such documented cases. Most theories involve things being sucked up by tornadoes or hurricanes and deposited elsewhere."

"What about the tears?"

"I sent a sample down to the BCA lab in St. Paul for analysis. It'll be a while before we have anything." He looked directly into Cork's eyes, and his own eyes seemed lustrous. "I'm going to do everything I can to prove there's a logical explanation. But if I can't, it won't be the first time I've seen a miracle."

"Yeah? How so?"

Gooding waited until the waitress had refilled his cup. Then he glanced behind him at the tables where the noise was the rumble of voices and the clatter of flatware on plates. Just slightly, he leaned toward Cork.

"Not a lot of people know this, and I'd just as soon you kept it to yourself. I was dead once."

Cork drew back to get a good look at Gooding. It was clear the deputy wasn't kidding.

"When I was six, my mother packed us up for a Christmas trip to visit friends up in Paradise, in the U.P. of Michigan. It's snowing like crazy, and the roads are ice. We're crossing a bridge over the Manistee River, and some guy swerves across the center line, hits our car, and we go through the railing, plunge right off the bridge. The river's covered with ice, but the car just busts right through. I can still hear my mother, screaming, then the car's full of water so cold it felt like a big hand had grabbed me and was squeezing the life right out of me. It was dark in the water under the ice. I couldn't see anything. The last thing I remember is this beautiful light, this beautiful peaceful light surrounding me, and I remember not being afraid.

"The next thing I know I'm in a hospital room. I open my eyes and the nurse there is crying, making the sign of the cross, saying it's a miracle. I'd stopped breathing for almost half an hour before they pulled me from that river and revived me. As nearly as I've been able to tell, there's been no residual harmful effect. I forget things now and then, but who doesn't?"

"You told me you grew up in a children's home. Your parents?" Cork asked.

"Killed in the accident."

"And you believe it was a miracle that you survived?"

Gooding thought a moment. "I know these things happen, that doctors say there's a medical explanation, the cold water shuts down the body, reduces the need for oxygen, all that. But believe me, when it happens to you, it's nothing short of a miracle." Gooding glanced behind him again. "Like I say, I'd just as soon you kept this to yourself. Especially now, with all that's happening here in Aurora."

"Sure, Randy. I understand. No problem."

Gooding stood to leave.

Cork said, "You and Annie friends again?"

Gooding smiled. "We had a long talk one night after youth group. I apologized, told her pretty much what I told you about Nina van Zoot. I think she appreciated that I trusted her. She's a special young woman, Cork." Gooding stood up. "Thanks for the breakfast. I owe you one."

After he'd finished his own breakfast, Cork headed to the sheriff's office. He wanted to have a talk with Solemn. When he walked into the department, he found Marsha Dross on front desk duty talking with a blonde in tight jeans, stiletto heels, and a red Tommy Hilfiger sweatshirt.

Deputy Dross said, "I can't authorize that. You'll have to talk to the sheriff."

"And he's not here," the woman said impatiently.

"That's right."

"What about his lawyer? If I get permission from him, can I talk to Winter Moon?"

"That would be a beginning," Dross said.

"Who's his attorney?"

"Jo O'Connor."

"Got an address for this Joe guy?"

"In the phone book."

"Thanks. You've been a big help," the woman said with sarcasm. She turned abruptly, glared Cork aside, and shoved out the door.

"Who was Ms. Charm there?" Cork asked.

"Journalist. Tabloid journalist."

"Oxymoron, isn't that?" Cork said. "She wanted to talk to Solemn?"

"Yes. And she's not the first."

"May I talk to him? On behalf of his attorney, that Joe guy?"

The deputy laughed and buzzed him through.

It was Cy Borkmann in charge of the jail that day.

"Has he been any trouble?" Cork asked.

"Winter Moon? Are you kidding? All he does is sit. Talks to you when you talk to him. Stands when you tell him to stand. Otherwise, it's like he's zoned out or something." He let Cork into the interview room, then went to get the prisoner.

When Solemn came, he stood just inside the door. He looked a little spacey as he smiled at Cork. The deputy locked the door and left them alone.

"How're you doing, Solemn?"

"Fine," Solemn said. "I'm just fine. But I've been wondering about you."

"Me?" Cork stood in the middle of the room, feeling oddly awkward in the young man's presence. "Never been better."

Solemn studied him awhile, that enigmatic smile never leaving his face. It was Cork who broke the silence.

"You heard about the roses?"

"Father Mal was here a little while ago. He told me."

"What do you think?"

"If you think about something like this, you've missed the point. You were at the cemetery?"

"Yes."

"Before you began to think, what did you feel?"

"That someone had gone to a lot of trouble for no reason that I could see."

"You felt that? Really?"

It wasn't true. What he'd felt when he first stood in the quiet of that cemetery, in the overpowering scent of roses, was something very much like awe. Then his thinking had kicked in, his twenty-first century mind, locked behind bars of skepticism.

"Did you and the good father come to any conclusions?" Cork said.

"He has his doubts. Mostly, though, he asked about my prayers. The priestly thing, I guess. He asked me if I talked to God."

"Do you?"

"All the time now. But it's not like praying, like I grew up thinking of prayer. I just clear my mind and I find that God is there."

"Kitchimanidoo?"

"The Great Spirit, if that's the name you want to use, sure. Words don't mean a lot. They get in the way." Solemn closed his eyes and was quiet for so long that Cork thought he'd gone to sleep standing up. "I grew up thinking Henry was some kind of witch. Everything I knew about religion was what I was told in church, and I didn't listen much. I wasn't ready for any of this, Cork. Now, when I clear my mind, the one question that's always there is, why me? And the answer that keeps coming back is, why not?"

He smiled gently. "Maybe that's what this is really all about. Jesus didn't come to me because I was prepared for Him. He came to me because He can come to anybody. I'd like people to know that. That's what I told Father Mal."

Solemn looked peaceful and convinced, and Cork found himself thinking about the kids he used to see at O'Hare in Chicago, the Hare Krishnas, beating their drums and chanting, so sure that they'd connected with the divine. How many of them now wore business suits, and took medication for high blood pressure, and didn't want to talk about their Krishna days? Fervor was something the young possessed, and then it trickled away. He thought about Joan of Arc. If somehow she had managed to escape the burning and live to see wrinkles and the other slow wounds of time on her skin, would she have ceased to hear God speak, laid down her sword, become some man's vessel carrying some man's child? He wondered how long it would take Solemn's certitude, his moment of grace, to pass and leave him as empty and lost as everyone else. Some part of Cork hoped that wouldn't happen, but mostly he was sure it would.

"Look, Solemn, the reason I came today. I'm still trying to figure who it was Charlotte was seeing before her death. I'd like to talk to her friends, get an idea if they had any inklings. Do you know who her friends were?"

"Real friends, I don't think she had."

"Who did she hang with?"

"Three people usually. Bonny Donzella, Wendy McCormick, and Tiffany Soderberg. She was tightest with Tiffany."

"You're still certain you don't know who the married man might have been?"

"No clue."

"Did she ever talk about her father?"

"Not much."

"When she did, how did she sound?"

"What do you mean?"

"Was she particularly emotional in any way?"

"Not that I recall. Why?"

Cork considered sharing his suspicions about the sexual abuse in Charlotte's past. But everything about Solemn at the moment felt clean and refreshed, and Cork figured there was no point dragging him through the mud. "No reason." He stood up. "I'm sure Jo will drop by later. You need anything in the meantime?"

"Everything I need, I have. Thanks."

Cork lifted the phone and called for Borkmann, who opened the door. Up front, Marsha Dross was talking with some people in the waiting area, a man, a woman, and a boy. The man wore old corduroys, the line of the wales worn and broken in places. His blue dress shirt was frayed at the collar and sleeves. The woman wore a light brown housedress with little chocolate brown flowers along the hem. The boy was in a wheelchair.

"We came down from Warroad," the man was saying. He gripped a blue ball cap in his hands, and turned it nervously while he spoke. "We heard about the roses and about the Indian who talks with Jesus. All we're asking is a minute of his time. We just want him to put a hand on our boy here, that's all."

Their son sat in the wheelchair with his fingers curled into claws, his head lolled back, his mouth hanging open. His mother stood beside him, looking past Marsha Dross, as if locked somewhere behind the deputy was the answer to all her prayers.

Cork walked outside without waiting to hear the response he knew Dross would give. He stepped into the sunlight of that late May morning and saw a television news van pull into the parking lot of the sheriff's department, and then another. He went to his Bronco, got in, and watched for a few minutes as the cameras and cables came out and two more vans arrived.

There was no way around it now. The circus had begun.

JUNE

21

THE NEWS OF THE MIRACLE went national. After that, every day, starting an hour or two after sunrise, the faithful began to gather in the park between the jail and Zion Lutheran Church. Their numbers varied as did the reasons they came. Some believed that the angel of the roses and the vision of Solemn Winter Moon were somehow connected, that Solemn was blessed, and that what had already occurred was not the end of whatever it was that God intended for Tamarack County. Some, like the Warroad couple who believed Solemn's touch would free their son from the curse of his body, came seeking a personal miracle. Others were merely curious and visited the now-famous cemetery, then joined the crowd in the park on the slim chance that during their brief stay they might catch a glimpse of Solemn and get a snapshot for an album. One day a vendor arrived selling minidonuts and corn dogs from a mobile stand. After that others showed up, hawking T-shirts and icons, snow cones and cotton candy. People put out lawn chairs and blankets and the park had the feel of a festival. Cy Borkmann told Cork that he'd talked with some folks who visited sacred sites all over the country, and who'd just come from Hillside, Illinois, where the Virgin Mary was reputed to appear in a cemetery every day but Tuesday. They hadn't seen the vision but were hoping in Aurora to be able to see the man who'd talked with Jesus, maybe even hear him speak.

Jo advised Solemn not to say anything publicly and to give no interviews to the media. Even so, a lot of information had already leaked. Maps purporting to show the location of Solemn's vision were circulated, and the reservation crawled with pilgrims seeking the footprints that Jesus, in his Minnetonka moccasins, might have left behind.

Mostly, these were outsiders. The natives of Tamarack County who'd watched Solemn grow up and who knew the darker aspects of his history didn't believe for an instant that he'd been tapped on the shoulder by the Son of God. Even though local business boomed, many residents of Aurora resented the reason for the intrusion and griped about the disruption of their own lives caused by the publicity.

They showed their sentiment in exactly the way Jo had feared. On an afternoon in the first week of June, with little more deliberation that it took to choose a new pair of shoes, the grand jury handed down an indictment of Solemn Winter Moon for first-degree murder.

"All a grand jury hears," Jo had explained to Solemn earlier, "is the evidence against you. All they see is the prosecution's case. There's no opportunity for us to challenge the assumptions the county attorney has made, to question the evidence, to cross-examine witnesses. The point of a grand jury is to make sure that such a serious charge as first-degree murder isn't made frivolously. Honestly, if I were on that grand jury looking at the evidence as Nestor Cole, our county attorney, will undoubtedly present it, I'd be hard-pressed not to indict."

"I'm glad you're on my side," Solemn had joked.

"I'm trying to prepare you for the worst," Jo explained. "If they indict, we go to work. We'll have a chance to make a trial jury see things from another perspective, to question everything the prosecution lays before them."

"I appreciate what you're doing," Solemn said.

To her client, Jo presented a positive image, but after the indictment was handed down, she shared her concerns in private with Cork.

"I'm thinking of moving for a change in venue."

They were sitting in Jo's office in the Aurora Professional Building. Outside, the sun hung in a cloudless sky and the temperature was a balmy seventy-five. Because the windows were closed and the building's central air fed an artificial coolness into the room, the feel of the early summer day was lost on them.

Cork shook his head. "Judge Hickey'll never agree. Maybe you can hope for a good jury selection."

"What I'd really like to have is something that will destroy the heart of their argument."

"Like what?"

"How about another suspect?" Jo leaned forward in her chair. "You've been asking all along, if it wasn't Solemn who killed Charlotte then who was it. I held you back because I was afraid if you didn't find anything, we would have hurt Solemn's chances for no good reason. Well, Solemn's got nothing to lose now. The prosecution has blinders on. They're not looking for anybody else. We can turn over any stone we want and see what's hiding there. It's time for you to do what you know how to do."

A smile dawned on Cork's lips. "You're turning the bloodhound loose? I can sniff anywhere I want?"

"Sic 'em," she said.

As soon as Jenny arrived at Sam's Place that afternoon, Cork apologized, left her to handle things alone, and drove to North Point Road. He parked in front of Arne Soderberg's house and knocked on the door. No one answered, but he saw Lyla's gold PT Cruiser in the drive, so he walked around in back. Lyla was in her garden, pruning bushes. She wore white cotton gloves, a broad brimmed visor that fully shaded her face, a yellow blouse, and tight white shorts. She pruned the branches with quick snips, and Cork couldn't tell if she knew what she was doing and didn't have to think a great deal about it, or if she was pissed and taking out her anger on the plants. Her back was to him. She bent over, bent low, and her tight shorts cupped her butt cheeks like a pair of lusty hands.

Cork walked closer and spoke up. "Lyla?"

Startled, she stiffened and quickly turned.

"I'm sorry," Cork said. "I knocked. No one answered. I'm looking for Tiffany."

"She's not home from school yet. What do you want with her?"

She held the pruning shears low in front of her with the blades pointed at Cork. If she were to lunge at him, she'd prune a part he would sorely miss.

He said, "To talk about her friend Charlotte Kane."

"Charlotte Kane was no friend."

"I've been told they spent a lot of time together."

"I don't understand what concern that is of yours."

"I'm consulting on Solemn Winter Moon's defense."

He'd decided that consulting was a good umbrella term for whatever it was he was doing.

"I'd rather you didn't talk to my daughter," Lyla said.

"Talk to me about what?"

Tiffany had come into the yard the same way as Cork, from the side of the house and soundless. She carried a graduation robe, a satiny green and gold, the high school colors.

"Charlotte Kane," Cork said before Lyla could respond.

"I don't want you talking to him," Lyla said.

"Do you think I have something to hide, Mother?"

"This is not our business."

"Oh, spare me," Tiffany said.

Mother and daughter locked eyes, glares slamming into each other like wrecking balls.

"Very well." Lyla said it as if instead of capitulating she were granting her daughter permission. She yanked off her gardening gloves and walked to the house.

Tiffany laid her gown over the back of a black wrought iron lawn chair.

"Graduation tomorrow night, right?" Cork said.

"None too soon," the young woman replied.

"Big plans?"

"University of Hawaii in the fall."

"A program there you like?"

"Yeah. It's called the get-the-hell-out-of-here-and-stay-warm program. What do you want to know about Charlotte?"

She didn't ask with a lot of interest, and Cork figured she was only talking with him because she knew it would irritate her mother.

"I've been told you were pretty tight."

She shrugged. "I guess."

"You spent a lot of time together?"

"What's a lot?"

"Why don't you just tell me about you and Charlotte."

Tiffany was dressed in a pair of faded jeans and a light blue sweater. The sweater seemed a little warm for the day, but it was a good color for her, and showed her figure well. She looked bored with the questions.

"We did some things together. Partied a little."

"She partied with Solemn Winter Moon for a while, too, then broke up with him. Any idea why?"

"He got to be creepy."

"What do you mean?"

"Always accusing her of seeing someone else."

"Was she?"

"Until she went out with Solemn, she didn't have a boyfriend. Her father was against it or something. I think she just got tired of Solemn. He could be weird sometimes. Moody as hell."

"Did she get along with her father?"

"Who does?"

"Did she talk about him?"

"Not much." A moment passed in which Tiffany seemed to be contemplating deserting Cork. Instead, she surprised him. "When we first got to know each other, just after she moved to Aurora, sometimes we'd spend the night at her place, a sleepover, you know. After a while, if we did one, we did it over here."

"Why was that?"

"Her old man was creepy." She seemed to like that word.

"In what way?"

"Always sneaking around, watching her. We'd be in a room talking and I'd look up and there he'd be, lurking in the doorway. She told me she thought he listened in on her phone calls. He was always giving her the third degree, where was she going, who was she going with." A deft sweep of her hand and she flipped back a strand of blonde hair that had blown across her cheek. "It's funny, though. She could say whatever she wanted to about him and her aunt, but let anyone else say anything and she went ballistic. She could be weird, too."

But not creepy, Cork guessed.

"Did she ever talk to you about suicide?"

"No way."

"Did she talk about things that were important to her?"

"Like what?"

"Anything. Life, love, plans after high school."

"She just wanted to get away from here. Like that was a news flash."

"Solemn's been charged with her murder. What do you think?"

"Maybe he killed her. The jealousy thing and all."

"Suppose Solemn was right, Tiffany. Suppose Charlotte had been seeing somebody else. Any idea who it might have been?"

"If I were you, I'd talk to Dr. Kane."

"Why?"

"He was, you know, like her shadow. If he did listen in on her calls, he probably knows a lot he hasn't said."

"Was she close to her father?"

"What's close?"

"Did they show affection? Give one another kisses, hugs, that kind of thing?"

"I don't remember. What difference does it make?"

"I just wondered if you ever saw anything between them that might have made you a little uncomfortable."

"Saw anything?" It took a few seconds before she divined the true intent of his question. She wrinkled her nose in disgust. "Ewwww. Now you're getting creepy."

"Just a couple more questions," Cork said. "You were at the New Year's Eve party out at Valhalla. I saw your name on the list your dad's people put together."

"So?"

"Did your parents know you were going?"

"Oh yeah, like they're going to let me go to an unchaperoned blowout at Valhalla. I told them I was at Lucy Birmingham's house for a New Year's sleepover, okay?"

"Did anything creepy happen at Valhalla? Between Charlotte and anybody?"

"Solemn and Charlotte argued a little. Nothing serious. That's it. Excuse me, but I have a lot to do for tonight. Are we done here?"

Cork could see she was finished with him in her own mind and would probably give him nothing more. "I guess so."

She picked up her graduation gown and went into the house.

Cork stood a moment in the garden that Lyla Soderberg had created. Roses dominated. They hadn't bloomed yet, but Cork was sure they would. Lyla had a way with roses, knew what made them grow. She seemed on less certain ground when it came to a family. But in that, Cork knew, she was not alone.

22

Cork left his Bronco parked in front of the Soderberg house and walked the quarter mile up North Point Road to the old Parrant estate, a huge thumbnail-shaped plot of land at the end of the peninsula, surrounded by cedars. Cork lingered on the drive, which was lined with peonies, and he took a good long look at the imposing house. An undeniable power emanated from all that dark stone, but it seemed to Cork a joyless energy, with anger at its heart. He thought about Judge Robert Parrant and his son. The father a brutal man, the son even worse. Violence, betrayal, death, these had been their lives and their legacy. Fletcher Kane and his family had fared no better. Charlotte was dead, and no sooner had she been buried than Glory took a powder, vanished without a clue. Cork understood. He'd probably have fled that doomed house, too.

His knock wasn't answered immediately. He waited in the deep porch shade, listening to noisy crows that had established a small rookery in the cedars down toward the lake. The door was opened a minute later by Olga Swenson, the housekeeper.

"Afternoon, Olga," Cork said. "Is Fletcher in?"

Olga Swenson wasn't a cheerful Swede. Before Kane hired her, she'd been a waitress and part-time cook at the Pinewood Broiler. Her dour nature had probably kept the tips minimal, which may have explained why she'd gone to work for a man like Kane. She seemed just about as thrilled to see Cork at the door as she'd been to see him park his butt on a stool at the Broiler.

"Yah."

"Could I speak with him?"

She appeared to view this as a burdensome request, but she stepped aside and let him into the foyer. "I'll get Dr. Kane."

She walked down the hall toward the room Cork knew was a study. She knocked, opened the door, then came back.

"He's not there."

"Upstairs, maybe?"

She scowled, turned, and climbed the steps as if mounting a gallows.

"Mind if I sit down while I wait?" he called.

Without a word, she lifted her hand and waved him in.

He wandered into the living room. He was about to sit on the sofa when a photograph on a bookshelf caught his eye. He walked over and took a look. It was of Glory and a young girl, maybe fourteen or fifteen. They were standing in the desert with a big pipe cactus behind them. Glory had been wearing a straw hat, which she held in her hand so that her face would be clear in the shot. The girl wore a baseball cap that shaded her features. Even so, it was clear that she had a large gauze bandage over the left side of her face, and that she stared unhappily at the camera. She looked vaguely familiar to Cork, but he couldn't quite place her. He took the photo down to study it more closely.

"He must've gone down to the boathouse."

Cork turned quickly. Olga Swenson had come downstairs quietly and was eyeing him as if he were a thief.

"I was just looking at the picture."

The housekeeper's expression softened just a little. "It used to be in Charlotte's bedroom. That room's closed all the time now. It seemed kind of lost there, so I brought it down. I don't even think Dr. Kane's ever noticed."

"Do you know who this is with Glory?"

"Her daughter."

"Glory has a daughter?" It was the first Cork had heard.

"Had. I think her name was Maria. They told me she died." She wiped her hands on her apron and nodded toward the lake. "Like I said, Dr. Kane's probably down at the boathouse."

"Thanks." Cork put the photograph back on the shelf and walked to the front door.

"I don't imagine he'll be thrilled to have company," Olga said.

"I'll take my chances."

After Olga closed the door, Cork stood on the porch a moment thinking about Glory and the daughter she'd lost. Was there a curse on the Kanes, he wondered.

The front of the house was well kept, but the long, sloping back lawn was a different story. The grass was badly in need of cutting, the blades grown tall, ready to seed. Making his way to the boathouse, Cork felt as if he were wading into a deep, green sea.

The view of Iron Lake from the end of the point was one of the best on the whole shoreline. The day was calm and the water hard blue. The only sound was the noise of the crows in the cedars. Fletcher Kane stood on the dock, casting a line into the lake. He was using a fly-fishing rod, casting as if the lake had trout. Iron Lake had trophy walleye and northern, fat black bass that lurked in the weeds, and sunnies and bluegills in the shallows, but it had no trout. Tall and awkward-looking most times, Fletcher Kane seemed a study in grace as he cast the line. His long body moved in some rhythm that beat in his head. Out and back, out and back, his long, mantislike arm cocked and released, and each time the fly at the end of the line touched the water at almost the same spot with no sound, no splash to mark the moment of delicate connection, only a widening circle of ripples that gently warped the blue steel look of the water.

Kane wore khakis and a flannel shirt with the sleeves rolled above his elbows. A brimmed canvas hat protected his head from the sun. Flies were hooked all around the crown like small, bright jewels. That Fletcher Kane was a fly-fisherman was something Cork hadn't known. Kane was a murky pool of unknowns, and the only reason Cork had sought him out was to stir things up and see what surfaced.

"Fletcher?"

Kane jerked and the fly at the end of the line popped back, falling far short of its mark.

"I'm sorry," Cork said. "I didn't mean to startle you."

"O'Connor. What do you want?"

"Just to ask a few questions if I could."

"About what?"

"Charlotte."

"Your wife sent you?"

"I'm consulting on Solemn Winter Moon's defense."

"I don't have a thing to say to you."

Kane glanced at the fishing line that lay on the surface of the water like a crack across a blue china plate. He began to reel it in.

"You won't return Jo's calls. She's just wondering if you know how we can get in touch with Glory. We'd like to talk with her."

"I haven't heard from her."

"You have no idea where she is?"

"At this point, you know as much as I do."

He'd finished cranking in the line. Water dripped from the reel and wet black spots appeared on the boards at Kane's feet.

"You mind telling me the name of Charlotte's doctor?"

"Why do you want to know?"

"Is there a reason I shouldn't?"

"Fiona Case."

"Did Charlotte ever talk about her teachers?"

"Why all these questions about Charlotte?"

"I'm just trying to understand your daughter better, Fletcher. It might help to understand her death. What about her teachers?"

Kane's jaw worked in a way that sent bony waves along his cheeks. Anger just below the surface. Cork wasn't sure he would respond.

"Only one that I recall. Her English teacher."

"Man or woman?"

"A man. I forget his name."

"What did she say about him?"

"That she liked him."

"Liked him a lot?"

"She thought he was a good teacher."

"And she mentioned no one else?"

Kane seemed to have hit the end of his patience. His eyes bugged out, and he spit his words. "What does this have to do with anything? Winter Moon murdered her and that's all there is to it."

"You know that for a fact? How?"

"You mean besides all the goddamn evidence? He threatened her before."

"When?"

"Just before Christmas. He came to the house. They argued. He grabbed her, made threats. I ran him off."

Cork knew this was Kane's perception of the incident and that Solemn told a slightly different story.

"Two weeks later, she's dead." Kane threw his rod against the side of the boathouse. "I shouldn't have run him off. I should have killed him."

"Did they argue often?"

"All the time."

"You were in the habit of listening in on their conversations?"

Kane took a quick step forward. In height, he towered over Cork. Rage burned in his eyes, the desire to strike. But he didn't. He balled his hands into fists at his side and said, "Just get the hell out of here. Everything I loved is gone. What more do you want from me?"

It was a question that, at the moment, Cork couldn't answer.

As he left the boathouse, a wind rose, blowing in from across the lake. Big clouds that had been sleeping in the distance all afternoon suddenly woke up and raced across the sky, their dark blue shadows ghosting off the water onto the land. In the myths of his grandmother's people, *manidoog* rode those shadows, spirits of the woods, sometimes playful, sometimes malevolent.

Halfway to the house, Cork paused as a great block of shade engulfed the lawn, turning the deep grass around him the color of a bad bruise. The crows in the line of cedars thirty yards away began to raise a ruckus, and Cork looked to see what the big deal was.

Snakes. Thousands of them. Slithering scales over slithering scales, wave after wave, an angry black sea, smothering the grass under the trees. Crying wildly, the crows took to the safety of the sky. Cork felt his own flesh crawling as he stared at the writhing mass sweeping against and around the cedar trunks. One snake he could tolerate. A whole fucking sea was terrifying.

A shaft of light struck the ground, and Cork looked up where the sun pushed through a split in the cloud. When he glanced back at the cedars, the snakes were gone. The crows were gone. And by then the cloud shadow was gone, too.

Carefully, Cork walked to the place where the snakes had been. He thought the grass might carry some mark of their passage, but the long, upright blades showed no sign of disturbance. He stepped to the cedars. Beyond them was the south shore of the point, all rock and water, facing toward Aurora. There was nowhere for the snakes to have gone except into the lake.

Far down the shoreline, the crows wheeled away like ashes in a wind.

23

DOROTHY WINTER MOON was in Jo's office in the Aurora Professional Building. Cork knew this the moment he pulled into the parking lot. The enormous orange International dump truck she drove for the county was there, dwarfing all the other vehicles in the lot.

When he knocked, Jo told him to come in. Dot sat in one of the client chairs. She wore bib overalls with a dusty yellow T-shirt underneath, and the tan on her arms was even darker from the grime of her labor. Her old steel-toed Wolverines looked battle scarred and her face looked worried.

"I was telling Dot about the pubic hairs," Jo said.

In the autopsy of Charlotte Kane's body, the medical examiner had combed the pubic area and found hairs that didn't appear to match the dead girl's. The evidence had been sent to the lab of the Bureau of Criminal Apprehension in St. Paul for DNA testing and to match against a DNA sample from Solemn. The report had come back that morning. The pubic hairs were not Charlotte's, nor had they come from Solemn.

"That's good, right?" Dot said.

"It's a good-news, bad-news thing," Jo replied.

Cork leaned against a windowsill and crossed his arms.

"The good news is that it indicates the last person to have sex with Charlotte wasn't Solemn," Jo said.

"The bad news?"

"Motive. The prosecution could argue that it proves Charlotte was seeing somebody else and that Solemn killed her in a jealous rage."

"Seeing who?"

Jo looked to Cork.

"That's what I'm trying to find out," he said.

"Can't you tell from the DNA of those pubic hairs?"

"We need a sample to match them against, Dot. And for that we need a suspect and enough evidence to request that a sample be taken."

"You don't have a suspect?"

"Not yet." Cork gave her a sympathetic smile. "How're you holding up?"

Tough as she was, Dot seemed to soften in her chair. She stared down at her rough hands. "People are out at my place all the time now, reporters, assholes, all the time taking pictures, asking questions. Somebody broke the deer on my lawn. I've been keeping Custer locked in the house. All those people around, they're driving the poor dog crazy." She looked at Cork, then past him out the window. "It's hard when I visit Solemn. He's my son, but he isn't. It's like a stranger stepped into his skin. We don't seem to know what to say."

"It's the situation," Jo said. "It's put a lot of stress on both of you."

Dot handed Jo several papers. "Anything else you want me to sign?"

"No, that's it."

Dot tugged a pocket watch on a chain from her overalls. "Got to get back to work. Spreading gravel out at the fairgrounds parking lot today."

"I'll let you know when there's anything new," Jo said.

"Thanks."

Dot gathered her hair back and jammed a red ball cap over it. Cork could hear the clomp of her heavy boots long after she'd closed the door behind her.

"Coffee?" Jo asked, rising from her chair.

"No thanks."

She poured a mugful from a stainless steel server. "Well?"

Cork sat in the chair Dot had vacated. "I talked with Tiffany

Soderberg. She says Fletcher Kane was creepy when it came to Charlotte. Watched her all the time."

"Fletcher Kane is creepy, period. Proves nothing." Jo sat down and sipped her coffee. "Okay, for the sake of argument, suppose there was something between daughter and father, that doesn't mean he killed her. You've read the statement he gave about the night she disappeared. He was home. His sister corroborated his story."

"And Glory's conveniently gone now. He claims he doesn't even know where. I'd love to have his phone records for the past couple of months. I'd bet there's a good chance we'd find a number for Glory. Have you heard anything about the phone records for Valhalla yet?"

Cork had recommended that Jo subpoena the telephone record of the calls made to and from Valhalla on the day of the fatal New Year's Eve party. He thought it might be enlightening to know whom Charlotte had talked to on the last day of her life.

"Nothing yet." She looked at him and he could tell she was mulling something over.

"What is it?" he asked.

"I'm just wondering about due diligence."

"What about it?"

"You seem to be looking at Kane and no one else. Isn't that exactly what you accused Arne Soderberg of doing with Solemn?"

Cork pulled a small notepad from the pocket of his shirt. He put it on the desk where Jo could see. Written on it were four notations: *Teachers. Doctor. Family Friends. Priest.*

Cork said, "According to the academic record I got at the high school, Charlotte had four male teachers while she attended. She talked about one of them in particular. Her English teacher, Alistair Harding. He taught a poetry class she took fall semester last year. Her only official extracurricular activity was the school literary magazine. Harding was the advisor. He probably had a good window on her psyche. I'll do some follow-up on him today.

"Her family doctor is Fiona Case. I think we can pretty much eliminate her as a suspect, but I'd still like to interview her."

"Unless I can bring a successful motion to compel her to talk, you won't get a thing out of her, Cork. Patient/client privilege. And the courts these days are extremely reluctant to allow medical records to be released or testimony to be given in instances where the victim's sexual past might be an issue."

"All right, then. We'll put Dr. Case on the back burner for now. How about family friends? I've been thinking a lot about that one. Glory told me that Fletcher didn't have friends. He had acquaintances, associates, colleagues, but no friends. And Glory, as nearly as I can tell, had only one close friend and that was Rose. We definitely need to talk to her."

"I already did. She doesn't know anything that would be useful. Glory was always very careful not to talk about the family."

"That probably means there was a lot to hide. What about St. Agnes? Were the Kanes involved in the church community other than to attend mass?"

Jo shook her head. "Not in any significant way."

"So they barricaded themselves in that big house and kept company mostly with one another."

Jo looked at the final notation on the notepad. *Priest*. "You're not serious about Mal."

"Mendax, Jo. She was angry with him for some reason."

"But Solemn believes Charlotte was involved with a married man."

Cork took his notepad back and stood up to leave. "In the eyes of a lot of his parishioners, he is married. Married to the church."

It was a busy day at Sam's Place. At a break in the action, Cork turned to Jenny and asked, "Mr. Harding was your teacher for poetry last fall, right?"

"That's right."

"Tell me about him."

Jenny put a basket of raw, frozen fries into hot oil. "He's a good teacher."

"What's he like?"

She shrugged. "He's very sensitive, I think."

"Sensitive how?"

"Intuitive. Kind."

"Married?"

"Mr. Harding?" She almost laughed.

"What's so funny?"

"Dad, he's gay."

"What makes you think so?"

She lifted the basket, shook the fries to rearrange them, set the basket back in the oil. "Aside from being not married, he's very neat, dresses nicely. And—well, it's just something you get a feeling about."

"A feeling," Cork said. "But no solid evidence?"

"I never asked him, if that's what you mean. Why all these questions?" She looked at him, and understanding came into her blue eyes. "Oh. Charlotte Kane's married lover."

It was sometimes difficult in the O'Connor household not to be overheard.

"You can forget about him, Dad."

"Because you think he's gay."

"He goes home to England every year over the holidays. He was in, like, London or someplace when Charlotte was killed."

A blue minivan pulled into the parking lot, and a half dozen teenagers piled out. Jenny turned toward the serving window. Cork scraped the grill and went back to this thinking.

Priest.

What did he know about Mal Thorne? What did anyone know? That he'd been in charge of a homeless shelter in Chicago and bore the scars of a knife attack by a couple of would-be thieves. Before that, a blank until his boxing days at Notre Dame. And before that, he'd been a kid from a tough section of Detroit. There were several important unknowns, among them the long period between college and Chicago, the reason a priest as capable as Mal ended up in a backwater place like Aurora, and why Charlotte was so angry with him.

When he had a few minutes, Cork went to the back of the Quonset hut and pulled out an old address book. It was a duplicate of the one he kept at home. He looked up a number, dialed long-distance to Chicago.

"You've reached Grabowski Confidential Investigations. I'm out of the office at the moment. Leave me your name and number and a brief message and I'll get back to you, pronto."

After the tone, Cork said, "Boomer, it's Cork O'Connor. Been a long time, buddy. I need your help. Give me a call when you can." Cork left two numbers, Sam's Place and home.

He'd just hung up and was about to return to the serving area up front when the phone rang. He figured Boomer had been screening his calls.

It was Jo. She'd just received a fax of the phone records for Valhalla. Cork told her he couldn't get away, but that he'd call Annie and have her pick them up on her way to work.

Things were busy the rest of the day, and it was late by the time Cork finally sat down at the old birch wood table in the back of the Quonset hut and looked over the phone records Annie had brought him. A lot of young people had known about the party. Several calls had been made from pay phones, so no way of telling who was on the line. The only items on the whole list that stood out for Cork were two calls placed from the home of Wilfred Lipinski, mayor of Aurora, one at 9:57 P.M. and another a 10:41 P.M. If Lipinski had teenagers who knew about the party at Valhalla, the calls would not have been odd, but all the Lipinski children were long ago grown and gone, and so Cork wondered. For a minute or two, he considered the possibility that the mayor might have been Charlotte's mysterious married lover. But the idea of Wilfred Lipinski, who at sixty-two looked about as kissable as a cod, making love to the young woman was too much for Cork to imagine, and he dismissed it.

When he finally locked up and headed home, it was after ten o'clock. The longest day of the year was only a couple of weeks away, and a bit of light still lingered in the sky, a thin blue memory of day spread along the western horizon. A shaving of silver, all there was of a moon, hung above Iron Lake. The night was warm and liquid, and the color of everything melted toward black.

He took a detour and cruised past the sheriff's office and jail. Across the street, the park where the believers and the curious gathered was almost empty. A few people still kept vigil. Cork recognized the couple who'd come from Warroad on the chance that Solemn's touch would heal their wheelchair-bound son. Such desperation, Cork thought. Although he couldn't bring himself to pray for them, he hoped that their own prayers were somehow answered.

Jo was already in bed when he got home, propped against her pillow with her reading glasses on and a stack of manila folders on Cork's side of the bed. As he walked into the room, she lowered the papers in her hand.

"Late," she said. "Everything okay?"

"Just going over the phone records."

He drew the curtains and began to undress. The house was quiet. The air in the room carried the scent of Oil of Olay.

"Find anything?" Jo asked.

"Not what I'd hoped." Cork hung his pants on a hook in the closet and tossed his shirt and underwear into a wicker hamper. "No calls from Kane's place that day."

"Do you still believe Fletcher's involved?"

"He's put up a wall around almost every aspect of his life. I can't help thinking he's hiding something behind it."

"He's not a warm man," Jo said. She cleared the files from Cork's side of the bed and set them on the nightstand. "And granted, he's odd in a lot of ways, but that doesn't make him capable of the kind of things you want to ascribe to him."

Cork pulled out a pair of red jogging shorts and put them on. "I haven't ascribed anything to him. But I don't think anybody in Aurora really knows Fletcher Kane. I don't think anybody knows what he is or isn't capable of doing."

Jo spoke carefully. "I'm not saying he's innocent, but I do think that if all you're looking for is the bad in someone, that's all you're going to see."

The image of the snakes on Fletcher Kane's lawn that afternoon still haunted Cork. He was sure that what he'd seen was simply a trick of the light as the wind passed through the long grass in the shadows under the cedars, but the unsettling feel of it lingered.

"There was one thing odd about the phone records," he said. "Two calls were made from Mayor Lipinski's place."

"Not so odd," Jo said. She took off her glasses and set aside the papers in her hand. "Wilfred and Edith had a New Year's Eve party. We were invited, remember? We declined. The calls were probably a couple of teenagers who'd been dragged to the party at the Lipinskis' but were more interested in the one at Valhalla."

"Probably," Cork said. He eyed the stack of folders Jo had moved to the nightstand. "What's that?"

"I'm going over all the statements given by the kids who were at Charlotte's party that night, looking for anything I didn't catch earlier. This is the umpteenth time. I think I can recite each one word for word by now."

"See anything?"

She shook her head.

"Going to brush my teeth," Cork said. "Be right back."

He went into the bathroom and began brushing. He'd done only half the chore when a thought occurred to him. He hurried back to the bedroom.

"What if it wasn't a teenager who made those calls?" he said.

Jo looked up from the papers in her hands. "An adult, you mean? What? Calling to check on a child she knew was at an unchaperoned party in the middle of the woods?"

"Not calling as a parent," Cork said. "Calling as a lover."

Jo thought about it. "Charlotte's married man? That might be a stretch."

"We won't know unless we pursue it."

Jo spent a few more moments weighing the possibility. "How do we check it out?"

"We need some information. The names of any teenagers at the Lipinskis' party, and the guest list. You're on the library board with Edith. Why don't you call and ask her?"

"I'll do it first thing in the morning."

Cork went back to the bathroom and finished with his toothbrush. He knew Jo was right, that if all you looked for was the bad in someone, that's all you'd see. Maybe his motive for focusing on Fletcher Kane wasn't the purest, but that didn't mean he was wrong in his suspicions.

Cork smiled into the mirror. His teeth, at least, were clean.

24

THE NEXT MIRACLE occurred the following morning and could have been predicted, Cork thought.

Deputy Cy Borkmann accosted Cork the moment he walked into the Pinewood Broiler for coffee and the news of the day.

"You hear about the healing?"

Cork was on his way to a stool at the counter. "What healing, Cy?"

Borkmann waddled along beside him and placed as much of his oversize posterior as he could on the stool next to Cork.

"Somebody got hold of the blanket Solemn's been sleeping on. Used it to cure a blind man."

"Whoa," Cork said. He signaled Sara and asked for coffee. "Start at the beginning, Cy."

"This morning just after sunrise, folks started gathering in the park across from the jail, the way they been doing every morning. When there's a good number gathered, a guy shows up with a folded blanket, and he says it's Winter Moon's, from his jail cell. He says, 'Does anybody want to be healed?'

"From what I gather, nobody got much excited at first. Finally Grover Buck speaks up."

"Grover Buck? He's the blind man who got healed?"

"I know," Borkmann said. "There's a lot not to like about old Grover, but he's sure as shit been blind since the mine accident. Got himself that settlement and all. Well, Grover speaks up and says he might as well give it a try. The guy walks over to him, hands him the folded blanket, and Grover wraps it around his face. At first, nothing much. Grover says, 'Well, maybe I can see some flashes of light.'

" 'Down on your knees,' the guy tells him, 'and pray to the Lord for a miracle.' Grover falls to his knees and starts praying, and in a minute he pulls that blanket away from his face and he's got tears streaming down his stubbly cheeks and he says, 'I can see. Praise the Lord, I can see.'

"Now anybody knows Grover knows he ain't the most holy man on God's earth, nor the most trustworthy. But the guy with the blanket holds up his hand in front of Grover's face and says, 'What do you see?' And Grover says, 'Three fingers,' and he's right. The guy takes a red bandana from his pocket and says, 'Now what do you see?' Grover says, 'It's a hanky. And it's red. By Jesus, it's red.'

"Well, that got folks interested. The next healing really got them going."

"There were two healings?"

"That's what I'm here to tell you. You know Marge Shembeckler?"

"Don't tell me her arthritis was cured."

"The woman got up from her wheelchair and walked. First time in years. After that, folks swarmed all over the guy with the blanket. He starts cutting it into little pieces couple inches square and selling each square for twenty dollars. As the blanket gets smaller, the price goes up. I heard that the pieces come out of the last couple feet were selling for a couple hundred dollars. Whoever that guy was, he made a killing."

"The blanket, it did come from Solemn's cell?"

"Yep. Sheriff's all hot under the collar about that. Shouldn't be too hard to pin down who took it, though. Not a lot of folks in and out of there at night."

Sara set a cup of coffee in front of Cork and he thanked her.

"A shame," Cork said. "Taking advantage of people like that."

"You don't believe in miracles?"

"Have you taken a good look at that crowd? Those are desperate people, Cy, ripe for a con. Is Arne going to investigate?"

"He put Gooding on it."

Cork left the Broiler and headed to the sheriff's department to see Solemn. The sun was high already and the day felt like a scorcher. In the park across the street, there was singing and praying and a lot of movement, as if all those bodies were charged with electricity, with possibility and hope.

When Solemn was let into the interview room, he offered Cork a smile that seemed to be missing the glory that lately had illumined it.

"Morning, Solemn."

"Hey, Cork."

"They treating you well?"

"No complaints." He took a chair and sat down at the table across from Cork.

"You know about the blanket?"

Solemn nodded.

"Any idea how it got snatched?"

Solemn sat at the edge of his chair, feet flat on the floor, his hands folded in his lap. He looked like a man waiting, maybe on a bus bench, for whatever it was that would take him to wherever it was he was going.

"It's too warm most nights," he said. "I keep it folded at the foot of my bed. While I was asleep, someone must've taken it."

"You didn't see who?"

"No."

"Sound sleeper."

"I am. Now."

"What do you think? About your blanket and the healings, I mean."

"If it's true, it wasn't the blanket."

"What then?"

Solemn thought a moment. A long one. "Their own belief maybe. Maybe an accident of timing. Not my blanket. Not me."

Solemn stared where Cork was standing, but what he saw seemed somewhere beyond Cork.

"They're looking to me for something I can't give them. I spent a few minutes with Jesus. We talked, that's all. I didn't get healing powers. I can't drive out demons. All I came away with was a little peace. My own peace. If they expect something from me, they'll be disappointed. Whatever happened out there this morning, it wasn't me. I'd know if it was me, wouldn't I? Wouldn't I know?"

His eyes drifted to the floor like feathers falling from a wing. "God," he said, "I hope it's not me."

25

ON HIS WAY OUT to Sam's Place the next morning, Cork dropped by Jo's office. She'd already talked with Edith Lipinski.

"She was curious about my interest in her New Year's Eve party," Jo said, "but I explained that I was trying to find out who knew about the party at Valhalla and how. I wanted to talk to any teenagers who'd gone to her party instead and see what they might know. It was thin, but she bought it. Turns out there weren't any teenagers there. And she does have a guest list. Two, as a matter of fact. One for all those who were invited and one for those who actually came."

"Bless her anal-retentive little heart," Cork said.

"I asked if I could look at them, hoping there might be some parents who had kids at Valhalla that night. She agreed to let me pick them up later this morning when she's back from her hair appointment."

"I'm the only one at Sam's Place today. Hard to get away. Any chance you could bring them out and we could look them over together."

"I think I can swing it."

The telephone began ringing as he unlocked the door of the Quonset hut.

"Sam's Place. Cork speaking."

"So how are things in Nowhere, Minnesota?"

Cork recognized the irreverent gravel of Boomer Grabowski's voice.

"Compared to the old days on the South Side, generally pretty quiet, Boomer. How about with you?"

"No complaints."

Boomer and Cork had been cops together in Chicago, working out of the same South Side district. Cork had moved to Aurora, his own choice. Boomer had left, too, forced out by circumstance rather than choice. He was a big man, from a family whose men had always worked the steel mills. His body was like something that had been forged out of iron. But it was only flesh and bone, and most of the bone in his right leg had been smashed in an accident during the high speed pursuit of an armed robbery suspect. Boomer had been forced to retire on a medical disability. Retirement, however, was not in keeping with Boomer's temperament, and he'd opened his own shop.

"How're things in the Windy City?" Cork asked.

"Wouldn't know. I'm calling from Miami. I just checked my messages back at the office and heard your vaguely familiar voice."

"Vacation?"

"You kidding? Who's got time? So what's up?"

Cork filled him in on Mal Thorne, and asked Boomer if he'd check on the priest's background. Anything he could find out about his time in Chicago and before, if possible.

"You really think this priest has something to do with the girl's murder?"

"Just checking out all the possibilities, Boomer."

"Yeah. You were nothing if not a thorough bastard. How soon you need it?"

"The sooner the better."

"Look, I'm down here for a week. You want somebody on it before that, I can make some recommendations."

"I think it'll hold for a week."

"Tell you what. I'll call when I'm back in the office. If you're still hot for me to trot, I'll hop right on it."

"Thanks, Boomer."

"Thank me after I've done the job. And after you've seen the bill."

* * *

Jo showed up a little before one o'clock, just as Cork was finishing with the lunch rush, and she gave him a hand, taking orders at the window while he worked the grill. By one-thirty, the line had vanished. Jo took from her briefcase the list of guests who'd attended the Lipinskis' party and handed it to Cork. He laid it on the stool the girls sometimes sat on when things were slow.

"What are we looking for?" Jo said.

"Anyone who might have had a connection with Charlotte."

"Someone young?"

"In the kind of relationship we're considering, age probably wasn't a factor."

They went down the list silently. The third from the last name caught Cork's eye.

"Son of a gun," he said.

"What?"

"Arne and Lyla Soderberg."

"What about them?"

"Think about it for a minute, Jo. Tiffany and Charlotte were friends. Or something close to it. Tiffany told me that because Fletcher Kane acted creepy, any sleepovers they had were at Tiffany's house. Maybe something got started there."

"Arne Soderberg and Charlotte Kane?" Jo made a sour face.

"It's not such a stretch," Cork said. "Stay with me on this. Lyla and Arne have a troubled marriage. No secret there. When Charlotte's body was found on Moccasin Creek, I saw Arne's face. All horror. I chalked it up to the fact that as sheriff he was still pretty green. But what if it was the shock of seeing someone he was involved with lying there dead?" Cork stood up, feeling a little fire in his gut, the spirit of the hunt awakened.

"You don't think Arne killed her?"

"I don't know. He could certainly have been her lover though."

"What about Fletcher Kane?"

"I'm not forgetting about him. But there's a possibility here that definitely needs exploring."

"The truth is you don't like Arne Soderberg any more than you like Fletcher Kane."

"I don't like a lot of people. I don't suspect them all of crimes. But a few more answers might tell us if we're on the right track."

Jo said, "What do we do?"

"I think you should have a talk with Edith Lipinski, find out if she remembers Arne making phone calls, when he left the party, anything that might be helpful."

"In order to get the lists, I had to tell her about the calls from her home. She's not stupid. If I start asking about our sheriff, she's liable to put two and two together very quickly." She laid her hand very lightly on his arm. "Cork, we need to be careful. The town is seriously divided. People have stopped talking to me, to one another. I've had some clients threaten to withdraw their business."

"You fought for the Iron Lake Ojibwe for years. You've been threatened before."

"It's not the threats. I don't care about that. I just think we need to be sensitive to the ripples we send out. If we point fingers and we're wrong, we may hurt innocent people, and folks here will remember that a long time."

"If we turn our backs, won't we remember that longer?"

"Who said anything about turning our backs? Just do what you do quietly, that's all I'm saying."

"I'm not discreet?"

"Sweetheart, when you get hold of something, you're a pit bull."

"I am, huh?" Actually, he felt a little flattered. "All right. But we have to do this quickly, too, Jo, before Arne realizes we've got him in our sights. Maybe while you talk to Edith, I ought to talk to Lyla—discreetly—to see if I can finesse anything useful out of her. Sound like a plan?"

"A plan," she agreed.

He shut the serving window and put up the CLOSED sign.

Cork drove south out of Aurora, then turned west onto County 7. After a mile and a half, he approached a small billboard that read WEST WIND GALLERY, RIGHT 500 FEET. He took the turn and followed a graveled lane through a stand of poplar.

The West Wind Gallery was an old barn that had been converted into a showplace for the art of Marion Griswold, a professional photographer. She was often commissioned by big magazines like *National Geographic* and *Outdoor Life*. Framed and in numbered editions, her photographs were sold in the gallery, which she owned with her friend Lyla Soderberg, and also in galleries in the Twin Cities and in Santa Fe. Her work had been collected and published in exquisite editions designed to elevate the appeal of any coffee table. A woodburned sign hanging beside the door indicated that the gallery was open from noon until 6:00 P.M. every day except Wednesday.

Marion Griswold lived in a log home of recent construction east of the gallery. It was a lovely two-story structure that had a shaded porch hung with geranium pots. The photographer's dusty Jeep Wagoneer sat in front of the house. Cork had expected Lyla Soderberg's gold PT Cruiser to be parked at the gallery, but it wasn't anywhere to be seen. A little bell above the gallery door gave a jingle as he stepped inside.

A voice sang out from a back room, "Just a minute. Be right there."

Cork was the first to admit that he didn't know art. But he knew what he liked, and he liked the photographs of Marion Griswold. She shot the great Northwoods. Wild streams, autumn foliage, wolves with breath crystallized on a subzero day. She was able to capture what his heart felt when he was alone in the woods, and he admired that.

"Cork," she said, smiling as she came into the main gallery showroom. Her hair was black and cut very short, which Cork figured was a benefit when she was out in the wild, tramping through underbrush looking for a good subject. Her body was wiry and tanned and full of energy barely contained. She wore cut-off jeans, a high-collar white shirt with the tail out, and tennis shoes without socks. She carried a large framed photograph that she leaned against the counter where the cash register sat. "Haven't seen you here for a while. Not since you bought that piece for Jo. She like it?"

"It's in her office, dazzling her clients."

"I like to hear that. What can I do for you? Interest you in another piece?"

"Not today, thanks. I'm looking for Lyla. I thought she'd be here."

"Normally. But Tiffany's graduating tonight, and Lyla's out shopping. Planning on whipping up a special dinner for the occasion. Anything I can help you with?"

Cork recalled seeing Marion's name when he and Jo had scanned the guest list. "Maybe," he said. "I wanted to talk to her about the New Year's Eve party at Mayor Lipinski's place."

"The night Charlotte Kane was killed." She gave him a look that told him she was pretty but not stupid.

"That's right. I'm hoping to help Jo put the whole night in perspective. I'm trying to find out if any of the parents whose children were at Valhalla knew about Charlotte's party."

"Not Lyla, I can tell you that. She thought her daughter was at a sleepover. Those girls were clever. Gave Lyla a cell phone number to call to check on them that night. You know how unreliable cell phones are up here in the boondocks. Of course, when Lyla did call and couldn't connect, well, that's just technology in the deep woods." She laughed, a soft liquid sound. "Bright girls."

"So Lyla didn't call Valhalla directly?"

"No reason to. She didn't know they were there. Till the next day when everybody realized Charlotte was missing, and Tiffany confessed to her little ruse."

Cork sauntered to the counter and eyed the framed photograph Marion had brought with her. It was a teddy bear in a garden.

"Going for the domestic look?" he asked.

"A graduation gift for Tiffany. That bear is her favorite. I shot it in Lyla's garden."

"Nice," Cork said.

"Nice? Art is passionate, art is touching, art is orgasmic. But art is never nice."

"Orgasmic?"

"You have no idea."

"You wouldn't happen to know when Lyla and Arne left the Lipinskis' party, would you?"

"Couldn't say about Arne. Lyla left at ten-thirty."

"You're sure?"

"Positive. I gave her a ride." Marion stepped back and cocked her head as she appraised the teddy bear among Lyla's flowers. "She and Arne got a little of Wil Lipinski's rum punch under their belts and started taking mean little potshots at each other. Nothing deadly, but Lyla'd had enough of it long before midnight. When she started to leave, she discovered that Arne had taken the keys to her car. He wouldn't give them back. Told her she was in no condition to drive. Frankly, he was right. I offered to give her a lift."

"Home?"

"That's what she wanted, but I saw how upset she was, so we came out here, rang in the new year, and then I took her home."

"And Arne kept the car?"

"He did."

"What time did you drop Lyla off?"

"Twelve-fifteen, maybe."

"Was Arne home?"

"I don't recall seeing the car. Could've been in the garage, I suppose."

"Were there lights on in the house?"

"I don't believe so." She fisted her hands on her hips, squinted at Tiffany's gift, and shook her head. "Nice?"

Cork said, "Isn't shooting a teddy bear a little dull for you?"

Marion favored him with a tolerant smile. "If you look at life with the right attitude, Cork, nothing's dull."

Cork met Jo at her office.

"Did you get anything from Edith?" he asked.

"Enough to be enlightening. Lyla and Arne had a bit of a tiff, and they didn't go home together."

"I know. Marion Griswold gave her a lift. Arne kept the car."

"Lyla told you?"

Cork shook his head. "Marion. What else did Edith say?"

"Not long after Lyla left, Arne made his apologies and he left, too. Get this, Cork. She said Arne seemed distracted, not his normal glad-handing self. And he asked to use her phone a couple of times. Said he wanted to check on his daughter but his cell phone wasn't going through. She directed him to the phone in her husband's study, off-limits to the party."

"Marion said she dropped Lyla off at home a little after midnight. She didn't see any indication that Arne was there."

"Okay." Jo put her hands together and bowed her head a moment, thinking. "Arne left the Lipinskis' house shortly before eleven. It's a good half-hour drive out to Valhalla. Around eleven-thirty, Charlotte told people she was going snowmobiling. But probably she went out to the guesthouse to meet her lover."

"Arne."

"Maybe. I've been rereading the statements of all the kids at Valhalla that night. Sid Jankowski and Evelyn Foley said that when they went to the guesthouse a little after one 'to be alone,' they heard the snowmobile taking off, and Charlotte wasn't in the guesthouse when they got there."

"The time frame works, Jo."

"Everything we have is circumstantial, Cork."

"Not everything. We have a trump card. The pubic hairs the M.E. combed off her body. Suppose they match Soderberg's?"

"Unless we can actually put Arne at Valhalla that night, I don't think we have enough to compel him to submit to a DNA test." For a minute, Jo stared out the window. Then her blue eyes widened and she said, "Oh, my god."

"What?"

"Tiffany Soderberg."

Jo grabbed a stack of manila folders from a corner of her desk. It looked like the same stack she'd taken to bed with her the night before. She thumbed through quickly, found the folder she was looking for, and opened it. She flipped a couple of pages and scanned the text.

"Here it is. In her statement, Tiffany says she got to the party early, around nine, and that she got a ride to and from Valhalla with Lucy Birmingham. She didn't drive herself."

"So?"

Jo held up her hand, indicating Cork needed to be patient. She located another folder and flipped through the pages, found what she wanted. Her finger followed the text as she spoke. "In his statement, a young man named Peter Christiansen says he didn't arrive at Valhalla until eleven. He wasn't going to stay at the party long. About twelve-fifteen, he tried to leave, but couldn't because his car was blocked by Tiffany Soderberg's car. He went back to the party looking for Tiffany, couldn't find her, drank another beer, and when he went outside again, her car was gone, and he left." She looked up at Cork. "If Tiffany didn't drive there, why did he think it was her car blocking him in?"

Cork thought a moment. "Because it was clearly a Soderberg vehicle."

"And what Soderberg vehicle really stands out?"

"Lyla's gold PT Cruiser."

"Let's find Peter and make sure that was the car."

"Then what?"

"Then we visit Arne and if necessary, play our trump card."

They located Peter Christiansen at the Iron Lake marina, where he had a summer job. After he confirmed the information they needed, they headed to the sheriff's department and caught Soderberg just as he was leaving his office. He seemed in a particular hurry.

"Clocking out already?" Cork cast an obvious look at his watch.

"My daughter's graduating tonight, O'Connor."

"A big celebration?" Jo asked.

"Lyla's got a special dinner planned. So whatever it is you want, it'll have to wait until tomorrow."

"I don't think this one can wait, Arne," Cork said.

Jo touched her husband's arm. "Of course it can. Congratulate Tiffany for us, and tell her we wish her good luck. We'll come back in the morning and talk."

After Soderberg had gone, Cork turned to Jo. "What was that about?"

"If he is the one," Jo said, "this may be the last good time he and his family have together for a long while. We can wait until tomorrow, can't we?"

They left the sheriff's department. In the park across the street, the crowd had thinned considerably in the summer heat. A few blankets were still on the ground in the shade of the trees. Music played on a boom box, but softly. A red helium balloon had escaped, and its string was snagged in the branches of a maple. Cork watched the balloon pull gently at the end of its tether. The late afternoon was still, like a held breath. All of them, those who waited in the park hoping for a miracle that would free them from their own tethers, whatever they were, looked toward the jail that held Solemn Winter Moon.

"Come on," Jo said. "Let's go home."

26

ARNE SODERBERG held a coffee mug in his hand and a look of contentment on his face. A slice of morning sunlight, lemon yellow, lay across his desk. The cool scent of pine drifted in through the open window. It was the day after his only child had walked across the high school stage and received her diploma, and Soderberg wore his satisfaction like a new suit.

Cork almost felt sorry for what Jo was about to spring.

"So, what's up?" the sheriff asked.

At Jo's request, Gooding was in the room. He leaned against a file cabinet with his arms crossed. Jo and Cork sat in chairs, the high polish of the sheriff's desk between them and Soderberg.

"I'm trying to get a handle on the situation between parents and the kids who were at Valhalla the night of the New Year's Eve party," Jo said.

Soderberg looked confused. "To what end?"

"Everything we know about that night helps us put it in better perspective. I'm wondering about Tiffany."

"What about her?"

"Did you know she was at Valhalla?"

"No."

"You didn't call her there to check on her?"

"Why would I, if I didn't know she was at Valhalla? She was supposed to be at Lucy Birmingham's house."

"You were at the Lipinskis' New Year's Eve party, is that right?"

"Yes."

"You didn't try to call Tiffany from there? I mean try to call her at the Birminghams'?"

"No."

"Edith Lipinski says you asked to use her phone. You told her you wanted to check on your daughter and your cell phone wasn't connecting."

"Then maybe I did. I'd been drinking a little that night. I don't really recall everything."

"I understand how it is at a party like that. Did you call the Birminghams' house directly?"

"I don't remember."

"If you'd called the Birminghams' house directly, you would have discovered that Tiffany wasn't there. Isn't that right?"

"I suppose."

"So maybe it wasn't Tiffany you called?"

The sheriff didn't answer.

"I thought perhaps it was really Lyla you tried to call?"

"Lyla?"

"Edith told me that you and Lyla had a bit of a tiff and Lyla went home early. I thought maybe you called to apologize to her, but didn't want to tell Edith that."

Soderberg thought a moment. "That could have been it."

"You called her at home?"

Soderberg said carefully, "I must have."

"And you worked things out, I hope. Cork and I have a rule." She smiled at her husband. "We try never to go to bed angry. Edith said you left the party shortly after Lyla, a little before eleven. So you went home still thinking Tiffany was at the Birminghams'?"

Soderberg gave a nod.

"Okay. Lyla left the party at ten-thirty. She got a ride from Marion Griswold because you thought she was too drunk to drive. You kept the car, that gorgeous PT Cruiser, right?"

"I thought this was about Tiffany."

"I'm getting to that. You did keep the PT Cruiser?"

Soderberg hesitated. "That's right."

"You left the party at eleven and then what? Did you go straight home?"

He considered her a moment, then said, "I think we're done talking."

"Just a couple more things. You told Edith Lipinski that night that you wanted to use her phone to check on Tiffany. But you didn't check on Tiffany, did you? And it wasn't Lyla you called either. She wasn't home. She was at Marion Griswold's place. Why are you lying about the calls you made?"

"I'd like you out of my office," Soderberg said.

"Phone records indicate that two calls were made to Valhalla from the Lipinskis' home the night Charlotte Kane died. I think you made those calls. Around eleven o'clock, you left the party and drove to Valhalla. We have a witness who puts Lyla's PT Cruiser at Valhalla in that time frame. Why were you there? I believe for a sexual liaison with Charlotte Kane. I believe you'd had a relationship with her for some time."

"That's ridiculous," Soderberg said.

"I also believe it's possible that you killed Charlotte Kane and planted evidence that would implicate Solemn Winter Moon. Were you angry with Charlotte for having an affair with Winter Moon? Or had Charlotte threatened you with exposure—you, the newly elected sheriff of Tamarack County?"

Gooding slowly uncrossed his arms. His gaze shifted to the sheriff.

The frail vessel that had held Soderberg's contentment that morning had shattered. The happiness had drained from his face, and he looked stunned.

"I killed Charlotte?" He frowned. "Maybe I kidnapped the Lindbergh baby, too?"

"Much of this we can prove," Jo said.

"How?"

"By matching your DNA against the results of the DNA testing that was done on the pubic hairs taken from Charlotte's body during the autopsy."

"This is ridiculous."

"Is it? You never bothered to widen your investigation beyond looking at Solemn Winter Moon. I think it was because you were afraid that evidence might be found that could incriminate you."

"That's bullshit."

"Did Charlotte threaten to make it all public? Was that why you killed her?"

"I didn't kill her."

"Or were you just blind with rage because she'd been with Solemn, had let him touch her in the same way you had?"

"Gooding, get these people out of here."

The deputy didn't move.

"You were at Valhalla that night," Jo said. "You had opportunity and motive."

"No."

"You used your position as sheriff to protect yourself."

"No."

"You loved Charlotte Kane."

He opened his mouth but the denial died before he spoke it. That was the moment Cork knew Soderberg had cracked, the moment he knew Jo had him. Soderberg stood up and put his hands on his desk and leaned forward like a tree about to fall.

"Get out of my office."

"I'm prepared to ask the court to compel you to submit to DNA testing."

"You wouldn't."

She opened her briefcase. "This is your copy of the motion. It sets forth all the evidence and the reasoning. When I leave here, I'll go directly to the county attorney's office and give Nestor Cole a copy. From there I head to the courthouse to file and to request a date for the motion hearing. This isn't a bluff. It will get public and ugly, Arne. Why don't we talk now?"

"I have nothing to say to you," he replied hoarsely. "Deputy Gooding, I told you to get these people out."

Jo rose from her chair. "We're leaving, but we'll be back, Arne. While we're gone, take a few minutes and think clearly. And get yourself a lawyer."

She turned and walked out. Cork followed and closed the door behind him.

Outside Soderberg's office, he said, "What now?"

"I make good my threat."

"At the moment, all we're able to offer is speculation."

"No, we're citing a number of incriminating facts from which very reasonable suppositions can be drawn." She looked back at the closed door. "Maybe he killed Charlotte, maybe he didn't. But of the rest, he's guilty as hell, I know it."

"You need me?"

"No."

"Do you think we should let Solemn know what's up?"

"I don't see why not. He's got more at stake in this than anybody. Would you talk to him?"

"Sure." Cork touched her cheek. "Have I told you how glad I am that you're on our side?"

Cork spent a long time with Solemn, laying it all out carefully. In the end, Solemn appeared troubled by the news. He stood up from the table in the interview room, walked to the door, and put his hands flat against it. He tilted forward until the crown of his head touched as well. He seemed to ground himself on the hard reality of the jail.

"Do you think he killed her?" he asked.

"My gut feeling is no," Cork said.

Solemn stared down at the gray sneakers worn by all the long-term guests of the county. "So. It may do me some good, but I imagine it'll pretty well mess up Sheriff Soderberg's life."

"I imagine."

And he did. Cork imagined Lyla like a withered fruit, sucked dry of compassion. And he pictured Arne on the streets of Aurora, a man people would pretend not to see.

"He never seemed to me to be very happy," Solemn said. "I can't help feeling sorry for him." He turned to Cork. "Is he a religious man?"

"No more so than most folks, I'd guess."

"I'll pray for him." He returned to his chair and sat down with his hands folded in his lap. "I'm still going to trial?"

"We'll have to see about that." Cork signaled Pender, who was on cell block duty that day. "If I were you, Solemn, I'd pray a little for myself."

Solemn looked up at him, looked out of the deep brown wells that were his eyes. "Some days that's all I do. It'll help me, praying for someone else." He hesitated, as if reluctant to say the rest. "Thank you for all you're doing. Only . . ."

"What?"

"Maybe some things that are secret should stay that way."

"Sometimes we just turn over rocks, Solemn. What's there is there."

Heading out of the department, Cork passed the opened door of the sheriff's office. Soderberg was not inside. Gooding came over from the front desk.

"The sheriff got a call from the county attorney a few minutes ago," Gooding said. "He took off right away. Listen, Cork, even if you could prove that he was with Charlotte Kane that night, it doesn't mean he killed her."

"Maybe not, but it'll raise a hell of a question in a jury's mind. I'll catch you later, Randy."

In the parking lot, he got into his Bronco. Although it was still morning, the sun was hot already. He rolled down his windows to let in air. He was about to crank the engine when he spotted Arne Soderberg sitting in his BMW, staring. The wing that housed the prisoners was in front of him, and he seemed to be looking at the dull brick wall. Cork watched for a few minutes until Soderberg started his car and pulled out of the lot.

The sheriff drove slowly. At Fourth and Holly, he ran a stop sign. Not fast, just drifted through as if he didn't see it at all. He headed out past the town limits and turned onto North Point Road. He pulled into the drive of his home, got out, and went inside. Cork cruised past the house, drove a hundred yards, turned around, parked, and waited.

Less than five minutes later, Soderberg stepped out. He backed from his drive and headed into Aurora. He skirted Oak Street, the county courthouse, stayed well away from the sheriff's department, and kept going south. At the far end of town, he turned onto Lakeview Road and wound his way up the hill to the cemetery.

At that time of the morning, the grounds were almost deserted. Just beyond the gate, Cork saw Gus Finlayson, the groundskeeper, standing in the cool shade of a big maple, tossing hand tools into a small trailer hitched to the back of a John Deere garden tractor. Finlayson waved as Cork passed. Far ahead, the BMW pulled to a stop under a familiar linden tree, and Arne Soderberg got out. By the time Cork's Bronco rolled up behind the car, Soderberg was already down the hill standing at Charlotte's grave.

For a long time, Cork sat in his Bronco. He watched Soderberg smoke a cigarette, then light another. He remembered the wonderful fragrance that had filled the cemetery the day the rose petals appeared. Now the air smelled of cut summer grass, a good scent, but not at all a miracle. After a while, Cork got out, and descended the hill.

Soderberg saw him coming. "Haven't you done enough damage, O'Connnor? Just leave me the hell alone."

Cork looked at the towering marble monument erected in Charlotte's memory. "She was a beautiful young woman, Arne."

"You don't know the half of it."

"I suppose not." He let a few breaths go by. "That day on Moccasin Creek when you saw her body, it must have been hard on you. You didn't know she was there, did you?"

Fingers of smoke crept from Soderberg's lips, stroked his cheeks and his hair, then lifted free of him and drifted idly away. "She was alive when I left Valhalla."

Cork nodded. "The problem is this. There's no way for you to prove it."

Soderberg reached into his pocket and pulled out a scrap of paper. Without a word, he handed it to Cork.

It was a receipt for the purchase of 13.6 gallons of gas, a credit card transaction bearing Soderberg's signature. It had been generated at the Food 'N Fuel at 1:27 A.M. on January 1.

Soderberg said, "I was in Aurora when Charlotte was killed. It was Winter Moon. I know it was that son of a bitch."

Cork handed back the receipt. "What are you going to do, Arne?"

Soderberg looked up, squinting at the sun. His face was full of deep lines, like a flat stone fractured with a hammer. "Funny how things change. Yesterday I had the world by the balls."

"Let me ask you something," Cork said. "The rose petals in the cemetery on Memorial Day. I've been thinking about that a lot, especially now in light of what you and Charlotte shared. I'm thinking it was you. Some kind of grand gesture. You used

Soderberg Transport and the department copy of the gate key, all for Charlotte. An amazing memorial. Am I right?"

"Go to hell," Soderberg said. He flicked his cigarette away. It tumbled end over end, trailing smoke and embers, until it hit the stone on the next grave down the hillside and exploded in a shower of sparks. "Go to hell and burn, you meddling son of a bitch."

27

CORK FOUND JO in her office.

"Well?" he asked.

"I filed the motion. Everything goes public now."

Cork sat down. "I just talked with Arne Soderberg. He as much as admitted the affair with Charlotte, but he insists he didn't kill her."

"Do you believe him?"

"It appears that he has an alibi. And, yeah, I guess I do believe him."

Jo picked up a paper clip from her desk and turned it round and round between her fingers. "I've been thinking."

"Don't hurt yourself."

He smiled; she didn't.

"Thinking what?"

"I don't like it, but I'm thinking maybe Arne isn't the only Soderberg we should be looking at."

Cork considered the implication and leaned forward, resting his arms on her desk. "Lyla?"

Jo shrugged. "She left the Lipinski party early. And if she knew about the affair, she had motive."

"Marion Griswold said she dropped her off around midnight. I suppose there was enough time for her to drive to Valhalla before Charlotte was killed."

In fiddling with the paper clip, Jo had bent it all out of

shape. Cork saw that it now resembled a figure eight. Or the symbol for infinity.

"We should probably talk to Lyla. But . . ." She hesitated. "I don't know. If she's innocent, if she really didn't know about the affair, it seems cruel to badger her."

"A few questions judiciously phrased and we might be able to put everything to rest quickly."

Jo looked up from the paper clip. "What does your gut tell you about this one?"

"That it will feel better after I've fed it a few answers."

"The truth is, mine will, too."

She tossed the paper clip into the wastebasket beside her desk.

When Cork pulled into the drive of the Soderberg home, he saw that Arne's BMW wasn't there, nor was Lyla's PT Cruiser. But a little red Miata was. Tiffany was washing it. She wore jean shorts and a purple Viking football jersey. A bucket of sudsy water sat on the drive. The water hose snaked out from a spigot on the side of the house. The end was capped with a brass spray nozzle, closed at the moment. Tiffany bent over the car with a big yellow sponge in her hand and worked at lathering the hood. When she spotted Cork and Jo, she actually smiled. It was a better reception from her than Cork had experienced . . . ever.

"Nice," he said. He put a hand on the sporty little car.

She beamed. "My graduation present."

"Congratulations," Jo said.

"Thanks."

"Is your mom home?"

"No."

"Any idea where we might find her?"

"She went to the gallery." Her eyes drifted lovingly back to her Miata.

"It's Wednesday," Cork said. "The gallery's closed."

"I'm just telling you what she told me."

"Thanks." Cork started away, then turned back and asked casually, "Have you seen your father lately?"

"No. He's probably at work."

"Sure."

After they got back into the Bronco, Jo took a long look at the young woman. "God, I feel so bad for her. She has no idea."

"I don't know," Cork said. "It could be that when the shit hits the fan, she won't be much surprised."

At the West Wind Gallery, Lyla's car was parked next to Marion Griswold's mud-spattered Jeep Wagoneer. Cork eased his Bronco beside the other two vehicles. Jo tried the gallery door and found it locked. They walked to the house and stepped onto the porch. Cork knocked at the front door, waited, knocked again.

Then the scream came.

It came from the south, from beyond a thick stand of red pine. Cork leaped from the porch and began to run in that direction with Jo at his heels. He could see a narrow, well-worn path through the trees and he made for it. He hit the stand of pine just as another scream cracked the morning air.

Where the path ended a hundred yards through the pines, Cork could see a sparkle of blue he knew to be Little Otter Lake. It was a small body of water, but Griswold owned the land all around it and had the lake to herself. He ran hard, not knowing what he was heading into, feeling the rush of adrenaline. He wished he were carrying his revolver and wished, too, that he'd warned Jo to stay back. God only knew what awaited them.

He pulled up quickly before he broke from the cover of the trees. He could see an old wooden dock thrust out from the shoreline into the lake. At the end of the dock stood a naked woman, beautiful and slender and so deeply tanned her skin was the color of deer hide.

There was splashing in the lake, a froth of white water a few yards away from the dock. In a moment, a head bobbed to the surface, and from the mouth of that head a little stream of water shot into the air.

Jo stood next to Cork, and they both watched as Lyla Soderberg climbed onto the dock, naked and laughing. She embraced Marion Griswold and they kissed. But only briefly before Lyla shoved Marion off the dock. As the woman hit the water with a big splash, Lyla let out a scream of delight.

Cork and Jo walked back to the house. They stood on the

porch where the geraniums hung in pots, and for a while they didn't say anything.

"I think that's the first time I've ever heard Lyla laugh," Cork finally said.

"It's the first time I can remember her looking happy." Jo tapped a geranium pot and it swung idly, casting a shadow that cut back and forth across her own.

"Do you want to leave?" Cork asked.

"No."

In a little less than half an hour, the two women came walking up the path through the pines. They were fully dressed, but hadn't dried themselves completely so there were places where Lyla's white silk blouse clung to her, showing pink skin beneath.

Lyla hesitated when she saw Cork and Jo, but Marion came ahead smiling.

"Been here long?" she asked.

"A while," Jo said. "How was the water?"

"Purely refreshing." Marion arched a dark eyebrow. "Maybe you should take the plunge sometime."

Lyla stopped at the bottom of the porch stairs and looked up. All the laughter was gone from her. "What do you want?"

"Just to ask a couple of questions," Jo said.

"I'm not in the mood to answer."

"New Year's Eve," Jo said. "When you and Marion left the Lipinskis' party together, where did you go?"

Marion said, "I already told Cork. She came here."

Jo said, "Is that right, Lyla?"

"That's right."

"Can you prove it? Either of you?"

"Now, why would we have to prove anything?" Marion asked.

"Lyla's name has been mentioned in connection with Charlotte Kane's murder," Jo said.

"My name? That's ridiculous. Why?"

Jo glanced at Cork. He nodded.

"Because your husband was having an affair with her," Jo said.

"That . . . that girl? I don't believe it."

"He pretty much admitted it," Cork said.

Marion gave a wicked little laugh. "She really was quite a lovely young thing. Bully for him."

"So you see, it's not so ridiculous," Jo said. "Killing your husband's lover, that's a pretty sound motive."

"Only if you love your husband," Marion said. "Lyla, tell these folks how you feel about old Arne. And maybe, while you're at it, how you feel about me."

Lyla shot her a look of horror.

"Relax, sweetheart. These people are not stupid." Marion mounted the stairs and sat in one of the wood rockers in the porch shade. "Like I already told you, Cork, we were here. A private New Year's Eve celebration. Just the two of us."

"You told me you took Lyla home a little after midnight."

Marion gave Cork a smile that was all innocence. "I'm afraid I told you a little white lie. Didn't want to raise any eyebrows. It was really three A.M. And I'll swear to that in court."

"Is that true, Lyla?" Jo said.

Lyla's gaze drifted from Marion to Jo. She gave a silent nod.

Jo said, "All right."

Lyla's legs seemed to go weak, and she sat down suddenly on the steps. She looked away from them all, looked past the hanging geraniums, looked toward the pines that hid the little lake where she'd been laughing.

"Charlotte Kane and Arne," she said to herself.

She wasn't laughing anymore.

28

NEAR CLOSING TIME at Sam's Place that evening, Cork got a call from Jo. Oliver Bledsoe had just stopped by to inform her that the Iron Lake Ojibwe had decided to bail Solemn out of jail.

A few minutes later, Bledsoe himself drove up in his gray Pathfinder, got out, and leaned through the serving window. "Got a minute, Cork?"

Annie was cleaning up, and she told her dad to go ahead. Cork stepped outside and walked with Bledsoe to the edge of the lake. The water and the sky were twins, both of them black in the east but silver along the western edge where there was still the faint ghost of daylight. The air was breathless, the water dead calm.

Bledsoe wore black Dockers, a white, short-sleeved shirt, and a string tie with a turquoise slide. His hair, like the night, was a mix of black and silver. He put his hands in his pockets and looked out at the water. "I've been authorized to arrange bail for Solemn."

"I know. Jo called me. When will you spring him?"

"We'll have the money tomorrow."

Casino money, Cork knew. He wondered if word of Soderberg had got out, and was that the reason for the change of heart.

"Why?" he asked.

"A lot of support for Solemn on the rez, what with these miracles and all."

"You don't sound convinced."

"I knew his uncle. About as good a man as I've ever known. Solemn, I don't know except by reputation, which, quite frankly, isn't good." Bledsoe shrugged. "Maybe all those years I spent on Franklin Avenue listening to the stories of drunks, Shinnobs and otherwise, have made me a poor audience for this kind of thing. I can't help thinking that Solemn's worked a sleight of hand somehow." He glanced at Cork. "But you know him better. What do you think?"

"He's never claimed to be a part of the miracles. He just claims he talked with Jesus."

"Not that anyone's asking my advice, but I'd say it's not a bad idea to hold on to a little skepticism where Solemn's concerned." He turned back toward the parking lot. "If you don't mind, I'd like you there tomorrow when he gets out. It could be a zoo."

Cork nodded. "Just let me know when."

As he drove home that night with Annie in the seat beside him, he considered what Bledsoe had said. That it was a good idea to hold on to a little skepticism where Solemn was concerned. Cork let that piece of advice roll around in his thinking.

He'd found Charlotte's married lover, but he didn't believe that he'd found her killer. At the moment, he had no obvious suspects. Except Solemn. Who had a motive, an opportunity, no alibi, and toward whom all the evidence seemed to point. Cork wondered if he'd simply been fooled? Was it possible he'd allowed himself to believe what he preferred to believe, against all evidence to the contrary?

"You're sure quiet," Annie said.

"Just thinking," Cork said.

Like a cop, he thought dourly.

Bledsoe called early the next morning and spoke with Jo before she left for the office. The plan was to post bail at ten so that Solemn would be released well before noon, which was when the crowd in the park usually began to swell. Bledsoe hoped to convince the sheriff to help spirit Solemn away without a lot of fanfare.

Dorothy Winter Moon was already waiting at the sheriff's

office when Cork and Jo arrived. She'd done herself up like a rodeo queen in cowboy boots, tight jeans, and red snap button shirt.

"I don't know if this is a good idea," she said. "People know where we live. They'll just make life miserable for Solemn and for me. At least here, things are under control."

Cork had the same concern, but he made a suggestion. "Maybe he should stay at Sam's old cabin for a while, Dot. Until this is over and things quiet down."

"If he'll go," she said. "I don't know what to expect from him anymore."

Marsha Dross had taken them into the sheriff's office to wait. A few minutes later Randy Gooding stepped in.

"Folks, things are a little up in the air at the moment," he said. "The problem is that we're temporarily without a sheriff. Arne Soderberg turned in his resignation an hour ago."

That didn't surprise Cork. "Seems to me," he said, "protocol dictates that the most senior officer assume temporary responsibility as sheriff until the county commissioners appoint a replacement."

"That's right," Gooding said.

Cork thought a moment. "Cy Borkmann."

Goodman nodded. "Cy."

The wattle-throated deputy. A nice man, a competent officer. But sheriff?

"Where is he?" Cork asked.

"That's part of the problem. He has the day off. Took his wife down to Duluth for some hospital tests. So . . ."

"No one is officially in charge." Cork summed it up.

"That's about the size of it."

"It's all process," Cork said. "Bail is posted, prisoner released. Doesn't matter whether we have a sheriff present."

"What about getting Solemn home safely?" Dot asked.

"We'll do our best to get him to a vehicle, but after that, it's out of our hands," Gooding said.

Bledsoe and the paperwork arrived about fifteen minutes later. "There's something going on out there," he told Gooding. "I think they know about Solemn."

Gooding went to the window and looked toward the park

across the street. "Jeeze, you're right. They're swarming this way."

"We should probably take Solemn out the back," Cork said. "Keep him out of sight of the crowd altogether."

Gooding stepped to the office door. "Marsha, see if we'd have any interference taking Winter Moon out the back emergency exit. Pender, go out front and keep the crowd away from the front door."

"Who put you in charge?" Pender snapped.

To which Dross, as she departed on her errand, replied, "Just do it, Duane."

Gooding turned back to the others in the sheriff's office. "Cork, if it's clear in back, why don't you go out and bring your Bronco around. Dot, Jo, it might be best if you just stayed put for a while. You, too, Ollie."

Dross came back and stood in the doorway. "The coast is clear in back."

A general buzz had begun outside the opened window, voices rising, and Cork left the office quickly.

Deputy Pender stood on the sidewalk, facing the crowd that pressed toward the jail, his hands on his hips, fists against the leather of his gun belt. As Cork stepped into the late morning sunlight, he saw Pender lift his right hand and hold it up, as if he were trying to halt traffic at a busy intersection. His left hand went to his lips, and he gave a long shrill blast on a metal whistle.

The crowd, as it milled its way across the street and onto the grass of the sheriff's department, reminded Cork of cattle crossing a road. At the sound of Pender's whistle, those near the forefront did, indeed, attempt to halt, but they were pushed ahead by those behind.

Pender gave three more whistle blasts. At last, the forward movement stopped.

"Go back to the park," Pender shouted. "I want everyone to move back across the street to the park."

The sugar-cinnamon smell of minidonuts drifted ahead of the crowd. Yellow balloons on long white strings bobbed above their heads. Somewhere near the back, a boom box was playing "Horse with No Name."

"Move back," Pender said. "I'm not going to warn you again."

The front line held.

Cork figured it was a good time to get his ass out of the way. He slipped behind Pender and headed across the grass to the parking lot. No one seemed to pay him any attention. All eyes were intent on Pender.

"Winter Moon," someone yelled. "We want Winter Moon."

"Let him out!"

"Let us see him!"

"Free Solemn!"

Free Solemn. They'd found the cry, and it went up in a chorus, from mouths that had never personally spoken a word to Solemn Winter Moon.

Cork drove out of the parking lot and turned away from the crowd that acted as a barricade across the street. He maneuvered around the block and pulled to the curb at the back of the building. The cell phone on the seat beside him chirped.

"How's it look?" Gooding asked.

"Clear," Cork said.

"Ten-four. We're coming out."

No sooner had Gooding hung up than Cork spotted a few people edging around the corner of the building. Among them were the Warroad couple with their wheelchair-bound son. Why they'd broken away from the crowd up front, Cork couldn't say, but there was nothing he could do about it now except hope that he was able to get Solemn away before anything serious occurred.

The couple wheeled their son toward the Bronco, coming as if they knew what was happening. Behind them, the other few who'd deserted the crowd hung back, their gazes shifting back and forth between the wheelchair and the crush of people up front.

The rear door of the building opened. Gooding came out, escorting Solemn, who'd changed from his county uniform into jeans and a white T-shirt. Twenty yards of open ground lay between them and the Bronco. They'd taken only a few steps when a cry went up from the people who'd stationed themselves at the building's corner, and the rush was on.

The Warroad couple arrived first, thrusting the wheelchair and its precious occupant between Solemn and the safety of the Bronco.

"Please," the woman said. She grabbed Solemn's hand. "Heal my son." She tugged at his arm, pulling him toward the boy. Her husband tried to grasp Solemn's other arm, but Gooding interfered.

"Move away, folks," he ordered. "Let this man through."

"Please," the woman said.

Solemn could not ignore her desperation. He looked down at the boy whose tongue hung from his mouth, whose eyes roamed, whose hands were locked in a vicious grip that held nothing.

"What do you want me to do?" he asked.

Cork heard the noise of the crowd rounding the corner of the building. "Get in, Solemn," he shouted.

Solemn's eyes had not left the boy. "What do you want me to do?"

"Lay your hands on him," the woman said. "Touch him."

The first of those who'd given the cry neared Solemn. Gooding put himself between them and Winter Moon.

"Stay back," he shouted. "That's a police order."

It made them pause only a moment.

Solemn reached out and laid both his hands on the boy's head. He looked at the woman, his dark eyes full of doubt. "Like this?"

The flood of people swept into view. The sound of their coming triggered those already near Solemn, and those anxious few shoved past Gooding. Solemn lost his grip on the boy and stumbled toward the Bronco. He slipped into the backseat and slammed the door as two bodies hurled themselves against it. Cork hit the power lock, put the Bronco into gear, and drove away from the wave of faithful sweeping around Gooding.

Two blocks distant, he finally asked over his shoulder, "You okay?"

Solemn didn't reply.

Cork glanced in the mirror, and saw behind him the face of a terrified man.

* * *

The whole distance to Sam Winter Moon's old cabin Solemn didn't say a word. Cork parked in the shade of the pine trees and got out. Solemn moved like an old man, slowly and in a daze. When he was out of the vehicle, he stood and stared at the cabin.

"I'll bring you whatever you need," Cork said.

"I touched him. Nothing happened."

"What did you expect?"

Solemn shook his head. "I told you they were looking for something I couldn't give them."

"I know, Solemn."

"It's gone."

"What?"

But Solemn didn't say. He walked toward the cabin and went inside alone.

Fifteen minutes later, Dot drove up in her blue Blazer. Jo followed in her Toyota.

"Where is he?" Dot looked toward the cabin. "Inside?"

Cork nodded.

"How's he doing?" Jo asked.

"Pretty shaken."

"You need anything, Dot?"

"No." She took Jo's hand, and Cork's, and thanked them. *"Migwech."* She went inside to be with her son.

"Anybody follow you?" Cork asked.

"No. They were all too confused, I think. It was pretty crazy back there."

"Tell me about it."

"Cork, I saw Fletcher Kane. He was standing across the street, watching when Dot and I left the building."

"What was he doing there?"

"I don't know, but he didn't seem happy." Jo looked at the old cabin where Dot and Solemn had sought refuge. "Do we need to do anything here?"

"I don't know what it would be. Let's go home."

29

LATE THAT AFTERNOON at Sam's Place, Jenny said, "Dad?"

Cork was scraping the griddle. "Yeah?"

"Dad?"

He heard this time how queer her voice was and he turned. Business had been slow. Jenny sat on the stool at the serving window with her headphones on, listening to a CD by a group called Garbage. Cork followed her fearful gaze.

In the parking lot stood Fletcher Kane, staring darkly at Jenny.

"I'll be right back, honey," Cork said.

He took off his apron and went outside.

Kane was dressed in a black suit, white shirt, black tie. He reminded Cork of an undertaker. In the heat, sweat trickled down his temples. His eyes stayed locked on Jenny behind the window.

"What is it, Fletcher?" Cork asked, not kindly.

"What if she were dead?"

"What?"

"Your daughter. What if she were dead?"

"What do you want?"

"You have no idea, do you, how that would feel?"

"Is that a threat?"

Kane finally looked at Cork. "They let him out."

"Solemn? Yes."

"He's not at his mother's."

A boat came up to the dock. The engine whined like a huge insect, sputtered, then died. The silence after seemed heavy.

"Why would you care?" Cork said.

"I want to know where he is."

"You think I'm going to tell you?"

Kane reached into the inside pocket of his suit coat and pulled out a checkbook and a Montblanc fountain pen. He unscrewed the cap of the pen and opened the checkbook.

"How much?"

"Are you serious?"

Kane held the checkbook in the palm of his left hand. With his right, he wrote out a check and handed it to Cork.

Twenty thousand dollars.

"Go home, Fletcher." Cork tore up the check.

Kane watched the torn pieces flutter to the gravel, then looked toward Jenny. "No idea," he said, and walked back to his car.

Cork went into Sam's Place and called the sheriff's office, asked for Gooding. After he explained the episode with Kane, he said, "Randy, he's right at the edge of something."

Gooding breathed deeply on the other end. "I'll have a talk with him. I'm not sure what else we can do. He hasn't broken any law that you know of, has he?"

"Not yet."

"You know how it is, Cork."

"Yeah, I know."

It was dark when Cork finally locked the door of Sam's Place and headed to his Bronco with the day's take in hand.

He went to First National of Aurora and completed the night deposit. As he prepared to head out of the bank lot onto Center Street, Fletcher Kane's silver El Dorado cruised passed. Cork waited a moment, then eased onto the street a couple of cars behind him.

It was a warm summer night. The traffic was primarily young people, teenagers mostly, cruising toward the Broiler, which stayed open until midnight, or to the new Perkins, which was open twenty-four hours. They'd sit in booths, drink coffee or Cokes, smoke cigarettes, and talk of things that mattered to them now. Jenny and her boyfriend would be out there somewhere, in the midnight blue '76 Camaro that Sean had bought as a junker and had brought back to life. For Jenny, the things that mattered would be books; for Sean, in that season, it would be baseball.

Cork had been young once, in Aurora. He remembered the explosive feel of summer nights, when, at fourteen or fifteen or sixteen your heart was big and your head was forgotten, when you believed you had it in you to do everything, when you felt like you'd never die but if you did that was all right, too, because it couldn't get any better than this, or any worse. Every corner on Center Street was a place he'd lingered, spotlighted by a streetlamp, hanging out with a half dozen other boys his age. Except he'd never hung out with Fletcher Kane. Kane was a loner, even then, a small kid with glasses, tending a little toward plump. He was bright, everybody knew that, but not in the least athletic. Cork couldn't remember if he had had a best friend, or even a good one. Once the scandal of his father's death broke, and word got out about the investigation Cork's father had been conducting, Fletcher Kane stopped going to school and Cork almost never saw him on the street.

Cork did remember one incident. A Saturday night a couple of weeks after his father had died, Fletcher showed up at the old Rialto Theatre. Cork was there, too, to see Sean Connery as James Bond in *From Russia with Love*. After the show, as Cork headed home, he saw Fletcher surrounded by a number of high school boys, who'd cornered him in the alley behind Pflugelmann's Rexall Drugstore. Cork ran hard to the sheriff's office, where he found Cy Borkmann on duty. The deputy was young, but heavy even then. He followed Cork back to the alley and broke up the gathering where the high school boys were in the process of "pantsing" Kane, forcibly removing his trousers to make him walk the streets in his underwear. Fletcher Kane never said a word of thanks, not to the deputy nor to Cork. He eyed them both while he put on his pants, as if waiting for them to take their own turn at humiliating him, then with as much dignity as he could muster, he walked on home. Two weeks later, Kane's mother left Aurora for good and took her son with her.

Fletcher Kane had been set that way in Cork's mind for thirty-five years. Then the tall man with long hands and deep pockets had showed up in Aurora. The boy, however, was still visible in the face, especially in the hard, dark eyes that even after more than three decades still seemed to be watching the town, as if ready to be hurt and to hurt in return.

Kane turned onto Cascade, circled back, and again entered the stream of vehicles on Center Street. What was he looking for? What was out there in the night that drew him from the solitary dark of his home?

Cork followed for nearly an hour, up and down Center, past the Broiler and Perkins, as Kane insinuated his El Dorado into the flow of cars packed with teenagers. He had no business tailing the man this way, but he was curious and also concerned. Everything he believed told him Kane needed watching.

Finally, the El Dorado made a left on Olive and headed west, away from the center of town. Kane took another left on Madison and two blocks later, turned the corner, and pulled to the curb in front of St. Agnes. Cork drove past and rounded the next corner. He parked and leaped from the Bronco.

A waxing half moon had risen, bright enough to cast vague, disturbing shadows. Cork kept to those shadows as he made his way back toward the church. In the moonlight, the silver El Dorado seemed to glow. The driver's door, when it opened, flashed like a signal mirror. Cork ducked behind a minivan parked on the street.

Kane moved like a man condemned, dragging himself up the steps to the doors of St. Agnes. His shadow went before him and touched the wood long before he did. He reached out and tugged at the knob. His right hand rose in a fist and beat against the door. He stepped back, and for a long moment stared at what was locked against him. Finally he turned and sat down on the top step. He bent forward, and his shadow bent with him while he and his darker self began to weep.

Cork knew that he was trespassing on something terribly private. He crept away, wondering if Kane wept for himself, for his own hopeless situation. Was he, perhaps, still grieving for his daughter? Or had he come to the church seeking something that the locked door prevented him from finding?

30

GOODING JOINED CORK at the counter of the Broiler the next morning. Cork was finishing his coffee. Gooding ordered a cup for himself and a side of whole wheat toast.

"Light breakfast," Cork said.

"Here on official business, sort of. Our acting sheriff asked me to find you, let you know a couple of things."

"Cy? How's he doing?"

"Holding his own, I'd say." Gooding leaned nearer to Cork. "If you haven't heard, you soon will. Arne Soderberg came into the office yesterday afternoon with his attorney. Gave a full statement. He admitted to an affair with Charlotte Kane. Said it began last summer, but he broke it off when he got himself elected sheriff. When she took up with Winter Moon, he got jealous, went back to seeing her. He admitted he was at Valhalla, but swears she was alive and unharmed when he left. He's got a receipt and a witness that place him in town in the time frame we believe she was attacked. Looks like a pretty solid alibi. He also admitted that the rose petals were his doing. Said the last promise he made to her was that when he was a free man, as in divorced from Lyla, I guess, he'd give her a bed of roses to lie in." Gooding looked down. "Soderberg. I should have been suspicious. He had money, transport, and a key to the cemetery. Pretty sloppy police work."

"Give yourself a break. You couldn't have known he had a motive. Who would have thought it?"

Gooding looked up again. "You did."

"What about the blood tears? Did he know anything about that?"

"Swore he didn't have anything to do with it. Doesn't know a thing about it."

"You hear anything yet from the BCA on the samples you took from the angel?"

"Mostly water and a little blood. Type O-positive, most common blood type. Nobody actually saw the angel weeping. The tears had already streamed down the monument when the crowd started to gather, so I suppose they could easily have been put there earlier by almost anyone. Somebody, maybe, who just wanted to add to the mystique. You could figure it any number of ways that have nothing to do with miracles."

Gooding's toast arrived. He opened a packet of honey.

"Cork, I've got to tell you, we still like Winter Moon for the girl's murder. Too much evidence against him. The CA's going ahead with the prosecution. You still believe he's innocent?"

"I do."

"You really care about that kid, don't you?" Gooding said as he spread the honey over his toast. "I wonder if sometimes we want to believe something so much that the truth can smack us right between the eyes and we don't even notice."

Cork sipped his coffee and ignored the comment. "You said you'd have a talk with Kane. Did you?"

"I went to his place yesterday. It was like talking to a lamppost. I don't know where Winter Moon is, but if I were you, I'd tell him to lie low right now. I think you're right about Kane. He's right on the edge of doing something stupid."

From the Broiler, Cork headed straight to Sam Winter Moon's old cabin. As he passed through Alouette on the rez, he saw Dot's Blazer parked outside LeDuc's general store. Solemn was in it, alone behind the wheel. Cork pulled up on the passenger side and got out of his Bronco. He walked around the back of the Blazer to the driver's side, and noticed the old pickup parked not far away, and the two men who occupied the cab. He went to the pickup and leaned in the window.

"Junior," he said. "Phil. What's up?"

The smell of beer came from inside the cab where Junior

and Philbert Medina sat. The two men were relatives of Dorothy Winter Moon, her mother's sister's husband's children from a first marriage. They were both mechanics in their father's garage in Brandywine, the other rez community. Junior wore a ball cap over his long black hair. Phil kept his own hair in a buzz cut. Both men cradled rifles on their laps and each had a can of Budweiser clamped in a free hand. They gave Cork big, stupid grins.

"Just getting ready for a little deer hunting," Junior said.

"Deer?"

"Yeah," Phil put in. "Waiting for a fat buck to come strolling onto the rez."

"Helping Dot out, are you?"

"That's what family's for, cousin." On the reservation, everyone was *cousin*.

"You know, I'd feel a lot better if you'd put away either the beer or the rifles." Cork paused a moment, then added, "You ought to put away both."

"What are you going to do? Arrest us?" Junior laughed.

Cork turned away and walked to the Blazer.

"Morning, Solemn."

"Hey, Cork." Solemn kept his eyes straight ahead.

"I'm guessing you already heard that Kane's looking for you."

"I heard."

"And Tweedle Dum and Tweedle Dee over there are your answer?"

"Phil and Junior were my idea."

Dorothy Winter Moon had come from LeDuc's store with a sack of groceries in her arms. She wore sunglasses against the glare of the bright morning sunlight. She stepped around Cork and opened the Blazer's back door.

"This isn't a good idea, Dot."

"You got a better one?" She set the grocery bag on the backseat and shut the door.

"Go to Henry Meloux, Solemn," Cork said. "You'll be safe with him, and maybe he can help in other ways."

"I can take care of my son," Dot said.

Cork looked at Solemn. "Is this what you want?"

Solemn didn't seem to hear. The two Medinas laughed at something, a loud and grating sound.

"Don't let go of it, Solemn," Cork said.

Solemn slowly turned his head, and Cork saw the hardness in his eyes.

"Let go of what?" Solemn said.

"What you found out there in the woods. That feeling. That belief."

Solemn regarded him for a long time. "What if it wasn't real?"

"Sometimes believing is all it takes to make a thing real."

"That boy in the wheelchair, his folks, they believed."

Dot scanned the street as if any moment she expected that Kane would leap out of the shadows in ambush. "We need to get back to Sam's cabin." She circled around the front of the Blazer and got in on the passenger side. "Let's go, Solemn."

Cork reached through the window and put his hand on the young man's arm. "Go to Meloux."

Solemn didn't answer. He started the engine and, when Cork withdrew his hand, backed onto the street and headed north out of Alouette. The Medinas followed in their truck.

Cork looked at the dust kicked up in Solemn's wake and wondered about the comment Gooding had made earlier. Maybe he did believe in Solemn's innocence simply because he wanted to believe. Was that enough to make it so?

31

AT NINE O'CLOCK THAT EVENING, Cork said, "Let's close 'er up, Annie."

It was Friday night, and they'd had a steady stream of customers for hours. Cork was tired.

Annie turned from the serving window, which was empty at the moment. "You know, you'd make a lot more money if we stayed open late, Dad."

"I don't want to work late. Do you?"

"Not especially."

"Well there you are. We'd both rather be poor but happy. Let's get the place cleaned up."

Half an hour later, Annie walked to the door of the Quonset hut. "See you at home."

"I'm going to put the night deposit together. If you wait a few minutes, I'll give you a ride."

"It's a nice night," Annie said. "I think I'll walk."

"Suit yourself."

The evening sky was sapphire. Cork walked to the door and watched Annie head toward town, following the path along the lakeshore toward the copse of poplars that enclosed the ruins of the old foundry. The trees were dark against the fading light, and Annie, against the horizon, was dark, too, and small and lovely. There were moments like this when Cork felt absolutely full, overflowing with love for his life, his family, his friends, this place he called home. He felt all that was familiar wrap around him like an old, comfortable quilt, and he didn't know how a man could be any luckier.

When he'd finished preparing the deposit, he locked up Sam's Place and headed into town. After the money was safely in the bank's keeping, Cork drove Center Street for a while. It was a busy evening. The streets were alive with traffic, teenagers and tourists and locals taking advantage of the summer night. Cork was looking for Kane's El Dorado, but he didn't see it, and in a way he was relieved.

He'd just turned on Olive Street to head home when his cell phone chirped.

"Cork, it's Jo. Where are you?"

He heard the concern in her voice.

"On my way home. What is it?"

"It's Annie. She's pretty upset. She's sure someone stalked her after she left Sam's Place."

"I'll be right there."

They were in the kitchen, the three O'Connor women, Jo, Jenny, and Annie. Annie sat at the table with a glass of milk in front of her and an uneaten cookie. Jenny had pulled up a chair next to her. Jo sat across the table. They all glanced up when Cork came in. Jo and Jenny looked worried. Annie looked scared.

"Hey, sweetheart, how're you doing?" He bent and kissed the top of Annie's head. Her hair still smelled of hot fry oil.

"Dad, some creep followed me home."

Cork pulled out a chair and seated himself. "Tell me everything from the beginning."

It was dark outside. The bulb over the sink was on. Night insects bumped against the screen trying desperately to get at the light.

Annie played with her cookie, turning it round and round on the table. Occasionally, her eyes flicked toward the bump and brush of the bugs at the window.

"I saw him the first time in the trees where the old foundry is. He was, like, crouching behind part of that brick wall that's still there."

"Why do you think it was a *him?*"

"I guess I didn't then. When I saw him the next time, I was pretty sure."

"Where was that?"

"In Randolph Park. I was walking along the trail that cuts through the ball fields and over the culvert. He was there in the trees along the creek."

"You got a better look this time?"

"Yeah. But it was also darker, so I couldn't really see much."

"Tell me what you saw."

"I think he was tall."

"Taller than me?"

"I'd say so, yes."

"Fat, skinny?"

"Kind of medium."

"What was he doing?"

"Just standing there, watching me."

"How do you know it was the same person you saw by the old foundry?"

"I just know it was."

"Okay. Go on."

"I started running then, kind of like I was jogging home. I just wanted to get out of there."

"Sure. That was smart, honey."

"Then I saw him again. He was waiting in the alley just before I got to Gooseberry Lane. There's a streetlamp there, but he stayed in the shadow of the Kaufmanns' big lilac hedge."

"Did you get a better look this time?"

She shook her head. "I only saw him because he coughed."

"Did he say anything?"

"No."

"Did you?"

"No. I ran. I mean I really ran this time."

"Is there anything you remember about him? Any detail? His clothing?"

"No."

"Did he wear glasses?"

"I don't know."

"Face hair?"

"I couldn't see."

She seemed distressed that she had no answers, and Cork decided to let it go for now.

"That's okay, Annie. You did just fine."

"This is Aurora," Jenny said. "We shouldn't have to worry about pervs here."

Cork said, "Until we know better what's going on, you both ride home with me at night, okay?"

"What if Sean gives me a ride?" Jenny said, speaking of her boyfriend.

"Fine. But he sees you to the door."

"Which he ought to be doing anyway," Jo said.

Annie held herself as if she were cold. "I think I'm going to take a shower."

"A good long hot one," her sister advised. "Wash that creep away. Come on. I'll go up with you."

Cork stood up and hugged her. "It'll be all right, I promise."

She seemed to believe him. "Thanks, Dad."

When the girls were gone, Cork sat with Jo at the table. He picked up Annie's uneaten cookie and began breaking it into pieces.

"What do you think?" Jo said.

"Annie's as sensible as they come. If she says she was followed, she was followed."

"Why would someone do that?"

The cookie lay in crumbs on the table in front of Cork. "Jo, there's something I haven't told you. I didn't think much about it until now. The other day when Kane was out at Sam's Place, he asked me how I'd feel if it were my daughter who was dead."

"And you don't think it was just a rhetorical question?" Jo was quiet a moment. "You think it might have been Fletcher?"

"Annie said the guy was tall. Fletcher's tall. He's always been odd, but he's way beyond odd now. I'm not saying absolutely it was Kane, but I'd be a fool—no, worse; I'd be negligent—if I didn't check him out. Jo, if he did have something to do with Charlotte's murder, who knows what he might be thinking now."

Jo's eyes drifted to the door through which her precious daughter had just passed. She nodded once. "Start checking."

32

NEXT MORNING, Cork stopped by the YMCA early. He found Mal Thorne in the weight room, wearing finger gloves and working a heavy bag. The priest worked out this way several mornings a week, keeping himself in shape. He might not have been the athlete he was when he'd boxed at Notre Dame, but for a man in middle age, he was all right. He wore a sleeveless T-shirt, and his biceps were hard and round as river stones.

Mal stopped when he saw Cork watching him. He smiled and, with the back of the leather glove on his big right hand, wiped sweat from his brow.

"What's up, Cork?"

"Got a minute?"

"Sure."

The room smelled of warm weights and hot bodies and bench cushions that went too long between cleanings. Except for Mal and Cork, the place was empty.

"I've been thinking, Mal. About the graffiti Solemn spray-painted on the wall of St. Agnes. That Latin word."

"Mendax."

"Right. Liar. I'm pretty sure it was Charlotte Kane who put him up to it."

The priest showed no surprise.

"Why do you suppose she did that?"

Mal laid a hand on the heavy bag, as if to keep it from swinging, which it wasn't. "Search me."

"Not even a guess?"

"Some people feel as if God has let them down, as if the promises of the Church are empty. I encounter that a lot."

"Did you encounter it with Charlotte?"

"Maybe."

"You're hedging."

"I was her priest, Cork."

"And her confessor."

"It's the nature of the job."

"Mal, Charlotte Kane exhibited behaviors that, in my understanding, are classic for a young woman who'd been sexually abused, probably on a long-term basis."

The priest tugged off one of his gloves, and started on the other.

"It occurs to me that you're also Fletcher Kane's confessor."

"I'm not going there with you, Cork. You know that anything told to me in confession is a sacred confidence."

"I'm concerned. If he was sexually molesting his daughter, he may be trapped in a behavior pattern that threatens other young women."

"I can't help you, Cork." A drop of sweat hung on the priest's brow. It gathered weight, plummeted, splattered soundlessly on the wooden floor.

"Someone followed Annie home last night. Stayed to the shadows where she couldn't see him clearly."

"You think it was Kane?"

"Is there a reason I should?"

The priest looked away and didn't answer.

"You know something about him and about Charlotte, don't you?"

"Charlotte's dead, Cork. Let the dead rest in peace."

"I don't think there's going to be much peace here until we know the truth about her murder."

The priest took a deep breath. "There's only one truth of which I'm absolutely certain. That none of us is without sin." He gave a final, ungloved blow to the heavy bag. "We're done here."

He walked away, leaving Cork wondering what it was the priest knew but wouldn't say.

* * *

At the sheriff's department, he found Cy Borkmann sitting in the chair that only a few days before had been occupied by Arne Soderberg.

"You look good there, Cy."

"Hey, Cork," Borkmann said, rising. "Come on in."

They shook hands.

"How's it going?" Cork asked.

"No complaints so far. Have a seat. By the way, that was some nice piece of work, connecting Arne with Charlotte Kane."

"You know how it is. Sometimes you get lucky. Any idea how Arne's doing?"

"Heard Lyla kicked him out. Me, I wouldn't necessarily consider that punishment. Gooding told you about the rose petals."

"Yeah."

Borkmann shook his head and his wattle wobbled. "Swear to god, you could give Arne a bucketful of wishes and he'd find a way to turn it into a handful of horse crap."

Cork smiled, then got serious. "Cy, somebody followed my daughter home last night. Scared her pretty bad."

"Attacked her?"

"No. Stalked is more like it."

"Did she see who?"

"It was too dark."

"Let's write up an incident report."

"Hold on a minute. I'd like to run something by you. Just between you and me. Off the record."

"Shoot."

Cork told him about his discussion with the school psychologist. "From what I gather, Cy, behavior like Charlotte's may well have been the result of long-term abuse. In all likelihood, it predated her involvement with Arne. I'm wondering about Fletcher Kane. I'm wondering what kind of relationship he really had with his daughter."

Borkmann's eyes saucered. He picked up a pen and made a brief notation on a scrap of paper on his desk.

"Listen, Cy," Cork went on. "Glory Kane was the only one who could corroborate her brother's alibi for the night of the murder. Don't you find it a little odd that she disappeared the day after Charlotte was buried?"

"I don't know that she disappeared. Headed off on some kind of trip, I understand."

"Conveniently vague, don't you think?"

"Maybe. Probably Arne never thought about tracking her down because she didn't seem important to the case. I mean, we had Winter Moon right from the beginning."

Cork leaned forward confidentially. "Understand I'm just asking a question here. But if Glory knew something or suspected something and Fletcher was afraid she might tell someone, what would he do? Do any of us really know him well enough to know what he's capable of?"

"You saying he killed her? And that now he's stalking Annie?"

"I'm not saying anything, Cy. I'm just thinking that if I were sheriff, it would sure be something I'd look into." Cork sat back. "Do you know anything about Kane before he came to Aurora?"

"Enough."

"Anything you can share?"

Borkmann thought it over. "Wait here." He got up and left the room.

Cork went to the window. Another gorgeous June day. Although Solemn was no longer a prisoner in the jail, the hopeful still gathered in the little park across the street. Grover Buck had received his miracle, apparently. And Marge Schembeckler. But what about the boy in the wheelchair and all the others, those still waiting for what their faith had promised them?

Borkmann came back with a manila folder in his hand. "This is what we've got on Kane. Graduated magna cum laude from UCLA in seventy-four, from Stanford Medical School in seventy-eight. Joined the staff of the Worthington Clinic in Pomona, California, in eighty. Became head of the clinic in ninety. Invested well. Widowed four years ago. Retired and moved to Aurora. No criminal record."

"That's it."

"Slew of awards for his work. Humanitarian guy. Gave his time to causes and such."

"Where'd you get this information?"

"Gooding interviewed him."

"Did Gooding check it out?"

"Not that I know of. The guy wasn't under suspicion. Again, Arne figured he had Winter Moon dead to rights."

"Look, Cy. I think Arne made a big mistake when he stopped looking beyond Solemn, but Arne wasn't a cop. He didn't think like you and I do. A cop would know better."

"Sure," Borkmann said. "Sure."

"I'm working with Jo on Solemn's defense, but what I really want, what we all want, is to nail the son of a bitch who murdered Charlotte Kane. I don't believe for an instant that Solemn's guilty. I'm going to keep digging. If I find out anything, I'll share it with you. I'm hoping you'll show me the same courtesy."

"Well now, Cork, you know I can't make any promises. But I'll sure do my best to keep you in the loop."

"That's all I'm asking, Cy." Cork stood up and reached his hand across the desk. "Nice doing business with you. Sheriff." He grinned.

33

CORK FELT A LITTLE SLIMY in the way he'd used Borkmann. On the other hand, he got what he was looking for. He knew now that the sheriff's people had no more information on Fletcher and Glory Kane than he had. That meant there was a lot of digging to be done.

During a lull in the rush at Sam's Place that afternoon, he stepped into the back section of the Quonset hut, called directory assistance, and got the number for the Worthington Clinic in Pomona. When he telephoned, the automated system told him the hours were 8:00 A.M. until 5:00 P.M. Monday through Friday. If it was an emergency, there was a number to call. He was free to leave a message that would be returned as soon as possible.

Cork left a message.

"This is Sheriff Corcoran O'Connor calling from Tamarack County, Minnesota. I'd appreciate talking with someone there about Dr. Fletcher Kane. This is in relation to a homicide investigation." He left his telephone number, said thank you, and hung up.

He knew he'd have to be careful about the sheriff part.

When he returned to the serving area, he saw Deputy Randy Gooding at one of the windows talking with Annie, both of them laughing. Gooding signaled him over. Annie stepped back toward the griddle, smiling happily.

"Cy sent me over, Cork. He thought you might want to know

that we finally tracked down Grover Buck," Gooding said. "Duluth P.D. is holding him."

"For what?"

"Soliciting the services of a woman he thought was a prostitute, but who was really part of a sting. I'd contacted them earlier, when Buck suddenly dropped out of sight right after his miraculous healing. They promised to watch for him."

"Did he drive himself to Duluth, now that the Lord has opened his eyes?"

"Yeah, right. His nephew. Same one who helped him count out the five hundred dollars he got for faking his healing."

"Who paid him?"

"Swears he never got the man's name. But get this. The guy paid him off in bogus bills, counterfeit C-notes, while the nephew's standing there, watching. What does a sixteen-year-old kid know about counterfeit bills?"

"What about Marge Schembeckler and her arthritis?"

"I talked to her a couple of days ago. She admitted she was back in her wheelchair the same afternoon she was healed. Stayed in her house after that. Ashamed, she says. Doesn't seem to be any connection between her and the guy who paid off Buck. I figure she just got caught up in the moment and willed herself to walk. At least for a little while."

"So the blanket . . ."

"Wasn't anything special after all."

Although he couldn't have said why, Cork felt a little sad that the hands behind the miracles had been revealed.

"Anybody else know this?"

"Not yet, but they will soon enough. Borkmann's giving a statement to the media."

"A shame in a way. All those folks who wanted to believe so badly."

Gooding leaned close through the window. "Cy told me about the discussion you two had in his office. I got to tell you, I think you're way off base about Dr. Kane."

Cork shook his head. "There's too much about him that when you try to add it up just doesn't total."

"Mostly, he's just a man who's suffered a lot and wants his privacy, I think."

Cork thought different, but he didn't want to argue the point. "How about a chocolate malt?" he said. "On the house."

At dusk, Jenny turned from her serving window and said, "Dad, there's something going on at the dock. Doesn't look good."

Cork stripped off his apron and headed out the door of the Quonset hut. As he approached the dock, he could see clearly what was happening. A couple of young men with a big new boat had tied up at the landing. They weren't locals and Cork didn't know them. They were sunburned and drunk. Cork figured they'd spent the day on the lake, drinking and trolling. On the water, they'd been trying for walleyes, but when they tied up at the dock, they went fishing for something else—a couple of local teenage girls who'd also tied up there. The women wanted none of it and were just trying to get up to Sam's Place, but the men had cut them off.

"Evening, Susan," Cork said as he stepped onto the dock. "Hey, Donna."

The men turned at the sound of his voice, unhappy with his interruption.

"Excuse me, gentlemen," he said. "Got a couple of regular customers here. I always give them first-class treatment."

He stepped between the two men, forcing them to the edges of the dock, and he offered his hand to Donna Payne.

"Well hey, Pops, that's what we had in mind, too," one of the men said, grinning. He had blond hair made stiff by the sun and the wind.

"I think I know what you had in mind," Cork said. "And first-class, it wasn't."

As the girls passed between the two men, the guy with the stiff blond hair grabbed Donna by the arm. "How about dinner on us?"

"How about a cold one on me?" Cork said. He shoved the man into the water, and with a quick turn, did the same to his companion.

"Go on up to Sam's Place," Cork told the young women. "Jenny will take care of you."

The two men sputtered and flailed in the water and grabbed at the dock. Cork stood looking down on them.

"I'd stay in that water a little longer if I were you. It'll help you sober up. Then you take your boat and you get out of here. This is my property, and as of five minutes from now, I'll consider you trespassing and call the cops. Believe me, they'll love hauling you in. They like giving fines to strangers with expensive boats."

Cork left the men treading water and headed back to Sam's Place.

The two girls stood at the window.

"Thanks, Mr. O'Connor," Donna said.

"You're welcome."

Inside Sam's Place, Annie said, "You got a strange call while you were out at the dock, Dad. He asked for Sheriff O'Connor."

"Damn. What did you tell him?"

"I said you were busy breaking up a fight."

"Did you tell him I wasn't sheriff?"

"No. I took a message for you though." She had a piece of paper in her hand. "It was a Mr. Steven Hadlestadt from the Worthington Clinic returning your call. He said you wanted to talk to him about a homicide investigation involving Fletcher Kane. I told him you were actually investigating the murder of Dr. Kane's daughter, Charlotte. He seemed really confused. He said 'Charlotte?' I said yes, Charlotte Kane. And he said something really strange, Dad. He said, 'I thought they closed the book on that murder investigation four years ago.' "

34

"SHE WAS MURDERED four years ago?"

"An investigation of her murder was conducted four years ago. Whatever that means."

Jo fell quiet on the other end of the line. She was in her office at home. Cork knew the window was open because he could hear Stevie in the backyard with some other children. They were yelling. A game of tag, it sounded like.

"Did you call him back?"

"I tried. No answer. I left a couple of messages. He told Annie he'd be in his office all day Monday if I wanted to call him back. Jo, I need to go out to California. I want to talk to Hadlestadt in person first thing Monday morning."

"Maybe he'll call before Monday."

"Maybe. But I still think I should go. Kane lived most of his life in California. It could be that a lot of the answers we're looking for are there."

"It means you'll have to fly out tomorrow. That'll be expensive."

"Would you want to cross-examine a witness over the phone?"

"You really think it will be worthwhile?"

"Yeah."

"Gut feeling?"

"Gut feeling."

"All right. I'll get on the Internet and see if I can get you a reasonable fare." He heard her breathe, a sigh like wind across the wire. "What's going on, Cork?"

"Your guess is as good as mine. With any luck, come Monday we'll have an answer."

He was distracted the rest of the evening, and thankful when it came time to close. As he was preparing the slip for the night deposit, Annie called to him from the front where she was finishing with the cleaning.

"Dad, Aunt Rose is here. She wants you to come outside."

"Tell her to come in."

"No, she says for you to come outside."

Cork put the day's take in a bank envelope and sealed it, then he left the Quonset hut.

It was almost dark. Rose stood in the gravel lot, waiting.

"This is a surprise," he said.

"I was out for a walk."

"Long walk."

"I seem to take a lot of those these days. Mind if we talk down by the lake? It's so pretty in the evening."

They strolled to the dock, where the water was smooth and dark. The town of Aurora lay along the shoreline to the south, and far across the lake to the east the lights of isolated cabins glimmered here and there like stars fallen to earth.

"What is it, Rose?"

She crossed her arms and looked at the distant lights. "Do you remember the first time we met, Cork?"

"Sure. Beef stroganoff and cherry pie. Best meal I'd had in years."

She laughed gently. "You always had a good appetite. I knew right away you were a man who could be trusted. In Jo's life, that was important and rare."

"You grilled me pretty good that night."

"You passed with flying colors."

A fish jumped. A splash of water, blue-black rings widening. Then the night was quiet again.

"Why Jo?" she asked.

"What?"

"What made you fall in love with Jo?"

"Her eyes for one thing. They were fire and ice at the same

time. Her brain. The way she talked so passionately about things. It didn't hurt that she was beautiful, too."

Rose breathed a sigh. "Men like a pretty woman, don't they?"

"Beauty comes in a lot of forms, Rose, and I'll tell you this. I've never met anyone with a more beautiful soul than yours."

In the dim light, she smiled at him. "Thank you."

"You clean up pretty nice, too."

She laughed again.

"Long walk just to ask about Jo and me."

"That wasn't the reason I came."

Maybe not, but it was certainly on your mind, Cork thought.

"Jo told me you're flying to California tomorrow. She said you think Fletcher might have had something to do with Charlotte's murder."

"I'm just following leads, Rose."

"What if you don't come up with anything?"

"I'll keep digging until I do." Cork leaned against one of the dock posts. "You know, Rose, you've always been the soul of discretion, but if you've got something to say, I wish you'd just spit it out."

"I can't."

"Why not?"

"I made a promise. An important one."

"To whom?"

"I can't say."

"Do you know something about Charlotte? About the Kanes? Rose, this is important."

"I know. But I can't tell you now. When do you leave?"

"First thing in the morning. Why can't you tell me now?"

"I told you that I knew you were a man who could be trusted. Well, I need you to trust me now."

If anyone else had put him in this position, Cork would have throttled them. But Rose asked little, and when she did, it was a request to be heeded.

"All right." He let out a huge breath that conveyed, he hoped, his frustration. "You want a ride back to the rectory?"

"I'd rather walk. I've still got a lot of thinking to do."

A breeze arose, glided off the water cool and fresh, lifted her hair. Cork saw how beautiful she was then, and how any man might love her.

She said, "I used to believe life was pretty simple. There was my family, my friends, and my church, and there wasn't much that prayer couldn't help."

"And now?"

"Some days," she said, "I wonder."

She turned away from the lake.

"I wish you'd take a ride," Cork said. "Until we know who stalked Annie, it might not be safe to be out alone so late."

She weighed his concern, and after a moment, she said all right.

"Wait in the Bronco. I'll get Annie."

Inside, Annie had finished the cleaning and was ready to go.

"What did Aunt Rose want?" she asked.

Cork gathered everything for the night deposit, shook his head, and said, "I'm not sure she knows."

Early the next morning, before he left town, Cork drove to Sam Winter Moon's old cabin. Blue woodsmoke rose up from the stovepipe, and the smell of frying bacon was in the air. Dot's blue Blazer sat under a birch tree. The cabin door opened as Cork walked toward it, and Solemn's mother stepped outside. She wore jeans and a blue and white Timberwolves T-shirt and held a spatula in her hand.

"Morning, Dot."

"Cork."

"Looking for Solemn."

"He's along the creek." With the spatula, she pointed toward the east.

"Where are the bodyguards?"

"Bodyguards?"

"Junior and Phil Medina."

"Solemn sent them away." She swung her free hand at a fly that was darting about her head. "Jo told me you're going to L.A. today."

"Yeah."

"I told Solemn. He didn't seem to care much. He heard about the miracles. That they were bullshit."

"How's he doing?"

She shook her head.

"Think he'd mind if I talked to him?"

"You can try. Hungry? I got pancakes and bacon coming up soon."

"No, thanks. I'll just have a word with Solemn then be off."

He found Winter Moon sitting on a stump a hundred yards down Widow's Creek. It wasn't far from the place where, months earlier, Cork had found the dead whitetail. All remains of the deer were probably gone now, eaten by scavengers and insects. Nature cleaning up, Cork knew.

Solemn sat slumped, his arms on his knees, his head down, watching the creek water run past a few yards away. He didn't seem to hear Cork coming.

"Solemn?"

The young man didn't turn, didn't move at all. "They don't believe," he said.

"A lot of people never did. Does that make a difference?"

"It's gone. That feeling I got in the woods. I've lost it. Why did it come to me if it was just going to go away?" He shook his head. "You were right all along. It was just a dream. Hallucination, whatever. All those people looking to me, they really were just a bunch of suckers."

Cork sat down on the ground next to the stump and looked at the water moving past, saw how the sky was reflected on the surface without obscuring the rocks beneath that formed the creek bed.

"Solemn, last winter I saw something that to this day I don't understand. It was right after Charlotte disappeared. I was part of the search team looking for her, but I got lost in a whiteout on Fisheye Lake. Couldn't tell up from down. I haven't been so scared in a long time. Then someone, some *thing,* guided me to safety. I never saw it clearly. It stayed just at the edge of my vision, but I felt it was Charlotte, and I don't know how that could have been."

"You believe what you saw?"

"I want to believe. I want very much to believe, but I fall way short. It saved my life, that's all I know, just like what you saw saved yours." Cork shrugged and stared beyond the creek where the forest lay deep as any secret he knew. "I remember something Sam used to tell me. He said there's more in these woods than a man can ever see with his eyes, more than he can ever hope to understand."

For a long time, Solemn didn't respond. Then he said, "Sam's dead."

"What I'm saying is that most people would give anything for a moment of the kind of certainty you had out there in those woods. What you experienced is a rare gift and one that gives the rest of us hope."

Solemn slowly lifted his head. There were tears in his eyes.

"I felt like I was overflowing. Now I wish it had never happened, Cork, because now that it's gone, I feel more empty than ever. And more alone."

Cork wanted to reach out and hold Solemn, but touching that way wasn't Ojibwe.

He stood up. He had a plane to catch.

"Go to Henry," he said.

He stopped in Aurora to gas up. As he headed south out of town, he drove past the sheriff's department and the park where the crowd had once gathered, hoping for a glimpse of a man who'd talked with God. The park was empty now. Whenever hope packed its bag and left for good, all that remained was a terrible emptiness, immeasurably sad.

That was something Solemn understood well.

Cork drove to the Twin Cities, and at two o'clock caught a plane to L.A. By the time he'd shuttled to the Hertz lot to pick up his rental and driven to his hotel, a quaint place called the Claremont Inn just across the city line from Pomona, it was nearly six o'clock. His stomach was still on Minnesota time and he was starved. After he checked in, he headed out in search of food and the Worthington Clinic.

He found the clinic first. It was a multiwing building of snow white stucco set in a sea of grass behind iron gates and a wall hung with bougainvillea. In the background rose the San Gabriels, copper green in the late afternoon haze. It looked like the kind of place only an Oscar or a million bucks would get you into.

He had a decent steak in a restaurant just off Route 66, then he drove awhile. He hadn't been in Southern California for years and what had bothered him then bothered him now. The orange groves had become subdivisions and parking lots, and even with all the freeways no one seemed to be able to get anywhere fast enough.

He returned to the hotel a little before ten, and saw from the blinking light on the room telephone that he had a message. It was from Jo. "Call me, sweetheart," she said. "I have some good news."

Although it was nearly midnight in Minnesota, Cork called immediately. Jo answered, sounding a little sleepy.

"I talked with Rose today," she told him. "After you left. She knows where Glory is."

"How?"

"Glory heard about the angel of the roses and called Rose last week. She made Rose promise not to tell anyone. And you know how Rose is when she makes a promise."

He did. And now he understood the discussion he'd had with his sister-in-law the night before.

"She talked with Glory today, and Glory asked her to have you call as soon as possible."

Jo gave him Glory's number.

Cork looked at the area code. "Where is this?"

"Iowa. Rose said that when you call you should ask for Cordelia Diller."

"Who?"

"That's the name Glory is using. She'll explain. One more thing, Cork. Dorothy Winter Moon's been getting a lot of threatening calls. People are pretty angry about the miracle business. A lot of them seem to blame Solemn, think he must've been in on it. He's gone to Henry Meloux's, by the way."

"Good. If anyone can help, it's Henry. How's Annie?"

"She's at the Pilons. Claire invited her for a sleepover."

"Make sure she's careful. Make sure both of the girls are."

"That's a roger."

"I love it when you talk cop."

"I miss you."

"Miss you, too."

After he hung up, he punched in the number Jo had given him for Glory Kane. The phone at the other end rang several times before it was finally answered.

"Rosemount. This is Sister Alice Mary."

"Sister?"

"Yes?"

"I'm trying to reach Cordelia Diller."

"It's rather late. Everyone is in bed."

"She asked me to call her."

"Is it an emergency of some kind?"

"I wouldn't call it an emergency, no."

"Then I'm sure she didn't intend for you to call near midnight. I'll see that she gets your message first thing in the morning. Is there a number where she might return your call?"

Cork gave her the motel telephone number.

"Sister Alice Mary, where are you exactly?"

"Just outside Dansig, Iowa, right on the Mississippi River."

"I guess I mean what are you? What is Rosemount?"

"We're a retreat center for Catholic women, particularly those who are considering entering a religious life."

"You mean becoming a nun?"

"That's certainly one of the options."

"Thank you, Sister."

Cork hung up and spent a few minutes trying to picture Glory Kane as a nun. God might be able to see it, he finally decided, but his own eyes were way too blind.

35

Cork didn't sleep well. He got up early and tried calling Glory Kane in Iowa. All he got was a busy signal. He showered, shaved, dressed, and tried the number again with the same result. He went to a little restaurant down the street from the Claremont Inn and ordered eggs Benedict. They weren't bad, and the coffee was good and strong. He read the *Los Angeles Times*. The sports page, anyway. The Twins had dropped a game back of the White Sox for the division lead. He returned to his motel room and tried one last time to reach Glory Kane. The line was still busy. He wondered just how popular a retreat center in the boondocks of Iowa could be.

At eight, he presented himself to the receptionist at the contact desk of the Worthington Clinic. A blonde with a Rodeo Drive walk showed him to Steven Hadlestadt's office. Hadlestadt stood up to greet him and they shook hands.

The man was younger than Cork had expected, early thirties. His head was shaved smooth of hair. He had a narrow face with intelligent, blue eyes. He wore an expensive-looking gray suit and a red silk tie.

"I admit I expected just a phone call, Sheriff O'Connor."

"It's important, so I came in person. Is it Dr. Hadlestadt?"

"Yes, but not M.D. I'm the clinic administrator. Won't you sit down?"

Cork sank into the soft leather of a chair. The office was

beautifully appointed, and through a long side window there was a stunning view of the San Gabriels.

"Before we go any further, may I see some identification?"

Cork pulled out his wallet and handed over a card.

"This is a driver's license," Hadlestadt said.

"That's right."

"May I see your law enforcement ID?"

"I don't have one at the moment. I'm the former sheriff of Tamarack County. I held that office for eight years. Currently, I'm working as a consultant on law enforcement issues."

Hadlestadt handed back the driver's license. "Then you're not actually a cop."

"Would you look at this, Mr. Hadlestadt?" Cork thrust at him a copy of the *Duluth News Tribune,* the April issue in which the headline read "Aurora Girl's Death Ruled Murder." The story ran with a photo of the young woman.

"Is that Charlotte Kane?" Cork asked.

Hadlestadt's eyes took in the headline, then scanned the story and the photo. "It certainly looks like her, but I don't see how that could be."

"Why?"

"For one thing, she died four years ago. Or at least that's what I thought. And for another, it says here she's only seventeen. Charlotte Kane would be twenty now."

"What happened to Charlotte four years ago?"

Hadlestadt put the newspaper on his desk. "You say you're a consultant. In what capacity on this case?"

"I'm working for the attorney whose client has been charged with the girl's murder."

For a moment, it appeared as if Hadlestadt was considering the advisability of answering. Then he seemed to give a mental shrug. "Charlotte disappeared. They found her car a couple of days later. Lots of blood, but no body. As I understand, it was a pretty awful scene. The police carried out a thorough investigation, but I believe they never did find out exactly what happened to her. It was a terrible thing. She was such a terrific kid."

"Did they ever find the body?"

"No. At least not as far as I know."

"Was Fletcher Kane ever a suspect?"

Hadlestadt tensed. "No. And I can tell you right now I'm not going to say anything that would reflect badly on Dr. Kane."

"Please understand that I'm only after the truth. A young man has been accused of murdering Fletcher Kane's daughter, who appears to have been already dead. Mr. Hadlestadt, all I'm asking is that you help me understand how that's possible."

Hadlestadt rocked back in his chair. For a few moments, he looked away from Cork and studied the mountains framed by the office window.

"What do you want to know?" he said.

"When you knew him, what kind of person was Dr. Kane?"

"Terribly demanding of himself and his colleagues. A perfectionist. Sometimes difficult because his standards were always so high. But absolutely wonderful with patients. Compassionate, understanding."

This last part caught Cork by surprise, though he tried not to show it.

"He hired me. I worked with him for several years. I have nothing but admiration for him as a physician and as director of this clinic." Hadlestadt leaned forward, put his arms on his desk, and laced his fingers. "When Dr. Kane took the responsibility of heading Worthington, it was a place that catered exclusively to a wealthy clientele, people who wanted to buy back their youth or who wanted things done to their bodies they thought God had overlooked. Kane changed that. He hired talented physicians and gave them resources. Over time we've become known more for the reconstructive work we do here on victims of physical trauma. Automobile accidents, burns, that kind of thing. Don't get me wrong. We're still Hollywood's favorite choice for a nose job, but that's not at the heart of Worthington anymore, thanks to Fletcher Kane."

"Why did he leave?"

Hadlestadt shrugged. "What happened to Charlotte. It devastated him. He never got over it. He seemed to lose a part of himself, the best part, honestly. He resigned as director, withdrew from the rest of us, from the social life here. He asked for a new staff, which was a bit odd, but we accommodated him. He became secretive about his work. Considering everything he'd been through, I suppose most of this was understandable. It didn't surprise me at all when he finally left."

"What can you tell me about Charlotte Kane?"

"Aside from the fact that everybody loved her, not much. Maybe you should talk to someone who was closer to her. Try her mother. I'm sure she'll be interested in this." He tapped the paper.

"Her mother?" Cork said. "I thought Kane's wife was dead."

"The marriage may have died, but Constance Kane is alive, I assure you."

She lived in a big house in Ganesha Hills, above the Los Angeles County fairgrounds. The place was hacienda-style, two stories of beige stucco with a red tile roof. The property lines were marked with tall cedars, in almost exactly the same way as the boundaries of the Parrant estate back in Aurora. There was a fountain in front, a porcelain maiden pouring water from an urn into a small pool. The maiden had a young, pretty face and blank eyes. Cork rang the bell. Constance Kane appeared immediately.

He could see Charlotte in the woman at the door. The same raven hair, the same facial structure—small nose, high cheekbones, strong chin. Attractive. The eyes were different, blue and softer, with tiny crow's feet. She wore a yellow summer dress and sandals.

"Mr. O'Connor?"

"How do you do, Ms. Kane?"

Her hand was small but firm, her nails well manicured and polished with an opal sheen.

"Won't you come in?"

Lilies filled a vase on a table in the foyer, and Cork walked into their marvelous fragrance.

"Would you care for some coffee, or perhaps some tea?" she offered.

"Thank you, no."

In the living room, she indicated a stuffed chair and Cork sat down. She took a place on the sofa, crossed her legs at the ankles, and folded her hands on her lap.

"When you called from the clinic, you said you had some information about Fletcher that you thought I ought to have. Is he all right?"

"In a way, that's what I'm trying to find out. I'm from Aurora, Minnesota, your ex-husband's hometown."

"You're mistaken, Mr. O'Connor. Fletcher is from Kansas."

"I knew him until he was thirteen years old and his mother moved him away. They left as a result of rather unpleasant circumstances. It doesn't surprise me that your husband might have chosen never to speak of that time in his life."

"I'm sure we're talking about two different Fletcher Kanes."

Cork had brought with him a photo he'd cut from the *Aurora Sentinel* that had run with an article about the family shortly after Kane came to town. The article had been vague, but the photograph was clear. He handed it to her. "Is that your husband?"

She looked at the photo and said warily, "Yes."

"He returned to Aurora two years ago. He brought a daughter with him. Her name was Charlotte."

"Charlotte?" Her eyes hardened and the crow's feet deepened. "Is this some kind of sick joke? You said you were with the sheriff's department?"

"I was sheriff of Tamarack County, that's where Aurora is, for eight years."

"But no longer?"

"No longer." Cork took out the issue of the *Duluth News Tribune* that he'd shown to Hadlestadt at the clinic. "I have something here I think you ought to see."

She took the newspaper from him and spent a minute reading. She studied the news photo intently. "Whoever this is, she isn't my daughter. She looks like my daughter, but she's not." Ms. Kane stood abruptly and walked to a piece of blond furniture that seemed constructed for the sole purpose of holding expensive knickknacks. She took from it a framed photograph and brought it to Cork.

"This is my Charlotte. You see?"

It was a professionally done portrait, shot against a soft blue background. At first glance, it appeared to Cork to be the same young woman whose picture was in the newspaper. But when he put the news photo and the other side by side he could see the differences. In the jawline, the ears, and in the eyes especially. The California Charlotte looked tanned and happy. The Minnesota Charlotte was pale, thinner, sullen. Still, it was possible that the differences could be the result of the poor quality of the news photo reproduction, or a differing state of mind when each shot had been taken.

"Their ages are different, too," the woman said. "My Charlotte would be older."

Cork said, "Would you be willing to tell me about your daughter and her disappearance? And about Fletcher?"

She stared at him. "If you're not a sheriff anymore, what does all this have to do with you?"

"A young man has been accused of killing Charlotte Kane. Our Charlotte. I don't believe he did it."

"Why do you want to know about Fletcher?"

"There are a lot of unanswered questions in the case. If that's not your daughter in the news story, you have to wonder why they look so much alike and have the same name."

She sat down and closed her eyes. Cork waited. Through sliding doors, he could see a wide deck, flower boxes filled with red and white blossoms, and beyond that the purple hills of a metropolis that stretched unbroken all the way to the purple horizon.

"Charlotte disappeared a week after her sixteenth birthday," she began slowly. She looked at her hands, not at Cork. "We'd given her a car as a gift. She'd just got her license. She left after dinner that evening to meet some friends at the library. She never came home.

"Two days later, they found her car. There was a lot of blood in the trunk. Charlotte's blood. They never found her body."

She raised her head. Her face was taut, but composed.

"It took me a long time, Mr. O'Connor, but I finally accepted that my daughter is dead. It was different for Fletcher. I loved Charlotte very much, but she and Fletcher had something special between them." She hesitated. "I don't know how well you know my husband."

"Not well at all, I'm afraid."

"You're not alone. I was married to him for eighteen years,

and I understood him no better on the last day we were together than I did on the first. Fletcher was a very private person, very closed. He allowed few people near him, and he let no one inside. No one except Charlotte. From the moment she was born, she somehow managed to open Fletcher's heart. I admit, I often felt on the outside of things, a little envious of what the two of them shared.

"In the weeks before she died, however, they were often at odds. Charlotte's grades were slipping. She was spending too much time with her friends. In Fletcher's view, anyway. Really, it was normal teenage testing, rebelling. The night she disappeared, they had a fight. About her clothes, which Fletcher thought made her look like a bum. It was the style back then. Holes in everything. She left, and never came back. Fletcher couldn't deal with her loss, couldn't stop blaming himself, although there was no reason for blame. It tore him apart. He got stuck in his grieving. In the end, we didn't just lose our daughter. We lost each other. Eight months after Charlotte disappeared, we separated, then divorced."

The phone rang.

"Would you excuse me," she said. She left the sofa and went to the kitchen. "Hello?" she answered. "Hi, sweetheart." She was quiet for a moment. "No, I said Thursday night. The tickets are for the nine o'clock set. Jill and Ed will meet us there."

Cork didn't like listening in. He took the photograph of Charlotte Kane and returned it to the shelf from which her mother had taken it.

"I'm sorry, Mr. O'Connor." She stood in the doorway to the kitchen and spoke from a distance.

"That's all right."

"This is all very difficult to absorb."

"I understand."

"I don't know what's going on in your town—what's it called?"

"Aurora. Minnesota."

She nodded. "But your Charlotte isn't mine. Of that I'm absolutely certain."

"You're not curious?"

She crossed her arms protectively. "I don't know if you've ever had to deal with loss. This kind, this overwhelming uncertainty. At first you live on hope. You pray your heart out. You don't sleep, don't eat. Days stretch into weeks, weeks into months. Finally, holding on to hope becomes like holding up the earth, and you just can't do it anymore. You have to let go. You have to grieve and move on. I haven't heard from Fletcher in over two years. I moved on. I'd hoped the same for him." She squeezed her eyes shut, as if experiencing physical pain. After a few moments, she went on. "Fletcher didn't just lose a daughter. I think he lost the best part of himself, and he was desperate to get that back somehow. He became obsessed with finding Charlotte, whom he didn't believe was dead. He saw her everywhere. In passing cars, on street corners, in the mall. I've heard that everybody has a double somewhere. So I suppose it's entirely possible that he finally found Charlotte's double, some young woman as desperate for a new life as he was for his old."

"Or he manufactured her."

It took a moment, but as she understood what he was suggesting, a look of horror dawned on her face. "Jesus. That's hard to believe."

"But not impossible. I understand your husband was a gifted plastic surgeon."

"You misunderstand. I think Fletcher was probably capable of something that desperate and bizarre. What's hard to believe is that he found someone willing to let him do it." She crossed the room and picked up the photograph of her daughter. "If that's what happened, I feel so sorry for her. Mr. O'Connor, when you find the answer, I'd like to know."

He left her standing in the middle of her beautiful home, looking deeply troubled.

36

After he talked with the contact officer, Cork had to wait awhile. Finally Sergeant Gilbert Ortega came up front and escorted him back to the homicide division. There was another plainclothes detective in a corner of the office, coat off, shirt-sleeves rolled back, fingers tapping on a computer keyboard. He glanced up when Cork came in with Ortega but went right back to his work. Ortega sat down at his desk and motioned for Cork to take the other chair.

"Minnesota, is it?"

"That's right."

Ortega scratched at the small, neat mustache that lay like a pencil line on his upper lip. "Never been there. Pretty, I hear."

"You heard right."

"Officer Baker said you're interested in an investigation we conducted a few years back."

"Yes. Vic's name was Charlotte Kane."

Ortega nodded. "I remember. All the evidence pointed toward homicide but we never found a body. What's the Minnesota connection?"

"The girl's father lives there now. His daughter was murdered. As nearly as I can tell, the circumstances were similar to what happened here."

Cork handed Ortega the Duluth newspaper. The detective glanced at the photograph of Charlotte Kane then scanned the story. "I'll be a son of a bitch. Emory, take a look at this."

The other cop stood up. He was tall and had one long eyebrow that stretched over both eyes. He left his computer, came to Ortega's desk, and read over the detective's shoulder. He whistled and wrinkled his forehead. His eyebrow split in the middle. He looked at Cork. "They have a suspect?"

"A man's been charged. I work for his attorney."

"What is it you want?" Ortega asked.

"Any information you can supply about your investigation four years ago."

Ortega gave a smile, thin as his mustache. "You're interested in the father."

"Wouldn't you be?"

"It's a cold case. I didn't work it."

"Buster," Emory, the tall cop, said.

Ortega sat back and crossed his arms. "Buster Farrell was in charge of homicide back then. It was his investigation."

Cork said, "Is he still around?"

The two Pomona cops laughed.

"Oh, yeah," Emory said. "Buster's around."

"He's retired," Ortega said. "Medical situation. But he stops by. All the time."

"Think he'd mind talking to me?"

"I'm sure it would be his great pleasure," Ortega said. "Why don't I give him a call and square it. Couple things, though. I want to make a copy of that article before you go, and I'd like to have the name of the officer in charge of the investigation in Minnesota."

Buster Farrell lived in a stucco bungalow, beige with brown trim, across the street from a small park. The walk was lined with flowers, the yard edged with a perfectly clipped hedge. A sprinkler turned lazily on the lawn, spinning out water that fell in jewellike droplets on thick grass. As Cork strolled up the walk, the cop opened the screen door and came outside. He leaned on a metal cane.

"O'Connor?" he said.

Cork stepped onto the porch. "Call me Cork."

"And everybody calls me Buster."

He wasn't old. Late fifties maybe. It looked as if his body had been heavier at one time, but had recently been whittled on. Cork shook his hand and felt an unnatural quiver in the man's arm.

"Come on in. Can I offer you something to drink? How about a beer?"

Inside, the house was all warm brown tones. It was a place stuffed full of mementos—bowling and softball trophies, photographs on the shelves and walls, painted clay figures and drawings on manila paper that looked crafted by the hands of children—but there was an ordered feel to everything. Buster Farrell shuffled into the kitchen and Cork took a moment to look at a photograph on the end table next to the sofa.

"That's my wife, Georgia," Farrell said, coming back with two long-neck beers in his free hand. "She's a schoolteacher. Playing bridge this afternoon. Plays a lot of bridge these days. It's not that she likes cards so much. Since I retired, I drive her crazy. Hope you like Coors." He handed a cold bottle to Cork.

"Coors is just fine."

"Sit down, sit down."

Farrell took a big stuffed chair for himself. Cork sat on the love seat.

Farrell twisted the cap off his beer. "I remember when this stuff wasn't pasteurized and it was hard to get outside Colorado because it didn't travel well. Helluva brew back then. Gilbert said you're interested in the Charlotte Kane investigation. Didn't say why."

The story in the *Duluth News Tribune* that Cork handed over told him why.

"I'll be damned." He put the paper aside.

Cork said, "I talked with Constance Kane a couple of hours ago. She says the young woman in that news photo isn't her daughter."

Farrell shrugged. "She's the parent. She oughta know. But you could've fooled me. If it's not her, then it's her twin sister. Which she ain't got, that much I do know." He tapped the newspaper photo with his finger. "Age is wrong, but she could've lied about that. I've seen girls I couldn't guess if they were sixteen or twenty-six, you know?"

"Can you tell me about your investigation?"

"What's your interest?"

"The guy who's accused of her murder, I'm working on his defense."

"You don't think he did it?"

"No."

Farrell sipped his beer and considered Cork. "All right." He settled back in his chair. "The department got a call from the girl's parents the first night she disappeared. The chief sent a couple of uniforms out. Folks said she told them she was going to the library. Later on, we turned up some kids who said different. She was going to a party up in the foothills, planned to score some weed before she headed out. Never showed at the party. For a couple of days, our guys come up with nada. Then Long Beach P.D. finds her car abandoned in a vacant lot, blood all over the backseat. That's when I got involved. We looked at every possibility. Known drug dealers in the Pomona area. Carjackers. Her friends, acquaintances."

"Her parents?"

"Them, too. Nothing. It was the worst kind of case. A nightmare for everybody. I raised a couple kids of my own. Think I didn't worry? You say to yourself, God save 'em from all the crazies in this world, because you can't be there to protect 'em every moment. I felt for her folks, I really did. They weren't bad parents. Wasn't their fault. Just one of those things."

"The blood in her car, could it have been a smokescreen? She just ran away?"

Farrell shook his head. "It was her blood, and there was buckets of it. And near as we could tell, there was nothing for her to run from. She was smart, popular, good parents, good friends. The weed thing? Hell, kids that age, they all seem to do it. I'd say it was just a drug deal or maybe a carjacking, something that went really bad. Kid was just at the wrong place at the wrong time. I'm guessing here." He picked up the newspaper and looked a long time at the photo. "Like seeing a ghost." He handed it back to Cork. "Whether it's her or not, I don't suppose it matters much. Either way she's dead for sure this time. Ready for another beer?"

"No, thanks. Anything else worth knowing?"

"You like her old man for it, don't you? It's what I'd be thinking if I were you. He's the constant in the whole equation. But I wouldn't be too quick to jump to any conclusions." He pointed at the paper. "That kind of tragedy, it lays folks open. You get a good look inside. I don't know what Dr. Kane was like out there, but here all I saw was genuine grief. Doesn't mean absolutely he didn't do it. No matter how long you've been in this business, you can still be fooled. I'd just be reserved in my judgment is all I'm saying."

"Thanks. Appreciate your perspective." Cork finished his beer in a couple of long swallows and stood up. "I should be going."

"One more thing."

"What?"

"Two Charlottes. If I were you, I'd think about the fact that Kane's a plastic surgeon. From what I learned in my investigation, one of the best. That ought to suggest something to you."

"It already has."

Buster Farrell walked him to the door.

"Miss it?" Farrell asked.

"What?"

"Being a cop."

"Never said I was."

"You were. I can tell." Farrell stared hard into his eyes. "Yeah, you miss it." He gave Cork a quivering, parting handshake. "Me, too."

37

CORK BOUGHT A U.S. ROAD ATLAS at a 7-Eleven on Murchison Avenue, then went back to the restaurant where he'd had breakfast. He ordered coffee and a BLT and opened the atlas. He located Dansig, Iowa, a small dot on State 26 just south of the Minnesota border. He wanted very much to talk with Glory Kane. Or Cordelia Diller, if that was what she was calling herself now.

When he returned to his motel room, he realized it was dinnertime back in Minnesota. He called home and was surprised by the voice that answered.

"Rose?"

"Hello, Cork."

"Did you drop by for dinner?"

"Actually, I'm preparing it. Ellie Gruber came back today. She's at the rectory now, so . . . I'm back here."

Back here, Cork thought. *Why didn't she say back home?*

"That's good, I suppose."

"Of course, it's good." Her voice brightened, the chipper tone a little forced. "Have you talked with Glory?"

"I tried to call," he said. "All I got was a busy signal."

"That's probably because of the tornadoes. Several last night in southern Minnesota, northern Iowa. Knocked out power all over."

"That probably explains it. Is Jo around?"

"She's coming into the kitchen right now."

"Good to have you home, Rose."

"Thanks, Cork."

A few moments of dead at the other end, then Jo came on the line.

"Cork?"

"Hi, kiddo. Full house again."

"Not entirely. You're not here. How'd it go today? Did you find out anything?"

"Fletcher Kane's a lot more complicated than I imagined. I don't know what to think now."

"What about Charlotte?"

"I believe there were two, and one of them may well have been manufactured." He told her the details of his conversations that day. "I spoke with Hadlestadt again. He said that with the amazing advances in facial bone reconstruction these days, it's not at all outside the realm of possibility. Highly unethical, but not illegal."

"He created a look-alike?" she said.

"It's possible he simply stumbled onto a girl who looked exactly like Charlotte, but what are the odds of that? Given that he was a desperately unhappy man, I think it's more likely that he used his skill as a surgeon to bring his daughter back."

"My god, that's so grotesque."

"I'll know more after I've talked to Glory. Or Cordelia. Christ, is anybody who they seem? How are things there?"

"No more stalkers, thank God."

"Don't anyone get lax."

"Don't worry. By the way, I've heard that Nestor Cole may withdraw the charges against Solemn."

"Why?"

"Word of your suspicions about Fletcher Kane's relationship with Charlotte leaked out."

"Cy Borkmann," Cork said. "Damn, he never could keep his mouth shut."

"What's being said about Fletcher isn't pretty. I think our county attorney is afraid the waters may be too muddy now for him to be sure of a conviction."

"Well that's something anyway." He took a deep breath. "Good having Rose back?"

Jo was quiet, then said, "We'll talk when you're home."

"All right," he said. "Love you."

"Love you, too."

He hung up, wondering why Jo was reluctant to speak about Rose.

He was getting hungry, thinking of dinner though it was still early, coast time. He walked to the window and looked out. A few ragged palm trees, too many cars, a dirty haze. A megalopolis full of people, and he still felt alone. He knew it was nothing compared to the loneliness of Solemn Winter Moon.

Cork walked back to the bed, sat down, picked up the phone and called Rosemount. This time he got through. The connection was scratchy, a sound like the crackle of tinder-dry brush. He asked for Cordelia Diller. In a minute, the woman he knew as Glory Kane was on the line.

"Glory?"

"It's Cordelia, actually."

"What's with the new name?"

"Not new. Old. Before Glory. Long before Glory."

"So why Glory?"

"We need to talk. Where are you?"

"California."

She hesitated. "Then you know about Charlotte."

"Not everything. How about you tell me?"

"I'd rather not talk over the phone."

"All right. I'm flying back to the Twin Cities tomorrow. I'll drive down to Rosemount as soon as I've landed."

She thought it over. "All right."

"I should be there midafternoon sometime."

"Cork?"

"Yes?"

"You think Fletcher is a good man?"

"People here seem to think so."

The dry brush sound filled the empty line for a moment. Then she said, "I used to think so, too."

38

CORK PICKED UP HIS BRONCO at the Twin Cities airport and headed south. In the bluff country near the Iowa border, he began to see the effects of the storms that had swept through two nights earlier. Great trees lay uprooted. High water had left tangled debris in the undergrowth along stream banks. Road signs hung bent on their metal frames. This was the Midwest and it was that season.

Cork drove through Dansig in the late afternoon. Near the south end of town, a warehouse stood with its walls ripped open, the corrugated siding broken and twisted. A mile farther, he encountered a sign, temporarily repaired with a thick binding of silver duct tape, that pointed east down a secondary road toward Rosemount Retreat Center. The road was a long, narrow lane bordered on both sides by windrows of tall western yews. In several places, a fallen tree lay in freshly cut sections along the shoulder. As Cork neared the Center, he heard a chain saw droning in the humid air.

Rosemount Retreat Center stood on a wooded bluff high above the Mississippi River. The buildings were all dark red brick and looked as if they'd been there since the Civil War. The trunk of a large oak near the entrance had split. Half the tree lay on the ground. The white wood deep at the heart was visible in a long gaping wound. Much of the lawn was littered with broken branches. In several buildings, the glass was gone from windows and temporary covers of plywood filled the empty panes. Cork parked in the lot in front of the main building where a green sign indicated OFFICE. He got out and stood a moment in the summer heat. The sound of the chain saw had ceased.

Inside, the air was cool. Cork told the woman at the reception desk that he was there to see Cordelia Diller and that he was expected. The receptionist made a call, told him it would be a few minutes, and asked if he would like to have a seat. He'd been driving for three hours, so he stood.

When she came in the front door, he barely recognized the woman he'd known as Glory Kane. Her hair was cut severely short and was no longer black but a soft auburn. She wore no makeup. She was dressed in a simple white blouse, jeans, and sneakers. A small black purse hung over her shoulder. She'd always been slender, but she looked even slighter now. She seemed to have lost something of herself, though it wasn't necessarily weight that was missing.

"Hello, Cork." She gave him her hand.

"Cordelia," he said.

"Let's walk."

He followed her outside, down a path that ran toward the river.

"Cordelia Diller?" he said.

She shrugged. "It's what's on the birth certificate. I changed it to Ruby James when I moved to Las Vegas."

"And Glory Kane?"

"That was Fletcher's idea. When I became his sister."

"Are you related to Fletcher at all?"

"No. His real sister died shortly after she was born. Some kind of complication related to her mother's pregnancy. There." She pointed to a wooden bench perched at the edge of the bluff. They sat down. She opened her purse, took out a pack of Pall Malls, and lit a cigarette. "Still trying to quit," she said, blowing smoke. "One more thing I'm working on changing."

The humidity felt oppressive to Cork. The smell here was different from up north. There was an odor of desiccation, of dead leaves and wet earth and slow rot. He missed the fresh scent of pines and the clean air as it came off Iron Lake.

"You can hardly breathe," she said, as if she'd read his thoughts. "That's how I felt every day I lived here."

"When was that?"

"A long time ago." She tapped her ash. "That's how I knew

about Rosemount. I was born in Iowa. A town called Winterset. You know Winterset?"

"No."

"Birthplace of John Wayne. He changed his name, too." She took a long draw on her cigarette and appraised Cork through the veil of her exhaled smoke. "Rose says you think Fletcher might have had something to do with Charlotte's murder. I don't know you, but Rose thinks a lot of you, and I think a lot of Rose. So I'm going to set you straight on a few things. I hope it does some good."

She fell silent. She was quiet for so long Cork began to think she'd changed her mind. Somewhere on the other side of the buildings, the chain saw started up again and droned on like one crazy cicada.

"It was a long and, believe me, unpleasant road from Winterset to Las Vegas. It doesn't matter how it happened, but I ended up supplying very rich men with very young, pretty, powerless girls. The streets of Vegas are full of runaways, kids thinking that with all that money floating around, there has to be a way to grab a little for themselves. It's the lights, too, and the sun. The kids, they're just waiting to be preyed on."

"Charlotte was one of them?"

"That wasn't her real name, of course. She told me it was Maria, but I'm almost sure that was a lie. She was the brightest. The one with the most promise. She had class. I guess I saw some of myself in her. I don't know what was true about her. She told me she was from St. Louis, that she'd gone to Catholic school there. Wealthy family, she said, but she hated them. Her mother especially. Her father started having sex with her when she was pretty young, and the mother turned her back on it. That part I'd guess is true. Old story with a lot of the street kids.

"She became the exclusive property of a regular client, a man named Frankie Vicente, well connected with the mob. He treated her special. Bought her things. Maria fell in love with the bastard. As much as a fifteen-year-old can fall in love with anybody. I tried to warn her, told her to be careful. I'd known Frankie a long time. He was handsome, charming. But he wasn't a man capable of love. If you crossed him, he became a sadistic animal."

She closed her eyes. The cigarette burned so low between her fingers Cork thought it would sear her. She must have felt the heat. She let it fall into the grass and crushed the ember under the toe of her shoe. Immediately, she reached into her purse for the pack of Pall Malls.

"Eventually Maria learned the truth about him. The hard way. She tried to get away. Ended up on the street in Phoenix. I don't know how he tracked her there, but he did. Sent his goons. They brought her back. Frankie beat her. Broke her ribs. Nobody leaves Frankie unless Frankie wants them to leave."

"She didn't go to the police? You didn't?"

She looked at him for a moment with contempt, then understood. "That's right. You were a cop. Well, the cops in Las Vegas are different. Frankie and his people own them."

She lit another cigarette and clouded the air in front of her.

Then suddenly the tears began to flow. She wiped at them with her free hand.

"Have you ever been scared, Cork? Desperate? I mean so scared and so desperate that you couldn't see any way out of something? You know how many times I thought about killing myself, and maybe Maria, too, just ending the misery for both of us. But I was too weak for that. So I mostly kept myself in an alcoholic stupor and let things happen.

"Then Maria did something that angered him. I don't even know what. He hit her with a whiskey bottle, the son of a bitch. Crushed her cheekbone, disfigured her horribly. Of course, he paid for the best plastic surgeon money could buy."

"Fletcher Kane," Cork said.

"Yes, Fletcher. Frankie told me to take care of it. Maria and I flew to California several times to consult with him. He was wonderful. Patient, kind. But hurt, too, you could see it. Over time, seeing him, listening to him, I trusted him. He was such a funny-looking man, but he seemed to have a good heart."

"You still think that?"

"Let me finish. Away from Vegas, I began to think about going back to that life, and I didn't like the idea. I didn't like the idea of Maria going back to Frankie. I didn't know what to do. I finally confessed everything to Fletcher, and he suggested a way he could help. He used a computer to show us how Maria would look after he was finished with the surgery. It was different, but still nice. He said if we changed her hair color, too, Frankie would never recognize her. And he said he would help find a place for us to hide.

"I know men. I knew that there was more to all this than his good heart. I didn't care. It was a way out. Maria, she finally understood about Frankie, and she was scared of him. So we agreed. The whole process took several months. We rented a condo not far from the clinic. Frankie never once visited. The son of a bitch didn't want to see her until she was pretty again.

"After the procedure, Fletcher set us up in another place, in Ventura. He let a few weeks pass so no one would connect our disappearance to him, then we all moved to Aurora."

"Did you know he'd altered Maria to look like his own daughter?"

"I knew he'd had a daughter who died. I didn't know what she looked like until we'd come to Aurora and I found some photographs he kept in a box."

"Did you know how she died?"

"Not until Rose told me that you'd gone to California and why."

"What did you think when you found out?"

"That you were wrong in believing Fletcher might have been responsible for Maria's death. Fletcher is not an easy man, but he's no murderer."

"How do you know?"

"He was with me the night Maria went missing. I was drunk, but not enough to pass out. We both went to bed around two. But you probably knew that from my statement. You just didn't believe it."

That was true.

"Did Maria know about Charlotte?" Cork asked.

"No. Fletcher didn't want her to know. I think he was concerned that she wouldn't understand or that it might scare her. I don't know, maybe he was afraid of letting her in on the secret, afraid she might tell someone."

"How did you feel about him using her that way?"

"We'd been used by men in a lot of ways, Maria and me. It didn't seem so terrible. At first. We all tried to be the family Fletcher imagined. But he didn't want Maria just to look like his daughter. He wanted her to be Charlotte. He told her how to dress, how to talk, what to say. He tried to get her to do things with him, the kind of things he'd done with his daughter. Biking, skiing, tennis. He was always correcting her. Sometimes he got short with her. She had a large birthmark on her hip, shaped a little like Florida. He wouldn't let her wear a bikini or a high-cut suit because it might show. He even suggested she have it removed, because Charlotte didn't have a blemish like that. He never understood, or maybe just never accepted that no matter how Maria looked and acted, she would never be Charlotte, and he didn't know how to love who she was. She understood that, I think, even though she didn't understand why." She shook her head. "Maria tried so hard to please him. She needed to be loved. Eventually she tried to get him to love her in the same way her father had. She came on to Fletcher, tried to use her body to get his love."

She closed her eyes, as if the memory or the talking exhausted her.

"What happened?"

"Fletcher was disgusted. Maria was confused. I was drunk. After that, he kept her at arm's length, but he watched her all the time. He got a little scary that way. Maria began to say she felt like a prisoner. The silence was suffocating. Toward the end, Maria was pretty messed up. I wanted her to see someone. You know, a therapist or something. But Fletcher wouldn't allow it. Sometimes I thought about taking Maria and leaving, but I had no money. And I was scared to death that if we left, Frankie would find us. Or Fletcher. He'd become so strange. Disgusted with Maria, but desperate not to lose her."

"Fletcher never did anything about Maria's advances?"

"You mean sleep with her? No. Believe me, I would have known. Maybe I wouldn't have done anything about it, but I would have known."

"Why did you stay? I mean after Maria disappeared?"

"I hoped she might turn up at the door one day, and I wanted to be there when that happened. I never had a daughter, and I wasn't any good at playing mother, but I cared about Maria. Once she was buried, there was no reason to stay. Fletcher was actually quite generous. Money is something I don't have to worry about now." She stood up and looked back at the Center.

"Rosemount is for women considering a religious life. You've got to be wondering how someone like me could ever think they might be able to serve God."

"I'm not thinking that at all," Cork said.

She dropped her cigarette and crushed it out. "I thought that Fletcher was offering a chance at a new life for me, for Maria. I thought that maybe we could all escape our pasts. I was wrong. There's only one way to start a new life, and that's by facing the truth. I don't know what's ahead. God hasn't shown me yet, but for the first time in my life, I'm not afraid."

She couldn't seem to decide whether to sit or stand. She began to pace.

"I've told you all of this because I owe Fletcher something. In his way, he tried to help. I'm hoping that now you know the truth, you'll be a little more compassionate toward him. I pray for him all the time. I know what it is to be lost. I think of him alone in that big, awful house, and I'm sorry for him. If it hadn't been for Rose, I never would have made it through all that."

"Did you tell Rose the truth?"

"I told her nothing. I wanted to. I knew she wouldn't judge me, but I just couldn't do it. She knew something was terribly wrong, though, and she did her best to be a friend. She helped me to believe there's good in me. And the sisters here, they're helping me, too. I know I still have a long way to go, but I believe I'm on the right road." She looked at Cork. "I don't know if Solemn Winter Moon is responsible for Maria's death—"

"He isn't."

"Either way, I'll pray for him. It's the best I can do."

Cork waited a bit to see if there was something more she wanted to say, but apparently there wasn't. He had the information he'd come for, so he got up to leave.

"I think I'll stay here awhile," Cordelia Diller said. "Give my love to Rose."

Cork walked to his Bronco. When he looked back, she was sitting on the bench again, a thin ribbon of cigarette smoke unraveling in the air above her.

He drove north for a couple of hours but was too tired to drive the final 250 miles to Aurora. He stopped in Red Wing and called Jo from a Super 8 motel to let her know he'd be home the next day. He ate a pretty good burger at a place called the Bierstube and drank a couple of cold Leinenkugels. It was dark by the time he came out, but he wasn't ready to turn in. He drove to a park on the Mississippi River, got out, and walked.

It was a clear night, the sky full of stars, the moon not yet risen. The river was a wide sweep of black with the far side lost in darkness. Cork stood in the quiet under a cottonwood on the bank.

Even after he'd talked to Cordelia Diller, he'd considered the possibility that Kane might have killed the second Charlotte because he couldn't control her, couldn't make of her the daughter he'd tried to resurrect. But unless Cordelia Diller had lied—and Cork didn't believe she had—Fletcher Kane had an airtight alibi. So Cork had to accept that he'd been wrong in his thinking. Although the manner in which the man had used Maria was unconscionable, of the particular sins Cork had ascribed to him, Kane was innocent.

He thought about the desperate minutes on the cold ice long ago in January when he'd been lost in the whiteout and the gray figure that had kept itself just out of his vision and reach had led him to the safety of his snowmobile. He'd sensed that it was Charlotte, and at the same time, it wasn't Charlotte. Now he understood. Somehow, the girl Maria had reached out to him, saved him. But why? Because he'd tried to save her, and like her had become lost? Or was it that she wanted him to find her killer, that she simply wanted justice?

If that was the case, there was a problem, because he had no suspects left. He believed the killer wasn't Fletcher Kane, nor was it Arne Soderberg, or Lyla. He still believed in Solemn's innocence. The crime was old and cold now. Cork wondered if this was one that would go unsolved. Sometimes you just had to accept it.

But not when the dead reached out to you. Not when you knew they demanded justice.

Far to the east, the moon lay just below the horizon, and its glow lit the sky like a distant fire. All around Cork, the night was still black.

39

HE WAS ON THE ROAD AT DAWN, and hit the outskirts of Aurora by eleven. The first thing he did was go to Jo's office. He closed the door behind him and she stepped into his arms.

"It feels like it's been forever," he said, drinking in the scent of her, Dentyne and the faint suggestion of Sunflower cologne.

"You look tired," she said.

"Strange motel rooms, hard beds."

"But you're home now."

"How's Solemn?"

"I haven't seen him since he left the jail. I talked with Dot yesterday. She's changed her telephone number. Too many people calling, saying cruel things. Some threats. Even if the charges are dropped, it won't make Solemn innocent in people's thinking. Are you going to tell Cy Borkmann what you found out about Fletcher?"

"Enough to clear his name." He laid his cheek on her shoulder. "You were right, Jo. If you're not careful, all you see in someone is what you're looking for. I probably ought to apologize."

She took his head in her hands and kissed him. Her lips were the best thing he'd tasted in days.

"You're a pretty smart woman, you know?" he told her.

She laughed gently. "I've been trying to make that clear to you for years."

He disentangled himself from her embrace. "I'm going to see Fletcher."

"Good luck, sweetheart."

Blue thunderheads climbed quickly out of the west as Cork turned onto North Point Road. He drove slowly past the Soderberg house. Lyla's PT Cruiser was there, as well as Marion Griswold's mud-spattered jeep. Arne's BMW was gone. Cork had heard that Soderberg had taken up residence in the family cabin on Lake Vermilion and had gone back to work for Big Mike. He wondered about Tiffany, how she was doing in all this.

As he pulled up to the old Parrant estate and got out, thunder rolled out of the distance. The wind picked up, and Cork could smell the coming storm in the air. It was a good smell, one that in his experience promised something cleansing and refreshing.

He knocked on the door. Almost immediately, Fletcher Kane opened it. He greeted Cork with an angry look and the barrel of a Remington shotgun.

"You've got to be the world's stupidest man," Kane said.

The Remington scared Cork. "I'm going to turn around right now, Fletcher, and just walk away."

"It's that easy for you? I don't think so."

Cork decided not to move. "I talked with Constance. And with Glory down in Iowa."

"What gives you the right to pry into my life?"

"I know the truth now. And I'm sorry."

"Sorry?" Kane said. "Sorry for what?"

"That a lot of bad things happened to you that you didn't deserve. I'm sorry that Charlotte's dead. And Maria. I'm sorry that I thought you might have been responsible, because I know now how much you loved your daughters."

"Daughters?" He frowned. "There was only Charlotte."

"I know you would never have done anything to hurt her."

The blue-black clouds had gobbled up the sun. The deep boom of thunder shook the porch. Cork waited. Kane stared at him. The black eye at the end of the rifle barrel stared at him, too. Cork tried to think if there was anything more he should say.

"Get out of here," Kane finally spit.

Without another word, Cork backed off the porch and down the stairs. He moved at an even pace, never taking his eyes off Kane. Big drops of rain thudded onto the ground around him and thumped against his skin. By the time he reached his Bronco, the rain was a torrent. He got in, wiped the drips from his face, and carefully left the drive. The whole time, Fletcher Kane followed him with the shotgun. When he was safely away, Cork finally let himself breathe.

Cork headed north out of town. The storm passed quickly, leaving a steaming vapor rising from the pavement. He turned onto a graveled county road and continued for several miles before he came to the place where the split trunk birch marked the trail to Henry Meloux's cabin. He left the Bronco parked at the side of the road and began the long walk in.

Half an hour later, he crossed the ruddy water of Wine Creek. On the far side, the air was still. Shafts of sunlight broke through the high branches like boards shoved down out of heaven to create a sanctuary. Whenever Cork entered the deep woods, he knew he was stepping into a sacred place. This was much the same way he'd felt as a child entering the church. It was not just the peace, although it was truly peaceful. It was more than the incense of evergreen all around him and the choir of birds in the branches above and the cushion of the pine needles like a thick carpet under his feet. There was a spirit here so huge it humbled the human heart. The Anishinaabe blood that ran through his body might have been the reason Cork felt this way, but he didn't think so. He believed that any man or woman who walked there without malice would feel the same.

He found Henry Meloux sitting on the ground, cross-legged, in the sunlight in front of his cabin. Walleye, his old yellow hound, lay in the shade not far away. Meloux held a small pine branch in one hand and a Green River knife in the other. He was carefully working the wood with the sharp blade. Walleye slowly got to his feet and shuffled out to meet the visitor, but Meloux seemed not to notice.

"Anin, Henry," Cork said, using the traditional Ojibwe greeting.

"Anin, Corcoran O'Connor," the old man said. He lifted the piece of whittled wood and squinted along its length. "I have been thinking this morning about your grandmother." With the tip of his knife, Meloux pointed to a place near him on the ground, and Cork sat down. The old Mide returned to his woodworking. "She was a beautiful woman. When I was a young man, I thought that someday she would be my wife."

This was news to Cork. Grandmother Dilsey had never spoken of it nor, until this moment, had Meloux.

"But one day a man with hair the color of fox fur came and opened a school on the reservation. His hair was not the only thing about him like a fox. He stole your grandmother's heart. If I had not already chosen to become a member of the Grand Medicine Society and to understand the way Kitchimanidoo means for his children to live together well upon the earth, I might have been filled with hatred for this man. I might have killed him in anger." The old man glanced at Cork, and a smile touched his lips. "Your grandfather was a lucky man."

"You're talking about anger, Henry. You know about Fletcher Kane?"

"I know."

"Is Solemn here?"

"Not here."

"But you know where."

Meloux cut a shaving from the stick.

"I'd like to talk to him," Cork said.

The old Mide lowered his hands and set the knife and the piece of wood in the dirt. "I will have to think about this." He uncrossed his legs and pushed to his feet. He began down the path toward the lake, and Cork followed.

They threaded their way between two high boulders and on the other side came to the end of Crow Point, where Meloux often set an open fire and burned sage and cedar. Iron Lake spread away from the rocky shoreline in a glitter of reflected sunlight. Meloux sat on a maple stump next to the blackened stone circle. Cork sat on the ground. The old man drew a tobacco pouch from the pocket of his worn flannel shirt. He offered a bit toward the four directions of the earth, then he took papers from the same pocket and rolled himself a cigarette.

He handed the pouch and the papers to Cork. They smoked a long time in silence. Cork had never known Henry Meloux to hurry a thing.

"What do you think?" the old Mide said at long last.

About what, Cork had no idea. He gave the question due consideration, however, and finally replied, "The more I think, the more confused I become."

Meloux nodded once and smoked some more. "What do you feel?" he asked.

"That I've been tricked."

"Who is the trickster?"

"I guess, Henry, that would have to be me. I let my feelings about Fletcher Kane get in the way of understanding things. Maybe I've misjudged everything because of it."

Henry Meloux regarded the last of his hand-rolled cigarette. "The head confuses," he said. "The heart misleads."

"So what's the answer?"

"There is a place between the two, a place of knowing."

"How do I get there, Henry?"

Meloux threw the butt of his cigarette into the ash inside the stone circle. "Follow the blood," he said. He stood up and began to walk away.

Cork had no idea what the old man's final words meant, but it was obvious that was all Meloux was going to say. About Solemn's whereabouts, he had evidently decided to remain silent.

Cork bid Meloux farewell at the cabin, scratched Walleye's head in parting, and started back. He was a little disappointed that he hadn't exactly accomplished what he'd come there for. He hadn't been able to talk with Solemn.

He followed the path through the woods and came again to the stream. He started to cross but in the middle stopped so abruptly that he slipped off the stone onto which he'd just stepped. He splashed into the calf-deep, red-hued, iron-rich water. Although the whites called it Wine Creek, Cork remembered that long ago, Henry Meloux had told him the Anishinaabeg had another name for the stream. They called it *miskwi*. The translation in English would be *blood*.

40

FOLLOW THE BLOOD, Meloux had said. A clever instruction? A test perhaps?

The stream flowed into Iron Lake a few hundred yards to the west. Cork quickly checked that stretch, found nothing, and turned back. For an hour, he followed the stream east, deep into the woods. The water coursed among low hills, through stands of spruce, pine, and poplar, raising a ruddy foam as it funneled between close rock walls and spilled into deep, sanguine pools.

He came at last to a long ridge of gray rock that lay before him like a wall. The stream seemed to issue from the slope itself directly out of a blackberry thicket that grew along the base of the ridge for as far as Cork could see. He walked left, then right, looking for a path through the brambles, but he saw no way. Eventually, he lowered himself into the water and began to crawl along the streambed, pushing his way among the thorns. The vines caught his clothing, snagged his hair, scratched his skin. He'd disturbed a horde of mosquitoes that added their own torment on top of the claws of the blackberry vines. The streambed was littered with sharp rocks that cut his hands as he dragged himself forward. At last, he cleared the thicket and stood up, dripping wet.

He faced a gap in the ridge where the stream had cut a narrow corridor. The breach, barely wide enough for a man to slip through, ran at an angle and twisted out of sight. Cork turned himself sideways and squeezed between the rocks, following the water. After a few minutes of slow progress, he came out on the other side of the ridge and found himself in a place he'd never been but recognized immediately.

The meadow was circular, contained within the hollow of a bowl created by a ring of granite ridges like the one through which he'd just passed. The hollow was edged with poplars and aspen and the ground was covered with meadow grass, tall and silky. Along the banks of the stream grew cattails. Not far away stood a makeshift sweat lodge, a frame of bowed willow saplings lashed together and covered with a tarp. Almost dead center in the hollow, a hundred yards from where Cork stood, a single rock rose out of the earth, a gray pinnacle far taller than a man. Seated in the grass at the base of the rock was Solemn Winter Moon.

Solemn watched Cork approach, and a crescent moon grin broke out across his dark face. "What happened to you? Meet up with a cubbing she-bear?"

"A blackberry thicket," Cork said.

Solemn was shirtless. He wore only khaki shorts. His boots and socks sat on the ground off to one side. His long hair was uncombed, wild. It had become a net that had captured much of what traveled on the current of the breeze. Dandelion fluff, a gossamer thread spun by a spider, a yellow dusting of pollen. Solemn seemed a natural part of the place he'd come to. On the ground beside him lay the small black Bible that Mal had given him in jail.

"Mind if I rob you of your solitude?" Cork asked.

"Nothing here belongs to me. That includes the solitude. Sit down."

The sun was almost directly overhead, but the air in the meadow felt cool. "This is where you met Him, isn't it?"

"He walked out of the trees over there." Solemn pointed toward the east, to a place near where the stream flowed into the hollow.

"Were you hoping He'd come again?"

Solemn smiled. "Yeah."

"Still hoping?"

"Not anymore."

"Lost hope?"

Solemn took a good look at Cork. "You ought to wash that blood off. Maybe have a drink while you're at it. You look thirsty."

"I am."

"The creek's clean," Solemn said. "It's what I drink."

Cork got up and went to the stream. He knelt, cupped his hands, and drank. The water refreshed him.

"I'm glad you dropped out of sight," Cork said as he cleaned his wounds. "Safer."

"I didn't drop out of sight. I ran. I came to Henry because I was scared."

"Fear is a good thing sometimes. Got an angry crowd back there in Aurora."

"I wasn't afraid of the people who think I fooled them. I was afraid I'd fooled myself."

"Did Henry help?"

"He led me back here. We built that sweat lodge, and Henry did what he could to bring me back to harmony. After he'd finished, he told me I wasn't done, that I needed to stay awhile, alone. I asked him if he thought Jesus would come again. You know what he said? He said, 'Expect nothing, because nothing is what's going to come.' " Solemn laughed quietly. "That Henry. He always means exactly what he says, but it's hard to figure sometimes."

Cork finished at the creek and sat down beside Solemn at the rock. "Jesus didn't come, did he?"

"Nothing came. Exactly what Henry said. But I know what he meant now. Nothing was going to come because it was already here. I had it all along. You know what it is, Cork?"

"No."

"That's interesting because the last time you visited me at Sam's cabin you told me exactly what it is. Certainty. I knew God. Or Kitchimanidoo, or whatever name we give to the spirit that binds all things together. I *knew.* And after that nothing else mattered. Not the old anger, the old hurts. Not yesterday or tomorrow. I didn't have to think about it, try to understand it. I just knew. It doesn't matter whether Jesus walked out of those trees or if I dreamed Him. What I received was a true thing. I know that God is."

He smiled up at the sky, and his face glowed as if he'd swallowed the sun. He looked at Cork and saw the doubt there.

"You're thinking, why him? Why Solemn Winter Moon? I wondered the same thing. I traveled a hard, dark road, but what I was given didn't come because of that journey. It wasn't something I earned from suffering. It was a gift, a blessing like the rain. I wish everyone could know that." He reached out and put his hand over Cork's heart. "I wish you could."

A breeze came up and stirred the grass in the meadow. Solemn removed his hand, and for a moment, Cork felt as if he were going to fall apart, as if all that had held him together was Solemn's touch.

"You came a long way to find me," Solemn said.

"To warn you." Cork told him about Fletcher Kane. Everything he now knew.

Solemn nodded. "There's a man's been walking a hard, dark road, himself."

"For a while, you need to stay here or with Meloux, until we've figured a way to deal with Kane."

"Why are you so afraid for me?"

"I just told you."

"I guess I mean why are you so afraid of me dying?" He opened his arms toward the hollow. "Don't you feel it here? The source? We come from a great heart, Cork. The heart of Kitchimanidoo, the heart of God. And we just go back into that heart. There's nothing to be afraid of."

"When you're looking down the barrel of a shotgun, Solemn, it's hard to hold to that philosophy. Believe me, I know."

"Maybe you should stay here awhile."

"I've done what I came for. I just hope it's done some good."

"I hadn't thought about leaving."

"Good."

"Thank you, Cork. Thanks for everything."

Cork stood to leave. He looked down at Solemn. "I wish Sam could see you now."

"Who says he can't?" Solemn pointed toward a thick stand of poplar at the base of the western ridge. "A couple of hundred yards south of the creek. See that break in the trees? There's a path over the ridge. Unless you have a hankering for another go at the blackberry thicket."

"Once is enough," Cork said.

Cork found the trail through the trees. As he topped the ridge, he looked back. Solemn hadn't moved. Nor would he. The place he'd come to was as good as any man could hope for, and far better than most would ever know.

41

CORK KNEW HE'D LEFT a remarkable young man in the hollow where the Blood ran. Solemn had taken hold of something—or something had taken hold of him—that had changed him profoundly. Cork, who struggled at every step trying to understand himself and the world, envied Solemn. Yet, as he left the woods and drove toward Aurora, there was a dark voice deep inside him that whispered, *It won't last. Back among men, in a little while, he'll be like us again.*

His children were happy to see him home, but no happier than he was to be there and to be with them again. He held them each in his arms. Lithe Jenny. Annie solid as a stone. Stevie, who could not keep his little body still. Cork closed his eyes and knew that to lose a child would be the cruelest blow. Although his head told him prayer was pointless, his heart couldn't help whispering, "Please, God, keep them safe, my children."

The house smelled of Rose's cooking. Pork roast with a citrus marinade, new potatoes, butter squash, and homemade applesauce. A welcome-home meal, she told him when he stepped into the kitchen. She kissed his cheek and smiled, but she was unable to hide from him that she stood in the shadow of some private sadness.

"It's good to be home again," he said.

"Wash up," she replied, turning away and wiping her hands on her apron. "Dinner's almost ready. Oh, and you got a call. A man named Boomer. He said to call him back."

Boomer Grabowski had promised to call as soon as he returned to Chicago, in case Cork still wanted Mal Thorne investigated. Cork considered whether that was necessary now. He'd identified Charlotte's lover, and it wasn't the priest. Not that he'd ever really believed it was, but he'd wanted to be thorough. And still did. So he figured he'd call Boomer after dinner.

As it turned out, he never got the chance. But it would have been far better if he had.

In the stillness just before sunset, he sat with Jo, rocking in the porch swing. Jenny had gone on a date with her boyfriend, Sean. Annie was at the park with Ilsa Hardesty, practicing their pitches. She promised to be home before dark. Stevie rode his bike up and down Gooseberry Lane making a sound like a race car. Rose was taking a walk by herself, something she did regularly now.

"She's quiet," Cork said.

"She's in love. She believes she's hiding it, but even the girls can see."

"Has she talked to you?"

"No."

"What will she do?"

"What can she do? He's a priest. He's already taken."

"Sometimes priests leave the church. Sometimes because of a woman. Do you think Mal feels the same way about her?"

"I don't know." She watched Stevie zip past on the street, his little legs pedaling as if he were being chased by a devil. "I keep thinking back to Memorial Day. I knew then and didn't do anything."

"What could you have done?" He squeezed her hand. "It's not your fault, Jo. When two hearts connect, there's not a lot anybody can do about it. We both know that."

"She's always wanted to be in love, to find someone to care about and who would care about her. Why did it have to be like this? Why is love always so painful?"

"It's not. Not always, anyway."

"Oh, Cork, my heart's breaking for her."

As the sun set, the street dropped into the shadow of approaching night. Cork stood up to call Stevie in, but before he did, he glanced down at Jo and said, "Aren't you supposed to put all this in God's hands?"

Jo shook her head. "I don't know. Sometimes He seems clueless."

Cork guided Stevie through bedtime preparations and read to him awhile. He heard the doorbell ring. A few minutes later, Jo came upstairs and parked herself in the doorway to Stevie's room. She looked concerned.

"What's up?" Cork asked quietly. Stevie's eyes had just drifted closed.

Jo motioned him into the hallway.

"Dot Winter Moon is downstairs. She's worried about Solemn."

Dorothy Winter Moon sat on the couch in the living room. Her face was shiny with perspiration. Errant strands of her hair were pasted to her forehead like black cracks.

"What's going on?" Cork said.

"Solemn's gone," Dot said.

"I know. He's up in the woods near Meloux's place."

"He came back," Dot said.

Cork sat down in the easy chair. "Tell me what happened."

"He came home late this afternoon, showered, changed his clothes. Then he talked to me, like we used to talk."

"What about?" Cork asked.

"About Sam, about a lot of things in the past. I told him I was fixing pork chops for dinner. He said he had an errand to run, then he'd be back to eat. He kissed me on the cheek. I can't remember the last time he kissed me." She was a tough woman, but she was near tears. "He never came back."

"Did he say where he was going?" Cork asked.

"To the place where two hard roads come together. I don't know where that is."

Cork said, "Did you check Sam's cabin?"

"Yes. He wasn't there. And I called everyone on the rez. Nobody's seen him. I checked the bars he used to go to. Then I came into town hoping he might have come by here."

"I'll bet he went back to Henry Meloux's place," Cork said. "I'm sure he's fine, Dot."

"You think so?"

"I'd call Henry, but he's got no phone."

Jo said, "Cork, would you be willing to drive out and check?"

Dot looked at Cork, and her almond eyes were full of hope.

"All right."

"Thanks," Dot said. "Thanks a million, Cork."

Rose walked in the front door. She took in the scene, and she said, "Are you all right, Dot?"

Dot shrugged. "My boy's missing."

"Cork thinks he's with Henry Meloux," Jo said. "He's going out to check."

Rose put her hand gently on Dot's shoulder. "It could be a long wait. Why don't I fix some coffee?"

"Damn, that would be nice," Dot said.

Rose glanced at Jo, saw the look of concern on her face, and suggested, "Why don't you come into the kitchen with me, Dot. I could use the company."

After the two women had left the room, Jo turned to Cork.

"Do you really think he's at Meloux's?"

"I hope so, but there's one place I'm going to check first."

"You think he's gone to see Kane?"

"I do."

"You'll be careful?"

"Of course."

Along the two blocks of the central business district everything except the Pinewood Broiler and the Perkins had closed for the night. There were still vehicles on the streets, kids on summer break with nothing better to do, tourists looking for a nightlife that didn't exist in Aurora.

He turned onto North Point Road and drove past the Soderberg house, which appeared deserted. The moon was just rising, a yellow blister festering on the dark horizon.

No lights were on at the old Parrant estate either. He hoped that meant Fletcher Kane had gone to bed. When he was near enough to see things more clearly, however, his uneasiness crystallized into fear. Solemn's black Ranger pickup sat in the circular drive.

Cork parked behind the Ranger and got out. In the light that leaked from the blistered moon, he saw that the truck was empty. A night wind came off the lake, rustling the tall bushes next to the house, scraping branches restlessly across the stone of the wall. Cork climbed the front steps onto the porch. He peered through a window where the curtains hadn't been drawn completely, but he could see nothing inside. He knocked at the door. The only answer was the creak of a loose porch board as he stepped back to wait. He tried the knob. The door was unlocked. He opened it.

The smell of pot roast greeted him, a pleasant aroma that seemed out of place in that unwelcoming house.

"Fletcher!" he called. "Solemn!"

He took a hesitant step inside. For Cork, the move had the dreadful feel of inevitability, for he recalled far too well the night only three years earlier when he'd entered the Parrant estate in just this way, only to find that a shotgun blast had scattered most of the judge's head across a wall. He waited for his eyes to adjust completely to the dark inside the house, then he walked ahead to the switch he knew was in the entryway. The lights came on, revealing nothing extraordinary. The living room was empty. In the dining room, the table was set for dinner, a big pot roast center stage. There was one dinner plate on the table, dirty. An opened bottle of red wine stood beside a stemmed glass that was half full. Cork went to the stairs and called up toward the second floor, "Fletcher! Solemn!"

He turned at last down the long hallway that led to the study, where the sight of violent death and the smell of spilled blood had awaited him before. His steps seemed loud in the silence of that house. He reached the study door, which was closed. He knocked, waited, then pushed the door open. Although the room beyond was dark, the trapped, foul smell told him everything. The stink of gunpowder, the stench of blood.

When he turned on the light, his worst fear became reality. The wall behind the big desk was stained with splattered blood and fragments of tissue and bone, still glistening. On the floor below, lay Fletcher Kane, all but his long, insectlike legs hidden by the bulk of the desk. His legs and the ugly blue barrel of a shotgun.

Sprawled on his stomach next to an overturned chair, dead center in the room lay Solemn, an island in a lake of his own blood.

Cork's knees threatened to buckle and he steadied himself against the doorjamb.

He staggered forward, knowing that everything was useless, that with all his blood spilled onto the hardwood floor, Solemn was already dead. But it was what you did, what you were trained to do. He dialed 911, then knelt beside Solemn and numbly reached to check for a pulse.

The moment Cork's fingers touched him, Solemn gave a small groan.

"Oh, Christ," Cork said. He went down on his knees, knelt in the blood. Carefully, he rolled Solemn over. The shotgun blast had obliterated his T-shirt and made a pulpy mess of everything under it. Solemn opened his eyes, only the width of a whisker, but enough that Cork knew he was conscious.

"Cold," Solemn said.

"Here." Cork sat down, took him in his arms, and cradled him. "The paramedics are on the way. Hold on. Just hold on, son."

Solemn looked up at him and tried to speak.

"Don't talk." Cork held him tenderly and whispered, "Please, God. Don't let him die."

Where Solemn found the strength, Cork didn't know. The young man's hand slowly rose, touched Cork's chest over his heart, held there a moment, then dropped to the floor where it hit with a hollow sound.

Solemn Winter Moon was gone.

"Oh, Solemn, Solemn," Cork said. He laid his cheek against the young man's blood-matted hair, and before he knew it, he was weeping deeply, grieving as he would have for a son.

42

CORK SAT ON THE FRONT STEPS, in the glaring wash of colors from the cruisers' blinking lights, drinking coffee Cy Borkmann had poured from the Thermos he always kept in his cruiser. The steps were broad, and the crime scene team had no trouble moving past him, in and out of the house. He was grateful for the coffee. The bitter taste of it was something familiar, grounding. Even so, he felt as if he'd taken a long fall and had left an important part of himself behind.

With Solemn dying in his arms, he'd said a desperate prayer, but it had done no good. Maybe if he'd believed, if he'd been sure of God the way Solemn had, it would have made all the difference.

It was ridiculous thinking, he knew. The kind of thinking that sprang from guilt and grief. From believing that he hadn't done enough to protect Solemn. From realizing too late how much he'd cared. He drank his coffee, and he remembered the small boy with fierce, dark eyes who'd loved fishing and Sam Winter Moon's jokes. He wanted to block from his memory the feel of Solemn limp in his arms, the sight of his chest shredded by buckshot, the helplessness that had led to a prayer unanswered.

Gooding came out and Borkmann followed him.

"Finished?" Cork asked.

"We're just about to bag the bodies." Borkmann heaved a sigh that sounded like the wheeze of a tired draft horse. "You take a good look at things before you called us?"

"Good enough, I guess."

"Notice the top of Kane's desk?"

"I didn't look that good, Cy."

"Nice cherry wood, but scratched up pretty bad. New scratches. Gooding, here, thinks they're from the recoil of the shotgun. I think he's right. I think Kane laid the barrel across the desk and pointed it directly at Winter Moon where he sat. The kid had to know what was coming. I don't see any way Kane could have sprung the shotgun on him sudden, a piece that big." He held off for a moment, as if waiting for Gooding or Cork to offer another theory. When they didn't he said, "Murder-suicide is what I'd say."

A cruiser door slammed, and Pender came up the walk.

"Dross just radioed. She finished interviewing Olga Swenson."

Borkmann glanced at Deputy Gooding and nodded approval. Immediately after they'd arrived at the house, Gooding had recommended to the acting sheriff that, despite the late hour, he dispatch someone immediately to talk to Kane's housekeeper.

Pender looked at his notes. "According to Ms. Swenson, she had dinner on the table at eight o'clock, which was a little later than usual, but she said Kane'd been keeping odd hours. After the food was out, she left. Didn't stick around for any compliments on her cooking. I guess the drill was that Dr. Kane bused his own dishes. As far as she knows, Kane was alone in the house. She also said that he still insisted on her fixing a big family meal even though he wasn't eating much these days. Getting pretty lax in all his personal habits, too. Sounds like he was definitely on the edge. Dross'll give you a full report back at the office."

"Eight o'clock," Borkmann said. "And what time did you get here, Cork?"

"Ten-forty-five."

"All right." Borkmann tipped back the brim of his hat. "Looks like, Dr. Kane made a pretty good dent in that pot roast on the dining room table. And that bottle of wine is better than half empty, so he took some time to mellow out good. Let's assume he started eating right after the housekeeper left, and took his time stuffing his face. Maybe half an hour. Now from what you say, Cork, Winter Moon left his mother's place around twenty hundred hours. If he came straight here, he'd have arrived at about twenty-thirty hours, just about the time Kane was finishing his meal, sipping on that last glass of wine. Winter Moon comes in. They palaver, end up in the study with the shotgun between them. I'm guessing time of death is going to be around twenty-one hundred hours. It's a miracle he was still alive when you got here, Cork."

Gooding had been conspicuously quiet. He leaned against one of the big stone pillars of the porch and stared down at his feet. Every once in a while, he shook his head, as if he were having a conversation with himself.

"Dot Winter Moon still at your house, Cork?" Borkmann asked.

"Probably. She thinks I went out to Henry Meloux's place. She's waiting for me to come back with word about Solemn."

Borkmann looked like he had bad indigestion. "Guess I better head on over and break the news."

"I'll do it, Cy."

"Part of the job, whether I like it or not."

"I think it'll be easier coming from me."

Gooding said, "It wouldn't be good for her to see you like that, all covered in blood."

"I'll stop by Sam's Place and clean up. I keep a change of clothing there."

Borkmann said, "All right. But come on down to the office afterward. We'll get a formal statement from you there, okay?"

"Fine."

Borkmann went back into the house. Gooding stayed a minute longer.

"Dorothy Winter Moon called the office this evening," he said. "I took the call. I went out to Sam Winter Moon's old cabin first. I should have come here, Cork. I might have stopped this."

"You didn't know, Randy."

Gooding looked down at a Bible in his hand. "This was in the living room. It's the one Winter Moon had with him in jail. I thought maybe his mother might want it." He gave it to Cork. "We don't see any way that it's relevant to the investigation."

Gooding turned away and returned to his duties inside the house.

Cork stared at the book. A small, New American Bible, white cover. A simple thing, really, but weighty enough in Solemn's thinking that he'd brought it to the scene of his death.

Why had Solemn come here? Did he hope he could ease Kane's suffering, take away his hate? Did he really believe that he could offer the peace he himself had found in Blood Hollow? If so, Cork wished he could think of it as something courageous, but in his grief, he could only think how tragic and useless a gesture it had been.

He lifted himself from the steps and started toward home, carrying the burden of the news that would destroy Dorothy Winter Moon's world.

43

SOLEMN'S WAKE LASTED TWO DAYS. It was held on the rez, in the community center in Alouette, with friends and relatives of Dorothy Winter Moon taking turns sitting with the body. The evening Cork paid his respects, he ran into George LeDuc, Eddie Kingbird, and old Waldo Pike standing outside the building, smoking.

"Boozhoo," LeDuc said in greeting.

"Boozhoo," Cork said to them all.

"Look at that." Kingbird grinned. "Just in time for the food."

Pike said, "Stick around awhile, Cork. Rhonda Fox is gonna sing. She don't sing good, but she knows the old songs. Not many left who do."

Waldo Pike had white hair, plenty of it. He stood with a slight stoop, not from infirmity, but from back muscles overdeveloped across a lifetime of wielding an ax and a chain saw, cutting timber for a living.

Cork said, "I'll stick around."

"Your grandmother used to sing," Pike said.

"Yes."

"I heard her once when I was a young man. It was when Virgil Lafleur passed on. Singers came from all over. A lot of people looked up to Virgil, came to pay their respects. Some all the way from Turtle Mountain. Your grandmother's singing, that was something."

Waldo Pike fell silent and smoked awhile. Cork waited

respectfully. Pike was an elder who talked on Indian time, comfortable with long silences, and Cork didn't want to show disrespect by leaving before he'd finished saying all he had to say.

"I'm hungry," the old man finally said. "How about we eat?"

Inside, the largest of the meeting rooms had been set up for the visitation. The casket was situated in front of a window with a view of the playground behind the community center. Flowers and cards had been laid out on tables on either side. Folding chairs stood in a half dozen rows before the casket. Along the sides of the room, small tables had been arranged, with a few chairs at each so that visitors could sit and eat. The food, a potluck affair, had been placed on several long tables at the back. Among the other aromas Cork's nose picked up were the good smells of fry bread, wild rice stew, and Tater Tot hot dish.

A couple of dozen people were in the room, some just getting into the food line, others sitting in the folding chairs, listening to Chet Gabriel, who stood at a microphone to the right of the casket. Gabriel was a poet of sorts, and he was reciting from a sheet of notebook paper he held in his hand. Cork knew most of those present, most of them Iron Lake band.

Dorothy Winter Moon was at one of the side tables. She wore a dress, plain blue. Cork couldn't ever recall seeing her in anything so feminine. When she was alone for a moment, he walked to her.

"Evening, Dot."

"Hi, Cork. Thanks for coming." Despite the dress and the circumstances, she seemed strong as ever.

"Jo will be here in a bit. She had a late meeting with a client." He glanced around. "Lot of folks."

"It's nice," she said. "Thanks, Cork."

"What for?"

"Doing all you did. Solemn thought a lot of you."

"I wish I could have done more."

"You couldn't have saved him, if that's what you mean. He knew what he was doing. He had his reasons."

Cork was sure it helped her to think so, and so he said nothing. Others came to the table to speak with Dot, and Cork left her to them.

When the poet finished to polite applause, Cork went to the casket, which was open. Solemn lay on a bed of white satin, dressed in the kind of dark suit Cork had never seen him wear, his arms uncomfortably stiff at his sides. A new shirt and tie covered his chest, but Cork knew the violation hidden beneath the thin cotton fabric. Solemn's face was a work of cosmetic art, given color with rouge and powder, like a wax figure in a museum. Whatever Solemn Winter Moon had actually been, reluctant saint or madman, this dressed and painted body was a million miles removed from that. Henry Meloux would have said that Solemn was already far along in his journey on the Path of Souls. Mal Thorne probably believed that Solemn had taken his place in purgatory, awaiting the day his sins would be purged and he could enter heaven. Cork had no idea where the spirit of Solemn now resided.

"I used to think he was a shame to the Ojibwe."

Cork half-turned. Oliver Bledsoe stood beside him, staring down into the casket.

"Now?" Cork asked.

"Now I think The People will remember him with great respect." He turned from the body. "Got a minute?"

"Sure."

"Outside."

On one of the tables that flanked the casket was a small dish full of cigarettes, and beside the dish sat a box of wooden kitchen matches. Cork took a cigarette and a match. Bledsoe did the same. Outside, they lit up. Cork had quit smoking a couple of years earlier. The cigarettes were part of the Anishinaabe reverence toward tobacco, *biindaakoojige,* and the old belief that the smoke carried prayers to the creator, Kitchimanidoo.

Bledsoe said, "I heard the sheriff's department is dropping the investigation of Charlotte Kane's murder. I heard that unofficially they're still pinning it on Solemn."

"Yeah."

"You think that's what happened? Solemn did it?"

"No," Cork said.

"Leaving it that way, it's not good," Bledsoe said. "Indian kid kills a white girl. You know how often that'll be thrown at us around here?"

"I know."

Bledsoe smoked for a while. People kept arriving, nodding or waving as they went inside.

Bledsoe said, "I talked with the tribal council. They want to hire you to clear Solemn's name."

Cork watched the cigarette smoke drift upward toward a clear, cornflower sky.

"All right," he said.

"Good."

"I was going to do it anyway, you know."

Bledsoe laughed quietly. "That's what George LeDuc said."

"That's why he's chairman of the tribal council."

Inside the building, a woman began to sing. The notes weren't pure, but the words were Ojibwe.

"Rhonda Fox," Cork said.

"Going back inside?"

"Wouldn't miss it."

The day Solemn Winter Moon was buried, a sun dog appeared in the sky. Not many people had ever witnessed this phenomenon, a rare occurrence in which sunlight, refracted off ice crystals in the atmosphere, created the illusion of a second sun. Cork had seen it only once, and then in winter, and had no idea why it was called a sun dog. He and Jo and the others who'd gathered for the burial stood at the graveside in the cemetery behind the old mission building deep in the reservation, staring east, marveling at the two suns in the morning heaven. The sun dog stayed until the casket was lowered, and the dark mouth that was the open grave had swallowed the body of Solemn Winter Moon. Then, as those who'd gathered to pay their final respects silently scattered, the false sun faded away.

That same day, Cork watched another man's body being lowered into the earth.

It was late in the afternoon. The air had turned hot and sultry. Cork parked his Bronco in the shade of a burr oak inside the cemetery with a good view of the road that wound up the hill from town. He could feel a storm in the air, forming somewhere beyond the western horizon, the thunderheads just now rising above the distant trees.

As he waited, he thought about Fletcher Kane. He'd been wrong about Kane in important ways, wrong because he'd blinded himself. He'd wanted Kane to be the kind of man capable of abusing his daughter. Kane wasn't, although the rumors about him persisted. Was it any wonder he'd gone over the edge? In the end, what did Kane have to lose? His life had already been destroyed. He'd lost what he most loved—twice—and in the end had even been robbed of the respect of the community.

What had been Cork's part in this? He had voiced suspicions, and they'd become rumors as a result of Borkmann's loose tongue. But Cork knew Borkmann and was well aware of the man's weakness where confidentiality was concerned. Was there a dark place inside him that had calculated this and used the sheriff to ruin Kane? How well did he know himself? Cork wondered. Christ, he thought, how well did anyone?

After a thirty-minute wait, he saw the line of cars, only a half dozen strong, making its way up the hill, led by a shiny hearse. Directly behind the hearse was Randy Gooding's Tracker. As the abbreviated procession came through the gate, Cork saw that Gooding was serving as driver to the priest, and he also saw that the priest wasn't Mal Thorne but old Father Kelsey instead. The cars followed along the narrow lanes to the place that had been prepared, a plot of ground far from Charlotte's grave.

During the service, the doddering priest bent toward Fletcher Kane's coffin. Cork couldn't hear what the priest said. The old priest was too far away, and his voice was a whisper that died in the heavy air. The service was blessedly short. As things came to an end, Gooding stepped to Donny Pugmire, one of the pallbearers, and the two men exchanged words. Then Pugmire took the old priest's arm and led him to his own car, while Gooding walked up the hill toward Cork.

"Didn't know you were that fond of Fletcher Kane," Cork said.

"Father Mal called me. He said they didn't have enough pallbearers, asked if I'd lend a hand. I didn't mind."

"Where is Mal?"

"Sick." Gooding watched the cars leave the cemetery. "You know, I thought that when I quit the big city, I'd seen the last of hard things."

"They're worse here in some ways," Cork said. "Here, when tragedy visits, it knocks on the door of people you know."

Gooding nodded toward the new grave. "I hope this puts the lid on tragedy for a while."

"You think it's over?"

"Borkmann wants the Kane girl's murder to go in the cold case files. I think that's a good place for it."

"You believe Solemn did it?"

Gooding was quiet for a while. He looked toward the cemetery gate where, as the last of the funeral procession exited, an old, tan station wagon entered and stopped. A man got out and stared across the field of gravestones. He shielded his eyes against the sun with his hand.

Gooding said, "I think in the end he came to see the world differently, but before that he was certainly capable of murder. I know the Ojibwe don't want to believe that, and for the peace of this community, which I care about a lot, I'm willing to let sleeping dogs lie."

The man near the gate got back into the rusted station wagon and began to maneuver along the lanes between the rows of the dead. As the vehicle drew nearer, Cork saw that there were two other people in the car.

"What if it wasn't Solemn?" he said. "What if some monster is still out there?"

"No homicides since January, Cork." Gooding shook his head. "No more monsters. My money is on the man who was buried on the rez today."

"Any objection if I were to take a look at the case file?"

"None from me. You'll have to clear it with Borkmann. Or maybe just be patient a couple of weeks." Gooding smiled. "I hear the board of commissioners is thinking of offering you the sheriff's job until they can put together a special election. You wouldn't need any permission then."

The tan wagon pulled to a stop a few yards from where the two men stood. Three people got out, a man, a woman, and a boy, maybe twelve or thirteen years old. They looked familiar to Cork.

The man approached hesitantly. "Sorry to bother you people, but I'm wondering if you could help us."

"Be glad to," Gooding said.

The woman wore a white dress with daisies on it. She held her hands folded in front of her, in a way that seemed to bespeak great peace. The boy hung back and stood a little hunched, as if he were tired.

The man said, "We're looking for the grave of someone who was buried today."

"Right down there." Gooding pointed toward the open hole into which Kane's coffin had just been lowered.

"Thank you," the man said.

"Did you know Fletcher Kane?" Cork asked.

The man turned back. "Fletcher Kane?"

Cork gestured down the hill. "The guy they buried today."

The man looked confused. "I thought it was Solemn Winter Moon."

"Winter Moon?" Gooding said. "He was buried out on the reservation this morning."

"Oh." The man looked back at the woman and the boy.

Cork suddenly realized who they were. "You're from Warroad."

"That's right. How'd you know?"

Cork's attention was suddenly focused on the boy standing beside his mother. "What happened to the wheelchair?"

The boy didn't reply.

"Go on, Jamie. Tell the man."

The boy stammered, as if words were new to him. "He healed me."

"Solemn?"

The boy nodded.

The woman hugged her son and looked deeply into his eyes. "That good man healed him."

"Just a minute," Gooding said. He walked toward the boy, who stepped back at his approach. "I'm not going to hurt you, son. I just want a closer look. I'm a policeman." Gooding knelt in front of the boy. "Show me your hands."

The boy slowly lifted his arms, and the fingers that had been curled into claws opened toward the deputy.

"Can you walk for me?"

The boy took a few steps. They weren't perfect.

"Tell me your name."

"Jamie Witherspoon."

"How old are you, Jamie?"

"Thirteen."

"You've always been sick?"

"Yes."

"Always in a wheelchair?"

"Yes."

"Your parents didn't put you up to this?"

"No."

Gooding stood up. "I apologize for that last question," he said to the boy's mother. "It's just that it's all a little hard to believe."

In the face of Gooding's doubt, her own face reflected nothing but love. "Believing is what it's all about."

Cork directed them to George LeDuc's store on the reservation, told them to tell LeDuc their story, and he would escort them to Solemn's grave. He also told them to ask George to guide them to the home of Solemn's mother. She would want to hear what they had to say.

As the old station wagon rattled out of the cemetery, Cork said, "You told me once that you're a man inclined to believe in miracles. So what do you think, Randy?"

For a long time, Gooding simply stared beyond the cemetery fence where the wagon had gone. Finally he shook his head. "I don't," he said. "Honest to God, I just don't know."

44

Cork arrived home to discover that Mal Thorne had apparently mistaken the front yard for a parking lot. The yellow Nova had jumped the curb, its front wheels coming to rest on the grass apron between the street and the sidewalk. Inside the house, Cork found Annie standing in the living room looking stunned.

"Are you okay?"

She stared at him. "Father Mal's here."

"I figured that. Is he sick?"

"Not sick," she said. "Drunk."

"Where's your mom?"

"She took Stevie for a haircut. Father Mal came after they left. I didn't know what to do."

"Where is he?"

Annie's eyes went slowly upward, but Cork knew she wasn't looking toward heaven.

"In Rose's room?"

"I heard them talking. He said he's leaving the priesthood, Dad. He said he's in love with Aunt Rose and he wants to marry her. How could he do that?"

"He hasn't done it yet," Cork said.

Annie looked deeply into her father's eyes, maybe hoping to find something there that would help her understand. "He's a priest. The church is his life."

High above them, in the attic room, something thumped.

"You wait here," Cork said.

He bounded up the stairs and down the hallway to the opened door that led to the attic. He heard grunting coming from Rose's room, the sound of a struggle. He took the attic stairs two at a time.

At the far end of the room, Rose's sewing table lay on its side and her sewing machine had tumbled to the floor. The whole mess was surrounded by a spill of fabric of a dozen designs. Amid the ruin, Rose and Mal Thorne stood locked in a desperate embrace. The moment Cork appeared, Rose peered over the priest's shoulder and her eyes grew huge.

"Help me," she gasped. "I can't hold him up."

Cork realized that Mal was buckling and all that kept him from falling was Rose's strength. He slipped his arms around Mal Thorne's chest, wedging his hands between Rose and the priest.

"Got him," he said.

The priest roused, enough to help as Cork walked him to the bed. Cork released his grip and Mal flopped on his back on the mattress. Rose lifted his legs and, with Cork's help, arranged him so that, more or less, he rested comfortably.

Mal wore brown loafers, no socks. His khakis were wrinkled. His plaid shirt was torn, a long wound in the fabric beneath his right arm. His breath was all Southern Comfort. Through heavy lids, he stared up as Rose leaned over him.

"I love you, Rose," he said, his tongue thick, his lips barely moving. "I love you."

"Shhh," Rose hushed him gently. "Just sleep."

Mal's eyes drifted closed. He mumbled something, and a few moments later, he was snoring.

Cork was breathing hard. "We're not going to be able to move him, Rose."

"It's okay." She reached down, tenderly touched Mal's cheek, the bristle of his red hair. "He can stay here for a while."

"I'd better check on Annie," Cork said.

Rose nodded, but she didn't take her eyes off the man in her bed.

While Cork was busy upstairs, Jo had returned with Stevie. Cork found her in the kitchen listening as Annie recounted, in a voice pitched at the edge of hysteria, what had happened.

"He's still upstairs with Rose?" Jo asked Cork.

"Yeah, but he's sleeping now."

"Sleeping?" Annie said.

"Actually, he's passed out on your Aunt Rose's bed."

"On her bed?" Annie looked mortified. "What are we going to do?"

"Let him sleep it off." Cork walked to the refrigerator and pulled out a beer.

"Then what?"

What, indeed? Cork wasn't happy with Mal, with this intrusion into his home, with the clumsy, thoughtless way the priest had chosen to make his feelings known. But he also understood the terrible conflict that must have been raging in Mal, dammed behind the calm face a man in his position had to maintain. He twisted the cap off his beer and took a swallow.

"It's not right," Annie said. "He's a priest."

Jo said, "Priests are just people, Annie. They have problems, too. They make mistakes, change their minds—"

"Aunt Rose won't let him change his mind. He's a priest." She caught the look that passed between her parents. "What?"

"Your Aunt Rose loves him," Jo said.

That seemed to set Annie back on her heels a bit.

Cork heard the creak of the stairs and saw Rose coming down from floors above. She walked to where the others had gathered.

"I'm sorry you saw all that, Annie," she said as soon as she stepped into the kitchen.

"You won't let him leave the church, will you?"

"Annie," Jo cautioned.

"You won't," Annie said.

Rose balled her hands together and closed her eyes, and for a moment it looked very much as if she were praying. "I think I'm going to have to talk to God about that one, Annie," she said at last. "I'm a little confused myself."

Annie, who'd never run from anything, turned away and fled outside, letting the screen door slam behind her. Rose took a step to follow.

"Let her go," Jo said. "She'll be fine. She just needs some time by herself to think."

Rose took a deep, quivering breath. "I could use some of that, too."

"Oh, Rose."

Jo crossed the kitchen and threw her arms around her sister. Cork stood drinking his beer, as bewildered by the events as everyone else.

He called the sheriff's department and caught Cy Borkmann just as he was leaving for the day. He explained to the acting sheriff what he wanted.

"I don't have a problem with you looking at the Kane girl's file, Cork. But promise me one thing. You come across anything we missed, anything important, you let me or Gooding know. Deal?"

"Deal, Cy."

"When do you want the file?"

"ASAP. Mind if I copy the material? That way I won't be a pest down there."

"I'll go you one better. I'll have a deputy make copies. It'll all be waiting for you."

"One more thing."

"Don't push your luck."

"Any chance of getting a look at the file on the incident at Kane's place?"

"What for?"

"Maybe nothing. I'd just like to have everything that relates in any way to what happened to Charlotte Kane."

Borkmann thought a moment or two. "All right. Can't see that it would hurt anything."

"Thanks, Cy."

"I hate making these decisions." Borkmann hung up.

An hour later, Cork picked up the promised documents. It was early evening by the time he returned home. Except for Jo, the house seemed deserted.

"Where is everybody?" he asked.

"Jenny's with Sean. I think they're going to a movie. Stevie's across the street playing in the O'Loughlins' tree house. Rose is upstairs, standing watch over Father Mal."

"Any word on Annie?"

"No."

Cork looked outside, thinking about the man who'd stalked his daughter.

"Don't worry," Jo said. "She's always home before dark these days. Are you hungry? I'd be glad to make you a sandwich."

"What have we got?"

"Ham and cheese on rye."

"I can make my own."

"Sit down. Relax." Jo walked with Cork to the kitchen. "Chips and beer with that?"

"Thanks."

Jo took a bottle of Lienenkugel beer from the refrigerator and gave it to him. On the kitchen table, Cork laid out the folders of material he'd picked up at the sheriff's department and opened the first file.

"You didn't happen to discuss a reasonable fee with Oliver Bledsoe," Jo said as she put a chunk of smoked ham on a cutting board to slice.

Cork took a long drink of cold beer. "I'd do this even if they paid me nothing."

Jo set a block of cheddar on the counter and, beside it, put what was left of a loaf of dark rye. "People are asking if you're ever going to open Sam's Place again. Some of them. The rest seem to be wondering if you're going to take the job as sheriff if it's offered."

"Which group do you fall into?"

"I don't fall. I stand firmly behind whatever you choose to do." She began to slice the ham. "Going to want mustard on this?"

"Do you have any advice?"

"It's best with mustard."

"About the sheriff's job."

"I have enough trouble keeping my own life in order. I know you'll do whatever's right for you."

Cork sat down and leaned back in his chair. "Want to hear a story, Jo?"

"Does it have a happy ending?"

"For a crippled kid and his folks, yeah."

"I'm all ears."

As he began to tell her about the family from Warroad, she sat down with him at the table. When he'd finished, she said, "What do you think?"

"That I should have done more to protect Solemn. Maybe he had been given a gift, Jo, something important to share. Now that gift is gone."

She reached across the table and took his hand. "These people, you're sure they weren't part of some con?"

"As sure as I am of anything right now. I'm not saying that Solemn had the gift of healing. Maybe his gift was just that he helped these people believe enough to make their own miracle happen. You know?"

"Yes."

"It's important to me that people think of Solemn in a good way. So it's important that everybody know the truth of what happened to Charlotte Kane."

"I understand. What can I do to help?"

"For starters, you can finish making that sandwich."

Later, Jo ran a bath for Stevie, and while her son played in the tub, she came down to the kitchen where Cork had the documentation of Charlotte Kane's death investigation spread out on the table.

"Any luck?" she asked.

"Nothing so far." He folded his hands behind his head and stared up at the ceiling. "One thing I keep going back to. The food wrappers at the scene of her death. The fact that some bastard sat there callously eating while she died. I keep asking myself what kind of ghoul would do that kind of thing?"

"A sin eater." Annie stood at the screen door, looking in. Night was beginning to settle in at her back. "Can I come in?"

"Of course, sweetheart," Jo said.

She walked in, her eyes tracing the lines on the linoleum. "I'm sorry for the way I behaved."

"That's all right," Jo said. "Are you hungry?"

"I'm always hungry."

"How about a ham and cheese sandwich?"

"I recommend it highly," Cork said.

"Thanks."

Jo got the things from the refrigerator.

"Just walk?" Cork said.

Annie shook her head. "I bumped into Randy Gooding and he walked me to the Broiler. We talked. Look, he gave me this."

She held out a drawing that had been done on the back of a paper place mat from the Broiler, a pencil portrait of her. She looked very pretty and a little sad.

"Helped?"

"Yeah, it helped."

"Here you go," Jo said.

Annie took the plate. "Is it all right if I eat in my room?"

"Sure. Just bring the dishes down when you're finished."

Annie moved toward the living room, then stopped and glanced back. "I love you guys."

"Good night, sweetheart," Jo said. She watched her daughter head upstairs and she smiled. "Think she's okay?"

"She'll work it out. Good head on her shoulders," Cork said. "And quite lovely. She gets that from you."

"Thanks, cowboy." She bent to where he sat at the table and kissed the top of his head. "I'm going up to check on Stevie and get him into bed."

Cork went back to studying the files, looking for anything he might have overlooked before or seen and too quickly dismissed. It took a while before something dawned on him. When it finally did, he grabbed the documents that dealt with the night Fletcher Kane killed himself and Solemn, and he scanned the autopsy report for each man.

He went to the telephone table in the living room and pulled out his address book. He took it back to the kitchen and made a long-distance call. Jo came downstairs just as he was finishing.

"Stevie's asleep," she said.

"Sit down, Jo."

She heard the taut pitch of his voice. She took a chair at the table. "You've found something."

"Maybe."

Jo looked at the phone on the table. "Who were you talking to?"

"Boomer Grabowski in Chicago. Remember him?"

"Sure. But you haven't talked to him in years."

"I called him last week actually."

"What about?"

"To see if he'd be willing to investigate Mal Thorne."

"Why?"

"It was part of due diligence. But he was busy on a case in Miami, and then my head got all turned around for a while and I didn't follow up with him right away. That was a big mistake, because Annie got me to thinking tonight, Jo. We believe that someone was with Charlotte and ate food while she died. Now take a look at this."

He handed her the autopsy report on Fletcher Kane.

After reading it for a minute, she asked, "What am I looking for?"

"Stomach contents."

"There's not much."

"Exactly. Olga Swenson set a good pot roast dinner down on the table for Kane the night he killed himself. Somebody ate a lot of that food and drank a good deal of the wine that went with it."

Jo's eyes went down to the document in her hand. "It wasn't Fletcher Kane."

"That's right."

"Solemn?"

"He'd been fasting for several days, and his autopsy confirmed that."

Jo frowned. "You're talking about Annie's sin eater comment."

"Yeah."

"Cork, that was just joking. A sin eater? That's crazy."

"Whoever killed Charlotte Kane wasn't exactly sane. Who told Annie the sin eater story?"

Jo thought a moment. "Father Mal."

"What do we know about him?"

"What do you mean?"

"Just what I said. What do we really know about the man who's the parish priest?"

"Why is this even a question? Because he told Annie the story?"

"Humor me."

"He's a good priest."

"He says he's in love with Rose. He wants to marry her. Is that the behavior of a good priest?"

"I like him."

"So do I, but that's not relevant at the moment. What do we know about his past?"

"He ran a homeless shelter in Chicago. I've heard he risked his life to keep money for the shelter from being stolen."

"Maybe that's the story he tells to explain his scars. Is it true? What else do we know?"

"What do we know about anybody except what they tell us? My God, Cork, some things you just have to accept."

"Not when murder is involved." He nodded at the kitchen telephone. "Boomer agreed to check out Mal, find out about the incident that resulted in his scars, anything else he can turn up about the priest's background."

Jo shook her head. "This feels wrong."

"If Boomer comes up with nothing, fine. No harm done."

"Why don't you just ask Father Mal where he was the night Fletcher and Solemn died?"

"He's dead drunk right now. And there's no guarantee he wouldn't lie." Cork sat back suddenly. "But there is someone who might be able to help. What time is it?"

Jo glanced at her watch. "Nine-thirty."

"It's not too late." Cork got up.

"Where are you going?"

"To the rectory to talk to Ellie Gruber. Jo, believe me, I'm hoping she's able to give Mal an alibi."

The housekeeper answered the door in her robe.

"I'm sorry to come knocking so late, Ellie."

"That's all right, Cork. I'll be up until Father Mal comes in. Was it him you wanted to see?"

"You, actually. Do you mind if I ask you a question about Mal?"

"I won't know until you ask me, now will I? Would you like to come in?"

"No, thanks, Ellie. This will only take a moment. I don't know how to phrase this delicately. Have you noticed him acting a little strange lately?"

"Well." She clutched her robe tight at her throat.

"I'm a little worried about him, is all," Cork went on. "A lot of us are. Do you have any idea what's troubling him?"

"If I did, Cork, I'd be doing my best to help him."

"Ellie, think about the night Fletcher Kane and Solemn Winter Moon died."

"Lord, that's one night I'd rather forget."

"Do you remember Mal? How he seemed?"

"That was a bad night, to be sure. He got a call and went out. When he came back, he was very upset. Then a bit later he got the call from the sheriff's office about Dr. Kane. What a terrible, terrible night."

"Do you know who that first call was from?"

"No."

"What time did he go out?"

"Oh, it must have been around nine."

"When did he come back?"

"About an hour and a half later."

"Did he say anything?"

"Not that I recall. He's usually so pleasant. He likes a little Irish coffee before bed, so I had everything ready. But he didn't want any. He went straight to his room. I'm worried, Cork. I pray for him a lot these days."

"I'm sure it doesn't hurt, Ellie. One more question. Did you spend New's Year Eve here with the fathers?"

"Lord, no. I have a life outside this rectory. I was with my late husband's family, out at Tower."

"So Mal and Father Kelsey were here alone?"

"I believe so. Father Kelsey was probably asleep by nine, so I'm sure poor Father Mal had to see the New Year in all alone."

"Tragic," Cork said.

Jo was waiting in the kitchen when he got home.

"Well?"

"The night Kane and Solemn died, Mal went out about nine. Came back around ten-thirty. Very upset, no explanation."

Jo picked up the phone and handed it to him. "Boomer Grabowski called. He wants you to call him back."

"That was quick."

"The execution of a good reputation goes fast around here."

Cork ignored her comment and punched in Boomer's number.

"Don't tell me you've already got something," Cork said.

"It's all in knowing who to call."

"Spill it."

"Remember Dave Jenkins?"

"Yeah. Shaved head, right? You used to call him Cueball."

"That's him. He's with homicide out of Area Two. Been there for a couple of years now. You hit the jackpot with the priest, Cork. Before he took over the unit, Cueball got assigned to investigate two homicides in Hyde Park. Somebody iced a couple of punks with rap sheets almost as long as my dick. Turns out, they were the primary suspects in the assault and attempted robbery of a priest named Father Malachi Thorne."

"Jesus."

"Yeah. The bust was bad, and they had to let the douche bags go on a technicality. But get this. Cueball says that for a while the priest was a suspect in those murders. Seems the guys were beat up pretty bad before their throats were cut. And guess who was a hotshot boxer back in college. The priest. Here's where it gets interesting as far as your situation goes. It wasn't the first time the priest had been connected with a murder investigation. Sixteen years ago, a children's home he was in charge of burned down. Arson. A fifteen-year-old girl died, name of Yvonne Doolittle. You sitting down, Cork? This Doolittle girl had accused your Father Thorne of molesting her." Grabowski was quiet a few moments. "You still there?"

"Yeah."

"Not enough evidence to build a case against him. The Church hustled him away from there and hushed things up." Boomer laughed softly. "One more thing you're gonna love. The Hyde Park killings? There was something real whacko about them. Seems the perp had himself a feast at the scene after he'd done the deed. Cueball did some digging. You know that knack of his for uncovering the truly weird? This time he looks for weird and Catholic, discovers there's some kind of old Catholic mumbo jumbo goes along with feasting over the dead."

"Sin eating," Cork said.

"That's right." Boomer sounded impressed that Cork knew.

"Another good reason Cueball liked the priest for the killings. In the end, your Father Thorne had an alibi they couldn't break. Also, there was another double homicide with the same weird MO, and it happened before the priest came to Chicago."

"Know anything about those killings?"

"No. You want I should ask?"

"Let's get everything we can."

"All right. But you know, Cork, if I were you, I'd put this priest away right now. He sounds to me like one sick bastard. For all you know, you could have your own little serial killer right there in Nowhere, Minnesota."

"Thanks for the insight, Boomer. I'll be in touch."

He reported everything to Jo who sat tight-lipped at the table. When he was finished, she stood up, walked to the door, and looked through the screen, where dozens of moths shuddered their wings against the mesh. She said nothing.

"It makes sense," he argued quietly. "Solemn thought Charlotte had been seeing a married man. Mal *is* a married man."

"I thought we knew who the married man was. Arne Soderberg."

"When I talked to Glory Kane—I mean Cordelia Diller—she told me that Charlotte—Maria—related to her father in a sexual way and that she'd come on to Fletcher, hoping to secure his love that way, too. Mal's not only married, Jo. He's *Father* Mal. And think about the graffiti on the wall at St. Agnes. Liar. Who do you suppose that was directed at?"

She spoke carefully and with her back still to Cork. "I know you think anyone is capable of murder. That's how you've been trained to think. I find it hard to believe that Father Mal is the kind of monster you've painted."

Cork followed her to the door. He put his arms around her and spoke quietly. "I wish I had your faith. In God, in people. I don't. I've seen too much, I guess."

"You believed in Solemn when no one else would."

"That was for Sam."

"In the end, it was for Solemn." She laid her head back against his shoulder. "And you believed in us, even when everything seemed hopeless. What do you think faith is, Cork?

I think it's believing in what you care about even in the face of all evidence to the contrary. I care about Father Mal. I want to believe in him."

"You still have to ask questions, especially the hard ones."

She stepped away from the door. "What about Mal? Tonight?"

"I'll take him back to the rectory."

"I suppose that's best. Let's not say anything about this to Rose. Not yet."

"All right."

She put her hands gently against Cork's chest, as if to feel his heart. "I know we have to be thorough and ask the hard questions, but I hope neither of us ever stops believing that the answers can be good."

They found Rose sitting in the rocker, which she'd pulled nearer to the bed where the priest slept. The lamp in the corner was on low, and a soft light spread across the room. Mal looked peaceful.

"How is he?" Jo said.

"He hasn't stirred."

"I need to wake him up," Cork said. "Take him home."

Rose looked as if she were about to object, then nodded her agreement. "It's probably best."

Cork leaned over Mal, caught the smell of sweet bourbon coming off his skin. "Mal," he said. Then louder, "Mal, wake up." He shook the priest's shoulder.

The man's eyes flickered open and his pupils swam a moment before finding solid ground on Cork's face. "Huh?"

"I'm taking you home, Mal. Back to the rectory."

The priest considered this, and while he thought, his eyes began to drift closed.

"Come on, Mal." Cork slid his arm under the priest's shoulders and hauled him to a sitting position.

"Oh, Jesus," Mal mumbled.

"Let me help," Rose said.

They swung his feet off the bed and together helped him up.

"I don't feel good," Mal said, swaying.

"Hold on to us." Rose positioned herself to one side; Cork took the other. Between them they managed to get him downstairs and out the door.

"My car," Mal said as he slumped onto the passenger side of the Bronco's front seat.

"We'll take care of that tomorrow," Cork said.

For a brief moment Mal worked on focusing, and he put out his hands to cup Rose's face through the open window. "I didn't want . . . ," he began, but seemed to lose the thought. "I'm sorry."

"Go home, get some rest, and we'll talk," she replied.

Cork backed down the drive, his headlights holding on Rose and Jo, stark and worried in the glare. No sooner did the Bronco hit the street than Mal leaned out the window and threw up.

"Sorry," he managed as he settled back. He closed his eyes and within a minute was breathing heavily.

Cork had wanted to question him, but that was plainly hopeless. He settled on getting him to the rectory and, with the help of Ellie Gruber, into his room and to bed.

As he headed back to Gooseberry Lane, he considered what Jo had said about believing in the people you cared about even when it appeared crazy to do so. Jo believed in Mal. Rose believed in Mal. So why didn't he?

45

NEXT MORNING, Cork woke to a gentle knocking at the bedroom door.

"Dad? Mom?"

"What is it, Jenny?"

"Can I talk to you guys?"

"Just a minute." Cork looked at the bedside clock. 7:30 A.M. He'd overslept, but not by much.

Jo stirred. "What is it?"

"Jenny wants to talk to us."

"What time is it?"

"Seven-thirty."

"Oh, my." She was awake. "I have to get ready for work."

"Come on in, Jen," Cork called.

Jenny stepped in. She was still in her sleepwear, a long Goo-Goo Dolls T-shirt that reached to her thighs. She stayed at the door.

"What is it?" Cork said.

"It's Aunt Rose. She's in the kitchen, crying."

"Rose?" Jo sat up.

"She won't talk to me," Jenny said. "She just cries."

"I'll be right there." Jo threw off the covers.

Downstairs, Stevie lay on the floor in front of the television, watching Nickelodeon.

In the kitchen, Rose sat alone. On the table in front of her was a cup of coffee and an envelope. In her hand, she held a piece of light blue stationery. She was sobbing quietly.

"Rose?" Jo knelt beside her.

"He's gone."

"Mal?"

"I heard his car this morning. When I looked out my window, he was driving away. I came downstairs and found this taped to the back door." She picked up the envelope from the table. Her name had been written on the front. "He left a note." She looked down at the stationery in her hand.

"Rose, would it be all right if I read the note? And Cork?"

Rose hesitated. "Please," Cork said. "It's important."

Rose handed it to her sister. Over Jo's shoulder, Cork read Mal Thorne's handwriting.

> *Dear Rose,*
>
> *Forgive me. I looked to you wrongly for a redemption that was not yours to give. This burden I carry, this gluttony for sin, is mine alone. I don't know if I've abandoned God, or God has abandoned me, or if we're mutually disgusted and have simply turned our backs on one another. I do know that I feel lost and need to find my way again. I'm afraid it may be a very long road ahead. But I will always treasure the lasting memory of the one true beauty I have known in my life, the one perfect thing. A flower called Rose.*
>
> *With the greatest affection,*
> *Mal*

"Gluttony for sin?" Cork said, his voice rock hard.

"What is it?" Rose said.

"It's nothing. Oh, Rose. I'm so sorry." Jo put her arms around her sister.

"He's leaving Aurora," Rose said. "He's talked about it, now he's going to do it."

"Leaving for where?" Cork said.

"I don't know. That's never been clear."

"I'm getting dressed." Cork started out of the kitchen.

He hadn't gone far when Jo grabbed his arm.

"I need to get some answers," he told her. "Before the chance is gone. You know I do."

He could see the struggle reflected in her face. Finally she released her grip.

The morning outside was deathly still, but high up, an unseen wind pushed scattered clouds relentlessly across the hard blue sky. The sun intermittently splattered the Bronco's windshield with blinding light, and Cork squinted to see his way. There seemed to be a restlessness in the atmosphere, but he chalked it up to his own unsettled mind.

He was surprised to see the Nova still in the drive at the rectory. He jumped from the Bronco as a huge cloud swept across the sun, and he waded through deep, blue shadow toward the rectory door. Ellie Gruber answered his pounding.

"I need to see Mal," Cork said.

Ellie wrung her hands and didn't answer.

"I know he's here, Ellie."

"He's in a state, Cork. I don't know." She looked behind her in a frightened way.

Cork put his hands firmly on her shoulders and urged her aside. "It'll be all right, Ellie."

He entered without her uttering an objection.

The door to Mal Thorne's bedroom was open, and Cork found him packing. A big suitcase lay open on the bed, and beside it a pile of clothing. The priest stood carelessly folding a pair of pants.

"Leaving Mal?"

The priest looked up, startled. "Cork?"

"Taking off without saying good-bye?"

"Yeah. I guess so."

"Where are you going?"

"Not sure." Mal went to the dresser and opened a drawer.

"Leaving the parish high and dry, aren't you?"

"There's always Father Kelsey."

"Right."

"The diocese will send somebody. Somebody better than me."

"You sound like you've lost your faith in yourself."

"You could say that."

"A gluttony for sin?"

The priest swung around. For a moment, he seemed upset, then it was as if he simply shrugged it off. He resumed his packing.

Cork stepped nearer to the bed. "Mal, you told Annie a story a while back. Something about a sin eater."

Mal Thorne stuffed a handful of assorted socks into the suitcase. "It's something I tell all the kids I work with. I use it as an example of how the substance of Christianity is sometimes warped by church doctrine. It's a little on the ghoulish side, but it gets their attention."

"You don't believe in sin eating?"

Mal glanced up. "This day and age you'd have to be a little crazy to believe something like that."

"I see. But it's perfectly sane to believe in, for example, a virgin birth?"

"Why are we having a theological discussion?" The priest squeezed his temples, as if pressing against a headache. He reached into the suitcase, pulled out a fifth of Southern Comfort, and unscrewed the cap. As he brought it to his lips, he said, "Hair of the dog and all that."

"Sure. Got a lot on your mind, I imagine."

"Glad you understand."

"Are Fletcher Kane and Solemn part of it?"

The priest took a long swallow. He looked at the bottle and shook his head. "Big help there, wasn't I?"

"The night they died, where were you?"

Mal Thorne hesitated. He glanced at Cork, then away. "I was here."

"At the rectory?"

"Yes." He bent to his packing.

"The whole evening?"

"I may have stepped out for a minute."

"Try an hour and a half."

The priest shot him a killing look.

"Where were you in those ninety minutes, Mal?"

"With all due respect, that's none of your damn business."

"Ellie told me you got a call about nine o'clock and hurried out. Was it Fletcher Kane calling? Did he call to tell you what he'd done? What he was going to do? Did you rush over there and find out you were too late? And did you sit down at the table that had been set for a meal and consume the sins of the two men you couldn't save?"

Mal Thorne stared as if he thought Cork had gone stark raving mad. "That's ridiculous."

"Is it? The two men who tried to rob you in Chicago, they were murdered after the attack. And whoever killed them ate their sins afterward." Cork leaned across the bed, pressing tight the space between him and the priest. "Tell me about Yvonne Doolittle, Mal."

The priest froze. His eyes went cold, his tone icy. "That's why you're here? You know, you're a real son of a bitch."

"That I am, Mal. In the pursuit of truth right now, I'd spit in the eye of God."

"Truth." The priest spoke the word as if he were cursing. "You've assembled a lot of facts, but you haven't come anywhere near the truth."

"Then enlighten me, Mal. I'm all ears."

The priest almost laughed. "Fine. Yvonne Doolittle. That poor, confused girl. She'd been sexually abused at home and in foster care. She saw me as a father figure. Unfortunately for both of us, to her a father also meant sex. When I wouldn't respond, she threatened me, and finally made those allegations. You see? I was no more help to her than I was to Fletcher Kane or Solemn Winter Moon. Or Charlotte." The priest seemed to go limp, as if he might fall, and he steadied himself by putting his hands on the bed. "Liar. The writing on the wall? That was directed at me."

"Why?"

"Charlotte came to me one day. It must have been November. She was so confused, so convinced that she was the most awful human being. All she wanted was to die, she said, because she loved someone who didn't love her back. You know how many teenagers I've heard that from? So what did I tell her? That time would take care of it. That she should put her trust in God, her father. That He loved her. That she was one of His treasures. She went absolutely crazy. Called me a liar. Said the church was a lie because fathers didn't love their children. They fucked them. She left and never came back. Not just to talk but even to worship. Gone from the church altogether until the night she broke in with Solemn."

From the dark forest of his own self-loathing, he stared at Cork.

"The whole truth and nothing but the truth, so help me God. Isn't that how it goes? All right then. While Fletcher Kane, in all his suffering, took his own life and the life of that remarkable young man, do you know where I was? I was with Rose." He looked up, his face screwed into a mask of pain. "With Rose, trying my damnedest to convince her to help me shatter my priestly vow of celibacy, a thing she would not do. How's that for pathetic? You don't believe me? Ask Rose. She won't lie to you. She's the finest person I've ever known."

Mal Thorne reached into his suitcase for the bottle of Southern Comfort.

"A gluttony for sin? Try pride, for example, so cocksure I could make a difference somehow. And to everything else, you can now add lust." He raised the bottle. Before he drank, he said, "I'm tired, Cork. I just want to be left alone."

A knock on the door frame brought Cork around, though the priest seemed not to hear. Ellie Gruber stood timidly in the hallway. She held a cordless phone in her hand.

"A call for you, Cork," she said. "It's Jo."

"Thanks, Ellie."

Cork took the phone. Ellie retreated.

"Hey," Cork said.

"Before you go crazy over there, there's something you should know. The night Fletcher Kane and Solemn died, Rose was with Father Mal. She swears it."

"I already went crazy. And Mal told me the truth."

"Oh." She was quiet a moment. "How's he doing?"

"Less than fair, I'd say."

"Is he still leaving Aurora?"

"I don't know."

"What a mess. You got a call from Boomer Grabowski. He asked me to pass along some information you wanted. He said the other murder victims in Chicago were a young, engaged couple. The case was never solved. He said it was interesting that the young man was a former priest and his fiancée was a former nun."

"Any names?"

"Yes. His name was James Trowbridge and hers was Nina van Zoot."

"Say that again."

"His name—"

"No, hers."

"Nina van Zoot." She waited. "Cork? Are you still there?"

"Yeah," he said when he was able to breathe again. "A nun, Boomer said? You're sure? Not a prostitute?"

"Definitely a nun. Boomer says to call him anytime. And he doesn't believe you've actually given up being a cop."

"Right."

After Cork hung up, he looked at Mal Thorne. The look alone seemed to sober the priest dramatically.

"Are you all right, Cork?"

"Randy Gooding?" Cork said.

"What?"

Cork took some time to rearrange his thinking, put things in place. "It sounds crazy, Mal, but Gooding may be our sin eater."

"Why would you say that?"

"He told me once about a woman he knew in Chicago. He lied about her in some respects and didn't tell me the important part, that she was murdered, and someone ate her sins."

"Gooding? I don't believe it. He's such a righteous young man."

Cork rubbed his forehead and thought out loud, "If it is Gooding, why would he kill the two men who attacked you?"

"You don't know that he did."

"You think all of this is just coincidence? When the murders occurred, he was working the FBI's Milwaukee field office, just a hop, skip, and a jump from Chicago. He was involved with one of the victims. Did you have any contact with Gooding in Chicago?"

"No."

Cork tried to put it all together, but there were gaps. Still, the direction of his thinking felt right. "I'm willing to bet he knew you somehow. I think he followed you here, and the sin eater killings continued."

"Why?"

"I don't know, but there's got to be a connection. We just haven't found it yet."

Cork started out the door.

"Where are you going?" Mal Thorne asked.

"To have a talk with our acting sheriff." He paused before he left the room. "What about you? Still taking off?"

The priest looked down at the bottle in his hand. He put the booze in the suitcase and closed the lid. "There's no way in hell I'm leaving town right now."

46

Cy Borkmann wasn't in his office. He'd gone to the village of North Star, Deputy Marsha Dross said, to confer with Lyman Cooke, chief of police there, who was interested in taking over as Tamarack County sheriff should the Board of Commissioners choose to offer him the position.

Dross shifted in her chair and picked up a pencil from the contact desk. "I was sort of hoping they'd offer you the job. I heard you might be interested. I hope you'll consider it. Having you back as sheriff, that would sit just fine with me."

"Thanks for the vote of confidence, Marsha. We'll see what the commissioners decide to do. Say, is Randy in?" He looked past the contact desk toward the heart of the department.

She shook her head. "He's not on until three today."

"Do me a favor, will you? It's important. Have Cy give me a call as soon as he's back from North Star. I'll be at home."

"I can try to raise him on the radio."

Cork considered it but decided he didn't have anything concrete on Gooding. He'd probably have to do a lot of talking to convince Borkmann, and he didn't want to do it over a radio.

"Don't worry about it, but when he comes back tell him we have to talk ASAP."

"All right."

"One more thing, Marsha. Any idea if Randy was on duty New Year's Eve?"

"If you give me a minute, I can pull the duty roster for that night."

"Would you?"

"Be right back."

A few minutes later, she returned.

"Randy was on from eight to three-thirty that day. One of the lucky few who had the evening off."

By the time Cork returned to his house on Gooseberry Lane, Jo had left for work. Jenny was in the kitchen, eating a bowl of Cheerios, still wearing her sleep shirt.

"Are we going to open Sam's Place today?" she asked.

"I've got something else on my agenda."

"You know," she said, "I've been thinking. If you hired Sean to help, Annie and I could pretty much run Sam's Place by ourselves. It's not exactly rocket science, Dad."

"Sean? Your boyfriend?"

"I don't know any other Sean."

Cork walked to the doorway of the living room. Stevie was still on the floor in front of the television, but he was working with crayons and a coloring book now and paying no attention to what was on the tube.

"The other thing is," Jenny went on, "if you don't open Sam's Place pretty soon, I'll have to find another job. I'm starting to dip into my savings account. You know, the one I've been putting money into for college."

"Where's Rose?"

"She got a call from the church office a little while ago. They needed her, so she walked on over."

"How's she doing?"

"I've never seen her so sad. Maybe helping out at St. Agnes will do her good." She paused a beat. "What about it?"

"What about what?"

"Hiring Sean?"

"All right. On a trial basis."

"Really? That's great." Jenny stood up. "I'll get changed and go tell him." She gave her father a huge smile. "I'm going to love being my boyfriend's boss." She put her bowl in the sink and started out of the kitchen. "Oh, Mom wants you to call her right away."

Cork walked to Jo's back office, to use the phone there. He wanted privacy to tell her of his suspicions about Randy Gooding. He was thinking that although he didn't know the reason yet, it all made a strange kind of sense. Gooding wasn't on duty the night Charlotte was killed. He could easily have heard about the party at Valhalla and posted himself out there, waiting for his chance. He could have stolen Solemn's wrench and picked up the Corona bottle Solemn had left in the snow. If he'd gone to Valhalla with murder on his mind, he'd probably stopped at a convenience store for the food he'd eventually consumed along with Charlotte's sins. As for the evening Fletcher Kane killed himself and Solemn, Gooding must have lied. He hadn't gone to Sam's old cabin first. He'd gone to Fletcher Kane's home, gone too late to stop the killings, but with enough time to consume the sins.

But why? What did he know about Gooding that would have pointed toward a motive for killing Charlotte?

He reached for the phone just as it rang.

"Cork? This is Mal. I'm at Randy Gooding's."

"Jesus, Mal, what are you doing?"

"I know how Gooding knows me. And there's something here you have to see."

"Is Gooding there?"

"No."

"I'm on my way. But if he comes before I get there, don't do anything stupid, okay?"

"That's a promise."

Cork hurried upstairs to his bedroom. From the top shelf in his closet, he took a metal lockbox and put it on his bed. He keyed in the combination and lifted the lid. Inside, wrapped in an oilcloth, was his S & W .38 Police Special. The revolver had belonged first to his father, who'd worn it every day while he was sheriff, and then it had been Cork's, who'd done the same during his own tenure serving the citizens of Tamarack County. There was a trigger lock on the weapon. Cork took the key from his key ring and undid the lock. He went back to the closet and pulled down a cardboard box. Inside was a basket-weave holster and gun belt, which he put on. From the cartridges he kept with the revolver, he took enough to fill the cylinder. He lifted the weapon to feel its heft, a thing he hadn't done in quite a while, and he slid it into the holster and pressed the thumb snap into place. There was a time when he'd worn the gun daily, when the weight of it on his hip would go unnoticed for hours. Much had happened in his life between that time and now. The .38 made him feel prepared for what might lie ahead. But he was also aware that the badge, which used to be a standard part of the ensemble and that was the unquestioned rationale for carrying the weapon, was missing, and in a way, he felt naked.

He stepped into the hall just as Annie came out of her bedroom. She looked still asleep, her hair a tangle in her eyes. She yawned.

"Morning, Dad."

Then she saw the revolver at his side, and her eyes crawled up until she looked with concern into her father's face.

"I have to go out for a while, Annie. Until Rose comes back, you or Jenny need to be here to watch over Stevie. Do you understand?"

"What's wrong, Dad?"

"Nothing, I hope. Just stay here," he said. "I'll explain when I get back."

He brushed against her in the hallway, barely a touch, but she fell back as if he'd shoved her.

He drove to Gooding's place, a block north of St. Agnes. Gooding's Tracker was parked under a big maple in front of Mamie Torkelson's house. Cork pulled to the curb across the street and got out. He checked the Tracker. It was locked.

A dozen years earlier, after her husband died, Mamie had turned her two-story home into a duplex and had begun leasing out the upstairs. Cork looked toward the upper floor, which Gooding now rented. The curtains were drawn.

The clouds that had been scattered most of the morning were coming together in an organized line that threatened rain. They advanced across the face of the sun, and the whole block around Cork dropped into a dark, blue quiet.

He didn't like the setup. It felt wrong, threatening. He reached down and thumbed back the safety strap on his holster, then started walking cautiously up the walk toward the house. Mamie Torkelson was nearly deaf. As Cork approached the porch, he heard her television blaring from the first floor, a commercial for Wendy's. He realized that he hadn't eaten yet and he was hungry. Suddenly all he could think about was eating. It was an odd thing, but he remembered it was like that sometimes in a tight spot. You thought of a thing and once your mind got hooked on it, you couldn't let it go. Even as you were telling yourself to focus, to concentrate because your life might depend on it, you were thinking about the other thing that had nothing to do with your immediate survival. As he mounted the steps toward the deep shade of the porch, he was sure he could smell hamburger grilling, and his mouth watered, and as he reached for the doorknob, he wanted the taste of a burger in the worst way.

Before Cork touched it, the door swung open. He stumbled back and his right hand dropped toward his holster.

Mal Thorne stepped out. When he saw where Cork's hand was headed, he brought his own hands up in surrender.

"Don't shoot."

"You shouldn't be here, Mal."

"I wanted to talk to Randy."

"That was not a good idea."

"It doesn't matter. He's not here."

Cork glanced back at the Tracker parked on the street. "What did you want to show me?"

"Upstairs." He waved Cork to follow him inside.

The stairway was dark, lit only from the light that slipped through a small window on the upper landing. Mal went ahead, mounting rapidly. Cork followed more slowly, eyeing the closed door at the top.

"You've been inside?" Cork said.

Mal nodded.

"How?"

"He didn't answer when I knocked, so I went downstairs and told Mrs. Torkelson that I was supposed to wait for him inside. She was reluctant. She told me she believes in giving her tenants complete privacy. But I was insistent and sincere and she opened it up." Mal reached for the door. "Nobody ever believes a priest would lie."

He slipped out of sight inside.

A moment later, Cork went in after him.

Like many of the homes in that area, the house had been built in the early 1900s, in a time of prosperity in Aurora, when the iron mines were operating day and night and the supply of timber seemed inexhaustible. The trim was all oak, stained and polished to show the beautiful, fluid grain. The window construction included leaded glass in most frames. The floors had been recently sanded and refinished to a mirrorlike gloss. Gooding had furnished the living room and dining room modestly. Everything seemed surprisingly clean for the home of a bachelor.

Mal stood across the room at a built-in hutch with a mantel. In the middle of the mantel sat a domed Seth Thomas clock, and flanking it on either side were a number of photographs in frames. Mal picked one up. "Take a look at this," he said.

Cork walked over and looked at the photo. The shot showed a group of seven adolescents, boys and girls, standing in a line on green grass in bright sunshine in front of a white clapboard building. The kids had their arms linked as if they were great friends. Standing behind them was a much younger Mal Thorne.

"Yvonne Doolittle is the girl in the middle."

She was taller than the others, and from the development of her body, appeared to be older. She was blonde, squinting into the sun, and very pretty.

"This was taken at the orphanage?"

"At St. Chris. St. Christopher's Children's Home. Outside Holland, Michigan. The kid on the end, far left. Does he look familiar?"

"Not really."

"He was only thirteen and small for his age. His name back then was Jimmy Crockett. He wanted desperately to become a priest someday. I'd never known a kid with a more profound sense, in his own mind, of what was right and what was wrong according to church canon, and he wasn't reluctant to tell you so. He made it his business to keep everyone on the straight and narrow. The kids started calling him Jiminy Cricket. You know, Pinocchio's conscience."

The bells of St. Agnes rang the hour, eleven o'clock. Because they were so near, the sound was beautiful and pure.

"Cork, his middle name was Randall. Imagine him a foot taller, a hundred thirty pounds heavier, and with a beard."

"Randy? But his name's Gooding."

"After the fire, the publicity generated a sympathetic response. I heard that many of the kids were adopted, even ones like Jimmy who were considered to have little chance."

"Why little chance?"

"His age for one thing. Teenagers aren't often adopted. His background for another."

"What about his background?"

"When he was little, Jimmy was in and out of foster homes. His mother was psychotic, frequently institutionalized. During her psychotic episodes, she believed she was the Virgin Mary. When Jimmy was six, she drove off a bridge with him in the car."

"Suicide? Not an accident?"

"No accident."

"Did Gooding know that?"

"Yes. Much of the time he was at St. Chris he was seeing a therapist." Mal put a fist to his forehead. "He was an artist even then. How could I not have recognized him?"

"He's entirely changed, grown into a man, a very big, very disturbed man. Did you ever see him after the fire?"

Mal shook his head. "The church snatched me out of there, and forbid me to have contact with any of the kids."

"What kind of relationship did you have with Jimmy Crockett?"

"He never knew his father. I think he saw me as a surrogate. A lot of the children did."

"Could he have been responsible for the fire that killed Yvonne?"

"Why would he?"

"Maybe he believed he was protecting you."

Mal's look turned dark as the possibility settled into his thinking.

Cork said, "The two punks who attacked you in Chicago. If Gooding killed them, it might have been for the same sort of reason. Maybe revenge in your name. But if that's true, why Nina van Zoot?"

"Nina van Zoot?"

"Another sin eater killing in Chicago. She and her fiancé."

Mal nodded toward the photograph. "Bottom row, middle. The thin girl, smiling. Nina and Jimmy were good friends. She became a nun, I heard."

"She left her order to get married, Mal. Her fiancé was a former priest."

"Why would Jimmy kill them?"

Cork thought a moment. "When he told me about Nina, he called her a prostitute and the man she fell for a pimp. He may have killed them because they broke their vows to the church, and he considered them criminals. I'm beginning to think he sees himself as some sort of policeman of God. If that's true, then maybe he followed you here to protect you."

"How did he find me?"

"When you were attacked by those two punks, was the story in the newspaper?"

"You kidding? A priest attacked? It was front page for a while."

"If he was a good agent, Gooding was reading everything in the news. Maybe that's when he became aware you were in Chicago."

"When he came here, why did he kill Charlotte?"

"I don't know. He was in charge of the investigation of the vandalism at St. Agnes. Maybe he figured out she was responsible and he interpreted it as an attack against the church. Maybe that's why he framed Solemn, too. His thinking is not exactly rational."

"There's more you should see."

Mal led him to a door that stood slightly ajar, and pushed it open wide.

What hit Cork first was the smell, sweet and smoky. Familiar. Cork realized it was the scent of the frankincense used during the services at St. Agnes.

The room was large, probably designed as a master bedroom when the house had been a single-family dwelling, but it was almost bare now. There was a cot with a thin mattress that looked handmade from a brown sheet. From the bits of straw that protruded at the open end of the mattress, the nature of the bedding on which Gooding slept was quite clear. Except for a crucifix above the head of the cot, the walls were empty. Next to the cot stood a small stand with a Bible and a candle. The candle had been burned to a nub. At the foot of the cot was a tiny table that held a white, enamel wash basin, a bar of soap in a small dish, and a clean, folded towel.

"Looks like a monk's cell," Cork said.

"One from the Middle Ages, maybe. Believe me, they don't look like this today." Mal walked to the closet and beckoned to Cork. "Have a look."

Inside, hung on wire hangers, were all manner of priestly garb. A number of thin rope fingers fell over the edge of the closet shelf above.

Cork reached up and took down a whip. It was a homemade device, a sawed-off broom handle twenty inches long, with four lengths of thin, jute rope tied through a hole near the end. Each length of rope was about three feet long and knotted every three inches along its length. The end of each lash was glued to prevent unraveling.

"A discipline," Mal said. "That's what I've heard it called. It's a scourge for self-flagellation. I've never actually seen one before." He looked around him at the spartan room and then back at the whip. "My God. This man sings in our choir. He's in charge of our youth program. How could we not have known?"

"Who he is, he's hidden well from everyone."

Cork put the whip back on the shelf.

Far back, in a corner too dark to be seen clearly, were two stacks of large sketch pads. The top pad on one stack looked as if it had been slashed with a knife. Cork picked up the pad and took it into the light of the room.

They were pencil drawings and charcoal sketches. Nude studies mostly. All of them of Charlotte Kane, and all of them cut in some way. Cork went through the sketchbook slowly, page after page.

"Did she pose for these, do you think?" the priest asked.

"No. I think he imagined her. According to Glory, Charlotte had a birthmark on her hip. It's not in any of these drawings. This is pretty obsessive stuff."

"He saw her in church every Sunday. My God, did it begin there?"

"Or maybe during his investigation of the vandalism at St. Agnes. I suppose it's possible Charlotte tried to play him then, came on to him. Whatever, it's clear she touched something in him that he didn't know how to control, maybe didn't even want to acknowledge." Cork flipped through the slashed pages. "If we're right about him, he's killed several times. I don't suppose he'd have any difficulty at all justifying in his own twisted thinking one more. What I don't understand is the sin eating."

Cork returned the sketch pad to the closet and picked up the top pad from the other stack.

"What are we going to do?" the priest asked.

Cork didn't answer. The sketches in the other pad froze his blood.

Mal saw the look on his face. "What is it?"

Cork held out a drawing toward the priest.

Mal Thorne's mouth formed a stupefied O. "My God," he said.

It was Annie. Annie naked on a bed, her face done in heavy makeup, her hands cupping her young breasts, offering them lasciviously.

Cork's thinking went rapidly over the events of the last week or so, and he locked on the tall figure who'd kept to the shadows, stalking Annie, and the fact that only the night before Gooding had just happened to bump into her. He dropped the pad into Mal's hands, went quickly to the phone in Gooding's living room, and called home.

Jenny answered.

"Is Annie there?" Cork said.

"Upstairs, I think."

"Check."

"Dad—"

"Go check. Now."

Silence. The static long and grating. Then Annie.

"What is it, Dad?"

"Are you okay?"

"Sure. Why?"

"Listen to me. Stay there in the house. Don't open the door to anyone, especially Randy Gooding. I'll be home in a minute."

"What's wrong?"

"Just do what I say. I'll explain when I get there. All right?"

"Okay."

Cork hung up.

"What now?" Mal said.

"We put everything back just as we found it. I don't want Gooding to know we're onto him. Then I talk to Cy Borkmann, who gets a search warrant, and we put an end to this."

Outside, the whole sky had been overtaken by storm clouds, and a wind was rising. Mal Thorne glanced back at the house.

"Think Mrs. Torkelson had any idea what was going on above her?"

"None of us knew about Gooding."

The priest rubbed a hand over his forehead and closed his eyes. "Jimmy Crockett. I never would have guessed. God, if only I'd . . ." The priest stopped there.

What was the use of trying to grab onto the past, hoping to change what no human could. The best thing to do was simply to let it go, but Cork knew that was easier said than done.

"I'm going to pick up Annie and then hit the sheriff's office. Want to come?"

"No." The priest looked toward St. Agnes. "I'll be at the church if anybody wants to talk to me."

"Rose is there."

"Really?"

"She got a call from the office this morning. I guess they needed her."

"From the office? I don't think so. Hattie's on vacation, and Celia couldn't come in this morning. Dental appointment. Nobody's been there all day as far as I know."

"Somebody called."

"I can't imagine who it would have been."

Cork looked at Gooding's Tracker parked on the street. He glanced toward St. Agnes, visible only a block away. And he remembered something.

"Gooding knows about you and Rose. Annie told him last night."

The priest squinted at Cork. "You don't think . . ."

Cork was already on the street, making for St. Agnes at a dead run.

47

Cork flew up the front steps of the church, the priest at his heels. The door was locked.

"The office," Mal shouted, and they veered across the grass to the office/classroom wing.

Cork grabbed the handle, but the door wouldn't budge. Mal pushed Cork aside, jammed his key into the lock. As soon as the door was open, Cork rushed inside, the priest a split second behind him.

The desk of the reception area was empty, the hallway dark, the wing dead silent but for the heavy breathing of the two men.

"Maybe he's not—" the priest began.

"He's here. They're both here," Cork said. "There's no other way to play it. Get on the phone to the sheriff's office. Get people here. Do it now, Mal."

Without waiting for a response, Cork headed down the short end of the hall, away from the sanctuary, toward the offices. He checked each room, found them all empty. When he came back to the reception area, the priest had disappeared. Cork had no idea where Mal had gone, but he hoped he'd made the call. He moved down the hall in the other direction, making sure each classroom was clear as he passed. Just before he reached the open door that led from the office wing into the church itself, he came to the stairway that led to the basement. He paused, considering whether to check the lower level first.

Then he heard Mal Thorne's voice coming from the church beyond the door.

The clouds that had blotted out the sun cast a darkness over the sanctuary, as if a blanket had been dropped on the church. The priest stood at the back, beyond the last pew. He faced the entry to a tiny chapel that was used for small weddings or other intimate ceremonies or services. Cork could see a candle burning in the chapel, but nothing else. From the way the priest spoke, Cork figured Gooding was in there. Probably Rose, too.

"Just listen to me for a minute, Jimmy."

"Jimmy?" The voice from the dark chapel. "Then you know?"

"I do. About Yvonne and Nina and Charlotte. About the rest."

"Do you understand?"

"I don't. This isn't the way of our Lord." The priest opened his hands, as he did when offering a benediction.

"Not our Lord, Father. Of His soldiers. Those who wage His wars, who protect His Church."

"You?"

"We are born damned, those like me, damned to kill in the name of the church."

Cork kept low, sliding along the front pew to the far wall where Gooding could not possibly see him. Silently, he made his way toward the chapel. He was clearly visible to the priest, but Mal Thorne gave no sign he'd seen. Cork took up a position at the end of the last pew. If Gooding could be drawn out, his back would be to Cork. Only once, Mal's eyes flicked in Cork's direction, acknowledging his presence. Cork held his .38 ready in a two-handed grip.

"No one is born to kill, Jimmy."

"Not true, Father. I was double born, raised from the dead for this purpose. Understand, though, that I'm not without compassion. Those that die don't die stained with sin. I can't pardon their transgressions, but I can take them away."

"By consuming them?"

"You showed me the way a long time ago at St. Chris. The story of the sin eater, that was a blessing to me."

"You don't want this sin on you."

"I'm not afraid to die, because when I stand in the light of God, all the sins committed in His service will be forgiven."

"Jimmy, Jimmy, this isn't the way. Not with this woman."

"I know how tempting they can be, Father. The handmaids of Satan."

"Because of Charlotte?"

"It was so easy for me to imagine having her. She tempted me to take my eyes off God. She played on the weakness of the flesh, Father. This harlot, too. She was sent to seduce you from your true bride, the church."

"You're wrong. This good woman would have nothing to do with me. The church has no better heart serving it than hers, I swear to you."

"You're too good, Father. You don't see the true abomination, but I do."

"You were always a good boy, Jimmy. You don't want to do this."

"Want? What I want is meaningless. I have been called."

Cork knew that reasoning with Gooding now was out of the question. He was a man whose holy mission, at that moment, was to send Rose McKenzie to hell, and if he had to give his own life in the effort, that concerned him not at all. He'd concocted a theology that covered all the bases, that left him righteous and fearless. A man not afraid to die was the most dangerous kind.

The darkness in the church seemed to deepen. Thunder made the floor and the pews shiver.

Cork signaled Mal Thorne, motioning for him to lure Gooding out. The priest's eyes rested on the revolver in Cork's hands.

"You'd best leave, Father."

"It doesn't have to be this way."

"Don't you understand? I was born so that it could be this way. I was raised from the dead for it."

"Don't do this, Jimmy."

"I have my duty, Father. And not even you can intervene."

The priest faltered a moment. When he spoke again, his voice had lost its pleading. "Not here, then. Not in God's house. You will not spill blood where the Blessed Virgin will have to see, where our Lord Jesus will have to look down on it from His cross, in this place He promised sanctuary to all His children. This thing must be taken outside. You take it out into the world where the sin is everywhere. You will do this, Jimmy. You will do this for me and for our Lord."

The voice from the chapel didn't reply.

"Jimmy," the priest said sternly.

"You're right, Father. Outside, then. But you move back."

The priest backed away until he reached the place where the center aisle divided the rows of pews.

Rose came first, her eyes wide with fear. A strip of silver duct tape sealed her mouth, and her wrists were bound with duct tape as well. Blood stained the collar of her white blouse. Gooding held her from behind in a tight grip and pressed a hunting knife against her throat. Below the blade, a thin line of blood ran down her neck

Gooding wore black. At first Cork figured it for the color of an executioner, but then he saw the collar and realized the man was dressed as a priest. Gooding urged Rose forward, and she walked with halting steps, her chin lifted above the knife blade.

Cork had a clear shot at Gooding's back, but he was afraid the bullet might go all the way through and hit Rose.

"Up the aisle, Father." Gooding jerked his head, directing the priest toward the front of the church.

Mal Thorne gave way.

Gooding reached the center aisle and executed a quarter turn so that he and Rose faced Mal. Far down the aisle, at the priest's back, stood the altar with its crucifix. Above the altar was a large stained glass window. On sunny Sunday mornings, the window blazed with light and a dazzling array of colors. At the moment, it was dark.

Cork remained crouched behind the last pew, his .38 trained on Gooding. The deputy pressed himself tight against Rose from behind. They were thirty feet from Cork. Because there was no separation of their bodies, he had no chance at a clean shot. His hands were shaking, from tension and from fear. Sweat crawled down his forehead, stung his eyes, and he blinked desperately to clear his vision. He knew if he pulled the trigger now, Rose was at great risk of being hit. On the other hand, if the deputy were to look to his left, he would see Cork and understand how the priest had deceived him, and he would do his duty, as he saw it.

Cork prayed for an opening, just one moment of opportunity.

And that's when it happened.

The clouds above the church parted. Light, suddenly brilliant, burst through the window behind the altar, and flooded the aisle with a blaze of gold that hit Gooding square in the face. Blinded, he let go of Rose and raised his left hand to shield his eyes. The knife in his right hand lifted from her throat.

"Rose," the priest screamed.

She twisted from Gooding and rushed into Mal's waiting arms.

Gooding lowered his hand and stood looking at the stained glass window, transfixed. Cork had the shot he'd prayed for, but he hesitated. Rose was with the priest now, the knife no longer at her throat. And Gooding was not moving. Maybe there was another way to end this.

But the blade was still in the man's hand, the steel still warm where it had pressed against Rose's flesh. She was only a few steps distant, an easy lunge, and Gooding was anything but predictable. And if what Gooding believed was true, that there were those born to protect, and damned in that birthing, then Cork knew he was one, too.

He squeezed the trigger. Twice.

The crack of the .38 seemed to shake the walls of the sanctuary.

As if the strings that had moved him all his life had suddenly been cut, Gooding dropped to the floor.

Mal Thorne let go of Rose and started instinctively toward the fallen man.

"Wait," Cork shouted.

He kept his revolver trained on Gooding, and he came forward. He could hear the note sung from Gooding's chest, the high pitch that was the leak of air from a lung shot. Gooding's hand was empty, the knife fallen near his feet. His eyes, a clear, crystal blue, stared straight up, as if they were focused on something beyond the beamed arch of the church ceiling.

Mal pulled the tape from Rose's mouth. "Are you all right?"

"Oh, Mal," was all she could manage, and she buried her head against his shoulder.

A moment later, Gooding's eyes closed. His body relaxed.

Mal said to Rose, "It's all right now." He gently gave her over to Cork, stepped toward Gooding, and knelt. "May the Lord pardon thee whatever sins or faults thou hast committed."

In the golden light that fell across Randy Gooding's forehead, Father Malachi Thorne traced a cross.

From outside the church came the wail of a siren, and the sound mixed in an eerie way with Gooding's final, whistling breath. Long ago, Randy Gooding had died and been brought back to life. Cork was pretty sure that this time he was dead for good.

JULY

48

HE STOOD ALONE in the cemetery.

Two hours earlier, the sun had risen and now the dew was evaporating from the grass, carrying upward the smell of wet, fertile earth. Scattered across the hillside below Cork lay the buried dead, seeds whose planting had brought forth a crop of stone.

North, in a grave less than two weeks old, lay the body of Randy Gooding. A hundred yards south was Fletcher Kane's marker, a block of white marble, small for a man who could have afforded a mausoleum. Down the hillside to the east stood the angel pillar that marked the resting place of the young woman whom Aurora had known as Charlotte Kane. The three graves were within sight of one another. Three points of a triangle, Cork realized. A closed shape. Completed. Explained. Understood, however, only as much as anything human could ever be fully understood. There were still a lot of questions in Cork's mind, but they were questions only the dead could answer now.

Gus Finlayson drove up on his little tractor, hauling a trailer full of garden tools. He stopped behind Cork's Bronco, got down, and came to where Cork stood.

"My favorite time of the day," the groundskeeper said.

"It's peaceful."

"Usually is. I figure that's why I see you here so much these days."

"Mind?"

"Why would I mind? Lots of folks drop by to spend some time here. This place, it makes you look at life a little different, I figure." Finlayson gazed across the headstones. "Some people seem upset about Gooding being buried in the cemetery. Like any of his neighbors here care. How's that saying go? Fences make good neighbors? You ask me, it's death does that. The dead, they're not prejudiced. They don't complain. And they never make too much noise." Finlayson scratched his nose with his thumbnail. "Heard the priest left town."

Cork nodded. "Taking some time to think a few things through."

He didn't know what to hope for. But if being together was what they finally decided, he thought he would be very happy for Mal and Rose.

"Guess everybody needs that now and again, even priests." Gus thought a moment. "Maybe especially priests. But then I'm Missouri Synod Lutheran, so what do I know?" He turned back toward his tractor. "Gonna be a beautiful day. You take 'er easy, Sheriff."

"You, too, Gus."

By the time Cork drove down the hill into town, Aurora had awakened. Traffic was moving on the streets. A few cars had already pulled into the lot of the IGA grocery store. Fishermen who'd been on Iron Lake since before dawn were being joined by pleasure boats cruising out from the marina.

He loved Aurora and understood why it was the kind of place people who wanted to escape from problems—of the world, of a big city, of a troubled past—came to. But there was no place far enough away to run from who you were. The secrets people hid from others, they still had to live with themselves. It was just as Cordelia Diller had told him on that high bluff in Iowa. In starting over, the best place to begin was facing the truth.

The truth about Gooding was something Cork would never fully know. A man cold enough to kill many times over, but also compassionate enough to consume the sins of Solemn Winter Moon and Fletcher Kane, freeing them, in his own belief, to stand unstained before God. He understood why some people might object to Gooding resting forever in Lakeview Cemetery. They thought he was evil, pure and simple. Cork didn't believe anyone was purely and simply anything. All human beings, it seemed to him, were a collection of conflicting impulses stuffed into one skin, trying somehow to find peace. Death was certainly one way.

He didn't go directly to the sheriff's department but headed first to St. Agnes.

He stood at the bottom of the steps looking up at the church doors. Over the course of his life, he'd crossed that threshold hundreds of times. Then horrible things had happened, and he'd turned his back on St. Agnes and all it stood for.

Two days before, he'd gone with Henry Meloux to Blood Hollow and in the sweat lodge there had worked with Meloux to restore a sense of harmony. At the end, when they emerged into sunlight, Meloux had said, "It's not finished. You're a man of two bloods, two people, a spirit divided. I think you still have a long road ahead of you, Corcoran O'Connor."

Now he mounted the church steps. Inside, he came to the place where Gooding had fallen. The carpet had been cleaned of blood, leaving nothing to indicate that a man had died there, killed by Cork's hand. But Cork knew, and he would never be able to cross that spot without remembering.

He stood almost where Gooding had stood and had held a knife to Rose's throat, and he looked where Gooding had looked the moment the light had filled the church and the man had stood transfixed.

What Cork saw was the window behind the altar, a stained glass rendering of Jesus, his right hand uplifted in blessing. The figure had always been there, during every service ever held in the church. Randy Gooding must have seen it a hundred times. So why, on the morning he'd held Rose's life in his hands, did he seem paralyzed? What did he see that day that he'd never seen before? Maybe he really was blinded by the light. Or maybe his own warped mind had conjured up a vision. With Gooding dead, there was no way to know for sure. Cork was more than willing to accept another possibility, however, one that the life and death of Solemn Winter Moon, the simple faith of people like Rose McKenzie and the family from Warroad, and the reality of his own experience while lost in a whiteout on Fisheye Lake had opened him to. It was possible that what had stayed Gooding's hand was nothing less than a miracle.

Near the confessional, the new parish priest waited. His name was Father Edward Green. He was an earnest young man, still a little uncertain in his manner. He was half Cork's age, and Cork had trouble thinking of him as "Father" anything.

"Thank you for agreeing to this," Cork said.

"No problem." The priest smiled.

"It's something I wanted to do before I put this on." Cork held out his badge.

"I understand. Welcome back to the church."

The young priest didn't really understand. It wasn't the church Cork was returning to. It was the journey. Meloux was right. In his search for that place where his soul would feel undivided and finally at peace, Cork knew he still faced a long road. He could have chosen any number of paths, but the religion of his youth and his family seemed to him as good as any other.

"Shall we?" The priest stepped into the confessional and pulled the curtain.

Cork entered the other side.

There was a moment of silence, then the priest said, "Go ahead."

Cork crossed himself, surprised how natural the gesture felt after so long an absence.

"Bless me, Father," he began, "for I have sinned."